S. R. Masters grew up around █████████
receiving a Philosophy degree fr█████████
moved to Oxford where he stu█████████
health. His short fiction and nov████████ published inter-
nationally. Labelled as 'a writer to watch' by Publishers Weekly,
he is also the author of *The Killer You Know* and *The Trial*.

www.sr-masters.com

X x.com/SRMastersAuthor
instagram.com/SRMastersAuthor
f facebook.com/srmastersauthor

Also by S. R. Masters

The Killer You Know

The Trial

HOW TO KILL WITH KINDNESS

S. R. MASTERS

One More Chapter
a division of HarperCollins*Publishers* Ltd
1 London Bridge Street
London SE1 9GF

www.harpercollins.co.uk

HarperCollins*Publishers*
Macken House, 39/40 Mayor Street Upper,
Dublin 1, D01 C9W8, Ireland

This paperback edition 2024
1
First published in Great Britain in ebook format
by HarperCollins*Publishers* 2024

A catalogue record of this book is available from the British Library

ISBN: 978-0-00-852015-1

This novel is entirely a work of fiction. The names, characters and incidents
portrayed in it are the work of the author's imagination. Any resemblance to
actual persons, living or dead, events or localities is entirely coincidental.

Printed and bound in the UK using 100% Renewable Electricity
by CPI Group (UK) Ltd

MIX
Paper | Supporting
responsible forestry
FSC™ C007454

This book contains FSC™ certified paper and other controlled
sources to ensure responsible forest management.

For more information visit: www.harpercollins.co.uk/green

For Mom and Dad

A Random Act of Kindness

The two children sat trying to throw stones into a terracotta pot at the other end of the villa's front courtyard. Granny's yells from inside echoed around them, but they were too concerned with the *pings* and *skitters* of their failures, and the hollow *conks* of victory, to notice.

And they'd heard it all before. No one had fed Duchess. Duchess would be famished. Duchess might die if no one fed her, oh *why* wouldn't anybody listen to her about dear Duchess?

But Duchess was already dead. She had been dead three years.

Skitter. Skitter. Ping. Conk.

'Well done,' the girl said. 'You're getting so good.' Her brother looked up, pleased.

Inside, their mother shouted back at Granny, a weak, exasperated sound. The siblings shared a look before turning their attention to the dwindling pile of stones. The girl threw one and it bounced off the rim. The boy threw the final one and it struck the edge of the pot.

Brushing dirt from his knees, the boy, never one to stay still for long, stepped out from the column of shadow running along the wall, intending to replenish the pile. He halted when their mother clacked through the beaded fly-curtain and strode over to the olive tree at the back of the courtyard. One hand covered her face, the other held a carving knife streaked with watermelon gore. The children watched her back, the rapid bobbing of her shoulders. Again, they glanced at one another.

'Are you feeling upset, Mum?' the girl said.

She made them wait before finally saying, 'I need you to take Granny out for a walk. I just… Granny just needs some fresh air.'

The boy made a face. 'Do we have to?'

The girl tried to guide the boy with barely perceptible head shakes. Now wasn't the time.

'I'd like you to, please. She would enjoy spending time with you.'

'No, she wouldn't,' the boy said. 'She doesn't know what's happening anymore. I heard you say that.'

The girl widened her eyes, but the boy was focused on the salmon patio tiles. Mum crossed the courtyard and knelt down before the boy, clutching the knife between her knees. The blade and her gaze jutted up.

'Sometimes I say things I don't mean when I'm over-whelmed,' Mum said. 'We don't know what Granny feels anymore. And we never will, so we must act like she feels everything. Do you know why?'

'No.' The boy couldn't hide his annoyance.

'Because it is the kind thing to do.' From inside Granny swore, and their mother looked back at the house. 'And even if it feels … pointless. Even if it feels like you are wasting your time. Well … the harder it feels, the kinder you're being.'

2

The children pushed their grandmother's wheelchair up the bumpy footpath to the cliffs overlooking the bay. Though the incline was gentle, they would stop periodically to apply the brakes and catch their breath. In earlier stages of her illness, Granny would go missing and often be found up here staring out to sea, no memory of where she was going or where she had come from. Mum said it was where her soul wanted to be, which was why she liked the children to take Granny up here.

If that was true though, Granny's soul had forgotten to tell the rest of her. 'Where are we going?' she would ask in a tone of complaint, no answer the children gave sufficiently satisfying to prevent the question being asked again moments later.

'Disneyland,' the boy answered once, and the girl did everything in her power not to laugh. Laughing at Granny would certainly not have been kind.

At the clifftop they walked a little way before pausing to rest, positioning the chair so grandmother could watch the azure sea smash the cliffs far below. The two sat on a patch of dry grass, legs crossed, squinting at the horizon.

'Do you really think Granny feels anything?' the boy said. 'I don't.'

The girl sighed. 'No.'

'Is it kind to let her live like this? If she was an animal, she'd be dead, wouldn't she? Either eaten or starved.'

'True. But we're different. Aren't we?'

'I suppose.'

A soft breeze blew across the clifftop, bringing with it Granny's hospitally smell. The girl recoiled, hating it and what it stood for. 'I think it's hard to know what the kind thing to do is sometimes. Remember when Duchess got caught in the trap? Grandad broke her neck and said you have to be cruel to be kind.'

The boy nodded. Though only eleven and twelve, everything they had been through, upending their lives to be in this strange country just to look after a relative who had barely spoken to them when healthy, had aged them. There had been a dreadful inversion of the natural order. Mum cared for Granny, and they cared for Mum. Making her sandwiches when she forgot to eat. Covering her up when she fell asleep on the sofa. Putting themselves to bed at night.

'Where are we going?' their grandmother yelled, jerking her body with such violence that the chair started rolling down the slight gradient towards the cliff edge.

The brakes. They'd forgotten.

Both children sprang up, grabbing a handle each and stepping on a brake before the chair had a chance to build up a catastrophic momentum.

They sat back down, nervous smiles on their faces. 'That was close,' the girl said.

'Just a bit.'

For a long time they listened to the ocean.

'Where are we going?' Granny asked.

'Nowhere now,' the girl said.

The two children looked at each other, still smiling.

'Sometimes,' the girl said, 'I think Mummy wants us to have an accident up here.'

'What do you mean?'

'I heard her say to Daddy once that it would be better for everyone if she were…' The girl lowered her voice, just in case, and flicked her head at Granny. '… dead. That your family was your duty, but that if she were gone there would be no choice. Then we could go home, and things would be normal again. We'd get Mummy back, and she'd get Daddy back, and we could live in England again. And you know, we would get money from Granny's house. Wouldn't that be the kindest thing for everyone?'

The boy thought about this. 'It would be kinder on Granny, too.'

'An accident?'

'Yes, an accident.'

After some time, they rose together without speaking. They each released a foot brake and returned to their patch of grass. The wheelchair didn't move.

'She's not really alive anyway,' the girl said, to reassure the boy.

'The harder it feels, the kinder you're being,' the boy said, to reassure the girl.

Granny shifted her body again, and the chair began rolling. It picked up speed, wobbling awkwardly on the uneven ground. Again, the girl managed not to laugh, even though it looked funny. The two children held hands.

Then the wheelchair reached the cliff edge, slowing down where the land levelled out and rubbing up against a rock which stopped it from making the final plunge. The children waited. Granny would likely jerk again. Only she didn't. She just stared out at the horizon.

The boy stood up and began to collect stones, bigger than those in the courtyard. He made a pile between them on the grass.

'Where are we going?' Granny asked.

They aimed at the varnished walnut panel on the back of the wheelchair. Some hit the wheels. Some missed. Some didn't.

Skitter. Skitter. Ping.

Conk.

PART I
A Mug's Game

ONE

Tessa

Tomorrow would either be the best day of their lives, or the very worst. First though, Tessa and Andy had to deal with *today*. Tessa hadn't even wanted to stay in London, let alone the flat, such were the painful associations with the previous times they'd been through this ... experience? Ordeal? Lottery? So as a distraction, without consulting a map they drove up the M40 and didn't exit until the outskirts of Oxfordshire. As they had often done on adventures early in their relationship, they let instinct guide them, turning down roads on whims and heading towards places with unique names.

Marsh Gibbon. Little Rollright. Unbelievably, too: Quainton.

Then they saw it: Nether Appleford. Andy joked that he'd always been partial to the nether regions, and with that the decision was made.

Two miles outside the village a small, colourful figure dangled from an old-fashioned signpost. Andy pulled the car onto the grass verge so Tessa could get out to investigate.

'It's a knitted Freddy Krueger,' she said with a half-smile on her return.

'Really?'

'Why not? Nothing says welcome like the 1980s' favourite child murderer.'

They passed the walled grounds of an enormous house, two signs at the front reading *Appleford Manor Hotel* and *Appleford Equestrian Centre*. A knitted Indiana Jones had been tied to the former, fedora and all. The narrow road descended, fields giving way to taller and taller trees either side of them. They spotted a knitted Darth Vader, a Legolas, and an Iron Man, before the road levelled off and they reached another sign.

Welcome to Nether Appleford
England's Kindest Village

'I'm sure we'll fit right in here,' Andy said with an exaggerated downward peer at his Napalm Death T-shirt.

Tessa smiled. 'That's some claim.'

They pulled into a car park and continued up the unmarked road on foot. Andy's massive hand reached out to her, and she took it. The band of nervousness squeezing her middle loosened.

Whatever happened tomorrow, it wasn't the end of the world. They would find a way through.

The road bent sharply to the right before straightening. There before them, was Nether Appleford.

'Oh, wow,' Tessa said, looking up at Andy. 'Did you know this was here?' From his dumbfounded expression and silence, she suspected not.

The village – if a single road could be called such a thing – lay in a valley between two steep forests. Fifty or so identical cottages, with netted thatched roofs and all painted a brilliant white, lined both sides of the road. At the foot of the road, a huge evergreen grew in the centre of a manicured lawn, behind which a lake glimmered in the late-spring sun.

They proceeded downward. Ahead, two children, a boy and a girl, ran across the empty road holding hands. The boy turned and stared with a single eye, the other concealed by a patch. Tessa smiled. How funny, she'd worn a patch around that age too, to correct a lazy eye. How long had it been since she'd thought about that? Some children at school had been so cruel about it, dashing all her hopes that it might go unnoticed. But hadn't that been her first experience of real kindness, too, when a group of boys asked her to play pirates with them before making her captain?

They came to a cloth-covered table, ten clipboards neatly arranged on top. Tessa picked one up. NETHER APPLEFORD MOVIE-THEMED CHARITY TRAIL, read the header. Beneath was a map of the village, ten numbers marking ten different locations. Number 1 was apparently near to where they stood. Tessa looked up. A slate tile adorned with a chalk '1' had been propped against someone's front fence. Beside it, two pairs of walking boots and a hiking pole had been decorated with tinfoil stars.

'*Star Trek*,' Andy said.

It took her a moment to understand. 'Bloody hell. That was quick. Isn't that technically a TV show, though?'

'It's a film, too. Give them a break, Tess.'

A donations box sat in the middle of the table. Tessa dropped in a pound and asked Andy if he thought it was enough.

He shrugged. 'They don't exactly look short of cash around here.' He scanned the road before gesturing to the clipboard. 'They've not even put what charity it's for. I'm not paying for their church roof.'

They followed the numbers around the village, writing down their answers as they went. One clue was in the village pub on the green, and they bought two large jam jars of local ale from an affable thirty-something sporting a red beard and a *Goonies* T-shirt.

'Do you know where the money for the walk goes?' Andy asked.

'Does it not say on the map?' he said, looking down at their clipboard. 'A bit of an oversight. Well, this time it's being split between a selection of food poverty charities. That's normally what we do. Pick a topic and then split it between a few. To be fair to all of them.'

'Do you do a lot of these things, then?' Tessa asked.

'Yeah, we do a couple of themed walks a year. And in general, we do loads for charity, a lot of it here, actually. Pub quiz, live music… The gents behind the film walk do a bi-monthly cult movie night upstairs. Charity's big here in the village.'

Clue number seven was in the village shop next door. It was the sort of fine foods store common in suburban London: locally sourced produce, healthy vegan ready meals, organic everything. Back outside, they headed across the immaculate green to a chapel-cum-village hall on the other side. A notice board at the front advertised a book club, something called School of Rap and Rock, and free computer coding lessons. It also declared:

Kindness Sermon Every Other Sunday
10 a.m.
All beliefs and religions welcome

They walked towards the giant, mushroom-shaped tree. Its ridged trunk looked like many smaller trees had merged. An attractive, Lycra-clad couple jogged by, Fitbits raised to wave hello, identical toothy smiles brandished with breathtaking sincerity. Tessa and Andy smiled back until the couple had passed before turning to each other with exaggerated horror.

'Are you a bit scared?' Andy said.

'It's like the hipster Stepford. Are you going to move me here and turn me into a gluten-free robot?'

Andy laughed and fell silent. Eventually, he said, 'Is it weird that I don't *completely* hate it?'

Tessa shook her head. 'Cult cinema nights sound good.' But it wasn't only that. Whatever it was, though, she couldn't exactly articulate it. She just kept picturing the boy in the eye patch.

'This is how they get you, though,' Andy said.

'I know. What's the catch?'

This close to the towering evergreen now, it became apparent that this was no ordinary tree. From the lower branches, which grew just above head height, dangled countless heart-shaped pieces of pink fibreglass, all covered in hand-written messages.

An information board explained that this three-hundred-year-old yew was known locally as the Kindness Tree, and villagers would report here the kind acts of other residents. An artfully crafted wooden trough topped by a glass cover ran along the bottom of the board, divided into little sections – one of which appeared to be a letter box. Inside were blank hearts and marker pens – pads of paper, too, headed with the village logo, apparently for leaving more detailed reports of kindness.

The logo itself, which they'd seen on their clipboard, depicted a tree from which a single large heart dangled from the left branches.

'I wonder if anyone's mentioned their logo looks like a hanging tree,' Tessa said.

'That's what happens here if you're not kind enough.'

Tessa laughed again before leaving Andy's side to walk amongst the hearts in the shady cavern of the canopy. Many hearts hung at eye-level, and she reached up to turn one so the message faced her.

Maria helped Lucas find Texas Ted when he had to wear his eye patch.

Tessa's throat tightened, and every last drop of her default cynicism evaporated.

'You okay?' Andy asked. She hadn't even noticed he was back at her side.

She blinked and wiped her cheek. 'No, *you're* crying at a stupid message on a heart.'

'Oh, love.' Andy went to hold her but she walked away, towards the lake, laughing it off.

'Come on,' she yelled back, 'let's get these last few clues.'

They found *The Dark Knight* (a suit of armour knitted with black wool) and *Silence of the Lambs* (a sheep with packing tape over its mouth) on the footpath circling the lake. Done, they walked back up the road to drop off their clipboard.

A slight woman somewhere between her mid-fifties and mid-sixties, by far the oldest person they'd seen today, stood talking to a young blonde woman with the same vaguely annoying bone-structure beauty as Tessa's sister, Maddy.

'Thank you, Olivia,' the older woman said to her, 'I'll see you in the pub.'

Beautiful Olivia took a moment to appraise the two of them approaching the table, before she departed the scene with an odd smile. The older woman faced them. She had neat grey streaks in brown hair tied back in an all-business ponytail.

'Did you have great success?' she said, reaching out to take their clipboard and flashing them the Nether Appleford smile with her wide, bright teeth.

'Think so, yeah,' Andy said. He reached into his pocket, removed his wallet and took out a note which he placed in the donation tin. Tessa did a double take.

The woman noticed the gesture and said, 'That's so kind of you.'

'When in Rome,' he said.

She studied Andy for a few seconds, her eyelids lowered. 'Have you been here before?'

Andy glanced at Tessa before shaking his head. 'Nah, never.'

She shook her head. 'You look very familiar. Never mind. Have you left us an email? Oh, yes you have, great. Well, if you win, we'll be in touch. I hope to see you back here again some time. Have you any plans for the rest of the weekend?'

After a short silence, Andy said, 'Yes, but nothing as nice as coming here.'

On the drive home they made some half-hearted attempts to take the piss out of Nether Appleford, but as London grew closer, they both fell silent. They listened to music to relieve the tension building in the car and Tessa stared out the window. If only they could get drunk when they got home. Or how great would it be, after all this time, to do something stronger? A couple of lines would be just the ticket.

But no, that younger, more hedonistic version of herself had been instructed to fuck off years ago. So perhaps she'd seduce Andy instead. That could definitely work. It had been a while.

'It was funny when that woman said she recognised you,'

Tessa said when they reached the outskirts of London, the strange little village not having really left her mind.

'I knew you'd pick up on that. I've honestly never been there before in my life.'

'So we just found that place.'

'We just found that place.'

'So you're not planning to turn me into a robot because we can't have kids.'

He turned to her, and she wished she'd stayed quiet. Disappointment, irritation, pity. It was all there on his face. 'We'll have none of that tonight,' he said. 'This time's the one, I'm sure of it.'

———

They fucked, but the whole thing was done too quickly. He was snoring beside her moments after, while she lay awake. While her eyes were closed for much of the night, so she couldn't be certain, she felt like she hadn't slept at all when her alarm went off at quarter to six.

She stepped out of bed and tiptoed across the carpet in the dark.

'Love you,' Andy said.

'Love you, too.'

In the en suite she weed into a cup and at the sink unpacked the test the clinic had given her, all of it routine now. She began the usual mental pep talk about how it didn't really matter what happened, yet her hands shook when she lifted the pipette and squeezed four drops onto the test cassette. The control line appeared. She watched for the test line. It would all be okay. Andy had a good feeling. So did she.

But why would *this* test work when so many others hadn't?

For a while she willed it to appear, and when it didn't, she sat on the toilet biting her thumbnail. It took time, that was all. Looking wouldn't help. And so what if it was negative? It didn't change anything for her and Andy. They had each other. They'd talked about it a lot over the years, and the worst-case scenario was total freedom.

Freedom from the endless What Ifs? Freedom from an unplannable future. Freedom from late-night feeds and the tyranny of responsibility.

All lies, of course. Not all freedom was good. Deep inside she didn't want to float anymore. She craved an anchor. Was that so shameful? To have a purpose not self-generated.

She got to her feet and looked again. The test line was still blank. But it had to come this time. It was that simple.

So she watched. Watched and waited. And waited.

TWO

Tessa

T he last person Tessa wanted to see was Maddy, but dinner with her sister had been in the diary long before this round of IVF. They probably should have rescheduled, but she'd not wanted Maddy thinking she was disorganised. With six o'clock approaching, Tessa prepared a risotto. Chopping onions. Grating parmesan. Mixing stock. Yes, distraction was probably good.

They'd already started laughing about it. Their shared gallows humour had kicked in almost as soon as she'd pried herself from his arms around mid-day, her throat and eyes still abraded from crying.

At least we can get smashed tonight.

The doorbell rang at exactly six, of course, and Tessa crossed the room to throw the assorted plastic waste into the bin before answering. The lid lifted, and Tessa froze. The pregnancy test cassette lay on top of the week's rubbish. The last time she'd seen it had been on the bedside table before she fell asleep in Andy's arms. He'd moved it whilst she slept.

She leaned closer, instinctively looking for a positive line even now. But as it had been the previous three times they'd been through this, white space prevailed. Forty grand in total. Their entire life savings. For this. All the specialists. The hospital in America. The injections, the womb scratching, the fibroid scraping. All the dashed hopes a person's sanity could handle.

'You getting that?' Andy shouted from upstairs.

She kept staring, wanting to watch for a little bit longer.

'I know what we talked about before,' Andy had whispered earlier, 'but it doesn't have to end here.' But they both knew this was the end of the line – bar some miracle or lottery win. She was forty early next year. They'd been in a cycle of saving, trying, and failing for over six years now. It had to end somewhere, and they'd both known, when their final six grand had yielded only one viable embryo, that it was now or never.

She stared at that white space. Apparently, never it was.

The thud of Andy's footsteps broke her concentration, but still she didn't look away. The kitchen door creaked open.

'Tess?'

He came up behind her. Saw. Understood. He turned her around and held her to his enormous chest. The doorbell rang again.

'I'll sort them,' he said, letting her go and taking the plastic waste from her hands. He pushed it into the bin and took off the lid. He tied the bag and lifted it out effortlessly.

'I'm sorry,' she said, pushing the heel of her hand into a damp eye. 'I'm being pathetic—'

'No, you're not.'

He left her, and she heard bustle and chatter at the door. She wiped her eyes and poured herself a large glass of white wine. When Maddy entered, skin glowing, naturally blonde hair shaped by some *actual* flipping haircut with highlights at the front, Tessa did her best to smile. She hugged Maddy before she had a chance to notice Tessa's own flushed cheeks and the silver hairs glinting beneath the harsh lights of the kitchen spots.

Andy entertained Maddy and her fiancé, Bhav, in the dining room while Tessa finished cooking and got tipsy. Every so often the conversation lulled, and Tessa would hold her breath, abdomen muscles clenched. She really didn't want them to bring up the IVF.

It wasn't as if they talked often. Since the time Maddy's favourite colouring pencil had been yellow and Tessa's black, the two had inhabited very different mental worlds. So Maddy certainly didn't know they'd gone back for a third round, let alone a fourth. But she knew they were trying, and because she was such a lovely, thoughtful ray of bloody sunshine, she might well ask how it was all going. And if she did … well, Tessa didn't know how she'd react.

So best it didn't happen at all. Every time the laughter quietened, and the talking slowed, Tessa would walk in with more drinks or snacks, to make sure the topic of IVF didn't fill the silence. How's things at the lab, Mads? Bhav, you still playing football? What was your accommodation like when you went to Spain?

She kept up the performance over dinner, Andy increasingly seeking out eye-contact as her new conversation topics became more random. But a lull came while Tessa was chewing, and Maddy and Bhav shared a secretive look before Maddy said, 'Bhav and I were wondering—'

'About the wine?' Tessa said, rice escaping her mouth and landing on the table. She swallowed. Maddy looked at her, eyes wide with confusion. 'It's not great, is it? Sorry, can you taste it in the food? Is that what you were going to say?'

'No,' Maddy said.

'Tastes great to me,' Bhav said.

'I shouldn't have cheaped out, sorry,' Tessa said. 'But you never know with the sale wines, do you? Are they on sale because they know you'll be hooked once you try it, or are they on sale because it's rubbish?'

Andy put his hand on her leg beneath the table. She put her hand on his and squeezed.

No one spoke. Maddy and Bhav were looking at each other again. Tessa panicked. 'What about you guys?' she said. 'Do you guys … cheap out on wine?'

Bhav shrugged and smiled. 'I cheap out on anything when I can.'

'Bhav's a bargain king,' Maddy said, assessing Tessa with kindly concern. 'Martin Lewis-level.'

Tessa forced another smile. Mads and Bhav had been together since meeting at university – typical that Maddy's first love had been her soulmate. They were giving each other that look again now, silently communicating.

'Guys,' Maddy said. 'We really wanted to catch up tonight because we'd been thinking about you a lot, and—'

Tessa faked a cough and held up a hand. She dashed to the kitchen, poured a glass of water, and waited for a new conversation to start.

'You okay, love?' Andy called out.

'Yeah, fine,' she replied, pinching the web between her left index finger and thumb where years of such attention had coarsened the skin. What must they all be thinking? She had to get a grip. If they brought up the IVF, so what? She could just say they were still saving. That was all it needed. A simple, one-line exit strategy. She skulked back in and sat down. 'Sorry about that.'

'We just really wanted to tell you in person, Tess,' Maddy said, and pushed her phone across the table. An image, a galaxy of black and white, filled the screen. Tessa tried to swallow. Andy put his hand back on her leg and squeezed, hard.

'It's a baby,' Maddy said after a beat, like Tessa didn't know. 'We're pregnant.'

Tessa closed her eyes. Opened them again. Maddy asked for water not wine tonight, didn't she? Her skin fucking glowed.

Of course. A baby. Maddy. Why the hell not?

She took a deep breath and tried her hardest to say the right thing. She even had the words lined up and everything.

But what she managed was, 'Oh, fucking fuck off.'

The excitement fell from Maddy's face. Bhav's jaw hung ajar. Tessa covered her mouth with her hand. But it was out now. They all stared at her. 'That was... Maddy, I'm sorry.' She instinctively tried to cover up. 'I was just messing around. I was—'

No, she couldn't do it. She stood up and left the table. Left the flat, down the stairs and through the back exit of the building. She sat down against the wall between two industrial-sized bins.

Where she belonged.

———

She didn't want Maddy to find her, but Tessa didn't send her away when she did. Maddy sat beside her on the floor.

'I don't know what to say,' Tessa said. 'I'm being a child. I'm so sorry. I'm ... happy for you.'

'No, you're not,' Maddy said. 'How could you be? Andy

explained. I feel like an idiot. I should have asked about you first—'

'Don't you dare be fucking nice about this,' Tessa said, her voice cracking. 'You couldn't have known. We didn't tell anyone.'

'I knew you'd been trying. That's why we wanted to be here to tell you in person. I'm just saying, Tess. I totally understand.'

Tessa wasn't sure she could bear this, not now. Her kindness. Her natural, unwavering kindness. And here *she* was, acting like she was a kid again; her jealousy at her sister's effortless successes boiling as violently as it had done all those times when her parents had asked her why she couldn't be more like Maddy.

'You know, I haven't had to come and find you since we were teenagers,' Maddy said, reaching out and hooking her little finger around Tessa's. 'Takes me back. The Todd sisters, out by some bins again.'

'What, Mum and Dad having a drunken argument in a restaurant?'

'Or in front of the PTA friends they were always so keen to impress.'

Tessa snorted a laugh. After a moment of silence, she asked, 'How far along are you?'

'Twenty weeks. I'm due in November.'

'You're not even showing.'

'Oh, trust me, I am.'

'Were you … trying?'

'Sort of. We didn't expect… I'm sorry.'

'Please don't apologise for me being a shit,' Tessa said. 'I'm happy for you. Really. It was just … a bad … bad…'

A bad day – was that what she'd been about to say? What a load of bollocks. This outburst, this behaviour… This wasn't the outcome of a single day.

'I'm just a bad person.'

'No, you're not.'

'Did you hear what I said in there? I'm toxic. If I were a baby, I wouldn't want to grow in me either.'

'Tessa, that's... Biology doesn't care about... Rose West had children.' She winced and Tessa laughed.

'I'm really happy for you, Mads.' She squeezed her sister's little finger with hers.

'You're not ... toxic.'

'Do you remember after Mum and Dad split up, and every so often Dad used to have us over at his shabby old farmhouse? And he used to abandon us in the garden to do chores while he watched the cricket. Like, hard, proper labour.'

Maddy put on a jolly-hockey-sticks voice. 'No passengers on this ship.'

'And we never wanted to go there, which is why he always met us in town and took us for dinner...'

'... and left us in the cinema.'

'But then, apropos of fuck all, he insisted we come over for the whole weekend once. Friday *and* Saturday. And I was about fifteen, you would have been eleven. We'd never done that before, and I just knew something was going on. So I put my foot down, and just said I wasn't going. Mum and I really argued about it, but I just dug in. And so you got to go to Thorpe Park, because Dad had won tickets and it was all meant to be a lovely surprise. The one nice thing he ever did for us, and I missed it because I expected the worst.'

'I remember that.'

'I haven't changed since then, Mads. I expect the worst so I can never be disappointed. But now it's like ... cynicism's a ... suit of armour, but ... the suit's been slowly poisoning me. Like it's lead or something. Does that poison you slowly?'

Maddy, a chemist for a biopharma giant, nodded. 'Yes, lead can do that.'

'Exactly. So now here I am. Full of lead. Sulking at home while everyone else is on a roller coaster. Telling my sister to fuck off after she tells me she's having a baby.'

'Today was just bad … timing. Anyway, you're just smart, aren't you? You ask questions. Don't accept things at face value. That's a good thing.'

'You don't believe that. You've always been the peacekeeper.'

'Yeah, but sometimes you've got to pick a side. Do you not remember what *actually* happened at Thorpe Park? He brought some young student of his to go with me while he did … well, went to the bar, I suspect. I threw up after one of the rides because I had heatstroke from working in that stupid garden the day before, and so we had to go home. I didn't sleep for days from the sunburn. You were fine, because you knew what he was like. You were clever.'

Tessa shook her head. 'Clever, right. Stubborn. Single-minded. Determined. Mads, do you want to know what I've never been called in my whole life? Kind. No one's ever said, "You know what, Tessa? You are so kind." Because, the thing is, I'm not.'

Maddy considered this. 'No one ever says you're kind to your face, do they? Doesn't mean they don't think it.'

'Do *you* think I'm kind?'

Maddy paused. 'Kind… Kind of. Yes, you definitely *can* be kind.'

Tessa snorted a laugh. 'People think you're kind *and* they say it to you.'

'I don't know—'

'It's fine, I'm not kind. I understand that about myself. Maybe I resented the way Mum and Dad were always giving

25

themselves away to all their causes and yuppie friends and their charity functions, projecting this perfect, happy family, then coming home, getting drunk and hitting each other. Ignoring us. But now my heart's black, and *Christ*, am I still going on about myself? Just fuck me. You deserve a better sister.'

Maddy shook her head. 'You were the oldest. You had to be tough. You didn't have an older sister like I did. And Mum and Dad … they weren't fair to you.'

Tessa had never heard Maddy say anything this candid before about the way their parents had treated her. Their disappointment in everything, from her looks to her grades, was made clear. She'd always believed Maddy wasn't even aware of it. She took a juddery breath to steady herself.

'I thought having a baby might squeeze some goodness out of me,' Tessa said. 'You know, the milk of human kindness and all that.' She squeezed her sister's little finger again and glanced down at her seemingly flat middle. 'It's amazing, Mads. Really. I'm going to be an auntie. The Todd genes will live on.'

'Not sure if that's a good thing or not, but thank you, Tess.' Maddy put a hand on Tessa's shoulder and looked at her earnestly. 'That's really … *kind* of you to say.'

'I see what you did there. But stop it.' Tessa clasped her sister's hand between her two. 'Or I'll tell you to fuck off again.'

Maddy gave a crooked smile, and Tessa recalled the pretty blonde she'd glimpsed in Nether Appleford earlier. They really had looked quite similar. Kindness, it would seem, was an underrated cosmetic.

That night they lay in bed, Tessa knowing Andy was awake but neither of them speaking. What more was there to say? Already inebriation was giving way to shame.

'Do you want some good news?' Andy said. 'We won a prize.'

'What prize?'

'That film walk thing we did. The village emailed this afternoon.'

'Really? What did we win?'

'A free meal at the pub.'

'Our luck's really turning, then.'

'Want to go back there? Might be a laugh.'

Tessa pictured the tree again, all the hearts spinning on the low branches. She pictured the little boy with the eye patch, before his face morphed into Maddy's, her eyes betraying the latent hurt she felt while trying to rise above Tessa's outburst. Lastly, she pictured the test cassette again, lying on a heap of rubbish.

Yes, she did. She wanted to go back quite a bit.

THREE

Tessa

At lunchtime the following Saturday, Tessa and Andy arrived at The Yew Tree to claim their prize. The tree, after which the pub was named, now cast a shadow over the whitewashed exterior and thatched roof. At the bar, the red-bearded barman, now in a Super Mario T-shirt, greeted them like old friends. He showed them to a table at the back of the main bar room – Andy ducking beneath the low oak beams – and left them with a menu.

On the wall nearby someone had affixed a stylish poster for *Heathers* to advertise the next movie night in the upstairs room. Tessa had watched the film repeatedly during university, wearing out a VHS tape that even then had been well on its way to being a relic. Shelves of books ran close to the ceiling: Shirley Jackson, Jonathan Coe, Anne Tyler, so many authors she'd read and admired. While they waited for their order, the sound system almost exclusively played classics from their youth. 'Black Hole Sun' by Soundgarden. '1979' by The Smashing Pumpkins. 'Enter Sandman' by Metallica. They were small things, but it was as if they were being wooed.

Neither of them commented. They shared rosemary chips and knowing smiles.

While they ate, Tessa became aware she was being watched. A woman in a yellow scarf and thick-rimmed glasses grinned at her from over by the bar. Seventy or so, her grey hair flowed from beneath a pork-pie hat. When Tessa glanced over to check a third time, the woman gave her a big thumbs up. Assuming she was asking about the food, Tessa returned the gesture. The woman clapped her hands, delighted.

Once they finished eating, the woman they'd met when they'd handed in their answers last week approached their table.

'I had a feeling when we met I'd be seeing you two again,' she said.

'Hello again,' Andy said.

'Andy and Tessa, is that right? I'm Ruth. Congratulations. How are you finding the food?'

'Lovely, thanks,' Andy said.

'Well, Aaron has a wonderful chef. We're very lucky, really.'

'Is Aaron the man that's been serving us?'

'Aaron's the landlord, yes.'

Tessa asked Ruth about the woman in the hat, who was now conversing with Aaron. Ruth looked over, nodded, and lowered her voice. 'Ah, well, that's October Allsopp.' She spoke like the name should mean something. When Andy and Tessa didn't react quickly enough, Ruth added, even more quietly, 'October owns Nether Appleford.'

'Owns?' Andy said. 'What, all of it?'

'Yes, we're an estate village. Everything from the manor down to the lake and all the fields you can see. There's not much that goes on here that she doesn't know about. But don't worry, I told her you were lovely.'

'Does she own the cottages?' Tessa said.

'Almost all of them, yes. The pub, the shop, the chapel. The village has been in her family for generations, although I should add, she's not your typical estate owner. She's not an aristocrat.'

'How interesting. Do the residents here rent, then?'

Ruth nodded. 'Lots of them work for the estate. Like me.' She grinned. 'Not all of them, though. I shouldn't say, but October looks after everyone very well, and people pay what they can afford. No one pays anything near market rates. And she props up this place, and the shop. It's all about the community for her.'

Tessa looked for October again at the bar, but she'd gone.

'Can we move here?' Andy said and laughed.

'Of course.' She laughed, too, perhaps humouring them, perhaps not. 'You certainly seem like our sort of people. Are you looking for somewhere?'

Tessa glanced up at Andy. 'Well…'

'It's complicated,' he finished. Ruth held up her hands to indicate she wouldn't press them.

For that Tessa was grateful, because how could you begin to explain to a stranger that your long-imagined future had been forever rendered a ghost place of empty swings, echoing schools and tiny beds made up but never slept in? That they really had no idea what they were going to do now, no longer imprisoned in baby-trying limbo. How could you explain that yeah, sure, moving somewhere completely different, with a completely different way of life, was one of the many ideas that had come bursting out from behind the dam of their uncertainty. And that they had even joked about moving to Nether Appleford, with today's trip being a semi-serious scouting mission. So, *were* they looking for somewhere? Yes, hypothetically, Ruth, yes, they were. But in reality?

'Is it really as … nice as it looks?' Tessa asked Ruth.

Ruth widened her eyes. 'It's even better.'

Tessa reached for her coffee, and the cuff of her long-sleeved top withdrew to reveal the black-heart tattoo she'd had done one drunk night at university. Before Ruth noticed, she brought the hand back without the drink.

Before driving home, they visited the Kindness Tree again, reading more of the acts the villagers had deemed laudable enough to report. Pep taking 'the kids' to the cinema. Dev looking at Lilliana's ear in the middle of the night. Olivia's inspiring generosity. That last name, Olivia: it had been the name of the razor-cheekboned blonde Ruth had been saying farewell to the day of their first visit. What incredible things must she have done for such a gush? She'd noticed that same woman entering the pub earlier, chatting jovially with Andy and Aaron when Andy had gone to the bar to double-check their drinks had been part of the prize. Tessa had again been struck by the paranoid notion that Andy somehow knew them all already, but dismissed it almost instantly – just more of the same old reflex cynicism she wanted done with now. Cynicism, and perhaps just a sprinkling of jealousy. Whatever it was, the lot needed to go.

They followed the footpath around the lake again, the piney air redolent of summer camping trips. Good memories, of getting the trains and coaches to the coast with her little friendship group at sixth form. Being away from home, ensconced in that shared bafflement of simply existing that bound young people so tightly. She'd not really had friends like it since.

'I'm getting the weird sense you're into this place?' Andy said.

'Are you?'

'You're smiling.'

She hadn't even realised. 'Do *you* like it?'

He hummed through a tight-lipped smile. 'It's cute, I'll give them that. The film nights. The charity stuff. The community vibe. But … could I live here? It all just seems a bit too … happy clappy? Been there, done that.'

She nodded, taking his point. She'd met Andy at a metal night she'd been doing the sound for – one of a number of cash-in-hand side hustles she'd done in her twenties and early thirties to pay the bills while trying to get various music projects afloat. He'd been drumming for one of the bands, and after the sound check he came to chat with her behind the board. Like her, he'd reached a liminal space in his life, torn between creative pursuits and stability.

Unlike her, he'd had a complete spiritual reversal a few years before. Following a devoutly secular upbringing, he'd joined the local church band as a drummer to earn some extra money and had fallen for the church's matey style of Christianity. One thing led to another, and he wound up being paid to visit schools to peddle Jesus to impressionable teenagers through 'cool' assemblies and charismatically delivered lunchtime discussion groups. All in service of something called The Question, a course designed to spread His word to the masses. But after his dad died when he was only twenty-seven, Andy found the 'God-shaped hole' he thought he'd filled empty once again. That hole, a reference to a U2 lyric, had been the guiding force in his life until then. But he wanted nothing to do with a God cruel enough to strike down a non-smoker with lung cancer before they'd turned sixty. A God like that deserved only disdain and resentment.

'You're probably right,' Tessa said. 'You know, I saw someone had given another person a heart for taking the time to give them a heart.'

Andy laughed. 'Exactly.'

She considered letting the subject drop, but after a moment felt obliged to explain herself to him. 'But, I don't know why, but yeah, I sort of do like it. The music in the pub … the books on the shelf. Like you said, the film night…'

'Uh huh.'

'And, I don't know, it just seems like … they try here.'

'Try?'

'Yes. They try. They don't just … perpetually abdicate.'

'You don't think we try? What have we been bloody doing the better part of a decade, then?'

'That's a different type of trying. That's trying because *we* want something. I don't know, I think I just mean … spiritual trying, or something.'

'Happy-clappy trying?'

She smiled. 'It's just easy, isn't it, to turn your nose up at a place like this? I always do it when I see people … making an effort. People giving a stuff. But why not kindness? Yeah, it's twee and a bit simplistic, but is it any worse than taking the piss and assuming the worst all the time? It's not even a decision with me, if I'm honest – it's a reaction. It's like, is this my best life?'

'I don't think you're doing too bad, love.'

'Okay, so my dad, right, he used to go to a newsagent to buy a paper, and he'd always slot a magazine for my mum inside so he didn't have to pay for both. He said the paper was too expensive anyway, and he wasn't going to be taken for a mug. That was such a big deal in my family. You couldn't get ahead in life if you were a mug. And it's weird, because even though I've rejected so much of how my parents could be, on some level I internalised that one value. In fact, I probably believed *they* were mugs for getting sucked into that whole upper-middle-class showboating rubbish they built their life around. But now … I've ended up thinking *anything* not obviously beneficial to me is a mug's game. It's not right, is it?'

Andy looked away, appearing to genuinely contemplate this. 'I do know what you mean,' he said eventually. 'But Tess, a lot of stuff *is* a mug's game. And I like taking the piss out of stuff with you. It's what we do.'

She didn't know how to respond to this at first. 'I know, and I'm not saying I want to stop taking the piss out of stuff. It's just … let's not hoard all the piss.' Again, Andy laughed. 'I mean, who am I to judge anyone? I don't know what I'm doing. And we must believe there's something good outside of just you and me. Otherwise, why did we even want kids?'

He fell quiet, and after a moment turned his head away from her.

'You okay?' she asked.

He looked back, a smile on his face but his eyes damp. 'Yeah. Fine, just … past tense caught me by surprise.'

And here it was. Proof, if more were needed, that she, at the very least, needed to change. She'd been so wrapped up in her own shit that she'd not even considered how Andy was coping. How he'd be grieving.

She stopped to hold him, squeezing him to her. 'I just … want to make a connection with the world again. We both need that, I think. When that woman said we looked like their sort of people… I've *never* been anyone's sort of person.'

Once he'd composed himself, he said, 'So what? Are you actually saying you want to move here?'

'I'm not saying that exactly. But … I know I want a change. So, maybe. Yeah. I mean, why not?'

FOUR

Tessa

O nce back in the car, Tessa looked up the village on her phone and found no properties for rent. They stopped at an estate agent in the nearest town and asked the two suited young men, suddenly alert now at their adjacent desks, about Nether Appleford.

'We don't really get anything from there,' the estate agent with stubble said.

'That's not because of us,' the estate agent without stubble added. 'It's more that you have to apply through the estate.'

'They have a waiting list,' the estate agent with stubble said.

'It can be quite selective, but I believe they do all that in-house. But we do have some other properties in similar locations.'

'Between us,' the agent with stubble leaned over his desk and lowered his voice, 'I've also heard there are all sorts of rules you have to follow there. But are you wanting a property that's exclusively rural?'

'What sort of rules?' Tessa said.

The agent without stubble said, 'It's not something we

handle. However, if you're interested in viewing something in that style of property, we had a thatched cob come on last week, not far away?'

Tessa declined, thanked them both, and the two of them returned to the car. Andy drove while she found the website for Nether Appleford. Simple, yet tastefully designed, the site prioritised images over text – a blurred shot of the street through tree branches, a view of the Kindness Tree from the water level of the lake, the pub's cosy interior. The little text there was focused on the village's history and its current commercial activities. The manor house now operated as a hotel and wedding venue. You could order produce from the organic farm online. If you owned a horse, you could use the Appleford Equestrian Centre, which offered tailored livery packages and was home to a specialist equine hospital. And of course, ever present on the site was the village logo, accompanied by the motto *Just Be Kind!* beneath it.

According to a small link at the bottom of the site, the web developer was *actually* called Dev – another name she recognised from the Kindness Tree. Beside this link, and one about site cookies, she found what she'd been searching for:

Our Community

She clicked through to a page of text which explained that in the eighteenth century, generous Lord Hinton had built Nether Appleford for his workers. Not only that, but he had agreed to pay for their healthcare and funeral expenses, too. To honour his warmth, there had long been a tradition of performing kind acts in the village, as well as twice-yearly fetes, and annual prizes for the kindest residents.

At the bottom of this page was another link: Interested in joining our community? Tessa clicked.

Nether Appleford is a small but welcoming community that values kindness above all else. Our residents often remain with us for a long time, and homes in the village are rarely available. However, if you are interested in joining our community, do drop us a line and tell us about yourselves. Should an appropriate home become free, we will be in touch. Please do not be offended if you do not hear from us, but we have a considerable waiting list, and must balance your requirements with what we have available.

A form followed. It requested an applicant name, a date of birth, the names of other householders, the ideal number of bedrooms required, all residents' professions, whether one required furnished or unfurnished premises, and whether one had any other specific requirements. A final box asked for the reason one wanted to live in Nether Appleford.

'Shall I just fill it in?' Tessa said. 'For a laugh. We can leave it in the lap of the gods?'

'You're not worried about the rules?' Andy said, taking one hand off the steering wheel to make speech marks around his last two words.

'I'm sure they were just talking about the kindness stuff. And Andy, I think we need rules.'

'We do?' He mulled this over and eventually smiled. 'Yeah, maybe we do.'

'Honestly, I think rules would do us some good.'

Tessa took some time off work at the beginning of the following week, wanting to float inside her own head for a while. While Andy insisted working through his grief, she stayed at home, half-heartedly trying to finish a composition on her laptop she'd been chopping and changing for what felt like months. Her music was just a glorified hobby at the moment. It brought in a bit of extra money to supplement her day job in music publishing. But with some attention, and with all these brand-new tomorrows to fill, it had the potential to be something more.

But she kept getting distracted, looking up Nether Appleford online and poring over the website. Repeatedly checking her emails for a response. Reading articles about the science of kindness. How good for you it was supposed to be. It was daft, and yeah, she was getting over-fixated. And she could tell Andy wasn't entirely convinced. He was giving her the same concerned looks he used to give her when she'd started experimenting with drugs to improve her compositions a few years back – one of the few bad times in their relationship. Andy was a creature of habit, and for the most part so was Tessa. But she *was* prone to a whim, she knew that. That part of her unsettled Andy, which was fine, especially as, yes, he'd probably been right about her mixing as many uppers and downers as she'd ended up doing – and the trip to the hospital had only underlined that.

Wanting to be kind, though: that wasn't a whim, was it? He had to see that if they weren't careful, they would become one of those couples that got so absorbed in their own world, they lost touch with reality. Once upon a time they'd had friends. They used to go out to the pub and have people over for dinner. They'd watched the news regularly and even got out of the house to get to an environmental protest once. But as some couples started families, or fled the expense of the city, they'd gravitated towards a more solitary existence of binge-watching boxed sets and property programmes while bitching about how crap the world was outside the flat. And Andy had to sense how easy it might be for their cynicism and dependence on one another to morph into misanthropy and nastiness.

What happened on Wednesday with Andy's new assistant went some way to making her case. The kid, Justin, was an eighteen-year-old Andy had reluctantly taken on as a favour to a friend. Justin's dad was in prison for killing a bloke in a pub row, and the kid understandably came with baggage. He'd been in trouble with the police a few times, but Andy wanted to do his mate the solid, so he gave the kid a chance.

But since starting, Justin'd been a bit of a nightmare. Talking to his mates on the phone at work. Calling in sick when he was obviously just hungover. This time, after having told Andy he was going out on the lash the day before, the kid had cried off work with a message in the wee hours of Wednesday morning, claiming his mum was *really* sick. Andy lost it. He was in the middle of a big job rewiring a row of Victorian terraces, and he was already behind. He'd called Justin straight away and fired him in a few short, angry sentences.

'He thinks I'm a mug,' he said after throwing his phone down on the bed, shaking his head before muttering something about his Tradechecker score.

It didn't take him long to regret his outburst. And while he still stood by his decision, he felt obliged to go over that morning and explain to Justin in person how much he'd let him down and how he couldn't go through life taking the mick out of people trying to help him. Of course, when he had arrived at Justin's mum's high rise, he'd watched grave-looking paramedics wheel her into an ambulance while Justin watched, distraught. Andy had spent the morning keeping him company at the hospital, feeling like a complete heel and already having undone the firing.

He'd called to tell Tessa all this just after lunch, and though she tried to make him feel better, she knew he was thinking about everything they'd talked about, and where they went next.

Not long after he hung up, her email pinged. She opened it hurriedly, and when she saw the subject line she held her breath. It read simply: YOUR APPLICATION.

Andy often had his phone off when he was up against it, and she hadn't been able to get through to him again the rest of the afternoon. At 4pm he called Tessa to tell her he was still tidying up and was likely going to be back late. He was on his hands and knees sweeping as they spoke.

'How is Justin's mum?' Tessa asked.

'Not doing great. I feel like such a bastard.'

'Oh, Andy. Listen, don't worry about being late. But I have some … good news, I suppose. I got a response from our application.'

It took him a moment. 'What, the village thing?'

'Yeah. They've got a cottage they want to show us. They said we can come this weekend.'

'That's mad.'

'They obviously liked the cut of our jib.'

'Jibs like knives, us.'

'So, what do you think?'

'What *do* I think?'

'Listen, I know you've got more doubts than me. I know you're thinking I'm being impetuous. But can we just … go and see it? And if you're not feeling it…'

He fell silent, for so long that Tessa quickly lowered her phone to check the battery hadn't died.

'No,' Andy said. 'I'm in.'

She paused. 'You're in?'

'Yeah. Hundred per cent.' She heard him shift the phone

and now his voice came through louder. 'But Tess, if we do it, we really should do it.'

'What does that mean?'

'If we do it, let's really try to be better. Let's not half-arse it.'

She paused. 'Of course. Yes. We'll do it.'

'And we'll hold each other to it.'

'Yeah.'

'We're not just going to show up and … buy a few rounds at the pub, and then start taking the mick. We're not moving house ironically, are we?'

Again, she paused. 'I mean, we might not even like the cottage.' He said nothing, and she knew he wanted her to understand that he was telling her this couldn't be some whim now. 'No. Of course, we'll try. We'll really try.'

'Cool,' he said, and she heard his sweeping resume. 'Then let's go and see a cottage.'

FIVE

Tessa

R uth met them outside number 34, a cottage situated in the middle of The Road – the actual name of the main street.

'You're the village estate agent, then?' Andy said, dressed today in his only shirt that Tessa insisted he wear, long sleeves to cover his tattoos, buttoned up to hide any offensive band T-shirt he might have chosen.

'One of my many hats,' she said with a slightly pained roll of her eyes, like they didn't even know the half of it.

The building was Grade II listed, and many original features had been preserved. An inglenook fireplace. Wooden doors with ring-turn latches. Exposed beams like those in the pub. Also like the pub, the ceilings and, in particular, the doorways, were built for the average height of a different era. Andy bobbed in and out of rooms. Tessa fully expected him to call the whole thing off on the basis of the cramped space alone, but he made enough approving noises for her to know he wasn't hating it. Andy disliked with silence.

'Originally these cottages were built for two families and divided down the middle,' Ruth said. 'This one has, for a long time, been merged, so it has three bedrooms. You wanted two or three bedrooms in the application, have I understood that correctly? Out of interest, did you want an extra room for the recording studio you mentioned in your application? I wasn't sure how many rooms exactly you wanted.'

Tessa looked at Andy. She noticed a bit of plaster stuck in his unkempt hair. 'Uh…' The silence started to grow into the room. She hadn't exactly known what to put on the form, especially after how Andy had reacted to her talking about trying for a family in the past tense. So she'd fudged an answer, at a time when she still thought she was messing around.

Andy gave an uncomfortable laugh. 'Well, I think the more rooms the better. We're just keeping our options open, really.'

'Children?'

He laughed again and glanced over to check in with Tessa. She smiled reassuringly but wished Ruth would get the hint. 'Well, never say never.'

'Oh, well, that's lovely to hear. Don't leave it too long, mind.' Finally sensing their discomfort, Ruth moved on: 'I only ask because there's something I'm quite excited to show you.'

She walked them to the back garden, which sloped up towards the woods behind the cottage. On a concrete platform at the rear stood a wooden cabin. Ruth took them inside, revealing a space twice as big as Tessa's current office-cum-recording studio.

'It's completely soundproofed, a gentleman that lived here a while back had us do it for his trumpet. You could scream and shout in here all day and no one would be any the wiser.'

'Well, that'll be useful,' Andy said. Ruth didn't react to his attempt at humour.

'The previous lady used it for a painting studio, though, as you can probably tell from the smell. But I'm sure an airing and few candles will sort that. Would it work for you, Tessa?'

She was blown away. 'God, it's ... just perfect.'

'Fabulous. And the cottage? What did you think?'

Tessa looked to Andy, and he nodded once approvingly, so she said, 'I like it. It's so lovely. But—' She had so many questions, particularly about cost. This was far bigger than they would be able to afford in their current circumstances, and Oxfordshire prices weren't markedly different from London.

But Ruth wasn't really interested in buts. 'And what about you?' She tilted her head up at Andy.

'It's wonderful.'

'Great, great.'

They trailed Ruth, who moved neatly and quickly, back through the cottage again and out to the front garden. She kept walking past their car on the drive, at which point Tessa and Andy stopped. Ruth turned and gestured for them to keep following now.

'Where are we going?' Tessa said.

Ruth smiled patiently and glanced at her watch. 'To meet the Kindness Committee.'

She took them to the chapel opposite the pub across the green. Inside five people sat on plastic chairs arranged in a circle before the chancel. Tessa and Andy were shown across a bare wooden floor to the remaining two empty chairs, their backs to the entrance.

Sitting opposite them was October Allsopp, no hat today, a pink streak visible now in her grey bob. 'Hello, Tessa and

Andy,' she said, patting her hands together. 'Did you just love the cottage?'

'It was really nice,' Tessa said.

'I knew you would.' Addressing Andy, October said, 'And you're an electrician?'

'Guilty as charged.'

'Ah ha. We've not had an electrician in quite some time.'

The room fell silent. She kept nodding, her watery eyes fixed on Andy. Tessa shifted in her seat. There had been no mention of this gathering when they'd received the invite, and regardless of the authority-neutralising circle they'd created, it very much felt like they'd been corralled here for inspection.

Ruth, who stood beside October now, coughed. Eventually October stood up. 'Well, over to you, Dev.'

October left in the direction they'd entered, and a baby-faced man in a black suit and tie introduced himself as Dev Chopra, he of the Kindness Tree fame, a local GP based at the surgery in the next village which also served Nether Appleford. From Andy's right the members of the committee introduced themselves anti-clockwise. Olivia Chambers (who was the spitting image of Tessa's sister Maddy) went first, telling them she was a teacher at the junior school in the next village. Aaron McGinn, the landlord of The Yew Tree, and today dressed in a *Stranger Things* T-shirt, went next. And to Dev's right sat a new face, Leo Shelton, a copper with a lantern jaw and duckling-fuzz hair. Other than Ruth, now occupying October's seat, all the members of the Kindness Committee looked younger than Tessa.

'So,' Dev said, 'we wanted a chance to meet you, and for you to ask us any questions you had about living in Nether Appleford. All of us are residents here, and our role is to oversee village welfare and act as a link between the villagers, the parish council, and the estate. We also actively foster the village ethos, which includes things like running the fetes, themed walks, and other events, as well as administration of things like the Kindness Tree and the annual prize-giving.'

'We do all the grunt work while everyone else is dreaming,' Leo said, his voice deep and gravelly. The others laughed. He sat back in his chair, arms folded, his tight lilac shirt open at least two buttons. His muscly upper body and smooth skin spoke of gyms and mirrors, although something dancing in his close-set eyes and his playful smile said he was partial to both a rock and a rave.

'That's certainly true.' Dev addressed Andy and Tessa again. 'So really this is about you two, to give *you* a chance to put *your* mind at ease. Get to meet some locals and ask any questions. We're not sitting here in judgement or anything. Does that sound okay?'

'Fine by us,' Andy said, sounding not in the least bit fazed. Tessa's gratitude for him being there quelled her anxiety. 'Is this an interview, though?'

'No, it's not an interview,' Dev said, sounding panicked.

'It's definitely not an interview,' Olivia said, leaning towards Andy. Tessa noticed she had a small mark on her nose where a piercing might once have been. 'That's not the atmosphere we're going for.'

'It's just about you getting our vibe,' Aaron said, a little bit of his northern accent creeping in on the last word. From somewhere around Manchester, maybe? 'To make it less formal.'

'That's it,' Olivia said. 'When you move in anywhere you rarely get to find out about your neighbours until you are in already. So, it's for you, really. That's the idea. Please don't feel any pressure.'

'Are other people viewing the cottage, too?' Tessa managed to say. 'How does it all work?'

'There are others looking, yes,' Dev said, glancing a little warily at his fellow committee members. 'But think of this more like a friendly chat. For *you*, like Olivia said. It's definitely not an interview.'

SIX

Tessa

I t was definitely an interview. Each of the Kindness Committee took turns asking questions: where did they live now? Why did they want to move away from the city? Had they lived in a village before? None were particularly challenging. Still, Tessa grew nervous. She gave brusque answers, trying not to give too much away one way or the other. She pinned her sleeve to her wrist with the opposite hand to stop it revealing her tattoo and noticed Andy kept looking over, wearing that look he'd been giving her at dinner with Maddy.

Perhaps because of this, their attention turned to Andy – wanting to find out more about his job. They mentioned the village's 'really old houses' and some of the 'ancient wiring', and talked about the committee's plan to make the village more environmentally friendly, keen for Andy's input. He told them about some work he'd done for some wealthier clients, but after a while trailed off, realising perhaps that Tessa was being excluded. Dev turned back to her.

'And Tessa, you're a… You work in music publishing,' he

said. 'Is that sheet music? Or have I got the wrong end of the stick?' Leo rolled his eyes at this.

'Publishing ... well, I'm doing that at the moment, and that's admin really, for a big company's song library, songs they own rights to. It's been good for making contacts, and I've been gradually building a portfolio as a media composer, too, sort of part-time. Music's my real passion. And it's got to the stage now where ... I've got enough work here and there that I'm going to try and see if it all comes together to pay the bills. Really focus on it.'

Andy reached over and gave her hand a squeeze. 'She's really talented. She used to play in bands, too, before I met her. Plays it all – guitar, piano, sings... She's a better drummer than me.'

'That's definitely not true.' She smiled at him. 'And you know, Jack of all trades, master of none.' The Kindness Committee apparently liked this remark, as they were all nodding along. It wasn't entirely her being humble, either. She could get by, but had never learned anything formally. She'd just spent a lot more time than was healthy on her own in the giant basement music room in her halls at university instead of going out.

'Is it a specific type of music you like or do?' Olivia said.

'I'm pretty open minded. Mainly sort of ... rock and indie.'

'Ah.' She looked disappointed.

'Olivia sings a mean "White Cliffs of Dover",' Aaron said. 'Do you remember, at the UNICEF karaoke night we did?'

'Yes, there's a lot of musicians in the village actually,' Ruth said. 'You're in good company.'

'Oh, I'm no musician,' Olivia said, folding her arms. 'I have a party trick. Leo, though, you play guitar.'

Leo rolled his eyes again. 'I can play about three chords, if that's what you mean.'

'Nonsense,' Dev said, 'I've heard you both. I'd not thought of it before, but we are a very musical place, although I will add, I'm tone-deaf personally.'

'Dev has more visual talent,' Aaron said. 'You know those posters for the film nights at the pub? Those are his.'

'Oh, was the *Heathers* one yours?' Tessa said.

'It was.'

'And he did the whole village website, too,' Aaron said. 'For free, too. That's the sort of thing Nether Appleford is about. Helping each other where we're able to.'

'I'm wondering,' Ruth said, having not spoken for a while, 'would it be worth talking to Tessa about our new project? She could certainly help with the musical element.'

Everyone fell silent, perhaps because Ruth had jumped the gun a little bit. Andy squeezed her hand again, and when she looked over, the warmth in his eyes told her he thought they were doing well here.

Eventually Dev said, 'We can definitely keep that in mind,' before quickly moving the conversation on to how it would be remiss of them not to mention how good Olivia was at knitting. And for ten minutes or so, the conversation continued in the same light-hearted, self-congratulatory way, before Dev started to bring things to a close by asking if they had any questions.

Tessa had plenty, but found herself clamming up, not wanting to make a mistake this late in the proceedings. She was grateful when Andy spoke up. 'Well, our big question, I suppose, is how much the place costs to rent. If that's not too on the nose.'

'No, of course, great question,' Dev said. 'If we offer the cottage to you, we'd ask you to make a proposal. We'd then put that to the estate, and they would either accept or give a counter-proposal. It's all about what *you* can afford.'

'Seriously?' Andy said. Even though they'd been made aware of this by Ruth, it still seemed too good to be true.

All the committee nodded. 'October is more interested in creating a happy community than making money,' Ruth said. 'Just so long as she has enough to pay for the upkeep of the village.'

'Anything else on your mind?' Dev asked.

'Actually,' Tessa said, 'an estate agent told us the village had … rules for people who live here. Is that true?'

All the committee looked at one another before bursting into laughter. 'No, nothing like that,' Dev said. 'No rules.'

'Other than, *Just Be Kind*,' Olivia said. 'Which isn't really a rule.'

'No, but it's important here,' Leo said, the matey mirth gone from his face. 'The world out there … it's not good, is it?' Given his job, and the way his eyes lost focus, Tessa could only guess at the sort of dreadful things to which Leo was referring. 'But in here, you know, it's different. We try hard to make it different. To look after each other.'

Dev nodded, his expression serious, infected by Leo's earnestness. He addressed them again: 'One last question from us, then, and this might seem a bit abstract, but, what does kindness mean to you?'

Both of them hesitated.

'There's no wrong answer.'

For the first time Andy looked unsure, somewhat cowed; the way he'd looked when talking about what had happened with Justin. Eventually, he spoke. 'Like your man said, it's looking after people, isn't it? I mean … just don't be a dickhead.'

Dev nodded slowly, and after it became clear Andy had finished, he looked at Tessa. 'Is that the same for you, too?'

'Yes,' she said. 'Less sweary but … more or less. Helping people. Being caring. Considerate.'

Again, Dev waited, nodded, and got to his feet. 'Right, then. It's been a pleasure to meet you.' He held out his hand and Andy stood to complete the shake. Andy looked quite pleased again, but Dev's handshake looked limp and perfunctory. Tessa didn't get up, even though the rest of the committee were standing. There'd been a weird dip in the energy in the room, and Tessa had the sense that they'd not said enough just now. That the question had been a final test which they'd failed.

'Tess?' Andy said.

'Actually,' Tessa said, 'can I just add something? Sorry, Andy, I just wanted to say this before we go, about kindness. It's about kinship, isn't it? Being part of a family.'

Everyone turned to her, and after a moment the committee sat down again.

'Kin. Kind. They've all got the same … etymology, is that the word?'

'Interesting,' Dev said.

'Andy and I were trying for a baby. For years, actually.'

Tessa could sense Andy staring at her now, trying to make eye contact. She reached over to take his hand, but kept her focus on the floor before the committee.

'But even though the tests said there was nothing *really* wrong with either of us, it hasn't happened. And … the thing is, I've never really had a close family. Our house was always full of people but it was … all noise and no substance. And I think wanting a baby was partly about wanting to be part of something … bigger than myself. To join the world. Kinship, you know?'

She didn't dare look up, knowing she couldn't go on if they were all gawping, horrified.

She looked up. Straight at Ruth.

It was hard to read her neutral expression, but it didn't deflate her. And did she imagine it, or did Ruth momentarily make her eyes bigger, encouraging her? She went on:

'Because I've never been a joiner. Ever. Even at parties as a little girl ... everyone would dance to the "Hokey Cokey", and "The Birdie Song" and "Agadoo", and I'd be thinking, *Please, God, tell me the "Hokey Cokey" isn't what it's all about.*'

Someone laughed, Leo maybe.

'And when I was at school ... I preferred older kids. I hung out with this small group of these cynical Gen Xers, even though people my age all call themselves Millennials. Or maybe they call us Xennials now, but anyway, that was fine – until they left, and I had no friends my own age. So, I went through school just on my own, being ... sarcastic and angry, only ever letting one or two people close to me at any time – though not too close. And I don't know if it was innate or a reaction to how much my family prioritised the outside world instead of home, whether it's even a choice or an accident, but ... it just carried on like that through university, through my twenties. I've been an island most of my life. But that's just it ... you can't just go through life being an island, can you? You need other people. Otherwise ... you go wrong. You get mean and mistrustful. And ... I don't know if we'll have a family or not, but whether we do or we don't, I want to be part of a place where people care about each other. Somewhere where things matter outside of my own head.'

She looked over at Andy, and saw his fear in the humour-less, embarrassed smile occupying his face. She gave him a tight-lipped smile to let him know she was fine. That this was just her, committing. Like she'd promised. It didn't do anything to change his expression, and she could see him racking his brain for jokey things to say to defuse the tension. Sensed him gearing up to evacuate her. But before he could, a voice rose from the back of the room. Tessa turned around to see October sitting on a plastic chair. She'd assumed she'd left, but had perhaps been there the whole time.

'What a wonderful answer,' she said, her voice echoing through the chapel. 'Wonderful. Do tell us, when does your current tenancy expire?'

PART II
Just Be Kind!

SEVEN

How to Kill with Kindness

A nd after Granny fell, everything that the two of us wanted to happen did. There was an initial period of shock and grief, of course, but that was always going to happen when she died, with or without our involvement. None of us are immortal, after all! Once my mother stopped blaming herself for sending us up to the cliffs – something we'd done many times before, sans incident –everything changed very quickly.

We returned to England to be with my father. My parents laughed and touched one another again. And finally, we had their attention. No one suspected the truth; if anything, we were tragic victims, and as such, were treated to far more yeses than noes compared to other children our age. We moved into a gigantic house, went on holiday often, ate ice cream every day! Best of all, we didn't have to live in the presence of mean-ingless suffering anymore. Everywhere we looked: kindness.

Do you have any idea how powerful we felt, darling? To be passengers, as all children are, one minute; then suddenly being in the driving seat of your life. Had things stayed the same, we might have convinced ourselves we'd done a terrible thing. But the changes were substantial, and we were high on our success.

We talked about it a lot, late at night in secret sibling meetings in one another's bedrooms once our parents were asleep. One of us would knock, *rat-tat-ta-tat-tat*, on our adjoining wall to call a meeting, and the other would knock *tum-tum* by way of reply, confirming they were still awake and would soon be in attendance. What we soon realised, was that too many people in life spent time muddled up about right and wrong. Philosophising about it, agonising over it, praying for forgiveness. But everyone knew kindness when they saw it, didn't they? When they really looked hard at a situation.

Now, obviously not everyone does look hard. And we soon came to understand our own difference in relation to others in that way. Most people went through life half-asleep, unable or unwilling to see the world as it was. *Dozys*, we called them. Others, like us, perceived everything. The secret desires, the unspoken conversations, and most importantly, the gaps in the social world into which you could insert yourself to bring about changes. People like this we called *Sharpies*.

Now, we also realised there were two types of Sharpies. Some were clear-sighted, but ultimately only used their insight to spin webs to serve themselves. These people we called *Spiders*. Then there were people like us, who chose to make kind changes.

Saints.

Yes, a bit grandiose, of course – but we were children. And by the time we were old enough to realise, the terms had stuck.

And so it was that we began to experiment with our new-found powers. Our ability to know 'true' kindness. Small to begin with, and largely at home. One particular babysitter was a Jekyll-and-Hyde character, who switched from being an angel in my parents' company to being a monster once they left. We tried to let them know this, but likely they believed we were making things up, thinking she was just the firm hand we needed. But she struck us both at different times when frustrated. On the head. Where it wouldn't show – a lesson I never forgot, incidentally. Spider logic in action. She rushed us to bed, skipping activities she would later tell our parents she had done with us, all so she could bring over her friend and they could talk inane sex-drivel while we listened on the stairs.

It was clear to us she was a danger to children, and simply wasn't cut out for a caring profession. With a little bit of help from my father's booze and my mother's sleeping tablets, we crept around the house one night to make sure that she and her friend were found in such a terrible state that she would never be employed in this capacity again.

Incidentally, I looked the woman up on Facebook and LinkedIn recently and discovered she's found a career in the prison system – which I think was a good outcome for her. In a way, I think we might have acted as a guiding hand.

Then there was Mr Eldon, the French teacher at school, who would often leave us alone with minimally explained work for whole classes while he hid in the stock cupboard conducting an affair with Miss Daley, or sipping from a hip-flask of whisky while reading a novel. Like the babysitter, he was another Spider. He got away with this for years, because kids thought it was brilliant having no teacher half the time. However, the man was married with children. And some of us, those with plans, wanted to learn. It wasn't kind to us, or to his family, and so, over a course of months, we snuck into cloakrooms while people showered after PE and collected several undergarments between us. We then stuffed these with an incriminating but anonymous note from a student into his desk drawer and tipped off the cleaner with another note.

Soon, Mr Eldon was no more.

When I researched him recently, I discovered he is still with his wife. Perhaps this scare strengthened their relationship. He now works in administration for a ferry company. Both of us, meanwhile, got top marks in French when we left, and I remember thinking the French of our classmates had also improved by the time exams came around – *c'était du gagnant-gagnant!*

I could recount many more incidents in our childhood and teens where we gradually flexed our muscles, but I'm sure you get the point.

Dozys. Sharpies. Spiders. Saints.

This is basic terminology and conceptual apparatus that you'll need when the time comes for you to take over from me. And I hope in telling you this, that you understand what I've done in Nether Appleford has been the work of a lifetime. And that, out of kindness, I want to give you a template, something I never had.

Let me ask at this point, darling, is this already chiming with you? Do you have your own versions of these terms already that you apply in your head but never say out loud? I'm never quite sure about what floats in the undercurrents of your mind, you can be so hard to read.

———————

Dredging through these memories, and thinking about my legacy, is quite emotionally trying – especially knowing how much there still is to do to get all my ducks in a row. With time as short as it is for me, perhaps I need to focus on telling you about my activities in Nether Appleford, both what has already happened here, and what is happening currently. It is so hard knowing what will be useful to you. What will work. But while the context is important, perhaps I'll try not to belabour it. The present is what is important for you to know really, isn't it? You need to know what lengths I've gone to for you. And you need to know how to do what I do to keep my work going.

Things are going to happen quite quickly now, I suspect. It might all be done before the end of the year. A new couple, Tessa and Andy, are moving here and they have been something of a catalyst in me finally writing all this down. I'm convinced with their arrival, I might have the final piece of the…

EIGHT

Tessa
___

D espite what October Allsopp had said at the end of their meeting with the Kindness Committee, Tessa left Nether Appleford glum. She'd blown things with her outburst. Where had it even come from? As with so much about the village, it had just felt right in the moment. Andy had been reassuring afterwards, but he couldn't keep his concern for her from his face.

'You know whatever happens, love,' he'd said on the drive home, 'we'll be alright. Me and you. Village or no village.'

She nodded, even though ever since she'd seen that boy with the eye patch, it was Nether Appleford or nothing. They needed this place, otherwise they'd just drift back into their orbit of negativity. Sometimes in life, you needed to trap yourself. And the village was just that: a benign trap that would make them see this change through.

Her worries were unfounded, and that evening an email pinged on Tessa's phone, inviting them to make a proposal on the cottage. They did, offering slightly lower than what they could afford, just to test the water. When they hadn't heard back that night, they considered upping it. But they stayed strong, and the next day their proposal – half of what they paid in London for their flat – was accepted.

Realising she might now be able to quit her job and concentrate on her own music, Tessa started to do the sums again. Andy didn't let her finish, encouraging her there and then to hand in her notice. She did it, and later, they celebrated with champagne in bed, and when they approached the bottom of the bottle, Tessa poured out the remaining liquid into her own flute.

'So you're finishing that, then?' Andy said.

'I was *going* to.'

'Are you sure you're ready to move to England's kindest village?'

Tessa stuck out her tongue. 'Absolutely.' She emptied her glass into Andy's and made a satisfied face.

He nodded gratefully, took both flutes from her, and poured the contents back into hers. 'I didn't even want it.'

They moved only a month later, on a sweltering Saturday in mid-July, their landlord keen for them to go so she could increase the rent. A party of Nether-Applefordians arrived to help them unpack the moving lorry, adding to the chaos with assorted welcome gifts. Cakes, food, bottles of booze. Around four hundred people lived in the village, according to the Wikipedia page, and Tessa felt like she'd met most of them by mid-morning. All five of the Kindness Committee were present at different points during the day.

That night, Aaron offered them another complimentary meal at the pub if they wanted a break. Exhausted from days of packing, and overwhelmed by the fulsome welcome, the last thing Tessa wanted to do was eat in public. But she knew Andy was right when he reminded her it was the sort of thing they'd come here to do, and so, after setting up their bedroom, they headed to The Yew Tree. It was already rammed with Friday-night drinkers, and Tessa felt watched. More people wanted to introduce themselves and tell them how great it was to have them here. Andy took it all in his stride, while Tessa resorted to bigger and bigger mouthfuls of wine to keep the smile on her face. Andy left a £20 tip, pointed to it when she frowned, and said, 'Paper kindness.'

The next morning, their hungover lie-in was interrupted by more locals popping by to drop welcome gifts and introduce themselves. It was a good thing too, as the Kindness Sermon began at 11am, and enough new neighbours had invited them that they couldn't really stay in bed. It was standing room only at the chapel, although an older couple insisted they take their seats, and walked away smiling before they could object. Aaron, dressed a little more formally today in a red-and-black plaid shirt, got up and spoke for twenty minutes about kindness in the food chain.

'Every pound you spend is a vote,' he concluded like some sort of political candidate, 'so vote wisely, and vote kindly.'

Everyone applauded, and began to drift out, lively discussion breaking out around them. They were almost out the door when Dev, in a black suit as always, took them to one side.

'What did you think?' he said. 'Quite unique, isn't it?'

'Yeah, really interesting,' Tessa said. 'It's a great idea. So different villagers do it every other week, is that right?'

'Spot on, yes. Give a little take on kindness. Do you fancy doing one?'

'Oh, no. Not me. I hate public speaking. I can play any instrument in front of an audience, but talk...' She shook her head.

'Ah.' He looked momentarily disappointed, but soon rallied. 'Well, never mind. We've actually got a different favour to ask you, to do with your music, actually.'

'Oh yeah?'

'Yes. I know you're probably still knee deep in boxes, but we're actually meeting in an hour and … well, if you could come along, just for five or ten minutes.'

Her head still throbbed, and what she wanted more than anything was a glass of water and her bed. But Andy was watching closely now.

'Of course, yes. I'd love to help.'

———

Two paracetamols later, she returned to the chapel and entered a small function room at the back. An old, damp smell lurked here, conjuring memories of the times Mum and Dad had flirted with Christianity, dumping her and Maddy at the Sunday School held behind the church in a half-used room just like this. The entire Kindness Committee and October sat around a circular table, greeting her with welcoming smiles. She took a seat that had been left open for her, and was offered squash, coffee, tea, water, biscuits, scones, and cake, all of which she separately declined.

'So, Tessa,' Dev said, 'we're currently in the process of procuring a Story Station for the village. Have you come across one before?'

'No, I don't think I have.'

'Well, Olivia saw a few in Oxford, and we've decided we'd like one here. To put in front of the Kindness Tree.'

'It's like a steel audio unit thingy, powered by a handle,' Leo said. 'Visitors can come by and turn it, and it'll tell the village's history.'

'Have you read about the history?' October asked. Everyone's attention hurried to her. 'About Lord Hinton.'

'I have, actually,' Tessa said.

'It's fascinating, isn't it?'

'Yes,' she said dutifully, 'really interesting stuff.'

October clapped her hands together once, pleased, then gestured for Dev to continue.

'So, we've ordered the machine,' Dev said, 'and Olivia, our English expert, she's put together with Aaron and Leo a very good written history. But it's turned out the actual recording of the history is an additional expense we hadn't planned for.'

'It's my fault,' Olivia said, 'I didn't quite understand the quote. It was very—'

'Nonsense,' Dev said. 'We all had a chance to point it out. Anyway, we were also hoping to have a sort of little score for each section of the history.'

'Right.' Tessa shifted her weight in anticipation of what was about to be asked.

'So is that something you could perhaps do?'

She cleared her throat and crossed her legs. 'It's... What did you have in mind? You want me to record a score?'

'Have we got it wrong?' Aaron said, sounding concerned. 'Is it composing you do?'

'Oh, no, that's right. I just was trying to work out if it was the history you wanted or the music.'

'Yes,' Ruth said. 'All of it, if that's possible.'

She crossed her legs again the opposite way, looked down at the table and began to squeeze the web of skin by her left thumb. 'How ... how long is the ... spoken section?'

'About forty thousand words in total,' Olivia said.

'Okay. And ... how many pieces of music were you—'

'About ten,' Leo said. 'With maybe a little theme at the start.'

'Would that work?' Dev said.

'It … could do, yes.' She didn't know what to say; what they were proposing was a month or two of work, at least. Time she needed to get her own new career started. But they were all looking at her now, big-eyed and hopeful. So the real question was, did they want all this done for free? 'Uh, is there any sort of … budget involved?'

The mood in the room shifted. Bodies stiffened and faces hardened. The silence grew poisonous. 'A budget?' Ruth said after some time.

'It's… I could definitely look into it. It's just, I don't know if you'd realised it's quite a lot of work.'

'Oh, right,' Leo said, nodding, Dev and he looking at one another across the table.

'I could do a good deal,' Tessa said. 'Mates' rates.'

'Well, that's very good to know, Tessa,' October said, 'and very kind of you to offer. I think that's given us what we wanted, don't you think, gang?'

The rest of the table began to nod, their smiles a cordial droplet in a tall glass of water.

No one spoke for some time, so Tessa felt obliged: 'It really is a lot of work, but I could easily do some sums for you.' She looked to Ruth for help, who nodded in a way that suggested she should probably leave now.

'Okay,' she said. 'Well, thanks for thinking of me. I'll get to those sums, then.' She stood up. 'And let you know.'

'Thank *you*, Tessa,' October said. 'Very helpful.'

By the Sunday evening, a few more gifts had drifted in, and they'd run out of storage space for food and drink. They were already throwing things away. They sat in the cosy lounge, curtains drawn, cross-legged on the floor in the light of a single floor lamp. Tessa told Andy about her meeting with the committee, and he laughed, reassuring her she'd been absolutely entitled to turn down the request.

'I haven't exactly said no,' Tessa said, 'but ... now I've got no day job, I really want to earn some money asap. Get working on a mortgage deposit together, finally – you know?'

'I know. That's fair enough.'

She sighed, unable the shake the stress of the whole weekend. 'And these gifts ... do we have to do something about all of them?'

'Do something?'

'I don't know, write our thanks on a heart and hang it on the Kindness Tree?'

'You want to write out that many hearts?'

'I don't know how it works, Andy. Do we send thank-you notes? Do we throw them a dinner party? Are they expecting something back?'

'You're overthinking it,' he said, not sounding entirely sure. 'This is just ... how they welcome newcomers.'

'I didn't expect it to be so full-on straight away. They don't even know us.'

Andy laughed. 'It's been intense. But you know, you sound a bit critical now. You need to be careful about saying things like that around these parts.' He'd put on an exaggerated Oxford burr. 'You'll be hauled up before the committee.'

She laughed. 'I just want to get this right. Do you not feel any pressure?'

His gaze became steely. 'No, they just expect us to get on with our lives and be nice people, which we are. Almost. Why don't you put something on the village WhatsApp? You been invited yet?'

She made a noise to indicate she had. 'I've not accepted yet.'

He frowned. 'Tessa.'

'I hate massive WhatsApp groups. It's like … jumping into a boiling cauldron. I don't know how to act in them. Please don't make me join. They won't care, will they?'

'"Mute" and "archive" are your friends.' He shook his head. 'But you can't just *not* join it.'

She groaned and lay down on the floor. 'I know.'

Andy joined her on his front. 'Hey, here's a thought. Why don't we just write up a single heart on the tree, thanking the whole village for the welcome?'

Tessa liked its simplicity. It felt right. She nodded. 'You're good at this, aren't you? You can come again.'

They kissed, and with the last of their energy, they christened the house.

NINE

Jayden

He woke up with his ear buds in, a young Kate Bush in his ears singing one of her melodramatic ballads. Someone was calling his name, and he rolled over. A face peered at him through his open bedroom door. He caught the end of an annoyed expression and the bloom of a cheery one.

He took his buds out and sat up. 'Hey.'

'Sorry if I woke you, Jayden,' Olivia said, stepping inside. She wasn't. She was always waking him up at the weekend. Keeping him on the straight and narrow, she called it. 'There's a new couple moving in and we're all going over to help them. Do you want to join us?'

Could he say no? Could he fuck. 'Yeah, sounds good. I'll get dressed.'

'Well, no rush. The lorry's not here yet. But I thought you'd want to have enough time to … get in the zone. There's half a grapefruit on the table, if you fancy.'

'Thanks, Olivia,' he said, even though he hated grapefruit, and he'd told her a million times.

She was trying her best. That's what he kept telling himself.

There were a ton of villagers roaming around the grounds of the cottage. He caught a glimpse of the new couple conversing with about six people, looking totally overwhelmed. He felt sorry for them. When he'd first turned up here, and that weird committee had thrown a welcome party for him in the chapel, it'd been too much. He'd had to slip out the back door to sneak a hit on his vape. Olivia had been annoyed, saying she'd been embarrassed when they couldn't find him. He hadn't really understood the big deal; he'd only been gone half an hour.

'Jayden, everyone here wants the best for you,' she'd said. 'In Nether Appleford, everyone worries together. Do you understand?'

He followed. What she was saying was that everyone here knew his story. Where he was from. And they were all watching him closely, in case he messed up.

Jayden helped get a few boxes off the massive lorry, and Olivia eventually ditched him to go talk to the new man, a massive piece of meat in a Queen T-shirt. Jayden liked Queen a lot, so that was interesting. Even more interesting, one of the movers handed him down a guitar case, which was too heavy and too long to contain a normal guitar. He had a good idea what was inside, and the corners of his mouth lifted.

'They want that in the back shed,' a voice said, and when Jayden turned he saw that copper Leo coming down the drive from the cottage. 'Side gate's open.'

Jayden nodded and walked off.

'Oi, kid. Did you hear me?'

'Yeah, I heard,' Jayden said. 'Around the back.'

'Sometimes it's nice to use words, Jayden.' Leo smiled, and winked as if they were in on some joke together, before climbing up into the back of the lorry.

'Okay,' he said and followed Leo's directions.

He'd messed things up with Leo when he'd arrived three months ago. The guy ran a rock-and-rap club every month, and he'd invited Jayden to come. As much as Jayden wanted to get back to playing music again, he'd not wanted to do it with a bunch of primary school kids. He'd been nice about it. Told him he liked to just play on his own. But after that the dirty looks came. And he started doing this weird, annoying-big-brother thing where he kept taking him aside to give him 'advice' that was basically just criticism.

After one of the first stupid Kindness Sermons Olivia made him go to, Leo came up after and said, 'Bit boring, wasn't it?'

Jayden laughed, thinking he was being friendly.

'Well, even if *you* think it is, Jayden, other people don't. People make a lot of effort when they do their sermon, so employ your face, yeah, and look like you're not half asleep. It's not hard, is it?'

Jayden shook his head.

'If it is, don't come to them.'

Next time he hadn't come, despite Olivia's disappointment. But not before he had spotted a broken latch on a chapel window and started sneaking in to play the Spanish guitar in Leo's music cupboard. It wasn't a bass, his preferred instrument, but it would do. But that only made things worse. Someone must have heard him one evening, because Leo burst in and caught him in the act. He told him he was lucky he didn't book him for breaking and entering.

'Olivia deserves better from you,' he'd said. 'She's giving you a chance that not a lot of kids in your position get. You even want a better life, Jayden?'

'Yeah,' he'd said, which was true, and what Leo wanted to hear.

He'd then taken him back to Olivia's and given him the

same dressing down in front of her. When he'd gone, and Olivia asked what she could do to help him settle better, he told her that having a bass guitar might help. She'd smiled, glanced up at the poster he had on his wall of the band Ghost, all spooky skeletons and lightning, and said she'd think about it. He didn't hold his breath. She had this funny thing about rock music, Olivia. Whenever he listened to it, she asked funny questions like, 'Why are all the lyrics so nihilistic?'

The garden of the new couple's cottage was empty, and he carried the guitar up to the big shed-like building at the back. The sliding door was open, and inside were even more guitar cases, what looked like bits of an electronic drum kit, and at least three amplifiers. Was the Queen guy some sort of rock star?

He set down the guitar on a sofa and stared at it. He looked behind him, making sure Leo hadn't followed him. He seemed to be around every corner in the village. But the garden was empty. He opened the zip of the case a fraction, saw four gleaming strings and a big fat head with the word *Fender* printed on it. Definitely a bass. He stared for a while before unzipping it all the way. As he'd expected, it was a Precision. A gorgeous, wood-finish Precision. Like the one Geezer from Sabbath played.

For almost a minute he just stared. Finally, he stepped forward and reached into the bag to pull it out.

'Don't even think about it,' Leo said.

Jayden cried out and turned to face him. Leo regarded him with those too-close-together pissholes on his face.

'I was just seeing if it was a bass.'

'I know what you were doing. You're like a book to me, Jayden. A really boring one.'

He stood aside and moved his head to indicate Jayden should leave. Not wanting to be alone with him, he did. He was across the decking and on the lawn when Leo called him by name. Jayden turned.

'Surprise me, one day,' he said.

Jayden nodded, and turned to get back to the front as quick as he could. That was when he noticed a silver key in the grass down by his feet. It looked like the sort of key that might fit in a sliding door.

TEN

Tessa

Andy had ported his Tradechecker account to Oxfordshire and already had work lined up. By the time Tessa woke at eight on Monday morning, he'd left the cottage. She made coffee and went out to her studio to fine tune her own workspace, testing the soundproofing, setting up her electronic drum kit, arranging her desk.

Things as she wanted, she ate lunch and walked down to the Kindness Tree where she wrote her thank-you on a heart. A woman she vaguely recognised sat on a bench overlooking the rubber-floored children's playground beside the chapel. She was looking over, so feeling friendly, Tessa walked across the green, still holding the heart.

'Hi there,' Tessa said, and the woman, olive-skinned, with a sleek, raven bob, smiled and put her phone into her bag.

'Hi, Tessa.'

She was pleasantly surprised the woman remembered her name and wanted to repeat hers back to her as soon as possible. But what the bloody hell was it? She was Aaron's wife, and her name had been something exotic, hadn't it? 'So … do I just hang this anywhere on the tree?' she said.

The woman smiled. 'Just find a spot and hang away. It's Benedita, by the way.' Tessa noticed a faint Mediterranean accent now she'd heard her name.

'I remember,' Tessa said. 'Thanks so much for … the help and the gift.'

'If you've ever any questions about village things, you can always ask in the WhatsApp group. Are you in yet?'

'Sorry, I haven't got around to it just yet.'

'You've been invited, no?'

'Yes, sorry. It's been a bit mad, the last few days.'

'I'm sure.' Benedita nodded with understanding, though she sounded like she didn't believe Tessa. Or was that just Tessa being paranoid?

'I'll get to it when—'

A child's roar cut her off. Both women turned. Running over from the direction of the park was a young boy, about four or five, with a mop of dark hair and dressed in a *Paw Patrol* T-shirt and matching trousers. He punched Benedita on her legs twice before running around the bench in circles. The woman laughed and rolled her eyes. 'He's full of energy today.' Tessa recognised the boy as the one who had been wearing an eye-patch the first time they'd visited. Now the patch had gone.

'Is this … Lucas?' Tessa asked, pleased with herself for making back some ground on the name-recollection front.

'Yes,' Benedita said. 'How did you know?'

'Your heart is the one I remember from my first visit. How is Texas Ted, Lucas?'

The boy stopped running and glanced at his mum warily. '*My* Texas Ted?'

'Yes. I was wondering how he was.'

'He's in prison.'

'Oh no, what did he do?'

Lucas met her gaze and whispered, 'He's a…' then yelling, finished with, 'MURDERER.' He laughed maniacally and resumed his laps of the bench.

Benedita was eyeing Tessa now with a hint of caution. 'You read our heart?'

Tessa didn't know what to say. Were you not meant to read them?

'Oh … I'm sorry. I just found yours really moving. What you said about Lucas's eye-patch. I had a lazy eye when I was little, you see, and I just … well. How is he? No patch anymore.'

Now Benedita cocked her head. 'No, his eye is better. But he doesn't have a lazy eye. He was injured playing.'

The boy roared again and ran towards Tessa. He tackled her legs with enough force that she had to lock her knees to stop him toppling her over. She looked down, 'Hello.' She ruffled his hair.

'Come on, Lucas, you might trip Tessa up.'

The boy stopped his rugby game and began to punch her thighs instead. Slowly, methodically, left, right, left, right, thump, thump, a little grunt escaping him each time. Tessa did now step back, laughing awkwardly. She didn't want to physically stop him, but his blows were beginning to hurt. She was about to say something sterner, but it was fine, because Benedita was up off the bench and coming over.

'Lucas, do you think Tessa likes that?'

'I'm a boxer. Boxers like punching.' He kept pursuing her with his fists.

Tessa looked pleadingly at Benedita, and she made an apologetic face in return, a frustrating hint of what-can-you-do in it. 'I'm so sorry, he's just … going through a bit of a punchy phase. He's not hurting you, is he?'

Realising that Benedita had no plans to intervene immediately, Tessa put out her palms to ward off his blows. 'Can you stop please, Lucas?' she said.

'He'll get bored in a minute,' Benedita said with a reassuring smile. 'He's got a lot of anger at the moment about rules. You can walk away. I won't be offended. We can catch up another time. It might be for the best. He's off school anyway because he's a bit tired, and if he's got a bug I'd hate for you to catch it.'

Lucas didn't seem tired. Now he threw a punch at her belly, hard. She caught his fist in hers, and in a firm, louder voice, which made little attempt to hide her annoyance, she said, 'Lucas, please can you stop hitting me?' She let go, but the continuing force behind the child's fist carried him past her unexpectedly. He fell on his face and immediately looked up with wet-eyed betrayal. After contemplating his options, he decided to cry. He got up and ran to his mother, who collected him up and rocked him against her. She cast a stern glance at Tessa.

'Sorry,' Tessa said, 'he was actually … sort of hurting me.'

'I did suggest walking away.'

'Right. Yes. Sorry, you did.'

'He could have been hurt, Tessa.' She buried her face into the boy's hair, and said quietly, 'It's not good for their brain architecture to be … yelled at.'

Tessa didn't know what to say. She opened her mouth and felt a twist of embarrassment in her stomach. 'I didn't exactly shout.' Realising this wasn't the right thing to say to save the situation, she said, 'Did I? Sorry, I … I don't have kids. You're right, my bad.'

'They need nourishment. Understanding. *Kindness. That's* how they learn.'

'Of course. Yeah, sorry.'

Benedita shook her head. 'It's probably my fault. I didn't know you weren't used to children. Will your *legs* be okay?'

They throbbed, and she would have matching bruises for certain. 'Yeah, they're fine. I'll live.'

'Will you apologise?'

She hesitated. 'I'm sorry.'

'To Lucas.'

She couldn't believe what she'd been asked. But now Benedita's eyes were narrowing, and Tessa just wanted this over. 'I'm sorry, Lucas.'

This just seemed to harden Benedita's resolve further. 'I think we should probably get home.'

Tessa felt hot, burning with embarrassment and anger. But she apologised once again, and headed back to the Kindness Tree, unsure about how her little act of friendliness had gone so wrong. With an unsteady hand she hung her heart up, using the attached gold string, and watched it spin and swing for a while, suddenly sapped of energy.

When she walked away, she had nearly cleared the canopy when from behind her she heard a soft thud. She turned. Her heart lay on the ground. After a moment she returned it to the tree, brushing the dry dirt from it first. For thirty seconds she watched it, expecting it to be rejected again. This time it stayed put, and eventually Tessa walked home, looking back just once to check it was still there.

ELEVEN

Tessa
___

Despite trying to laugh it off with Andy, the encounter wouldn't leave her mind. Given it had been her first real attempt at kindness here and it had involved the eye-patch boy, it had all the hallmarks of a sign. But she wouldn't let it throw her. Nether Appleford was her benign trap, wasn't it? And one reason for coming here was precisely to negate her tendency to Cassandra and flee at the first sign of trouble. The stakes were simply too high now.

Contracts and commitments: these were things she'd come to appreciate on the road to middle age. Like marriage. She and Andy had never taken that step, partly because of laziness, but also because of the paperwork and expense (things which greatly weakened the power of portents). Had her parents ever married, their fickle mother might not have buggered off to live in Australia, thereby depriving her and Maddy of some much-needed security in those vital late-teen years. By the by now, but not forgotten.

Over the next week she pulled herself out of her funk and doubled down, deciding she'd aim to get her first heart on the

Kindness Tree before the big summer fete in late August. Ideally, she wanted to beat Andy, show him her commitment – although he was spending quite a few of his evenings after work on various small electrical jobs he'd picked up frequenting the village pub.

'Are they paying you for some of these?' Tessa asked one night, a little disappointed they wouldn't be able to hang out.

'Unknown,' Andy said with a toothy grimace.

'Is it kinder to ask for money before or later?'

'I think I've made a rod for my own back. I've done a few for free already, so if I start charging now...'

'Yeah, but ... you'll end up doing the whole village for nothing.' He nodded, clearly well aware of the situation. She was being mean-spirited again, wasn't she? She changed course. 'They'll offer to pay you sooner or later, I bet. And you know what, maybe that's what they'll do if I did agree to do this Story Station thing.'

'You still thinking about that?'

'No. Not really. Just ... you know, no passengers on this ship.'

Tessa joined the WhatsApp group, adding her congratulations to the hundreds that would appear whenever anyone had a birthday or whatever. It was a real job, but she made the effort – putting a Post-it Note on the inside of her phone case that read *Don't be a sociopath*. She started looking around for ideas on how to be more kind, visiting the tree often, reading articles, and printing off a list of one hundred kind acts and sticking it to the fridge.

Once her wounds were licked, she started by trying to right the wrongs she'd already committed. She bought a copy of the

Paw Patrol movie on Blu-Ray and some *Paw Patrol* wrapping paper – reasoning what was left might also come in useful once Maddy's baby arrived – and walked down to the pub one mid-week afternoon. Not knowing where Lucas and his family lived, she asked for Aaron at the bar and handed him the present.

'What's this?' he said, his usual welcoming smile nowhere to be seen. He looked it over front and back.

'Well, I don't know if Benedita mentioned, but Lucas and I fell out in the park. It was about a week and a half ago now.'

'Yeah, she did mention.' He kept his gaze on the gift and his expression remained neutral.

'Was he okay?'

He put the gift down on the bar and nodded. 'Oh, he's fine. Ben's just … a typical scientist. We're just very into giving our two a lot of developmental space to make their own mistakes. It's what the science says you should do.'

'Right, that's … really interesting,' she said. 'I didn't know about that.'

He looked at her now, not in the same warm way he'd done when they'd first arrived in the village, but it hinted at thawing. 'What's the gift then? DVD?'

They weren't going to have a Blu-Ray player, were they? They used VHS because it didn't hurt the kid's eyes or some-thing. Didn't watch television at all, only listened to it. She could sense it coming. But that didn't matter: it was the thought that counted.

Tessa told him what it was, and he sucked in air through his teeth and slid it back across the bar at her. 'The *Paw Patrol* movie?'

'Yeah, do you already have it?'

'We don't, no. We don't actually let him watch that one. We stuck it on once but … have you seen it? It's very … author-itarian.'

'Authoritarian?'

'Not many shades of grey. And the gender stereotyping is all over the place.'

'Okay, well that's no good. It's just... He was wearing the top when I saw him.'

'Oh, he does have one, doesn't he? That'll be the grandparents. We never chuck presents away. Waste not, want not.'

She shrugged. 'Well, I'll send it back and get something else.'

'It's okay. Don't worry about it. Water under the bridge.' Noticing a wet patch on the bar, he walked over to grab a tea towel and wiped it away.

'If you're sure. I'd like to make it up to him.' Aaron shook his head. 'Well ... I am sorry about it all. But, you know, I was thinking about the music you wanted me to do for the Story Station thing. I'm up for helping, if you still want. It's actually not as much work as I'd thought initially.'

'It's fine,' he said, throwing the tea towel over his shoulder and avoiding eye contact. 'It's actually been sorted now.'

'Oh no, that's a shame.'

He shrugged. 'Well ... it's all worked out, so... Listen, appreciate you coming. Did you want a drink while you're here?'

She declined and left, convinced as she did that Aaron's gaze was on her back.

When she got to her studio, she tried putting the pub encounter behind her by mixing a demo for an Ed Sheeran-wannabe from Kent. As she'd hoped in giving up the day job, having more time for freelance work had made a difference already. SoundGreat, a site linking musicians to producers, had been providing her with more proposals because she was completing more projects, and her ranking had considerably improved. Most of it was just stuff for rich kids with too much money and time but, added to the royalties from library music compositions she'd sold over the years, and her recently monetised YouTube ambience channel, it gave her a firm enough base to build on – especially in combination with their rent being so much lower.

She tried choosing between two similar-sounding vocal takes, listening to both four times before giving up. She couldn't get her ear in for the whirring of her mind. She plugged in her guitar and started hammering out a five-chord riff, the repetitive action bringing relief after her frustrating visit to the pub. She liked it enough to start shaping it into a short, punky song, and was soon setting down a drum track and some guitars.

She'd lost track of the time, and was laying a bass track when Andy startled her by banging on the door glass. He picked her up and carried her back to the cottage where he'd prepared dinner, a defrosted lasagne given to them by Ruth on their first day.

'What were you up to in there?' Andy said. 'You seemed a bit lost in it. Sounded heavy.'

'Yeah. I … just had some energy to burn.'

'Not a commission, then?'

She frowned. 'No. But I could use it as a library track if it's any good.'

Andy nodded, and she felt obliged to explain herself, so recounted her interaction with Aaron. It was only when she finished that she called that obligation into question. She'd never before felt the need to justify what she did musically to Andy. It was strange she had just now.

He didn't pursue the line of questioning, though, and he reassured her that Aaron and Benedita would cool off.

'Misunderstandings are bound to happen in a new place,' he said.

'It's just annoying because I was only trying to be kind.'

'Oh, I know. Just … I'm sure it will get easier. Let's take our time.'

That was easy for him to say, though.

Later that evening Andy had another job to do, over at October's cottage. Tessa wanted to go back to her song, use her alone-time to finish it while she still had the energy. But she also wanted to rid herself of the ickiness of her earlier encounter at the pub, so in the end she went back there, desperate to end the day with a positive interaction. Who knew, maybe she could convince them to reconsider her offer to do the Story Station music?

When she entered the porch between the two pub doors, the muted rumble of lively punters gave her pause. She pushed on, and once through the next door the chatter wasn't as fulsome as it had seemed. Or had the place quietened on her arrival, like some wild west saloon?

No, she was just being paranoid. She stood at the bar and waited for a while, watching Aaron further down the bar talking to Leo the copper. He eventually looked up and saw her, said something, and Leo looked up, too. He nodded, held up a hand to her, and the two of them looked away. Eventually a young woman, maybe still in her teens, served her with the sort of warm enthusiasm Aaron had first shown. Tessa took a jam jar of pale ale to a booth with a view of the room and looked around for friendly faces.

That was when she spotted Benedita sitting with Olivia. They'd been looking over, and immediately they both turned away. Benedita leaned down to say something softly to Olivia before walking off with a smile and farewell wave. On her way to the exit, she passed Dev and his partner, sat at a table by the window. She leaned down to say something to them, too, stood up and looked straight at Tessa.

For a while Tessa waited for someone to perhaps come and say hello. All these people here had probably been in or around her house on moving day. Where had all that good will gone? Could Tessa really have turned them all against her this quickly? She shook her head. This was paranoid, cynical thinking again. No such thing had happened. They were just giving her space, or perhaps they assumed Andy might be heading over soon and were biding their time.

Still, she lasted another ten minutes before the feeling of being on show got the better of her. Some sort of easy listening compilation was on the house sound system tonight, and now James Blunt was trying to convince her she was beautiful. She set her jam jar down on the table, a quarter of her drink left, and headed home through the darkening valley.

Back in her studio, the faint smell of spirits and paint had now been replaced by the familiar smell of hot amplifiers and plastic drum pads. The red switch on the bass amp shone. She flicked it off and sat down. When she cleared the screensaver on the computer, a black vertical line moved on the screen from left to right. Her recording software was still running, and she now had a two-and-a-half-hour track of an empty room, courtesy of Andy's interruption earlier.

She pressed the space bar, halting the recording. She started to look back through the last few minutes of the track, repre-sented on screen by a slender rectangle. Sound was represented within the rectangle as a zig-zagging line, not unlike a heart-beat on an ECG: the taller the line, the louder the recorded sound. A few spikes appeared from when she'd entered the studio just now, but as was to be expected, the rectangle was filled with the sonic equivalent of a flatline.

Curious as to what the mics might have picked up in her absence, given the soundproofing, she quickly scrolled through about forty minutes of silence. But when she reached the point in time when she would have been arriving at the pub, she let go of the mouse. A series of jagged lines appeared on the track. Scrolling back a little bit further, she found whatever event the mics had picked up. It went on for almost two minutes.

Tessa clicked at the start of where the first large peak appeared and pressed the space bar. Through the speakers on her desk, she heard the familiar pop and roll of the sliding glass door. The sound made her turn to the actual door, but it remained closed. On the recording the door slid shut. At first she heard nothing. She reached over and turned the knob on her speakers.

Now she heard something. Breathing. Rapid breathing.

She wanted to believe this was Andy. But the breathing grew louder as whoever the intruder was came close to the ambience mic she'd set up by the bass amp. She could hear the soft pad of footsteps on carpet, too. This person was prowling around the room. She spun on her chair to study for evidence on the floor but saw nothing.

Her eye had been off the zig-zags on screen, so when the moan came she jumped because the speakers were turned all the way up. She turned them down and listened. A chill settled around her heart. A mournful, nasal sob, like a wounded animal, filled the room. Then abruptly, it stopped. Shortly, the sound of the door opening and closing preceded another few hours of silence.

Tessa stopped the recording. Then she noticed that another brief spike appeared between the doors opening and the cry trailing off. She turned up the volume and played it again. The intruder had whispered something, but it was too quick to hear. She cut the snippet, slowed it down, boosted the volume. The whisper, lower and drawn out now due to the effects, spoke again like some tortured, angry demon. And this time she made out two words. 'Kill her.'

TWELVE

Tessa

S he called Andy from the kitchen and his phone started buzzing on the lounge coffee table. Not knowing where October lived, she paced back to the pub to ask someone. She had to know if it was Andy in her studio earlier. Trying to freak her out, perhaps. A mean little uncharacteristic prank.

The Road had no streetlights, and the dark and quiet felt oppressive until she ran into Leo walking home from the pub. He nodded at her, and when she nodded back his face softened with concern.

'Everything alright, Tessa?' he said, slowing down.

The unexpected compassion in his voice halted her. 'I'm just looking for Andy.' She was out of breath. 'He said he was at October's but I've got no idea where she lives.'

'Want me to walk you over there?'

She hesitated, taking in the size of him. He wasn't a giant like Andy, but his job probably gave him the fitness and confidence to appear more imposing. Perhaps picking up on her concern, he added, 'Honestly, it's only over there.'

'Yes,' she said, worried he might be offended. 'Please.'

On the way, Leo told her that October, wanting no special treatment, had moved from a wing of the Manor Hotel years ago and now occupied half of a cottage near the green.

'She's pretty special,' he said.

They knocked on her door and waited, and Leo explained that the other half of the cottage was occupied by Amara, the young woman who worked for Aaron behind the bar. He didn't think she paid any rent because October, having taken a shine to her at a climate change rally, had decided to support her through an environmental course at nearby Oxford Brookes.

October answered the door wearing a toucan-themed dressing gown and a bright pink scarf. She looked smaller, and somewhat frailer, without her hat and glasses.

'Oh, it's you, Leo,' she said, and the two hugged.

'Hello, my darling,' Leo said. 'We've come to rescue Andy from you, is he here?'

'I'm afraid Andy left half an hour ago,' she said, looking to Tessa. 'He wasn't here long. He told me I've got to get a new electric heater as mine's a bit naughty. Is everything alright? You look a mite haunted?'

'It's fine. I'm fine. I just… I needed to ask him something. Did he say where was going?'

'No, not to me.' Her hands came together and she shook her head. 'Well, I'm sure he'll turn up? He's probably just gone for a walk. I wouldn't blame him. The village is lovely at night.'

Back to square one, Tessa and Leo left October's and stood together on the pavement.

'And you didn't see him in the pub?' Tessa said.

Leo shook his head. 'Now, tell me it's none of my business, but I'm not sure I believed you just now about being fine. I've seen that look before plenty of times.'

'Oh, it's probably nothing,' she said, trying to sound light-hearted. 'I'm just overreacting, I think.'

He shrugged like it was no big deal to him whether she told him what was going on or not, and again it felt like she might offend him if she kept putting it off. Besides, why not tell him? He was a copper, and one she knew too. And since Andy had decided to go AWOL, what else was she supposed to do? That voice had freaked her out, and she didn't fancy going back to the cottage alone. So she told him while he nodded along, listening carefully.

'Well, Andy will turn up. And you're probably right that it was him. But you can't be too sure.'

'If he says it wasn't him, though, should I call the police?'

'I think the best thing is that I come back now and take a look?' Leo said. 'Then we can decide. What do you think? Andy might even be back now if he did go walking.'

But he wasn't. Because Andy didn't do walking unless it had purpose, and she'd known that. So Tessa took Leo out to her studio, and while she set up the computer to play back the recording, he casually studied the door and the decking by the entrance.

'Was this locked?'

'I thought so,' Tessa said. 'But I got distracted … so maybe I left it open.'

'Well, that probably won't fly with your insurance. I'd lock it every time you come and go.'

She nodded, feeling a little surge of embarrassment. 'I definitely will now.'

He stepped into the room and started eyeing her instruments. 'This really is some set-up.' He knelt to look at the guitar propped against an amp. 'Shame we couldn't get you in on the Story Station. I bet it would have sounded good.'

Off guard, she said, 'I… Uh…'

'Never mind. I'd definitely keep this place secure, Tess.

Even in Nether Appleford, you need to be vigilant. People hear "kindness" and think we're a soft touch.'

'Do you think that's what this was? A burglary. I don't think anything's been taken.'

'Might have been someone casing the place. Maybe they realised they were being recorded and fled.'

'I doubt they'd have known. The screensaver would have been on.'

He gestured for her to play the recording. He listened to the two minutes of noise, nodded, and looked back around the room.

'Don't you think it sounds like, *Kill her*?' Tessa said. 'Like, maybe, *I'll kill her*.' She performed the line through gritted teeth.

'It's hard to tell, being honest with you. It's very quiet. You know what, before you put a report in...' He paused. 'I've got an idea. I think I might have a suspect, you know.'

THIRTEEN

Tessa

They rang the bell for number 55, Olivia's cottage. Unlike Amara, Olivia had a whole cottage to herself, despite having no family. Did that mean she was even more well-liked by October?

'In some ways I hope I'm wrong about this,' Leo said, smiling in a way that suggested he believed he wasn't. 'But basically, Liv's taken in this fifteen-year-old lad, bless her. But we're starting to think he's a bit of a wrong 'un.'

'We?'

He leaned his head to one side, suggesting the answer was obvious. '*You know.*'

Tessa didn't like the implication of this remark. The notion of the committee all sitting around judging someone else in the village got her hackles up.

'Anyway,' Leo said, 'he's been caught a few times in places he shouldn't be. Doing things he shouldn't. Needs a dad really, a bit of discipline. But he's not exactly on the village wavelength, if you get me.'

Not sure if he'd been getting at something with that

remark, she waited a beat and said, 'You know, I wish I'd just said yes now to that Story Station thing.'

He didn't look at her but nodded once. 'That's not a bad approach to have here, Tess. Just say yes. Sort the rest out later.'

Olivia opened the door before Tessa could react to this. She greeted them with a surprised smile. Her gaze shifted from Leo to Tessa briefly before jerking her head back to Leo, like she'd glimpsed Tessa naked.

'Hi, Olivia, sorry for the late call. Is Jayden about?'

Her face fell. 'Jayden? He's upstairs, why?'

'Can we come in?'

They slipped off their shoes and entered Olivia's cottage. The lounge wasn't too dissimilar to Tessa's own, but for the citrusy smell and the white cat curled up on the sofa. IN A WORLD WHERE YOU CAN BE ANYTHING, BE KIND, read a print on the wall. A pile of school paperwork was strewn across her coffee table and a basket of knitting needles and wool was tucked beneath.

Leo explained Tessa's predicament, and every so often Olivia glanced at Tessa apologetically. Leo was just about done when a figure appeared in the kitchen doorway. Tessa turned, expecting the mysterious Jayden. But it wasn't. Instead, there was Andy.

He held up one hand in a greeting, while in the other one he clutched a screwdriver. 'Hello, hello.'

'Hi,' Tessa said. 'You're here.'

'I asked him to come and have a look at our shonky extractor fan,' Olivia said.

'Oh,' Tessa said. 'I thought… Did you go back home while I was at the pub earlier?'

Andy crossed the room to stand beside her, shaking his head. 'No, I just caught what Leo was saying while I was finishing up. That wasn't me in your studio, love. Why didn't you call?'

She scowled at him, partly because she didn't understand why he'd just stayed in the kitchen now instead of coming straight out when she'd arrived. What was that about? 'You left your phone at home.'

He patted himself down and smacked his forehead. 'Oh, bugger. Sorry. What a donkey. You're okay?'

'Yeah, I'm fine.' She looked up at Leo, who gave them both an awkward smile.

'Look,' Leo said to Olivia softly, 'I know Jayden's a good lad, but given … you know, what we know about him, is there any chance he might … have gone over there out of curiosity tonight?'

'Oh, there's every chance.' She rolled her eyes and reached up to grip the cross around her neck. 'I went out for a drink earlier.' She addressed Tessa. 'I was gone literally an hour at most. But he's asked me more than once about your studio ever since your moving day.'

'Would you mind if we just cleared it up?' Leo said and gave Olivia an encouraging nod.

Olivia spun around with a weary sigh and called up the stairwell for Jayden. About a minute later a tall boy ducked into the lounge, arms and legs spidering out from a baggy Chats T-shirt. He remained stooped, staring at Olivia's spotless white carpet. Tessa recognised him from that first day now. He'd been wearing a Ramones T-shirt, and she'd thought how cool that was.

'Hi, Jayden,' Leo said.

'Alright, Leo.'

'Jayden, matey, listen. You like music, don't you?'

Jayden snuck a look at Tessa. 'Yeah.'

'And what do you know about Tessa here?'

95

He shrugged. 'You mean her sick bass?' Despite his youth, his voice was low and steady, with no trace of pubescent cracking. In those few words she picked up his Brummie accent and a barely concealed caution.

'Yeah?' Leo chuckled. 'Do you play bass?'

'Used to.'

'Would you like to play Tessa's bass?'

He shrugged again, clearly sensing a trick, but also keeping his options open in case an offer might be afoot. It broke Tessa's heart a bit to watch. 'It's nice, yeah.'

'What did you think of her little studio?'

'Yeah, sick.'

Tessa shifted on the spot, not entirely comfortable with the tricksy nature of the grilling.

'I bet you'd kill to jam in there. Turn all the amps up and really … make some noise.'

The kid snorted, and a little smile crept on his face. One of his upper teeth was missing. 'I don't think she'd like that much. Not how I play.'

'No, she probably wouldn't.' Leo turned to Tessa briefly before he dropped the good cop act and said to the boy, 'Listen, Jayden, you didn't steal anything. You just wanted a look, didn't you?'

The boy gained an inch in height. 'You what?'

'You went in there tonight to have a little look around. It's okay, matey, you're not in trouble. We're just asking for Tess's peace of mind.'

'Nah. You've got the wrong man, officer.'

'Listen, don't be a smart-arse. Put yourself in her shoes. She's just moved here. She finds out someone's been to her studio. Now she's worried that some … creep's prowling around her place while she's out. Do you know what it feels like to have strangers in your house, Jayden? Maybe when you were growing up, yeah? Bet it felt horrible. All she wants to know is who it was, no harm done. Do you get me? So do the kind thing. Help us all out.'

He looked like he was about to say something again but then he caught Olivia's scowl and reconsidered. After a pause, he looked at Tessa. 'How did you know someone went in?'

'I heard a recording,' Tessa said, not happy that she had been made a part of what felt a bit like bullying now.

Jayden sighed and began to wilt once more. 'If I say I did it, can I go back upstairs? I'm not in trouble, you said.'

'No, but don't say it if it's not true,' Leo said.

'Fine. If it makes everyone feel better, I went in there. Can I go now?'

'Why did you go in there?' Leo said.

'Wanted to see her sick bass again.' He made no eye contact with anyone.

'You going to do it again?'

'No.'

'What do you say to Tessa, Jayden?'

For a long time the kid said nothing. He sighed, and Olivia closed her eyes like she was saying a silent prayer.

'It's fine,' Tessa said. 'I'm just glad … I know now.' He looked up at her. 'Thanks for being honest.' They locked gazes, and she smiled, trying to psychically project to him that she thought all this was a little bit shitty. He had a nice face. Aquiline. Pale. Intelligent. 'I like your T-shirt, by the way.'

He looked down, shrugged, and said, 'Sorry. Can I go now?'

Leo turned to Tessa and Andy now, the thin smile on his face saying, *Job done.* Tessa felt obliged to smile back. But none of this really added up. If Jayden had been involved, what had all that moaning been about? And despite what Leo heard, someone had said *Kill her.* Why would Jayden say that?

She was putting her shoes back on in the hall when Olivia stepped in to join her, Andy and Leo.

'I'm really sorry about this,' Olivia said. 'He's not quite as settled here as I'd hoped. He's just very bloody minded about all things music. I'm really trying hard to broaden his horizons a bit more.'

'Honestly, it's fine,' Tessa said. 'Like Leo said … it's more peace of mind. Do you think he was being truthful?'

'Oh, it's right up his street. He got caught breaking into the village hall one night, trying to have a go on the little guitar in the kids' cupboard. He's got form.'

'It's a ukulele,' Leo said.

'Right,' Tessa said. 'It's just, he didn't play any of my instruments.'

A what-more-do-you-want expression flickered on Olivia's face. Then with a shrug and a smile she said, 'I should probably go have a chat with him.'

Leo bade them farewell, and Andy reassured Olivia he'd come back soon to fix the extractor fan.

Once home, Tessa took Andy to her studio and played him the clip.

'You can hear that, can't you?' she said.

Andy pushed out his lips. 'I know what you mean, but it sounds like it could be anything, really, Tess. *Kill them*, maybe.'

'Not better.'

'Well, *Chiller*, maybe. *Killer*. As in, this set-up is killer.'

'I can hear it clear as day. Sounds more and more like, *I'll kill her*. Or maybe it is *kill them*.'

'You know what it's like after you listen to something a few times. I had this mate, Micky Holmes. Micker. He was into this thing where if you played famous speeches backwards you could hear hidden messages. Like Bill Clinton going on about the economy, and backwards he says, "Two tits in the front row" while his eyes flick towards some bird. You can hear anything, if you want to.'

Tessa laughed. 'Maybe. But then, why was he moaning and like, crying?'

'If you're really interested, why not ask the lad?'

'I don't want to bother him again. He looked harassed, frankly. And I don't know…' She wanted to tell him she didn't believe he really did it, but she had no reason to doubt what she'd heard other than a gut feeling – probably brought on by how unsettled Leo had made her feel before they'd entered Olivia's cottage. She knew Andy would say Olivia and Leo knew the kid better than she did. And that she should trust their gut instinct over hers. So instead, she changed the subject to something he was interested in. 'That's not a real thing, is it? Reverse speech?'

'I swear, Micker was on about it for weeks.'

They got on the internet, and spent an hour falling down a reverse speech rabbit-hole. When they were done listening to each other's backwards voices on the computer, Andy insisting he could hear Tessa imparting the message *Let's do doggy*, the two of them returned to the house, showered, but by the time she'd finished shaving her legs he was asleep – something he often did once the clock passed ten.

It was almost eleven now, but she wasn't tired. She walked through the empty house, keeping the lights off. In the back bedroom she looked out into the garden, and for a while she stared at what looked like a figure standing at the very back, where a low wire fence separated their grass from the woodland beyond. It was an eerie effect, but like with the recording, the longer she looked the less certain she became about what her senses were telling her. It was obviously just a fence post or something.

Eventually she gave up. She watched television downstairs, and on the way to bed later she stopped in the landing. Daring herself to do it, she returned to the spare bedroom and peered out the curtains, just to check one last time. Only this time, the black figure had gone.

FOURTEEN

Tessa

The sight of blood in her knickers the following morning scooped out her purpose and enthusiasm. Andy and she hadn't had that much sex since the move – well, if she was honest, since the IVF failure really, their lovemaking not having recovered its groove following years of baby-trying – so it wasn't as if her hopes had been high. Still, without fail she heard her father's voice in her head, as she did every month, chiding her the way he'd done when she ate a bag of crisps or a packet of sweets too fast.

Once they're gone, Tessa, they're gone.

Despite her best efforts, the morning was practically a write-off work-wise. Her concentration just wasn't there. She kept scrolling through the village WhatsApp group, catching up on anything she'd missed. The closest thing to drama was a message about whether there would be fireworks at the summer fete this year. Usually, the village didn't allow fireworks, because it wasn't kind to the village's dogs, but the latest flyer had featured an image of some fireworks. Alas, the whole thing was resolved when Dev, the creator of the flyer, confirmed that the 'fireworks' were actually shooting stars, and that there would be no fireworks at the fete.

Needing some air, she examined the place by the fence where she'd seen the figure last night. The ground on the other side was muddy in patches, and imprinted a few feet away was what might have been a footprint. It was too smudged to be certain, and she couldn't see any others. But given the wall of trees ahead, in which anyone might be hiding and watching her, she didn't venture over to look closer. It had been a shadow on a shadow, really. Just her mind being extra-vigilant for person-shapes in the aftermath of what happened in her studio.

After lunch, she went out for a walk. The blue recycling bin, which she'd used this morning, had been moved to the end of their drive by one of the neighbours. Further down The Road, she passed a silver Tesla parked by the kerb, and someone had left a note on the wipers. Signs of a little discord in the village? Tessa leaned over and read: *Jitesh, your flowery dress really suits you! Carly.*

Kindness was everywhere she looked, and with the Kindness Tree nearby, why not hang a heart to thank Leo for his assistance last night? She made it as far as Olivia's house before stopping, the previous evening's encounter returning to her in vivid detail.

Did she really want to reward what Leo had done? Suppose he *had been* right about Jayden. It still didn't justify grilling the kid in front of two strangers. He wouldn't get away with that in his job. And why had he done it, exactly? At the time, and up until they were standing in Olivia's lounge, it had really felt like he'd been acting out of concern. But there had been something showy about what he'd done, too. Something of a performance.

Just say yes. Sort the rest out later.

'Blugh,' she said to herself and turned back. She passed the note, the bins and their cottage, and continued up The Road, not ready to go home yet. Something niggled at her, something she didn't want to give oxygen to because it was coming from that little black part of her heart. But was all this stuff they did in Nether Appleford really kindness? It wasn't exactly setting her soul alight with inspiration. It all seemed more like … niceness. What the difference was between the two wasn't obvious, and who knew, maybe niceness gave rise to kindness? But there was a difference, and she suspected it was why she'd not just said 'yes' to the committee's request to compose their soundtrack.

However, that wasn't all that bothered her. Some of what she'd seen wasn't even niceness or kindness, was it? Maybe Leo thought he was being kind to her or to the village, but it hadn't been kind to Jayden. But even without all that eye-of-the-beholder stuff, she kept coming back to that word: performance.

Still, what wasn't a performance once you left the safety of your own head? And perhaps people like her needed performance to rouse them from their apathy. Was doing nothing better than doing something performatively kind? Besides, it wasn't as if everything in Nether Appleford had been uninspiring. She couldn't deny that Olivia fostering Jayden *was* genuinely inspirational. It hadn't entered Tessa's mind in any serious way before, not least because she'd always taken for granted having a child of her own, but maybe fostering might be something to investigate. No doubt it would be challenging, but it would be rewarding, too. And if the kid liked The Ramones, even better.

Near the end of The Road, not far from where they'd parked on their first visit, she caught sight of the opening to a laurel-lined public footpath. It looked very much like it led up to the woodlands behind the house. The far end wasn't visible, and when Tessa walked down to investigate, the growing shadows halted her. Even though there was a cottage on the other side of the hedge, the atmosphere created by the dark and the susurrating leaves unsettled her enough to turn back.

At the adjacent cottage, Tessa stopped at the end of the driveway and peered past the overgrown laurel encroaching the entrance. An older woman in shorts and a vest top stood outside her front door examining a pile of boxes. Short and plump, with a pleasingly squashed face topped by spiky silver hair, she reminded Tessa of a troll doll. She called out a greeting and the woman took a hand from her hip to wave.

'Do you know if this footpath goes up into the woods?' Tessa said, pointing to where she'd just come from.

The woman approached her, and Tessa entered the drive to shorten the distance. Once beyond the hedge, the state of the cottage's very un-Nether Appleford lawn caught Tessa's attention. The rusting remains of a white van sat in the middle of shoulder-high grass. Other objects stood out at the lawn's edge. A pile of crumbling bricks. A tin of paint. A hammer. All of this had been obscured from view, as had the full extent of the crates, clothes, bags, bins, bike wheels, furniture and appliances flowing out from either side of the front door like the house had been sick.

'Yeah, runs right up to the woods,' she said, her words twanging with an Oxford accent. 'Pain-in-the-backside walk, though. Goes along the ridge behind the gardens, and if you keep going, you'll get to Bicester, if you can be arsed.'

'So could someone, in theory, get into the gardens that way?'

'Why, you planning on burglarising someone?'

Tessa laughed. 'Yeah, I can see how that might have sounded strange.' Tessa had assumed that, like everyone else in the village, the woman might know who she was, might even have been there on their first day. Apparently not, though. 'I'm Tessa. Me and my partner moved into number 34 a few weeks ago. I was just wondering if you can get into the back gardens from up there.' It still sounded weird. 'Like, if it's safe.'

'Ah, 34.' She raised her eyebrows dramatically. 'The *Beddingtons*'.'

'Sorry?'

'The couple that lived there before you. Nice couple. Shame really, all that.'

Tessa couldn't resist the bait. 'Did something happen?'

With her hands on her hips, she stretched, arching her back until she winced with pain. 'No, nothing interesting. They just split up, moved on. That's all I meant. I'm sure you're bloody lovely, too.' She held out her hand. 'I'm Kath, in case you're interested. I'm the village dinosaur, been here as long as the village itself, some say. I shouldn't worry about your garden either. Someone would have to be awful keen to go that way rather than round the front.'

'That's good to know,' she said, although that was precisely her worry.

Up until then, Tessa had been trying hard not to stare at the surrounding junk, but something near the front door grabbed her attention now.

'Yeah, I know it's a pigsty,' Kath said, sounding suddenly shameful. 'I'm slowly sorting it all out.'

'No, I wasn't—' Tessa pointed at a glittering silver object beneath four stuffed black bin liners. 'Is that a bass drum shell?'

Kath glanced over her shoulder and nodded. 'There's a whole kit about the place somewhere.' She shrugged like what she'd just said might be a myth handed down through generations. 'But as you can see, it's like *Where's fuckin' Wally* round here.'

'Do you play, then? The drums.'

'Play. Teach. Buddy Rich's Snare Drum Rudiments. Did all that. But went down the fuckin' pan with the rest a long way back. It's space, is the problem.'

'So … was it jazz you played?' She heard herself emulating Kath's pattern of talking and inwardly rolled her eyes at herself.

'I played everything, my love.' She made a show of puffing out her sizeable chest. 'I was in a progressive rock band that supported Queen in '71, don't you know.'

'Really?' Tessa smiled, unsure if she was being conned. 'Do you miss playing?'

'I miss a lot of things. I'm *missing* a lot of things. But, I'm working on it as fast as one person can, so you pass that on, if anyone's asking.'

She wasn't about pass it on, but had a sense of whom Kath was talking about. 'Do you live here on your own?'

'Since my husband passed. Just me, myself and I.' Something like embarrassment crossed her face as she seemed to hear herself and not like it. 'Speaking of which, better get back to it, my darling. You take care here.'

Tessa thanked her, and watched her go back to the boxes, lifting one with great effort and depositing it five metres to the right. Her hand went to her back and she winced again.

Not entirely sure what she'd be getting herself into, Tessa said, 'Do you need a hand?'

Kath waved her hand dismissively. Tessa kept watching. She didn't want to go, feeling an overwhelming urge to invite her around to the studio. Let her drum on the electronic kit. But she needed to be wary of whims, and so for now she bit her tongue. She'd find out a bit more about Kath first. Get the back story before committing. Perhaps it wasn't entirely in the

Nether Appleford spirit, but so what? If she was going to let the village spirit in, she didn't want it to possess her.

Over dinner, she asked Andy if he'd heard anything about Kath. All he knew was that she wasn't exactly the toast of the town, given the eyesore her cottage had become in the years since her partner died. She'd once been an active community member, supposedly, but these days she kept herself to herself. She kept promising to tidy her place but had made no great strides towards accomplishing that. Now the neighbours were getting restless. The committee had offered to help her, but she had repeatedly promised she'd do it herself.

'How long's it been like that?' Tessa said.

'A decade, maybe. Dev was saying to me the electrics haven't been done in there for a very long time. Did you see inside the place? It's wall to ceiling with stuff, apparently.'

'That's so sad,' Tessa said.

'If she won't accept help, though...' He shrugged.

'I'm thinking of starting a band with her,' Tessa said.

Andy laughed before realising she was being serious. 'So what, you on guitar and her on drums? Like the White Stripes.'

'And a bassist too.'

'Who's your... oh.' He ripped off a piece of kitchen roll and wiped his mouth.

Tessa grinned. 'It could work. I don't know how good Jayden is, but I could get him up to speed.'

Andy nodded. 'So you're going to hook up with the two village pariahs, then? That's very ... on brand.' He started grinning.

'On brand? That's exactly *why* I should get involved with them, isn't it? If they're pariahs.'

'Hmmm.' He shook his head. 'What you going to call yourselves?'

'The Blackhearts.'

'It's good, but I think Joan Jett might have something to say about that.' He paused, smiled mischievously, and said, 'So I was talking to Olivia yesterday.'

'Oh yeah?'

'And she was asking if you could knit?'

'Knit?'

'Yeah. Needles. Wool.'

'No, I can't flipping knit.'

'Well … maybe you should consider it. They have a knitting circle. They listen to podcasts and knit and … they do all the little knitted creatur-ey things for the themed walks.' He was still smirking, but Tessa couldn't help but think part of him was being serious. That this was his roundabout way of telling her to try a bit harder.

'I'm not fucking knitting. No, I'll stick to my band, thanks. Do what you know. Like you helping people with their electrics.'

He swigged from a bottle of beer and nodded. 'Speaking of which, I said I'd go to Olivia's again tonight to sort that fan for her.'

'You will charge her, won't you?'

He studied her, his eyes narrowing a little. 'I suspect so.'

'Do you have to go?' she said, leaning forward and trying to sound seductive. 'We could … have an early night or something.' She really didn't want to be alone tonight, period be damned. Not after what had happened the night before.

'I promised her, Tess. But I'll try and hurry back. You'll be alright though, yeah? Do you want to go to the pub and I could meet you there later?'

She shook her head. She didn't want all those eyes on her

again. No, she'd get some work done. An hour or so before bed. The time would fly. Her intruder had likely been Jayden; she was just probably over-empathising with the kid because he was awkward. Because he was a bit like she'd been, if she was honest. But now the matter had been dealt with, there wasn't really anything to worry about. Andy would be back before she knew it.

'Just take your phone please,' she said, and he pulled it from his pocket and waggled it in the air.

In the end, the studio felt too isolated, too exposed, illuminated as she was in the glass door like an exhibit. So she brought her laptop to the lounge and worked on it with her headphones. Between fizzy beats and snaps of swooping synths, Tessa heard a sound she initially took to be the dishwasher in the kitchen. When the sound intensified, she took off one can and listened. It was chucking it down outside. Andy was going to get soaked. Teach him for abandoning her.

Before she returned to her work, another sound drew her attention to the front door. It was as if something had brushed briefly up against it. She waited for Andy to enter, and when he didn't, she felt a little prickle of cold on her neck. She got up, walked to the hall, and peered through the peephole. No one was there. Just rain pattering on the door was all it was, nothing to fear. She re-entered the lounge and something thudded softly against the bay window.

Tessa approached the window, and after a steadying breath, she slowly pulled back the curtain. A white face she'd never seen before, eyes wide and wild, stared back at her. Tessa screamed.

FIFTEEN

Tessa

B efore Tessa had overcome her shock, someone knocked at the door. Through the peephole Tessa saw a woman with jutting cheekbones and an overgrown blonde pixie-cut, the roots of which were now dark. The woman bobbed on the doorstep, her face alive with hundreds of barely perceptible movements. She knocked again.

The woman didn't look physically threatening. And what if she was in trouble, or a villager she'd never met coming to tell her something had happened to Andy? Tessa opened the door and the woman grinned with teeth exposed by receding gums. Her head poked out turtle-like from an oversized puffer coat, the dark colour of which accentuated her pallid complexion. This was noticeable not just on her face, but on the two bare legs beneath the mid-thigh hem.

'I'm so sorry, I didn't mean to startle you.' Her voice was light and faintly plummy. 'I could see a light, but I did wonder if anyone was home. Would it be possible to use your loo?'

'The loo?'

'Yes. Could I? I've been … driving and I must have lost my

way on these roads.' Again, the woman smiled with her long teeth. She now appeared to be leaning slightly to her right, as if to peer around Tessa and inside the house.

Tessa wanted to direct her to the pub. Because why had she come here, to a cottage in the middle of the street? She'd have had to pass all those other houses first. And she'd have passed the hotel on her way in, too; that would have been a more obvious place to stop. Her black little heart was at it again, screaming at her to dismiss her and shut the door. But her conversation with Andy was fresh in her mind, and sending her packing would be very 'on brand'.

'Yeah, of course, come inside.'

The woman stepped into the entrance hall. She placed a palm on Tessa's shoulder. 'Thank you.'

Without instruction, she turned left into the lounge, trailing raindrops and a sour smell. Tessa followed. 'If you carry on through, the loo door is in front of you.'

The woman stopped, nodded, and started to look around the lounge. When after a few seconds she was still doing this, Tessa pointed at the lounge's rear door. 'Just through there.'

'You have a tattoo?' the woman said, looking at Tessa's wrist. 'What does it mean?'

'Nothing,' she said, and put her arm down by her side. 'Just a drunken mistake.'

'Well, I wouldn't say that's nothing. I was drunk when I met my husband.'

Tessa laughed politely, but gestured with her eyes to the hall beyond the door to get the woman moving. But now the woman was staring at her Spanish acoustic guitar lying across one of the sofas. In this light, the redness of her eyes made it look like she'd been recently crying. Sorrow crossed her face briefly before she shook her head and finally walked to the toilet.

She was gone for five minutes, and Tessa had already started regretting her decision. She grabbed her phone, just in case, and drifted into the hall at the centre of the house. From behind the bathroom door she heard a hollow *thunk*. There came another, and another.

'Is everything okay?' Tessa received no reply. She approached the door now, and looked down at the base with a heavy pressure in her chest. 'Are you alright?'

'Fine. I'm fine.' The woman's voice sounded panicked. 'I'll be out in a minute.'

The pressure grew, and Tessa stood back by the front window to be nearer to the door. Where the hell was Andy? Why had he left her alone after what had happened?

But this wasn't really his fault. She should have trusted her instinct at the door and left her—

The sound of the bathroom light cord being clicked was followed by the woman's reappearance in the hall.

'I'm so sorry,' she said, stepping into the lounge wearing a knowing smile. Instead of leaving, she pulled back the sleeve of her coat and approached Tessa, offering her wrist. 'What do you think of that?'

To create space Tessa stepped further into the lounge and the woman now blocked her route to the front door. On her wrist, in around the same area as Tessa's own tattoo, was a faded pink butterfly.

'Isn't that funny?' the woman said. 'Same place.'

'Was yours a mistake?'

'It was so long ago, who knows? Anything can feel like a mistake or a miracle depending on the day, don't you find?'

Tessa again smiled politely and glanced towards the door.

'Is the guitar yours?' the woman asked. 'Do you work as a musician?'

'Uh, sort of.' Such a strange non-sequitur. 'I should get back to working, if I'm honest.'

'Do you like it here, in Nether Appleford?'

Tessa didn't know how to answer the question. Too many alarm bells were sounding now. That this passing, lost stranger could recall the name of the village perfectly. That she'd leaped to the conclusion of Tessa working as a musician from a sole guitar. And what had she been doing in the bathroom?

'Did you know people here, before you moved?' she asked.

Tessa stared into the eyes of her guest and let the tolerance fall from her expression.

The woman looked away, laughed, and brought up her hand to her chest where she clutched it defensively. She blinked, started looking around the room, and tears coated her eyes.

'They've really done nothing to it.' Now bitterness leached from her voice.

'I really need to get on,' Tessa said, convinced now that this woman, and not Jayden, had been the person that broke into the studio. Had been the person watching her in the garden last night. *Kill her.*

The woman held up a palm. 'I'm sorry. Let me explain. Can I explain? I'm… I think I want to warn you. I think that's it, really. They're not who they say, these people. There's cruelty here. Rich seams of it." She looked around the room again. "Honestly, I feel like … like I could just k—' The woman clenched her fist and forced her mouth closed.

Tessa swallowed. *Kill?* Had she been about to say could kill someone?

'Okay, listen, my partner's home soon, and I really would like you to leave now.'

'I lived here. Before you. In this house. I'm so sorry I lied, but I needed to check if they'd been true. Which of course, they hadn't. Not at all. Honestly, I could...' She shook her head. 'And I needed to retrieve something.'

'What do you mean? What did you leave?'

'It doesn't matter. I have it now. But ... I wanted to meet you, too. My *replacement*. But ... I don't understand. You are so like me. What does your partner do?'

'Please can you leave now.'

'Is he useful? My husband was useful. To them, I mean. He did their accounting.' The woman stepped towards Tessa. In response, she took a step back. 'You see, I think that's how it works. If you're useful to them, then you can stay. If you're not... They got rid of me. Once I wasn't needed. And it's not just me. Ask the right people, there's others they've done it to, I'm sure. Do you know Kath? I saw you speaking with her earlier. Talk to her. They've done far worse than what they did to me. Ones they don't want anymore. It's the committee, you see.'

'The Kindness Committee.'

'Them. Or maybe it's all *her*. October. I don't know. But you need to know, if you're no use to them...' The woman glanced again at the guitar. 'Are you useful, Tessa?'

Annoyance now overwhelmed her fear, and Tessa raised her voice. 'I'd like you to leave. And I'd like you to give back any stuff you've taken, too. If it's yours, I'll confirm that and make sure we can give it back to you.'

'No,' the woman said, straightening up and appearing to come back from whatever dream world she'd been occupying. 'It's mine. It was something my husband could never see.'

'What have you taken?' Tessa said. 'Is it in your coat?'

The woman took a step towards her, face contorted, and yelled, 'No, it's mine.'

Tessa flinched and backed up, expecting an attack. But she

lost her balance, fell, and pain flared as her head struck the top wall around the inglenook fireplace. She landed on her side, wincing at this fresh agony. The woman was approaching her now.

'Oh, now look,' she said, managing to sound both confused and irate. 'This wasn't supposed to happen at all. No.'

Tessa's head hurt a lot, but she needed to get to the poker on the other side of where she'd fallen because this woman was dangerous. Something was missing behind her eyes, and she'd known it the moment she'd looked through the peephole.

Kill her.

The woman was just centimetres from Tessa when she stopped and turned around. Someone was humming outside, behind the door. Andy. Yes, it had to be, because a moment later his keys went into the lock.

'Andy,' she shouted, 'call the police!'

The woman gave Tessa a surprised look, which quickly curdled into despair. Then she ran towards the back of the house, and a moment later Andy burst in.

'Call the police! She ran out the back.'

He ran to her and knelt down. 'Jesus, Tess. Who the fuck—'

He didn't wait for her to respond. There was blood on the hand that had been touching her head.

'Stay still, love.'

He got up again and dashed to the kitchen, coming back with a tea towel which he pressed to her wound. After she talked him out of chasing after her, he called the police.

Sometime later, flashing blue lights filled the lounge and Andy left her on the sofa to go and greet the police outside. Only they'd driven straight past the cottage, and were now down at the end of The Road. Shortly after, they were joined by an ambulance, and when both vehicles didn't turn around and come back up, he told Tessa he was going to go down to get them.

'Don't you dare bloody leave me.'

She nearly said it again, but judging from his contrite silence, she hadn't needed to. So they walked down together, Tessa still clutching the tea towel to the back of her head. When they noticed the crowd gathered on the green, they exchanged a look. They remained silent when they got close enough to see that an officer had erected some cones at the edge of the grass. Someone in the crowd asked softly, 'Is it Eleanor?'

'Oh, it's just horrible,' Benedita said from in front of them, turning to walk towards the pub with tears in her eyes.

The commotion appeared to be about a woman with short hair, sat beneath the branches of the Kindness Tree, head and body to one side, a stretch of something long, thin and taut connecting her neck to one of the branches. Except she wasn't sitting, was she? That cord was holding her up.

'That's her,' Tessa said, her voice flat and weak. 'That's the woman who broke in, Andy.'

SIXTEEN

How to Kill with Kindness

$\cdots$ **A**nd this Eleanor Beddington business is a perfect opportunity to illustrate some of the things I'm trying to impart to you. Kindness is not a science, my darling, although neither is it entirely an art. Perhaps, as a comparison, architecture comes close. Meticulousness, method and measurement are essential – and yet heart, in all its fickle, fallible glory, is required, too. When your heart leads, though, mistakes occur – and there is no doubt that this is the category into which Eleanor Beddington fell.

One of my rules is that you cannot be truly kind until you are kind to yourself. So while the Beddington couple were ultimately my choice, I made the decision with the best intentions, and due diligence was done. Eleanor's full health records were not obtainable to us in time, and so we were oblivious to her poor mental health until it was too late. And her partner, an accountant, wasn't exactly the most garrulous gentleman. She didn't use social media – apart from to occasionally advertise her 'art' – which is usually where you would spot warning signs. Given these omissions, can you really blame my soft soul for thinking an artist might bring joy to our village? Alas, I can live with my oversight. And, more importantly, once I understood her true nature, I made amends.

In my defence, Mr Beddington fitted in as I had imagined – if you'll excuse me another leap back to the past. He was thoughtful, with a well-managed creative streak. He participated in village life, and offered his professional expertise to others free of charge – including to the committee. His insights were key to a number of decisions made about the village's economy. He also had the right temperament. The openness and malleability needed to be part of a functioning community built around specific values. In short, a Dozy.

But it soon became apparent Eleanor was an ill fit. Possibly even a Spider. She spent much of her time alone, painting. When she did participate in village life, it was clear to all that she was an alcoholic, and a mean-spirited one at that. She would disparage her husband, other villagers, the village itself. Not in overt or demonstrative ways, but with sniggers or eye-rolls or veiled remarks that perhaps her husband didn't notice, but I certainly did.

Then, at the winter fete, she and her partner had a very public row. I would later learn she had muttered something mean-spirited about our village ethic, because she supposedly objected to us spending money on good food and drink. Mr Beddington, a little tipsy, had challenged her on this, so she had stormed off. The next morning, I found that someone had scrawled the following quotation on a sole heart hanging from the tree:

> *Where God erects a house of prayer,*
> *The Devil always builds a chapel there;*
> *And 'twill be found upon examination,*
> *The latter has the largest congregation.*

I'm not sure if Eleanor credited anyone with the intelligence to understand her quotation – the words belonged to Daniel Defoe – but I did. I removed the heart before anyone could see it, and took it to Mr Beddington, who confirmed the handwriting was Eleanor's. That night, a great row was heard by the surrounding neighbours, and the following morning, he left her.

This hadn't been my intention, and I had hoped he would remain and *she* would leave. I perhaps underestimated the amount of gunpowder in the keg, and anticipated having more time to engineer a satisfying outcome. The kindest outcome. But as I would learn, her ongoing rejection of our village was perceived by him as a personal attack on their relationship. In coming here, they had agreed to start a different, purer life than the one they'd lived in the city – this much we knew from their introductory meeting with the committee. It's a common enough tale among our residents, but as far as he had been concerned, this was a matter of life and death, due to her problems. And she was thumbing her nose at it.

Six months prior to coming to Nether Appleford, Eleanor had attempted to overdose. She told me this as we drew close to one another in the aftermath of their separation – an arrangement I made my first order of business. I visited her often, flattered her painting skills and considerable intellect, and despite her best efforts, I forced my way into her affections. We talked in depth about the periods of blackness that would descend upon her unannounced, stripping the world of meaning and leaving her with the task of continuing to exist with what remained.

'I think he believed a change of scenery would cure me,' she told me in her garden one afternoon, smoking a cigarette and staring at some point in the sky. 'I don't think he accepts it's a part of me he has to live with.'

'You were a sum to be solved,' I said, only repeating back to her what she'd already told me.

'Yes,' she said, feeling understood.

'You can't change who you are.'

'Exactly.'

Of course, I fully believed in her breed of black dog, and yet at the same time understood how infuriating such a thing must be to someone close to her. The entitlement of it. The immovable mass of it. Of course, I conducted the most rigorous of contemplations, but it seemed to me that, and I do not write this lightly, perhaps the kindest thing for everyone, given their lack of dependents, his waning affection, and her staunch individualism, would be if she did just offer up her neck and let the dog bite.

I'll never forget her saying to me, 'Do you know what it's like to smell Autumn changing into Winter, and simply be tired of it?'

But our villagers, good people that they are, rallied around her at her time of need, perhaps taking my lead. And in turn, she responded. She came out to the pub and moderated her drinking. She attended a film night. She offered to paint a mural in the chapel, which the committee began to consider.

Of course, only I knew her true feelings about our village. Had seen what she had written on that heart. We were the devil's congregation. When I asked her about it directly, telling her the white lie that the entire committee had seen it, she said:

'I don't know why I wrote it. I was in a low place. Perhaps I was jealous that people here found selflessness so easy.'

I laughed, and made a show of smiling with just the right hint of knowing and mischief to unlock her true thoughts. 'I'm not sure I believe you.'

She smiled back, looked up the sky again, and after some

time, said, 'Perhaps I just think kindness is more of a nature than something you do.'

'I can understand that,' was my reply, and an honest one. Because of course, it is likely true. Certainly, the things I do are in my nature, and I do not need the constant reminders of trees covered in hearts, and posters bearing slogans urging people to practise random acts of kindness. All of that is for other people. But there is only room for one person-of-ideas in a community of this size. One philosopher. For Nether Appleford to work, for there to be *coherence*, residents must have a more accepting disposition.

I acknowledge now that I mistook her quietness at her introductory meeting for artistic timidity. Really though, inside she sat there despising us all as much as she despised herself. And I know from bitter experience that her type of disposition doesn't change. She may have found the comfort of strangers useful in the aftermath of her husband's departure. But eventually she would revert. Like the smells of changing seasons, she would tire of us.

Despite the community's growing attachment to her, I was able to make my point heard in private conversations. As you know, darling, I know enough about everyone's business to make sure that the kindest outcome prevails. Which it did. The fact was, it wouldn't be kind to the other residents if we allowed her to remain in her large house paying a fraction of the rent. It would sow discord. And a temporary reduction simply kicked the can down the road. Allowing her first refusal on a smaller premises, should one ever come up, was the compromise I allowed, knowing the likelihood was by that time Eleanor would have moved on.

And I may also have shared with some that Eleanor did not really like living here, which seemed to smooth over any doubts.

So I broke the news to Eleanor over a glass of wine at her cottage, and of course, she did not take it well. One glass became two, became three. She had grown attached to the village now, undoubtedly because of how we all reacted to her setback. She also still held out hope that Mr Beddington would return to her soon. But she certainly couldn't afford the full rent.

'Could you not get them to reconsider? Please? We're very close to a reconciliation.'

The desperation in her voice told me this was likely fantasy. 'I am so sorry, but the decision has been made. Sometimes to be kind, the committee can seem ... quite cruel. If I had any more sway, I would use it. But they would very much appreciate you being out of the cottage by the end of next month.'

Never be afraid to use the committee this way, my darling, to absorb the blows – it is its purpose.

'Next month?' She fell silent for some time, giving minute little shakes of her head, like they might dislodge a useful thought. Then, one came: 'Do you have people ready to move in? Already?'

Given she sounded distraught now, I told her that no, we had not been so calculating. It was true, but we'd started the process of looking.

'Can I stay until then?' she asked. 'Who knows, perhaps by that point my situation...' She glanced at the portrait of her and Mr Beddington. 'Things might have changed.'

'I'm afraid there's a plan to freshen up the cottage,' I improvised. 'They want to paint and tidy. There's much we'd like to change. I'm so sorry. It's ... what the committee have agreed.'

She snorted at this, and for a moment I felt exposed. But she started to cry then, and the blame was directed at herself.

So, I tried placating her with the agreed first refusal on a smaller residence, but I sensed she knew her time was up here.

I genuinely believed the matter was concluded then, and never envisaged her returning so soon. Perhaps I had hoped her reconciliation wasn't all the stuff of fiction. And if it was, and one day the black dog went for the jugular, at least she might go out quietly and with dignity. But instead, she came to my home the other evening, confused and distressed. It had been barely two months since we'd moved her on. She wore a man's puffy coat – presumably once Mr Beddington's – which hung off her even bonier frame.

'I don't understand,' she said, once I had sat her down and calmed her a little by holding her to me and stroking her back. 'The committee said they would repaint it first. But people live there, a couple. I've seen through the window. It's not changed.'

'I know. I know.'

'Why?'

I stared at her a long time, at her overgrown fingernails and at the white flakes of skin in her hair. This misery, it stretched out through time in both directions. It had burrowed deep into her like a parasite and become part of her. It would infest others too. What hope could there ever be once you found the simple beauty in life boring? I'd been too gentle before, instead of being *truly* kind. I understood that then.

'They lied,' I said. 'I'm sorry, but I was tricked. I think they had someone ready all along to replace you. I tried to change their minds.'

She closed her eyes, nodding. 'Was it something I did, then? Something I said. Obviously, they couldn't wait to get rid of me.'

'How have you been coping recently, Eleanor?' I said.

'Not well,' she said, sniffing and wiping her eyes. 'Being honest. Damien has met someone. So that's not been great.'

She gave a bitter laugh. 'I'm living … in a flat, I guess you'd call it. It's one room. There are kids in the alley outside my window. They deal drugs and shout at three or four in the morning. Once I would have hated it, but now I just don't care. Sometimes I think about confronting them. I think about one of them perhaps attacking me.'

'Are you having thoughts like that often?'

She shook her head, although I sensed this was unrelated to the question. 'It comes. It goes. Same as always. I've told you, it's like another person lives inside me. And when they're in control, all the spark goes from the world.'

'Is that how it feels now?'

She nodded. I took her hand. 'It is this sort of thing, this unpredictability, that the village can't handle. People here are simple, or at least they crave simplicity, and you are not simple. You are, in their eyes, sadly, a *timebomb*. An accident waiting to happen.'

She stared at me, a little shocked. I went on.

'We spoke with an expert, someone to guide us, but in confidence he told us that in cases such as yours, nothing could really be done. That drugs and therapy, and any treatment really, it's all just … a postponement.'

'A postponement.'

'Of the inevitable. Because, Eleanor, what you have is a … how did he put it? … not an illness, but an awakening. In those moments of darkness, your brain is tearing down the fantasy world of values and meaning that our brain chemistry creates for the rest of us in order that we keep on going, and procreating. What he told us, is that you, sadly, are seeing the world for what it is. I personally didn't think that can be right, but obviously I'm in no position to argue. That isn't my area of expertise.'

'No.' She stared into the space between us. 'No, I suppose not.'

'This is why the committee wanted whatever future awaits you to happen … elsewhere.'

'Oh.'

'I'm sure they thought this out of kindness. For your safety. But Eleanor, we've always been honest with each other, and I'm not prepared to lie for them.'

'I understand.' She sounded dreamy now. Dare I say, hypnotised. Although I do think much of this was shock, rather than any particular skill on my behalf.

'I'm sure you can see it from their position. If they truly believe that what you have is … forever, they are bound to act decisively. Wouldn't you?'

I offered her tea, but she declined and rose to leave, my admonishment of the village's callousness still in her ears. I didn't really expect things to happen so quickly – my instincts are sometimes better than even I realise – but after our talk she visited her old cottage, terrifying the wits out of our important new residents.

I knew from her previous 'lows' that she had hidden something in her old house that might have helped her achieve her goals, a remnant of a previous 'near miss', but never would I have believed she'd actually go there to retrieve it that night. It may unfortunately slow down my plans for Tessa and Andy a little, but hopefully not by much. But really I couldn't have scripted things any better – although I likely would have prevented her defiling the tree. But my point in all of this is, darling, a kind person is a flexible person. Because you never know when you will be …

SEVENTEEN

Jayden

O livia worked as a supply teacher three days a week, and because Jayden couldn't join the local school until September, he was left alone with a load of homework books. He respected Olivia for trusting him enough to let him stay unsupervised, especially after all that shit Leo came over and accused him of, so he always tried to have something to show her when she got back. But maths was doing his head in today, and he wanted to go out in the sun and have a little puff. Life was short, wasn't that the lesson from that woman hanging herself?

It had been three weeks since it happened. He'd not seen much from the upstairs window, but he'd seen enough to keep him up at night. People hugging each other on the green. A black shape hauled into an ambulance. Faces with hollow expressions. The mood around the village was still black, and ever since it happened people had been coming over to Olivia's at all times of the evening to have these little meetings on the patio of her garden. Doorbell ringing. Doors slamming. All these voices. It was like living with a dealer again.

They'd not acknowledged it yet, but one good thing that might come out of it all was that now everyone might realise Leo and that new woman had been chatting rubbish when they'd come over, accusing him of breaking into her studio. He'd heard from Olivia that she'd been stalking the new couple for weeks, and that the studio used to be her art room. Had to be her, didn't it?

Funnily though, he *had* thought about breaking in. Especially when he'd gone back later that morning and found out the key in the grass *was* for the sliding door. But he couldn't be sure who was watching him, especially Leo, and so just to prove to them that he wasn't a bad kid, he'd simply left it in the lock.

He stood up and stretched. He went upstairs to his bedroom and took his vape off charge. He pulled out a lockable suitcase from under the bed and returned the charger. From the case, he took out a cherry-flavoured e-liquid and started filling the tank. The doorbell rang. Jayden jumped and spilled some of the liquid. Some landed on the carpet, even more on his suitcase. He swore, finished his top-up, and packed away everything but the vape. He pocketed it and the doorbell went again.

He expected it to be one of the committee. When Olivia worked, one of them would usually pop over to check on him. It was often Ruth (they got her doing all the shit jobs), but sometimes it was Aaron or even October. Once it had even been Leo, dressed in full uniform. His abdomen tightened. God, not him today.

But it wasn't any of the committee. It was Tessa, standing in the sun wearing a Ramones T-shirt and a sheepish smile.

'Hi, Jayden,' she said. 'Sorry to disturb you.'

He turned his mouth down and shrugged. 'Olivia's not here.'

'I've come to speak to you, actually. I wanted to apologise.'

'Oh.'

'It wasn't you that broke into my studio, was it? I mean, I know it wasn't. It was the lady who, uh, passed away. Did you hear she came into my house that night?'

He nodded.

'I didn't think the way we approached it was very … kind. I should have known better. I trusted the wrong people. So I'm really sorry.'

He shrugged again and nodded once.

'And if you could forgive me and we could start again, that would really mean a lot to me. As I know you like The Ramones, and … well, I do too. Obviously. And, us Ramones fans ought to look out for each other.'

This actually made him smile, but he wore it cautiously and quickly.

'Does that mean you *do* forgive me?'

'Yeah,' he said. 'Sure.'

'Brilliant. Thank you, Jayden. I appreciate it.'

She nodded and waited like she wanted him to say something else. He wanted to say something too, because if he didn't, she'd go. And Tessa actually seemed alright. It was a pretty decent thing for her to have come here and said all that to him.

'I did want to play your bass, you know,' he said. 'It's proper sick. I didn't, but I know why they thought I did.'

'Is that why you admitted to it?'

'Nah.'

'Why did you, then?' She wasn't making it an issue, he could tell. She sounded interested.

'You lot had already decided.' With a shrug he added, 'Pick your battles.'

When she'd gone, Jayden bounded down the back garden. Who knew, maybe he and Tessa could become friends, and she might invite him around to use her gear? He hopped up onto a patio chair and scaled the rear fence, landing on the patch of sloping land that formed a footpath of sorts between the back gardens and the rising woodland behind the cottages. Most of the gardens had tall fences, so it was a good place to puff in peace.

It was interesting what Tessa had said about what Leo had done not being very kind. When he'd come to Nether Appleford, he'd read about their whole kindness thing and thought it might be quite cool. Made him consider doing more nice things for other people. But since meeting Leo, who was such a big part of that committee, he'd started thinking maybe it was all a load of shit. Something about that stupid tree reminded him of influencers who did videos where they cured blind children and gave wodges of cash to homeless people. It was great in theory, but it was all for the clicks. It felt fake – unlike what Tessa had just done, which he'd instantly known was for real.

It wasn't just the fakeness, though, that bothered him about Nether Appleford. What had Tessa said again? She'd trusted the wrong people. Not person. *People.* Was she on about the committee? If she was, it synched with something else Jayden had been feeling lately.

He started walking along the back fences, searching for the spot where the stingers thinned so he could get into the wood. Sometimes he overheard conversations in the gardens, Dev on the phone talking to his sister about his financial troubles, Leo talking to someone about the 'luscious tits' on the woman he'd arrested the night before. One evening, the night after that woman died, he'd been coming home when he overhead Olivia in the garden talking with a few of the committee. He couldn't make out much because they'd all been murmuring and whispering, but he definitely heard Olivia whisper, 'It was all our fault, wasn't it?'

Aaron, a soft sort of guy usually, had said, 'No, of course not,' and he'd been raging.

They'd all gone in after that, so he'd never got to find out if they'd definitely been talking about the art woman. But he didn't really doubt it. Olivia said she'd lived in the village not long ago, and she'd had to leave when she couldn't pay her rent. What had gone on there, then?

He found a spot in the trees and sat down. He took out his vape, and was about to take a puff, when he heard a clattering sound nearby. He jerked his head left and right. He was still alone. A little while later he heard another clatter. Walking back later, he heard it again, accompanied this time by a strange little yelp, like a parrot had been strangled. It was coming from Leo's garden. He took a risk, and peered through a little hole in his fence. Over by Leo's allotment, was a small metal cage, and inside was a squirrel, flicking its tail and darting from one end of the cage to another.

Curious, he went back later that evening, wanting to find out if the squirrel was still there. If he could work up the courage, he might even sneak in and let it out. But when he got near he could hear Leo's voice.

'... and you can't go around nicking people's food off them.'

He was fucking lecturing the squirrel. Jayden started laughing, and had to put a hand over his mouth. Quietly as he could, Jayden approached the hole in the fence and looked in. Leo was sitting with his legs crossed by the cage, shaking his head and grinning.

'If you were a human, mate, we'd have to go through a whole rigmarole court case before we could set you right. But *unlucky*, you're a squirrel.'

Leo stood, bringing the cage with him. The squirrel, sensing something was up, starting darting around again, lashing its tail violently. Unmoved, Leo took the cage over to a water butt by a shed. Jayden didn't need to watch the rest. He backed away, heart thundering. He heard the cage go into the water. That fucking psycho, what a massive—

Kate Bush started singing 'Running Up A Hill'. It was the ring tone he'd set for Olivia. In a panic, he pulled out the phone from his pocket, and the song played even louder. It was a good ten seconds before it was silent again.

'Fuck,' Jayden mouthed, and stared at the hole in Leo's fence. Was someone there already, looking back at him? He couldn't be sure. Hoping not, he ran.

EIGHTEEN

Tessa

The next time Tessa allowed herself to truly look at the Kindness Tree, it had been three weeks since the break-in. Now it looked chastened and apologetic, stripped now of the fibreglass hearts so that the year's prizes could be awarded at the summer fete. What had become a bouquet pile ringed the trunk. She walked hand-in-hand with Andy, towards the green and the sounds of music and chatter.

In the immediate aftermath of Eleanor Beddington's suicide, the committee had postponed the fete, but following some 'soul searching', it was announced on the village WhatsApp group that celebrations would and *should* go ahead after all, to both honour Eleanor's memory and help the village grieve and move on together.

Tessa wasn't entirely sure if it was the right decision, and seeing the tree again only made her unease burrow deeper, but in a spirit of togetherness she wanted to show her face. The village, and particularly the committee, had been supportive about what happened to her that night in their attentive, by-the-book way. The whole Story Station thing seemed to have been forgiven, and Ruth had even popped by to apologise to her.

'I got carried away and shouldn't have put you on the spot that way,' she said, adding cryptically, 'I think sometimes we're all … *I'm* always so eager to … make a contribution that I don't always reflect.'

Even Benedita and Aaron had popped around for a doorstep check-in, no outward signs that they were still holding a grudge.

Despite this, Tessa still wasn't ready to forget what Eleanor had said about the committee either. *Rich seams of cruelty* wasn't a phrase you forgot in a hurry.

'You alright?' Andy said, catching her staring. She nodded and leaned into him.

When they reached the fete itself, spread across the green between the tree and the lake, Andy screwed up his face at the sound of an off-key troubadour belting out 'Wonderwall' through a squeaking PA system.

'Maybe I should go and help them adjust the levels for him,' she said.

Any anger she'd felt at Andy's absence that evening had been swallowed by the tragedy that ultimately played out. They'd grown closer. More touching, more kissing. A little sex, too. Even spending more time in the evenings together when work allowed.

In retrospect, there had, perhaps, been no danger at all to her from Eleanor Beddington. The injury Tessa had sustained had been accidental and hadn't even required stitches. And while that didn't change how things felt at the time, the village consensus, that she had been a troubled soul that they'd never been able to quite touch, made her a problematic villain. Tessa had heard from multiple sources about Eleanor's isolated life in the village and her separation from her husband. And clearly she'd held some animosity towards the village and October about the nature of her departure. All that stuff about them not being *true*... *Kill them. Kill her.* Either way, Tessa was convinced now that the remark had been Eleanor lashing out at them not her.

The police had taken Tessa's statement on her return from being checked at the hospital. They'd found nothing on Eleanor's body, and so the theory was the item she'd retrieved from their bathroom was the home-made noose used to end her life. She'd stowed it in the cavity beneath the bath, and the noise Tessa heard inside was likely the side panel being removed. The noose's specific design – made from a climbing cable and a resistance band, and cut to a particular length – spoke of plans abandoned. It took Tessa some time to shake the thought that it had been there during the months they'd been living there, as it did the woman's admission to her that she had been hiding it from her husband.

They ran into Dev and his wife, Jitesh, in front of the tombola stall. He greeted Tessa with a soft touch on the arm and a conciliatory expression. He'd been one of the first to come to visit her and she'd been surprised at how moved she'd been. Andy, distracted by the smell of the barbecue, excused himself to get food, while Jitesh got caught up in another conversation.

'I'm glad you decided to come.' He looked around at the tables, the bunting, the entertainments. 'I think this was the right thing to do, don't you?'

'It all looks amazing.'

Tessa guessed everyone in the village was here. She even caught sight of Jayden, looking grumpy leant up against the back wall of the pub, and of Kath sitting on a bale of hay in front of the stage. It was only then she looked up and understood who the current entertainment was: it was Leo and his acoustic guitar.

'I just wish she could have seen this,' Dev said, casting a glance over to a table on which a blown-up photograph of Eleanor had been erected behind a donation box. Carnations, gladioli and roses in different arrangements had been left both on top and beneath the table. Tessa had stopped listening to him, and when she snapped back into the conversation, she had no idea what he was talking about: '... which is silly of me to say, because you know rationally that a thing like this wouldn't make a difference. My sister had depression, and it's an illness. Isn't it? Still.' He paused, and unsure if he wanted a response, Tessa nodded. 'People here cared for her. Before she left, it really felt like she was growing into village life.' He sighed and shook his head. Then, looking right into her eyes, added, 'We know it takes some people a while.'

Tessa studied Dev's face. Was he talking about her now? Had that comment been pointed, or an attempt at reassurance? Cruel, or kind?

'Did Eleanor leave here on good terms?' Tessa said. 'You know, when she moved out.'

'We thought so, yes. Why do you ask?'

'She made me feel like I'd stolen her home.'

Again, he touched her arm. 'Tess, none of this is to do with you at all. I know it's hard, when things like this happen, not to look for something you could have done differently.'

'It's not that so much,' she said, a little frustrated by the suggestion. 'She just ... didn't sound like someone who wanted to leave.'

'Well ... I suppose she couldn't afford to pay the rent on her own once her husband had gone. So, in that sense, perhaps you symbolised that to her in some way. Again, not your fault at all.'

'And the committee couldn't help her?'

'Oh, it was discussed how we might. We talked about a few options. But in the end, she took matters into her own hands and left of her own volition.' He shrugged again, touched her arm once more, and said, 'Go easy on yourself, Tessa. It really wasn't your fault.'

By the time Andy and she had idled around the oval of tables on the green, played hook-a-duck and Aunt Sally, the call came to gather around the stage for the prize giving. During Ruth's nervous preamble, Tessa zoned out, still ruminating on the things Dev had said. It wasn't until Andy's name was called out, and he stood up to rapturous applause and whoops, that she understood he'd won something. He was on his way to the stage when Tessa realised she wasn't clapping, and that a few villagers, Amara and Leo, were looking at her.

Andy was encouraged by Ruth to make a speech, and he stepped forward to the mic looking directly at Tessa with an amused WTF expression.

'Uh.' Everyone waited in silence. Tessa glanced around again and saw smiling, encouraging faces. Someone whooped. Andy laughed. 'Cheers. Well... Most Promising, eh? Don't think I've ever been called that before.' Everyone laughed. 'I don't really do speeches. But yeah, cheers to the committee and everyone for this. For making me and Tess feel really welcome.' He glanced at her again and she smiled back. 'It's lovely to get this, but getting to do the work I've done for a few of you has just been an excuse to get to know you better.' She heard a tremor in his voice, and again, he looked at Tessa. She nodded encouragingly. 'Oh, your bills are in the post.'

Tessa felt heat in her face, worried he'd taken her wide-eyed nodding to be a hint that he should mention payment. But his remark got a big laugh and she relaxed. Andy held up his trophy to indicate he was done, and left to an even bigger reception than he'd received going up. This climaxed with whole village bursting into a chant: 'Just Be Kind! Just Be Kind!'

He sat beside her again, and Tessa rubbed his back, pleased at least one of them had made a good impression here. Not only had he beaten her to his first heart, she'd actually lost count now of how many he'd received. Whereas she was still awaiting her first. He smiled, looking at the little silver cup like he'd won an Ivor Novello. Silence fell over the crowd, and October Allsopp stepped up to the microphone wearing a chastened version of her omnipresent grin.

'It's so lovely to have you all here,' she said. 'Gosh, what an eventful few weeks, eh?' She dipped her head before continuing. 'I don't want to dwell too much on the challenges we've all faced. For some, they are very fresh indeed.' Tessa had been looking at the bale of hay in front of her, but with dread she now raised her head to see October looking at her. When she met her gaze, hoping to move her on, October nodded. 'Tessa, you did a very kind thing welcoming Eleanor, in her distress, into your home that evening. I hope you know that we know that.'

Now heads were turning her way, and God, why was October doing this? She had to make it stop. Tessa copied her nodding, and October closed her eyes. 'I'm sure Eleanor's husband, who is here with us today, appreciates that one of her last encounters was such a kind one. Thank you, Tessa.'

Now a man near the front was looking her way and smiling appreciatively. This seemed to go on for minutes, although likely it was mere seconds. Then mercifully October moved on, revealing that the Kindest Resident prize this year, the big one, was being suspended in Eleanor's memory. Everyone applauded, although when the chanting resumed, Tessa stayed quiet.

On her way back she ran into Leo coming out of the pub. He held up his guitar and beamed at her. 'You not sticking around for my second set?'

'I've just got … something to do at the cottage. I'll be back in a bit.'

'Great.' He waited, perhaps awaiting a compliment from her. When none was forthcoming, he gave a quick glance around and leaned towards her. 'How you been?'

'Fine, I think.'

'Yeah, good. Good. Listen, I heard you went and spoke to Jayden.'

Tessa paused. 'I did, yeah. Have you been over?'

Leo looked confused. 'I don't see why I would. He lied to us, didn't he? We might've known it was Eleanor sooner if he'd just been honest. We might have been able to help her.'

Was he really trying to blame Jayden now? 'I don't think that's—'

'Listen, Tess, did you mention any of that when the police were over? Us going to speak with Jayden, I mean?'

She looked into his eyes, noticing the red capillaries at the corners. 'I didn't mention you, no.' She hadn't wanted to get him in any trouble.

He nodded, neither confirming nor denying whether he approved of that. Then with a salute of his guitar, he headed back to the fete.

Tessa watched him walk off. What a bastard. How dare he suggest Jayden was in any way responsible? If anything, Leo falsely accusing the boy had been the problem. So if he wanted to open that door… But that was just it, no one was to blame, were they? First Dev insisting she not blame herself, now Leo blaming Jayden. If they wanted to blame anything, why not the little voice in her head that had overridden her gut instinct that day? *Say yes, sort the rest later.* Why not blame Nether Appleford?

She sought out Jayden, who was hiding around back of the chapel. She'd seen him disappear that way not long after the ceremony finished.

'Hey, Ramones friend.'

'What have I done now?' he said, a hint of a smile at the corner of his mouth. Beneath his dark coat he wore a Fleetwood Mac T-shirt, God love him.

'Nothing. I just wanted to know something. Can you really slap a little bass?' It was a gamble, referencing a daft line from a decade-old Paul Rudd film. But if he was a bassist, he might know it.

His smile broke out in full then, and he finally looked his age. 'Yeah, I can slappa the bass.'

'Want to try out for my band, then?'

His eyes grew wide and almost immediately he looked away. 'Serious?'

From over on the green, Leo started to play, and from the sound of the chord progression he was either doing 'Wonderwall' again or 'Boulevard of Broken Dreams'. Or, God no, was that 'Fly Away'?

'We could do a bit better than this,' Tessa said. 'Couldn't we?'

Jayden didn't laugh. He nodded.

NINETEEN

Jayden

H e came back from Tessa's buzzing. They'd sounded like a proper band. And that Kath, she was an absolutely amazing drummer. And okay, Tessa hadn't let him play the Precision, but he was perfectly happy with the bright-red Epiphone. It had sounded heavy as fuck through that pedal, and now she'd even let him take it home to practise.

He went to his bedroom and found that 'My Generation' song they'd been doing on his phone. He listened to it carefully, searching for any variations in the two-chord pattern he'd use to impress them next time. The ball of his thumb hurt, and when he lifted up his hand to his face he saw he had another burst blister. His downward bass technique kept rubbing against the wood.

The doorbell chimed, and he straightened up and paused the music. It'd been two weeks since he'd watched Leo murder that poor squirrel, and he'd been starting to think he'd got away unseen. But he was still edgy, not helped by his nerves about starting his new school next week and the nicotine withdrawal he was feeling from staying clear of that land behind the fence.

Turned out it was Andy again, coming to fix the kitchen extractor fan. He'd been over a few times before, fixing a light, fixing a broken shower. Jayden had tried chatting to him about music once, but he'd not seemed that interested in talking. When he went downstairs later to grab a snack, Andy was still there talking to Olivia. She sounded different, all lively and excited. He slowed down at the bottom of the stairs.

'I still have belief in something,' Olivia was saying. 'But … I mean, I don't go to church anymore. So, I feel a bit of a fake wearing my crucifix. What about you? Do you … have any belief?'

'A long time ago I did.'

'Since I've lived here … in the village, I've just not felt the need for it as much. My parents were religious, so that was some of it. They didn't like rock music at all, and so I only ever listened to classical, growing up. But … there was this U2 song a boyfriend of mine played me, and it had this lyric about a God-shaped hole, which always stuck with me. I really got that, you know. A God-shaped hole. But now, that hole sort of feels full.'

'God-shaped hole – you serious?' Andy sounded like she'd told him he'd won the lottery.

'You know it?'

Jayden walked in and the two of them didn't notice. Andy was showing her the tattoo on his arm of those same lyrics. It was weird. And a bit embarrassing. Olivia grabbed the arm, telling him to get out of town. Jayden yanked open the fridge, jars clinked in the door, and they both turned around to see him.

'Hi, Jayden,' Olivia said, sounding suddenly deflated.

Jayden smiled and nodded. He took out an orange-juice carton and swigged from it. 'Please could you use a cup?'

Realising what he'd done, he held up an apologetic hand.

'Jayden, let's get your opinion,' Andy said, gesturing for him to come over to where he stood in the corner of two kitchen counters. 'Do you see this?' He pointed up to the slats on the extractor-fan cover, his eyes momentarily glancing towards Olivia. 'Do they look a bit warped to you?'

Jayden first looked at Olivia, but she stood now with her arms folded, avoiding his gaze. When he looked up, he saw that, yes, two of the slats looked warped. One bent upwards slightly, the other downwards. 'Yeah.'

Andy removed a wooden spoon from a pot of big utensils and poked it into the gap created by warped plastic. 'We can't decide. What do you think? Doesn't that look like it fits perfectly?'

It definitely did. And again, he glanced at Olivia, who kept looking at the counter. 'Maybe.'

'Maybe.' Andy nodded with an exaggerated expression of curiosity. 'Well, thanks Jayden. Good to get your input.'

It wasn't until a bit later that Jayden wondered if Andy had been blaming him. By that time he'd gone, and increasingly aggravated about the notion, Jayden grabbed his vape and stormed into the back garden. So they were still looking to blame him for everything. Perfect. He found a place a bit further back in the woods – just in case – and let the nicotine soothe him. He was almost done when he heard crunching leaves and bracken behind him.

Before he could react, his new companion said, 'You know I have the right to confiscate that from you.'

He didn't turn around. He knew who it was. A moment later Leo came and sat beside him, dressed in his uniform. Jayden turned his head to look at him, caught a whiff of

142

mingling aftershave and sweat. He held eye-contact, brought his vape up to his lips, and took a hit. He turned the other way to exhale. Then, resigned, he handed over the vape without looking.

'For the best,' Leo said. 'Nicotine addiction is money down the drain. Is that your only one?'

'Yeah.'

'Where'd you get it?'

He shrugged. 'One of my mum's friends had a little side thing going on selling them. He gave me one as a birthday present.'

'Nice bloke. What was his name?'

Jayden shrugged. 'Didn't know it.'

Leo laughed. 'Did he give you the liquid too?'

'I'm giving up anyway.'

'Good to hear.' Leo snorted, and spat to one side. 'I'll be round to pick those up.' He paused before adding: 'Maybe I'll come when Olivia's out.'

'Okay.'

'Only because she'd be gutted to hear you'd been sneaking around behind her back, breaking the law.'

'Fine.'

'Or maybe I won't.' Leo let that sink in. Then he brought up the vape to his lips and inhaled. 'Just horrible. Honestly, mate. This is for your own good. I know you'll be angry with me now, but trust me. This sort of shit is economy. You've been bumped up to first class, and you need to start acting like it. There's a real chance Olivia might take you long-term if you … sort your act out.' He stood, knees clicking. 'You'll probably have withdrawal for a few weeks. Chew gum and keep your hands busy, I'd suggest.'

'I've got school starting next week.'

'Well, that'll take your mind off it, then. Oh, and Jayden.

Sometimes animals get injured, yeah? And the kind thing to do is put them down. Not everyone understands that, Jayden. But do you?'

'Yeah.'

'What's that?'

'Yeah, I follow you.'

'Good. Listen, a lot of people around here, Olivia especially, they don't know the world you've come from. They think they do. They think kids like you can be *saved*. I'm not convinced. I think if you see some of the shit you've seen, you're broken. I see it all the time. But I'm also an optimist. So maybe keep your head down, mouth shut, and stay out of this wood, and maybe, just maybe, you can prove me wrong. And you know what, Jayden? I'd like that.'

The first week was bad. He couldn't sleep and was tired all the time. Concentration was difficult at school. He chewed his way through endless packs of gum and played with a fidget spinner he got from the school nurse. A few kids tried making friends with him, but he found them irritating without knowing why. He knew Leo had waited for this exact moment to do this. That's why he hadn't visited straight away. He wanted to teach him a lesson.

One afternoon, Leo came over when Olivia was out. He stood over Jayden while he unlocked the combination lock on his suitcase. When it opened, he bent down and said, 'Good lad,' and patted his head. Jayden flinched, and Leo looked annoyed. He bent over, picked up the bottles, and left without another word.

He was irritable around Olivia, too, so he hid away in his room. One night she wanted a 'talk' about the band Ghost, who he loved and often listened to. She didn't like that their lyrics were about Satan, didn't understand that the band were being funny. He tried explaining, but she told him flat out she'd rather not hear them out loud in her house. He nearly lost it with her, and it took all Jayden's willpower not to kick off. He agreed to her terms, telling himself he'd just listen on his buds.

The second week was better. He still needed the gum and the fidget spinner, but he was getting better sleep. The jams were helping, too, and for their duration his symptoms temporarily abated. One night, though, the sore patch from his bass playing was throbbing, and his mind chose this moment to start torturing him. What he wouldn't give for a quick puff now! He remembered spilling that liquid on his suitcase and the carpet. Would it be possible, if he put a bit of water on the dried spill, to suck out the combined liquid and get a tiny hit? Just to get him to sleep.

He got up and pulled his case out. That's where the biggest spill had been. Hey, maybe there was even a liquid bottle inside that had been overlooked. That had fallen into a side pouch or something. He rolled the combinations into place and popped the locks.

He lifted the lid and saw there *was* something inside. His heart began to race, because it wasn't anything good. He was in big trouble.

TWENTY

Tessa
_____

I t felt right. For the first time since moving to Nether
Appleford Tessa had, not a buzz exactly, but a spine-
cracked-true sensation of life aligning. It had started almost as
soon as she'd begun playing music with Jayden. After she'd
checked Olivia didn't object – which she hadn't seemed to,
although she'd not been as enthusiastic as Tessa expected either
– Tessa listened carefully to what he'd taught himself, chose
some songs that fitted his aggressive strumming style, and gradually built up his confidence over a few weeks so that when she
suggested bringing a drummer over to their next session, he
wasn't fazed.

He'd probably not expected the late-sexagenarian lady with
the untidy cottage to walk in the next time they met up, but if
he'd had any scepticism about Kath's ability, he didn't let it
show. He might have been braced for the worst when she shuffled over to Tessa's electric drum pads and held her drumsticks
in a crab-like traditional jazz grip, groaning when she sat down
and straightened her back before tapping out a _rat-tat-ta-tat-tat_
on the snare pad, followed by a lame _boom chish_ on the bass

drum and high-hat. But as soon as she'd started working around the kit properly, sticks purring paradiddles across the rubber surfaces while a computer turned each strike into a corresponding drum sound that burst from Tessa's speakers, his mouth fell open.

At the start Jayden had seemed agitated and a bit quiet, but after a while he appeared to mellow out and really started enjoying it. Tessa singing and playing guitar, they stuck to simple stuff, grinning at each other when they knew they were about to get all the way through a track without messing up. Stuff like Green Day's 'Brain Stew'. The Who's 'My Generation'. Tessa had encountered enough drummers over her years in the industry to know that technique didn't always translate into an ability to keep the beat. But Kath was a metronome. She had it all except stamina, and they needed a good ten-minute break every so often so she could get her breath back. But that just meant the three of them had time to bond, sharing music and stories. They'd meet once or twice a week, usually on a Tuesday and Thursday night between six and seven, so that Jayden had time to decompress after school.

Andy found the whole thing amusing, at least initially. As September went on, though, he increasingly found Tessa's unwavering enthusiasm for the band puzzling.

'What's your endgame with those two?' he asked her one night, the two of them on opposite ends of the sofa, gazing at the telly.

'Do I need an endgame? As long as everyone's getting something out of it…'

'And what are *you* getting out of it?'

She shrugged, knowing there was too much to articulate. 'It's just making me feel useful. And I'm playing music again, not doing it on a computer.'

'You know, if you wanted a band … we could have started

jamming again.' He shrugged. She stretched her legs across the sofa and kicked him gently.

'Aw, are you jealous?'

'Maybe.'

'Well, we can have a band too, my sweet. I didn't know you were so keen.'

'Like we have time to do that.'

True enough, but was he also implying that it was her band's fault? He still wasn't saying no to the increasing number of evening freebie jobs in the village, and it wasn't a bad thing that her own work was taking off now, so picking a fight over Kath and Jayden felt wide of the mark. They were just busy, that was all.

'Olivia says you've bought the kid a bass guitar and amp?'

'No, I just loaned him that knackered old Epiphone I wasn't using, with a mini-Marshall.'

'She says it looks new.'

'I just restored it a bit.' Andy gave a single nod without looking at her. 'He's a nice kid, Andy. His story ... it breaks your heart. And all he wants to do is play music.'

'I'm sure he's great.' He paused to sip from a can of lager. 'Not sure he likes me, though.'

'What makes you say that?'

He shook his head and shrugged again. 'I'm just a bit worried about you getting too attached to him.'

Tessa sat up. 'Why?'

'Just a feeling. I'm not sure Olivia thinks it's working.'

She brought her feet back, irritated by her name coming up yet again. 'Has she said something to you about that?'

He turned to meet her gaze. 'No, nothing specific. It's just what I've seen myself ... you know, I've been over there.'

She studied his face until he turned away. It was like he was trying to bring her down to earth, which at this point, after everything she'd been through lately, she didn't really need. She was still having nightmares and morbid daydreams about Eleanor Beddington.

She fought the urge to suggest that *they* could foster Jayden, if Olivia didn't want him. Still, what was he up to, being such a buzz kill? The feeling she had playing music with those two was everything she'd come here to feel. That Epiphone restoration had taken up a lot of time, which she'd done with kindness, and it had made her happy – and now she was getting told off for it.

'Well,' she said eventually, setting it in stone now by speaking it out loud, 'hopefully he'll be here for the Christmas fete, at least. My *endgame* is doing a show there.'

'A show.'

'A gig, yes. So the village knows what a pair of legends those two are. And we're going to bring the house down.'

One evening, when Kath's back hurt too much for her to join them, Jayden asked Tessa whether he had ever seen Kath's cottage. When she nodded, he asked how it had got that bad.

She chose her words carefully. 'I don't know exactly. I think maybe it's hard to get rid of things if they remind you of someone you love. Grief can take over if you let it, and maybe she's become a bit isolated from anyone who might be able to help.'

He nodded like he might have some idea of what she was talking about. 'No one likes her here, do they?'

'I don't think that's true. Why do you say that?'

'Just a vibe, innit. They reckon it's not fair that she keeps saying she'll tidy up her place and never does.'

'Who says that?'

'Olivia.' He shrugged. 'I think it's harsh, though. If it reminds her of her dead husband, give her a break.'

'Well, I tend to agree. Although I can't imagine Olivia thinking that.'

He made a face like she was crazy, then seeming to catch himself, turned back to the bass guitar he'd been packing away. 'Anyway, they can't touch her, can they?'

'Touch her. What do you mean?'

'You know, get rid of her. She owns her place.'

'I really don't think anyone wants to get rid of her. And I didn't think anyone owned here except October.'

'That's what Olivia said. It's why they don't just move her on. She owns it.'

When she looked online later, she found that up until the late noughties there had been cottages for sale in Nether Appleford. Then after that, none at all. That was interesting, especially as it meant Jayden had been right. That lent the other claims he'd made an extra sheen of credibility. Apparently he had been listening to Olivia carefully.

She wanted to ask Kath about the history. In fact, she'd been wanting to ask Kath about a lot of things, given what Eleanor Beddington had told her to do. But Tessa hadn't quite found the right moment. She was nervous about bringing up the words of a woman who had been at her lowest, and she didn't want to upset Kath by dragging up potentially bad memories. She also didn't want Kath thinking this whole band thing had been a ruse to grill her.

But … *rich seams of cruelty*. It kept coming back to her. When she reflected on her recent interactions with Leo and Dev. When she thought back to how Aaron and Benedita had behaved in that first week, and how the pub had fallen silent. And now there was Olivia, and all this stuff about Kath. None of it felt quite right, and perhaps the time had finally come to ask some questions.

It was an unusually hot evening in early October, and Jayden left her and Kath in the studio to go back to the cottage to use the loo. The inrush of air was a relief in what had become a sweaty, Lynx-scented sauna. Tessa turned to Kath, who sat breathing heavily on the drum stool.

'How's your back?' she asked.

'Been better.'

'Can I ask you a question?'

'Better be a good one, with that build-up.'

'No, it's just … none of my business. But Jayden said something… Do you own your cottage? Or did he get the wrong end of the stick?'

'Definitely none of your bloody business,' she said. After a moment she let her deadpan expression relax. 'I do, as it happens. Used to be a few of us owned around here, before October took over the estate. She came in, though, and bought most of them out.'

'I wondered if it was something like that.'

'She's a lady with plans, isn't she?'

'But she didn't buy *you* out?'

'Nah. Last one standing, though I reckon they'd love me out.' She started laughing.

'Did they ever offer?'

'Oh, the offer's "always on the table", apparently. And it's a good one, too, to be fair. But when it was all first happening, my Malcolm was ill. And we weren't going anywhere then, not with him in a wheelchair. Then when he passed… Appreciate it doesn't much look like a home, though.'

Tessa nodded, understanding. 'So, if you had to guess, why do you think she bought the others out?'

Kath leaned over, grunting as she did, and picked up a water bottle from by her feet. She drank a mouthful and narrowed her eyes. 'Why you interested in all this, if you don't mind *me* asking a question?'

Tessa reached over and grabbed her own bottle of water for a sip. 'Did you hear that I saw Eleanor Beddington the night she died?'

Kath nodded. 'I heard that from her husband when he was down here for the fete.'

'I spoke to her. I know she wasn't well, so I wasn't sure whether to bring this up, but she mentioned she knew you.'

'Yeah, we got on.'

'She said I should come and talk to you.'

'About what?'

Was it really okay to bring this up? It felt a little icky. Yet what was the harm? Kath knew the context, especially if they'd been friends. She might even get something out of hearing Eleanor was thinking of her that night. Although Tessa couldn't kid herself. Her driving force now wasn't kindness but curiosity.

'It was hard to understand all of it,' Tessa said. 'But she said something about the committee getting rid of people that weren't … useful to them. She used that term, *useful*. She said they'd done it before, and you knew something about this.'

Kath mulled on this, frowning. 'Did she think they'd got rid of her then?'

Tessa nodded. 'I think that's what she was saying.'

Kath took another gulp from her bottle and belched. 'Boy will be back soon. Maybe later we need to sit down and have a proper chat, if you're really interested in what Eleanor and I used to talk about.'

'So is there actually something to this?'

Now Kath smiled. 'Something to what? The idea they'll get rid of people they don't want here? You don't even know the half of it, my darling.'

TWENTY-ONE

Tessa

After they finished, Jayden packed Tessa's Epiphone into its case and stood at the sliding door waiting for Kath. He often walked her back, despite it taking him out of his way.

'You don't need to always be fussing over me,' Kath said. 'I'm just going to talk to Tess about a few things and I'll get myself back tonight. You get home, you. And leave that door open when you do.'

He shrugged and nodded, perhaps a trace of hurt behind his nonchalant lip-purse. He held up a hand and left, another welcome breeze blowing in from outside. The two of them waited a minute and continued packing away before finally Tessa said, 'So how did you know Eleanor?'

'We used to talk every now and again. Got to know her first after one of the Christmas fetes. She'd been getting through the mulled wine like it were going out of fashion and there were a lot of eyes on her, if you know what I mean. Her husband was too busy chatting with the committee to notice her wobbling around on her own, but I got chatting to her and she ended up following me home like a stray. She wanted to come in, so what was I to do? I squeezed her back into my place for a few cups of tea and a chat.'

Tessa tried picturing where in Kath's cottage they would have done this. She'd only been inside twice, but the things outside the front had been nothing like the chaos within. Boxes and paraphernalia were piled almost to the ceiling in some places. To get inside she'd navigated a labyrinth of haphazardly stored personal history. Newspapers, plastic bags, bubble wrap. Even her kitchen had been dangerously crowded, stacks of old letters leaning towards the gas hobs. Occasionally, heart-breaking glimpses of an older life stood out. A photo album open, full of long-faded snapshots of a sunny holiday. A collection of sheet music scattered across the hood of a half-concealed piano. A calendar on the wall from the year after Malcolm died. Like she'd tried to go on, at least for a while.

Kath continued: 'I could see her looking around at all my stuff, and eventually she comes out and, I remember, she says, "This place looks like the inside of my head." We both had a laugh, and got to talking about … you know … life. Things getting on top of us and feeling a bit outside of things in the village. All that. I don't mind saying that it's not been easy since Malcolm. And we sort of connected about … that type of thing. Head stuff.' She looked away from Tessa and sighed. 'Big old misery party, it was. Anyway, long story short, we ended up on a ketamine trial together.'

Tessa burst out laughing. 'Sorry, what?'

'Don't you laugh, you git.' Kath was grinning.

'A ketamine trial. Really?'

'Yeah, they been testing it out at the hospitals round here, you know. For … head stuff. She came over and said we should try it, and I thought at worst it might be a laugh. Done a few naughty things in my time, but never that one.'

'I've read about trials like that, but… Did it work?'

'Well, I have to say, I got a lot out of it. Nothing's done what that's done for me. I'd go so far as to say it's the only thing that's worked. That's made me feel normal.'

'Did they keep you on it?'

'Nah. I'm on some waiting list or another for something, but not holding my breath.'

'Did it work for Eleanor?'

'She said so, yeah.'

Tessa nodded, absorbing the implications of what Kath was saying. 'How can they just leave you dangling like that?'

'It's a tease, is what it is.' Kath blew air into her cheeks while the rest of her deflated. After a moment, she said, 'So what else did Eleanor say to you about the village, then?'

'I know she didn't like it much. What was it you two used to talk about?'

Kath raised her eyebrows, stood up, and came around to sit on the worn-out sofa against the back wall. 'Well, if you didn't think me mad before—'

'I definitely don't think you're mad.'

'Well, see how you feel in a bit.'

'Okay.' Tessa smiled, trying to project openness.

'First things first, the idea that this village was built on kindness … well, that's bollocks, for a start.'

According to Kath, the version of the village's history on the website was missing a few important details. John Sackville, the owner of Appleford manor and estate, had indeed built Nether Appleford in the late eighteenth century and housed his estate workers there. But whether kindness had anything to do with it was up for debate. Kath contended that the village of Appleford, standing just outside the manor wall, both spoiled

Sackville's view and meant locals were wont to chuck things into his grounds when dissatisfied. So he had bought out every resident, and demolished the village, building a new one out of sight down in the valley.

'What they don't tell you at the spring pageant, is that some villagers didn't want to move,' Kath said, 'and one stood his ground and flat-out refused to go. No one could prove it, but most people knew who done the deed when the chap's house were burned down. So there's your starter for ten. Why do the committee keep trotting out this make-believe version of what happened here? It's not hard to find out what really happened. I think it tells you a lot. *Just Be Kind*, my arse.'

Tessa's mouth fell open. Kath went on, explaining the estate changed owners down the years, ending up in the hands of a renowned industrialist at the turn of the twentieth century. From there it was handed down through October's family until she got it a decade back – her brother should have inherited it, but he died in the years before.

'So when October took over,' Tessa said, 'she basically did the same thing as the founder. She bought out all the owners.'

'Yeah, well, like then, there were a few of us who weren't interested. There was me, of course. But there was this other fella, too, an older bloke, Willy Mortimer. He was a bit of a history buff. He's the one who told me first about John Sackville. And his great, great, great-uncle or something was apparently, so he says, the chap John Sackville burned out of his place all them years ago. And Willy loved all that, and he wasn't having it when he cottoned on that October wanted to buy him out. I heard they offered him twice what the cottage was worth at one point, too, but would he take it? Bollocks, would he. He'd paid off his mortgage and had all the money he needed, thank you very much.'

'Who's they?'

'Well, by then they had the committee going. October'd already booted out a few villagers she didn't really see eye-to-eye with, ones who rented. And she chose the committee from new villagers she'd hand-picked herself.'

'They booted people out. How is that legal?'

'Rents.' She launched her index finger like a rocket. 'Easy as pie. And it was obvious she was targeting the ones that weren't into all her kindness stuff. Discounts for people she liked, too. And that's likely why I think she wanted rid of the owners, so she'd be able to have her sort of people in. Cleanse the place. When they finally got rid of Willy, all the committee you know were in place, I think. Olivia was the newest, and I can't remember if she were in yet.'

'What happened with Willy?'

'Well, after a few years he got pretty bitter about all the changes. Nether Appleford was just a quiet village where people kept themselves to themselves all the years he'd lived there. Yeah, they had a bit of history with the kindness stuff, but October really went at it like the proverbial bull in the proverbial china shop. Everything was about bloomin' kindness.'

'So, like what?'

'Well ... that tree, for a start. Everyone heard she was giving rent discounts to people she liked, so people were going at that hammer and tongs, trying to get in her good books, putting every little thing they'd done up there. Elbows out, you know. People offering to do menial volunteer work around the place that really she could afford to pay for. Doing up that hotel, and the horse place. People traipsing in the woods picking up litter and putting the bags on their lawn so everyone knew how much work they'd done. I know that sounds like good things they were doing, but you know, it wasn't a kind atmosphere. They used to do paper hearts then, and you'd find them all up and down the street like autumn bloody leaves. *I fed my cat this morning. I took my kids to school. I didn't eat chocolate for Lent.* It was a competition.

'Then she had her little charity dinners at her house, and only invited her favourites. And of course, everyone noticed the people she liked also happened to be useful, too. You know. People with trades or professions. And when new people came in, they'd always have useful jobs, too. Ones October'd get them doing for free or discounts around the village.'

Recalling what Eleanor had said to her, Tessa nodded and said, 'I'm bloody useless, but my Andy's an electrician.'

'And has he been doing stuff around the village?'

'Yes.'

Kath nodded. 'Anyway, Willy didn't like all the change. And I get it, because if you liked it before, then all this made you feel like an outsider. Trouble with Willy though, he was a drunk, and he didn't always express himself in the most gentlemanly way. He got himself barred by Aaron from The Yew Tree in the end because he used to cause so much grief. Man was in his eighties, but he was scrappy. Committee found a load of them hearts all pulled down more than once, and it wasn't a mystery who done it. But I'm getting ahead, because what got him most angry was the fact his daughter somehow found out about him turning down the double-your-money offer. And someone had whispered to her about his drinking, and about the couple of times he'd fallen on his face in The Road.'

'So … were they trying to call into question his capacity?'

'There was a fire in his kitchen. He swore blind he never used a hob, and a fridge of ready meals spoke to that, but the fire brigade got here quick and said a dishcloth had caught on the burner. He wouldn't have it, and accused the committee of doing it to him while he was sleeping, because it were one of them that called 999, saying they'd seen it from outside. He got nasty with people in the village, banging on the door of the estate office, being aggressive. Now, I'd always liked Willy, but I could see that they had rattled him. In the end his daughter gets involved, she gets them out to do an assessment on him. For his head. Leo was there for it, in uniform, and he said later that Willy'd been talking gobbledegook when they went in. Wasn't making sense.'

'Wasn't Leo being there a conflict?'

'I don't know. This is Leo's patch, that's what he'd say. But weird thing was, Dev was there, too.'

'So, what happened?'

'They sectioned him, and he was in a psychiatric hospital for a while. The daughter was the one that came here when the place sold. Well-to-do type, blazer, heels, straight hair. Apparently, she now had decision-making power for him. Laughing and joking, she was, down at The Yew Tree with members of the committee.'

'So they set Willy up?'

'Make of it what you will. Maybe you reckon it sounds like the committee were just worried about him. That's probably what they were telling themselves, that they were being kind. Here's the thing, though. His place was over the road from here. So, I watched them cart him off that day. And I saw how he was that morning, and I heard him muttering to himself. He was saying they'd poisoned him. Clear as day.'

'Poisoned.'

'Yeah. And he was lots of things, Willy, and maybe he wasn't well in the head, what do I know? But you'd struggle to find someone here tell you he talked gobbledegook. Even when he was three sheets to the wind, he wasn't one slurring his words. He knew what he was saying. What I seen that morning … I don't know, watching Leo and Dev leading him off like that … it left a bad taste.'

Tessa fell silent. She had asked Kath for this, but now she didn't know what she wanted to do with the information. It was bordering on gossip, and even if it was true or half-true, what were the immediate ramifications for her? Kath, seeming to sense her hesitation, started to nod.

'Listen, that's just for starters. And my back… I probably need a lie down. But if you want to look into it, go find out what happened to Jamie Saunders, or Hattie Milner. Or any of the ones who left here after October took over. If he was still alive, I'd tell you to speak to Willy. But yeah, going back to Eleanor, she felt like the place was a bit off, and to make her feel better, to let her know that she wasn't imagining it, I told her some of this stuff. I thought I was helping, but who knows, maybe I made it worse. But I never really knew where she fitted in with their plan. She wasn't like the ones they usually choose. My guess was that they really needed the husband for some reason, that's what I've never worked out.'

'Can I ask you something?' Tessa said.

'God, you do like a build-up, don't you?'

'Do I seem like the type they usually pick?'

Kath paused, long enough to convey her true feelings. 'You're fine, you want to take what I say with a fat dose of salt. After what happened with Willy, I've always worried they'd come for me. If they really did do that to him … it was ruthless. And I know how they feel about the state of my place. But the fact they haven't yet … maybe it's not as sinister as what I've thought.'

Just then the curtain they'd pulled back to block out the low sun earlier in the afternoon moved aside. Jayden walked in through the open door, with the biggest smile Tessa had ever seen on his face. Tessa looked at Kath, both of them silently asking the other how much he had overheard.

'I knew it,' he said. 'I knew there was something wrong with this place.'

TWENTY-TWO

Jayden

'I think it's like *Hot Fuzz*,' he said, rubbing the burning ball of his thumb. 'You ever see that? It's funny.'

Kath, walking beside him, shook her head. 'Who's in it?'

Jayden loved that about her. When she didn't know what he was talking about, she never got defensive or made him feel stupid about his interests. She always listened. But he couldn't remember the names of anyone in it other than Simon Pegg, even though she might know some of the older actors. He didn't want to get his phone out to look because he knew she didn't like it. 'Ah, don't worry. It's just about a crazy village like this one.'

She tutted. 'You still on about that? You shouldn't have been listening.'

'I know.' He'd felt bad about doing it. But they asked him to leave, so he thought they might be talking about *him*. And right now he *really* needed to know whom he could trust. By the time he realised they were talking about Nether Appleford, he couldn't stop. 'But you're right, there *is* something wrong with this place. I know it. And all that committee hate me, so, you know. Maybe they'll come after me somehow. Try and get rid of me.'

'Don't talk wet. You're a good lad.'

He had to laugh at that. He so wanted to tell her about everything that had happened to him with Leo. And about what he'd found in his suitcase two weeks back. But as much as he trusted Kath and Tessa, telling them would make him a burden. A problem to solve. He liked being their friend, that they didn't patronise him and act like he was a bomb that might go off. For the first time in ages, he had a place to go where he didn't have to always be on best behaviour. If he told them what he'd found, that would all change. Besides, he didn't need their help. He could help himself.

'Someone needs to catch them in the act,' he said, swapping his bass guitar over to the other shoulder. 'Have they ever, you know, really hurt anyone?'

'Don't be daft. Tess just wanted a bit of village history, that was all. Just forget about what you think you heard.'

'I didn't *think* I heard nothing.' He let that sit for a moment, let her know she couldn't just dismiss him. 'I know what you were on about. *Kindest Village in England*, my arse.'

Kath laughed and shook her head. 'Your hand still hurting you?'

He hadn't realised he'd been rubbing it again. He held it up to look at the raw skin. She grimaced.

'It's not too bad. I'm sorry I listened in on you.'

'Let's forget it. You're a scamp, we knew that already.'

'A scamp? Isn't that a fish?'

She laughed. They reached the end of her drive and walked up towards the cottage. Seeing all the boxes and junk everywhere broke his heart. Happened every time he saw it. He'd offered to give her a hand with tidying it; the urge to do something for her was powerful. But he'd known from her big eyes, and how she'd gone all breathless after, that she didn't want any of that stuff touched. It was like a part of her body or something.

And he got that. He'd never met his dad, and all he'd known of him was his old bass guitar and a faded *Quadrophenia* T-shirt. When Mum had let that dick Vim sell his guitar … well, it'd sent Jayden over the edge, hadn't it? She might as well have cut off his arm.

But maybe if Jayden couldn't help with her cottage, he could help in another way. That's what Tessa had suggested he do when he talked with her about kindness the other week. She'd understood his point about the showiness of Nether Appleford. But her view was that if your desire to be kind was strong and genuine, and you were sure of the consequences of your actions, kindness could be a good thing.

'How do you know, though?' he'd asked. 'Like, how do you know you're not just doing it…' – he nearly said 'for the clicks' – '… to make people like you?'

'I don't have an easy answer,' she said. 'But maybe if your first thought about doing something kind is to tell everyone about it—'

'You mean, like, putting it on a tree?'

'—you might have other motivations.'

An idea struck him now, a mad one based on what he'd overheard Kath and Tessa talking about earlier. It was strong, and genuine, and the consequences would be that it killed two birds with one stone. He could do something kind for Kath, and solve the problem he'd found in the suitcase.

They reached Kath's door, and he was about to put his idea to her. But at the last second he bottled it.

'You wait here,' she said, and disappeared inside. A few minutes later Kath emerged holding out a pair of fingerless leather gloves. He stared, so she shook them at him. 'They were

Malc's. He used them to help his hand cramps when he was driving.'

Jayden took the dead man's gloves. Not wanting to offend her, he slipped a hand into one. It fitted perfectly.

'You look confused,' she said. 'It's to stop you catching your hand on that bass.'

He looked down and realised then that the glove was covering his sore patch. Affection burned in his chest, and he thanked her. It wasn't enough. He wanted to hug her, but instead, he decided to go for his idea.

'I'm so sorry about your … you know. All that stuff you were saying about … you know, with the ket.'

It took her a second to get what he meant. 'Well … never mind that.'

He smiled at her. To let her know he wasn't judging her or anything. Older people could be funny about mental health stuff, he got that. 'I could get you some.'

She frowned. 'You what?'

He dropped his voice close to a whisper. 'Some ket. I could get you some.'

She stared at him a moment and burst out laughing. 'Very funny.'

He couldn't help smiling because she was. 'Nah, I'm serious.'

She pointed at him, put on a playful scowl, and said, 'Scamp, if I ever saw one.' And with that, she closed the door on him.

———

She hadn't believed him, had she? He stomped home. Had she thought he was joking? Or didn't she think he was capable of hooking her up? *Stomp, stomp, stomp.* If she didn't think he was capable … well, that really didn't sit right with Jayden. People never believed him, even though most of the time he was right about stuff.

Like when he'd lived with Mum, people hadn't believed him then. Because he passed exams, and he knew how to sort his hair and his uniform the way his grandad showed him, everyone at school assumed he was fine. They somehow didn't notice his cuts and bruises. The two broken bones. And once, a burn. He'd tried telling people, especially after Grandad died and he couldn't escape to his place in Oxford when things at Mum's got really bad. But the police, the doctors, the social workers, the teachers … they heard what they wanted to when he told them Mum didn't hurt him.

Because *she* never did, not directly. She forgot about food all the time, and didn't notice when he got nits and appendicitis. But the people she ran with, the ones she muled for, who got her drugs, the ones that would live in their house: they hurt him. And like Kath just now, those that could do something never believed him enough to act. Thought he was a … scamp, whatever the fuck that was. And in the end, when no one believed you, it was easier to just go along with what *they* wanted to believe. Pick your battles, as Grandad had taught him.

Well, he had picked one in the end. The one that had brought him here. Mum had let one of her 'friends', that prick Vim, sell Dad's bass. He'd got into debt with a violent local gang of some reputation called the Benton Boys, and Mum had no choice. Once Jayden had silently punched his anger into a pillow, he researched and hatched a plan. Turned out, all the organisations involved in his care, the schools, the police, the hospitals, didn't really talk to each other. The police didn't have the medical notes, and the nurses and doctors didn't have the police reports. And no one knew *what* was going on at his school. So he'd show them, make them understand his life. Mum high and scrunched up on the sofa like an old crisp packet most of the day, in a flat that smelled like a mix between gas and piss. A situation so bad, she'd now drawn the attention of the fucking Bentons.

One night, when Vim next seemed out-of-it but not too-out-of-it, Jayden said *No* when the bloke ordered him to go and pick up a Chinese. Then he'd got right in Vim's ugly face and told him what he thought about him taking advantage of his mum. Like he planned, the guy smacked him about. But Jayden made sure to keep going on about how bad he smelled and how dense he was, so Vim really went at him. Then, when it was over, and he knew he wasn't going to die, he walked three miles to the police station in Marlstone – because the local station was closed – opened his mouth at the reception desk to recite, 'I think my parents are a danger to me and I need taking into care,' and allowed the blood that dribbled onto the desk to do the talking.

Two days later he'd been driven down to Oxford by his social worker, his ears still ringing and minus one tooth. Even then they'd not quite believed him, though. He kept having to tell her that his mum *wouldn't* miss him. That she *wouldn't* want to get better and have him back. She'd been the best mum she could be in the circumstances, and he loved her in a way that made him hate himself. But she needed help, like he did. And … she didn't love Jayden the way mums were supposed to love their sons. She loved drugs.

Weeks later they all met up to find a way forward: him, his mum, the social worker, a copper, a teacher from the school, and Olivia. Finally, they all saw it. Mum didn't ask about his bruised face. She didn't act pleased to see him or try to hold him, despite having not seen him in the time between. She sat on the sofa, only mildly more with-it than usual, glancing down at her phone every so often like she was expecting a call.

'Babe,' she'd said to him, making eye-contact just the once, causing Jayden's heart to dumbly open in anticipation of an apology and a commitment to change. What she said was, 'It's not you, it's me. I'm just not the right person to be your mum.' Then she'd looked around at the others, hope glinting in her eyes like she'd just spied a crack rock, and said, 'You need to have him off me. I definitely consent or whatever.' Then, glancing around the room like the place belonged to someone else, she added, 'It's just not the best place for him here, is it?'

He'd told himself later that Mum had put on an act. Been vile to secure his future. Out of kindness, funnily. But he was never sure, and he thought about her saying those things daily.

———————

At Olivia's cottage, he set down his bass to retrieve the key from his pocket and realised his still-gloved hand had been locked in a tight fist. Inside, the lemon scent that usually reminded him a little of urinals was now overlaid with something like burned plastic. He followed his nose to the lounge and looked at the stairwell. The twin plug socket at the base was charred and a little melted.

'Uh, Olivia.'

She came running in, and when he showed her she nodded. 'I've seen, yeah. Can you still smell it then? I got rid of the lamp and isolated it on the switchboard, but I've asked Andy to come and have a look. Place is falling apart.'

Andy again, really? Something odd was going on there. Was it possible she *liked* him, and was breaking stuff herself to get him over?

'Everything okay?' she said. 'You look cross.'

He said nothing and nodded, and after a moment she sensed he wanted to be alone, so left him. They'd not been getting on recently, partly because of what had happened with his suitcase. When he opened it that day, there had been a decent-sized bag of weed inside – he knew the smell well. Straight away he'd hidden it in the attic, recognising a set-up when he saw it. Sure enough, Olivia randomly came in after school the next day, asking what was in the suitcase. He demanded to know why it mattered, and they got into a whole thing about trust, and because she just kept repeating that she wanted to 'keep him on the straight and narrow', he dug his heels in. Finally, she told him she'd heard he'd been vaping in secret, and demanded he open it. When he gave in, and she saw there was nothing inside, she ran off crying.

Upstairs he put his bass in the cupboard and summoned Ghost through his ear buds. He lay on the bed, still low-key riled about Kath's reaction to his idea. His reached to rub his hand and found the glove instead. He smiled, anger abating.

He just shouldn't have brought up the idea with her in person. Like Tessa said, he should just do it. He knew the plan was a good one. He'd just have to *show* Kath he was for real. Two birds. One stone.

He began to scroll through the numbers on his phone until he saw the name Rags. Rags had been the first name in this contact list, back in the day. He was the reason Jayden even had a phone. Rags had also been the one who'd given him his vaping stuff, and in general had always been decent to Jayden. Turned out not all Mum's friends were total shits, even if they did have dodgy side-hustles like selling stolen phones and counterfeit vapes.

Rags's main hustle, though, had been selling ket. The story went that some mate of Rags found out he had Alzheimer's and offed himself. But because he'd always liked Rags, because

Rags had been a nice guy, he'd left him a code for his lock-up. Rags had gone out there one night and found it filled with all these bottles of liquid ket. Tens of thousands of pounds' worth that just needed cooking up. Rags once said to Jayden that if he was thinking about going to university one day, he could earn some pocket money dealing at parties for him. Jayden *had* thought about sixth form and uni, but he was pretty convinced he'd be making his living playing bass by then, so had declined.

Point was, Rags liked Jayden. And Rags was the sort of person that liked a trade. A little bit of weed for a little bit of ket? Why not? Jayden had been around enough weed to know the bag he'd found – large enough so that if Olivia had found it, she would have suspected he was dealing, not taking – was worth something. Surely Rags would go for it.

Two birds. One stone. Kath could treat her 'head stuff'. And Jayden could turn something shit into something positive. Fuck you, Leo.

Because it was obviously him that had planted the bag, wasn't it? Maybe in league with October or some of the other committee members. Leo had already seen the suitcase when he stole Jayden's vape liquid, hadn't he? And he was the only one who knew about the vaping. He'd obviously come back, snuck the bag in, then told Olivia that he had some suspicion or another about Jayden – job done.

He supposed Olivia might even have been involved – who knew, with the village's history? – but that wasn't the obvious solution. The obvious solution was that Leo wanted Jayden gone because he didn't like him, and so had created a situation he knew people would buy, given Jayden's background.

But Jayden had foiled him. At least this time.

He got up, quickly checked the still empty suitcase again, and jumped back on the bed. He stared at his phone and let the music fill his head. He didn't really want to think about what might happen next, especially after what he'd heard Kath and Tessa talking about. No one had come for the drugs yet, and Olivia hadn't mentioned the suitcase again. But Leo probably assumed Jayden had chucked the weed down the toilet or something similar, and was now biding his time. Devising a new, even worse plan to get rid of Jayden.

But what could be worse than planting drugs?

No, he wasn't going to think about it. What could he realistically do, anyway? Ruling out Kath and Tessa, he had no one to turn to. And he wasn't naïve enough to think anyone would believe him anyway. Even if they did, they'd make him go to the police. And if he told them Leo was trying to frame him, it was his word against Leo's. And Five-O looked after their own.

No, the best plan was to make the drugs disappear. He stared at Rags's name again. Rags had been around a bit. What would *he* advise? Maybe he should ask him. He touched the name, bringing up his number. With his thumb he pressed the green call button and pictured Kath's face when she saw what he'd done for her. When she realised that Jayden was for real.

TWENTY-THREE

Tessa

By the next day Kath's illuminating revelations had dulled like morning-after glow sticks. Once she was alone, their revelatory power felt more like a manifestation of Tessa's problems adapting here and Kath's grief. The two of them needed to be more careful, especially around Jayden. It was irresponsible to talk that way about people they all knew, and what if those wild accusations got back to Olivia, or to October and the committee? She should have just let the whole thing drop. But she couldn't help herself.

She looked up Jamie Saunders and Hattie Milner online when she was meant to be working on a pitch for an exciting Hollywood film score that had landed in her inbox. She found nothing.

Weeks passed, and the warm evenings were no more, as October became November. She went out more and started asking questions, carefully, at the pub, at the bonfire-night festivities on the green (sans fireworks), at the film night. It was at the latter she finally found out about Jamie Saunders, having seen his name as a contact at the bottom of an old poster up at The Yew Tree.

One of the founders, Pep, gave an expletive-filled introduction to that month's film, *Jaws*. When he concluded with, 'We are the Nether Appleford Film Society, and this is *Jaws*,' a group picture of all the organisers briefly appeared on screen before the society logo and the opening credits. They were all holding pints, flicking Vs and pulling faces at the camera. Nervous laughter broke out in patches across the room before being consumed in the rising applause for the film. The photo had been up for just a few seconds, but Tessa had seen that the cause of the laughter had been a shark's head crudely pasted over the face of someone standing in the lower-left corner.

Catching Pep at the bar alone during the intermission clutching a beer, she complimented his introduction and asked about the shark's head.

'What, the thing on the photo?' He spoke with a London accent that was much softer off stage than on. 'I think we need to take a new one now, that joke's stale as bollocks.'

'I didn't get it.'

'That was Jamie, the lad that did our projections before Mark. He was *disgraced*, so we've had to pay a bit of a homage to it ever since.'

'Disgraced?'

'No one's told you about it?' He leaned forward, smiling, so close she could smell his pint. 'We were doing a night here, end of last year, *Final Destination*, and he's got the intermission video up' – he gestured at the screen where a strange mish-mash of surreal images and videos played while a fifteen-minute counter ran backwards – 'and suddenly the screen goes down, and his desktop's up. Jamie was out the back smoking, and someone goes off to get him, because this is a typical Jamie balls-up. Suddenly, the mouse starts moving and up pops a flipping porn video, with him in it.' He shook his head. 'Of course, this lot starts cheering, but then they realise his Mrs is in the audience.'

'It was her in the video?'

Pep shook his head slowly. 'Anyway … he wasn't our projectionist the next month.'

'So I don't quite understand. Was the video just on there and started itself?'

He took a sip of his beer and looked around, wary now. 'Someone stuck in a memory stick and ran. He said later that someone had filmed him and set him up. I don't know if that was legit or what. But whether his Mrs set him up, I mean, out of revenge… It didn't look like that, though – *she* looked as surprised as anyone. She was standing as close to me as you are, and I saw her face.'

'Oh no.'

'Anyway, covering him up was our little gesture of solidarity after what happened. You know, to his Mrs.'

'Does she still live here then?'

'Yeah.' He frowned now, and looked around the room. Lowering his voice, he said, 'She's ordering from Aaron right now.'

Tessa turned to the upstairs bar and the person he'd been talking about was now looking right at her. Olivia smiled, and Tessa smiled back.

———

More gossip. That's all it was. But her curiosity was ravenous now, and she had more questions. Like, who had been the person that found out about Jamie Saunders's affair? Who had gone to the film night to make sure he was shamed in that way? Pep had wandered off that night looking a bit uncomfortable when she'd tried asking more questions. So after one of their jams, she spoke to Kath about it.

'What makes you think the committee was involved?' Tessa asked her. 'Why would they do that so publicly to Olivia?'

'I don't have all the answers. Maybe they thought you've got to be cruel to be kind. Maybe Olivia was in on it. I can't say for certain it was them involved. But Jamie was another odd fit in the village. He wasn't a recluse, like Eleanor. You'd see him about at things. But he was a sore thumb in other ways. He was quite … old-fashioned, I suppose. With his values. One of those blokes that's always out in town with his mates, drinking. Then when he was around her, he was always … quite posses-sive. Know what I mean? Maybe they took against that. Olivia brought him in, too. He wasn't interviewed. She met him after moving here. So there's that. I just remember thinking, *He's not long for here.* So it was weird being right.'

Tessa nodded, still unconvinced. The only real connection to the committee was Olivia, which wasn't much. The event was extreme, so she could see why it made Kath think of the committee, or at least the version of the committee Eleanor and she had come to believe in. But it was no smoking gun.

It didn't stop her wanting to know more about Hattie Milner though, and because tonight Jayden was off on some errand he was being very cryptic about, Tessa brought her up.

'I couldn't find anything out about her,' Tessa said. 'People didn't seem to know her, or were pretending not to. I was starting to get a bit self-conscious – you know, thinking up reasons to ask questions about these people.'

Kath sniggered. 'I didn't mean for you to go at it like Poirot. Can't say I'm surprised people want to forget her. Hattie Milner worked up at that equestrian centre doing all the accounts and payments and that. I spoke to her once or twice, and she was alright. A bit brusque, but in that way you know where you are with a person. She did a lot in the village, too, helping out, organising things for the committee. But she had a fall-out with them about a year or so back. They were doing one of them charity walks, and she thought that they should stop giving money to all the big charities with plenty of money, and instead give some thought to the most effective way the cash could make an impact. I didn't think it sounded like a bad idea. Anyway, she was funny. She wrote a letter to the whole village and posted it to them. Saying the committee weren't considering her proposal and would they consider signing this petition she'd put up by the tree.'

'Did anyone sign it?'

'What do you think? I did, and maybe a few others out of sympathy. But six months later someone up at the horse place found a list in her work drawer of all these credit card numbers. And it turned out she'd supposedly been writing them down when people gave her them on the phone, all these rich people using those stables and the hospital. She'd been using their cards to make little transactions here and there, they said. Ones they wouldn't notice on their own, but together they added up to serious money.'

'So, she was arrested?'

'Yeah, initially. But nothing ever came of it. They couldn't prove it was her list or even that it was her taking the money. It was all going into some internet bank thing that had a fake address. But the odd thing was, she'd only been taking the numbers for about six months or so, they reckoned. So, either she did it because she was peed off at the committee for not listening to her, or...'

'Someone wanted rid of her.'

Kath played a punchline sting on her kit and grabbed the high-hat with a sad smile.

Ba-dum-bum-chhh.

TWENTY-FOUR

Jayden

It was a bright Saturday morning, and he'd agreed to meet Rags in Oxford. Andy was already over, talking to Olivia while pretending to fix the socket. They thought they were being quiet, but they'd left the stairwell door open. He didn't catch everything from up on the landing, but he heard enough. Andy suggesting Jayden had done something to the socket for attention. Olivia telling him it was her fault, that Jadyen was reacting to her finding him so alien, and that something motherly she'd expected to kick in just hadn't.

Jayden sighed, completing his emptiness. But he'd heard worse.

They started talking about rock music, and how much of a bad influence it was on Jayden. This made him clench his teeth. Olivia was making light of it, saying it was because her religious parents only let her and her brother listen to classical music growing up. That they'd been told rock music was akin to devil worship. But Andy wasn't even trying to put her right about it, even though he was supposedly a rocker.

Then Olivia said, 'He acts so … different after he's been

with Tessa. Almost … bolshy. Which I suppose is good for his confidence, but … is that the right type of confidence? I feel it turns him against me.'

Surely Andy would speak up now. But still he didn't.

Well, if *he* hadn't heard enough, Jayden had. He walked downstairs and into the lounge.

'You're awake,' Olivia said.

'Hi, Jayden,' Andy said.

His massive torso was squeezed into a pristine white shirt. Her lips were glossy and lipstick red.

Jayden grunted an acknowledgement at them and walked through the room. As he did, he noticed Olivia was framing some pictures on the floor. One frame she was repurposing, and he'd seen it before, hidden at the back of a drawer in the kitchen. The old photo was one of her and her old boyfriend, which now lay face up on the sofa arm. When he saw it, he did a double-take, and after processing his surprise, he sputtered a laugh of disbelief. The bloke looked like Andy. How had he not noticed *that* before?

———

He trekked up The Road skittish, head flicking left and right, forward and backward, eyes wide for trouble. It was the first time he was doing something unpredictable since finding the drugs, and if he were Leo, he'd have been watching closely for any unusual movements like this. He passed Ruth and October talking on the pavement. They fell quiet, nodded at him, and continued talking once he'd gone by. Jitesh and Dev glanced up from their gardening to wave and watch. And when he reached the end of the cottages, Leo's car drove past, and the man himself stared at him through the window.

But he didn't stop. So Jayden kept walking, waiting for Leo

to turn around to confront him. Ask where he was going. Search him, maybe. Nothing happened.

Not that he'd have found anything anyway. Because Jayden was one step ahead of Leo. Last night he'd snuck out down the backs of the cottages, just in case, and left the drugs hidden in a tree hollow near the bus stop. It cost him three hours of sleep, but better safe than sorry.

It took him the best part of an hour to get to the bus stop and locate the tree, and in that time he convinced himself the drugs had been found already. But they were where he'd left them. And when no one came leaping out to catch him in the act, and the bus even turned up on time, he took a seat at the back and held his head high. He'd made a plan, and it was going to work.

———

Rags had aged in the year since Jayden'd seen him. He had the same Shakespeare beard and floppy brown hair, still dressed in scruffy double-denim and winkle pickers. Around his neck he still wore a child's teething necklace, a small twist of purple silicone given to him by a long-gone girlfriend's toddler. But he'd shrunk somehow, and when he smiled, deep lines appeared all over his face. They hugged at the entrance to Christchurch Meadow, and walked down towards the river.

'I'm sorry about you and your mum,' Rags said.

'It's fine.'

'She's a good woman deep down, but ... well, you know. I heard that Vim fell out with the Bentons.' He sucked air through his teeth. 'I'm just glad you're being looked after. You are being looked after, aren't you?'

'I've got a roof over my head.'

Rags nodded thoughtfully. 'That village you're in, Nether Appleford, looks proper posh.'

Jayden shrugged. 'It's okay.' He didn't want to talk about the village. Not yet anyway.

'Are they all hippies or something? All that kindness bollocks.'

'Yeah, kind of.'

'So who is she, kiddo? This girl you want to impress? Rich, I'm guessing.'

'Nah, it's not like that,' he said with a little laugh. 'It's this old lady. Her husband died and she says ket's what works for her mental health.'

'Oh.' He sounded genuinely surprised. 'Okay.'

He shrugged. 'She's just kind to me. So I want to be kind back, you know.'

'Well, how fucking sunny is that. Good lad. And she's not going be bothered by a fifteen-year-old boy bringing her drugs?'

Jayden shrugged again and frowned. 'She won't grass.'

'Right, right. But she might wonder who your supplier is.' Rags's left index finger twitched a few times, as if he was firing an invisible gun into the ground.

'Nah, I'm just going to give it her without telling her it's from me. I'm not stupid.'

'No. You're definitely not that, kiddo.'

Before the following silence grew too big, Jayden said, 'So … I've got the stuff in my bag.'

'Yeah, yeah. We'll get to that. So this is just a one-off, is it? If she's using it to self-medicate … what happens when she runs out?' His finger went again. Twitch, twitch, twitch.

Jayden hadn't really thought about that. He didn't even know how much a medical dose of ket was. He started stiffening up and looked down at his battered red leather boots. 'Not really sure. See how it goes.'

'See how it goes. Okay. Okay.'

They started following the river around to the left, and Rags pointed to a deer standing in a field on the other side. When they found a secluded spot, the two of them sat down on the bank. Rags looked around, reached into his denim jacket, and pulled out a decent-sized bag of ket. Jayden's heartbeat quickened. It was happening. Rags looked around, unzipped Jayden's back-pack, and put the drugs inside.

After a while, Jayden said, 'You going to take your bag?'

'Where did you get it?' Rags said. Twitch, twitch, twitch.

'You wouldn't believe me if I told you.'

'No? Give it a spin, see what you win.'

Jayden had a lie already prepared. 'I stole it from a weed-smoking copper. He smokes in his shed at night, and I hopped his fence and grabbed a bag.'

Amused, Rags said, 'You robbed a copper?'

'Well, I thought, he's not going to report it, is he? And he's a dick.'

That made Rags laugh hard. 'See, you're smart. And weed-smoking coppers, that's good information, Jayden. You're a font of wisdom.'

'A what?'

'Listen, I don't want your weed. You keep that. Treat yourself.'

'Nah, you serious?' He didn't like that, and his appetite for his half-eaten sandwich shrivelled.

'I'll be honest with you, kiddo. When you first called I was pleased to hear from you, but I wasn't planning on calling you back. But when I read about that village you're in, I had an idea. So I was wondering whether maybe you wanted to be my man inside. Get me some information.'

'Information. Like what? Why?' Jayden couldn't imagine how Nether Appleford might help a guy like Rags.

'Well, I don't want to get you in too deep. Not just yet. But you'll probably be able to guess.'

Not knowing what to say, and not seeing anything but playfulness and warmth in Rags's eyes, he said, 'Yeah, I can give it a go.'

'Great,' Rags said. 'And if it doesn't work, no bother. I'll forget about the ket, consider it a late or early birthday gift or something.'

'Oh, my days. Serious?'

'This village you're staying in, Jayden. It has this kindness thing, doesn't it?'

'Yeah.'

'Do they practise what they preach there? Is everyone always doing kind things?'

'Sort of.'

'Only sort of?'

'It's a big part of living there, yeah, but, you know, sometimes people say they're being kind when they're actually just being … you know … they just want something.'

'So they like being *seen* as kind.'

'Exactly.'

'Good. See, *that's* useful.'

'Yeah?'

Rags smiled. His fingers twitched again. And now Jayden did notice something drifting across his face that he didn't like. But he ignored it, and kept looking interested. Because what did it matter what good old Rags was up to, now that he had ket for Kath? 'And you told me about a slightly bent copper. That's really good to know.'

'I reckon he's more than slightly bent. I reckon he's … a fucking circle.'

183

Rags gave another hearty laugh. 'And Jayden, are all the businesses in the village run by the estate. Do you know?'

'Nah, but I could find out.'

'Yeah, could you?'

'Definitely.'

'Great. Because I really want to find out more about that Equestrian Centre. I think that place could be very useful to me.'

TWENTY-FIVE

Tessa

She sat in the kitchen with a bowl of soup the day after her jam with Kath, a late lunch following completion of a mastering job for a death metal band. The quiet in the cottage was unsettling by comparison, and it was little wonder Eleanor Beddington and Kath crept into her mind.

Everything she'd been told was circumstantial, she knew that. No matter how compelling it had felt, none of it was any more convincing than a sign. The best thing to do now was just let the whole thing drop. Her curiosity was satisfied now, wasn't it? She was only ever going to get one side of this story, and as Kath had said, she had to take it all with a big dose of salt. Without more evidence, what could she do? She wasn't going to upend their life based on hearsay.

And okay, she hadn't made the greatest start in the village, true, but since she'd refocused her efforts, she thought she was making good progress. They weren't going to come after her, or whatever. And while she hadn't received a heart on the tree yet, and she still felt watched when she was out sometimes, surely what she was doing with Jayden and Kath was being appreciated by at least *some* of the village. And if they didn't see the good just yet, she was convinced they'd come around eventually.

She finished her soup and put the bowl in the sink. She was on her way to the studio again when she noticed an envelope on the mat by the front door. The post in Nether Appleford came early each morning, and she could see from where she stood that there was a handwritten name on the front in a neat yet, with its oversized loops and curly flourishes, playful cursive.

She opened it and found a note in the same handwriting. Tessa began to read, and a withering cold began to ripple through her body.

Dear Tessa,

I really believe in you, and your desire to be a kinder person. I know that it isn't as easy as it looks, and that sometimes effort isn't always rewarded. I wanted you to know, though, that I see and admire your effort, especially after everything that has happened to you recently. You're a real tryer. However, I do think you might be better off putting your energy into differ- ent, more rewarding, projects. Sometimes the best of our plans have uninten- tional consequences. And our quest for understanding can rub feathers out of joint. Kindness can be something of a balancing act, I think. But maybe you might find your efforts better received if you broadened your horizons?? It's just a thought, and know that I am rooting for you whatever you choose, and think you have all the makings of a great Nether Applefordian.

Best regards,

A Sympathetic Friend

Working was out of the question now, but her studio was as good a place to fume as any. She read the note many times, her hands shaking, in no doubt that this person was talking about what she'd been doing with Kath and Jayden. She wanted to talk to someone, to Kath perhaps, but she worried this might upset her. Might confirm all her worst suspicions.

Tessa's jaw ached from clenching her teeth, and she'd started squeezing the web of her thumb repeatedly. Who the hell did these people think they were?

Well, quite, *who were they?* That was a good question, wasn't it, and one she couldn't believe she hadn't asked before. She opened her browser and started her search with 'Dev Chopra' and 'doctor'. The first hit was an article from a local paper up north.

Manipulative Leeds GP suspended for lying about qualifications

It was him, without a doubt. There were photographs, although the piece itself offered little more than the headline. At a GMC hearing, Dev had apologised, blaming the made-up elite qualifications with which he'd garnished his already healthy CV on competitiveness with his older sister, a successful surgeon.

Unable to find much more on Dev, she searched for Leo next. Another hit. Another article with a photo confirming the name belonged to the same Leo Shelton that sat on Nether Appleford's Kindness Committee.

PC cleared of assaulting protester

This piece, from twelve years ago, also featured pictures of the victim's heavily bruised arm and shoulder, and of the extendable baton Leo had used to create the injuries. The judge in the case had ruled that the force Leo had used, caught on camera so not itself in question, was appropriate for self-defence.

Tessa paused to make a cup of tea. Because she had to get some perspective. It didn't mean *anything* that two of the five committee members had had a few troubles once upon a time, did it? Even if it *really* felt like she was on to something. Would it really matter a jot if she found dirt on all the committee members? Everyone had secrets. She ought to stop.

She didn't. Next up was Ruth.

And there it was – in the *Mail*, no less. Ten years ago. She'd been prosecuted for climbing into her neighbour's garden at night and burning down a tree after a long-running feud about spreading roots. She'd pretended a bonfire in her garden had got out of control but had been caught on another neighbour's security camera.

With a disbelieving smile, Tessa looked up Aaron, and was making her way through an article about the sophisticated premium-rate phone-number scam he and his sister had been convicted for running fifteen years back, when the door to her studio opened and Andy walked in. Her face grew hot and she moved the mouse to close down the browser.

'You coming in for tea?' he said.

Tessa looked down at the corner of the screen. It had gone 6pm. She once more moved to shut down the window but before she could, Andy's hands began massaging her shoulders.

'Is that … Aaron?'

The picture of the landlord's beardless face appeared near the bottom of the screen. 'Yeah.'

Andy fell silent, obviously reading now. His hands slowed down kneading and withdrew.

'Why were you looking this up?' His voice was flat.

It was a fair question, and one for which she had no easy answer. So, she spun around on her chair and told him what she'd found out about the committee. When she finished, she realised she'd still not put her search into context, so she kept talking, telling him about Jamie, and Hattie, and Willy, right back until she got to Eleanor, at which point she showed him the letter.

Andy sat down on the sofa, read it, and put it down beside him. He scratched his beard, his gaze focused on some space between them. But he said nothing.

'Don't you think it's all a little strange?' Tessa said.

His mouth opened and nothing came out, so he closed it. A moment later, he tried again, 'I mean … I thought we were coming here to…' He shook his head.

'What?'

'No, forget it.'

'You don't find this weird?'

'I find it weird you're sitting here, supposed to be working, and instead you're doing deep dives into the backgrounds of people who've done nothing but try and make us feel welcome. I find it weird that we've moved to this place to try and live a different way, and you're making friends with the two most … difficult people in the village while concocting conspiracy theories about everyone else.'

'Difficult. What's difficult abo—'

'You know what I mean, Tess. I didn't even want to come here. But now I'm making the best of it. I'm putting aside all my doubts and negativity, and actually, you know what, it's working for me? Other people aren't always arseholes.'

She stared at him, not sure where all of this had come from. 'I'm not saying they're arseholes, Andy. I'm saying they're all criminals, or more-or-less criminals. And they're sending me letters telling me I'm doing kindness wrong. That *is* weird, come on.'

'Why? We're in England's kindest village, for fuck's sake.

Don't you think forgiveness is a big part of that? Don't you think that, maybe, when those people decided to move here, they might've had in their minds that the people here might not hold their past against them?'

It would also make them easier to manipulate. Vulnerable. Eager to please. But she didn't say that. Because she knew he had a point.

'This is what you always do, Tess. And we said we'd call each other out on this stuff, didn't we? So here I am, calling you out.'

How well he knew her. She *did* always do this. She'd been getting uncomfortable here, hadn't she? So immediately she'd gone searching for the edges, for the loose threads so she could pull at them. And why, so she could feel superior to everyone?

'I just thought it was interesting,' she said. 'But sorry, you're right, it makes sense they'd come to a community like this. But … I am trying. I really am, and I'm sorry if it doesn't seem that way, but…'

Andy shook his head. He didn't look at her. 'Well … it doesn't. And I know you're still dealing with what happened with that woman. With what she said to you. That was frightening, but … I should probably back off before I say something stupid.' He stood up and crossed the room.

'Don't do a storm-off,' Tessa said with an exasperated laugh.

'It's been a long day. I've got to go over to Olivia's as well.'

'Olivia's again?'

'I think her whole place might be fucked. I'll get that done and … maybe we can do a reset tonight.'

'I can cook something now, if you want?'

'It's fine.' He slid open the door. 'I won't be long.'

He parted with a meagre smile, although the strength of his anger at her lingered long after the door slid shut.

Tessa turned around and stared at the screen. She released a breath she'd been holding and dwelled on her sudden emptiness. She closed down the article about Aaron, and hovered over the shutdown icon. The studio was silent, and she became aware of herself and her surroundings.

Fuck it. She opened the browser back up, and typed in the final committee member she hadn't checked.

Olivia Chambers.

She stared at the text for a while, but she didn't press enter. The cursor blinked. She looked up at a photograph of her and Andy in Tenerife that was pinned to her corkboard. He looked handsome and happy, talk of babies still a few years away. She closed the window down and went into the house to plan a mind-blowing meal for when Andy got home. A make-up meal. Followed by make-up sex, perhaps.

TWENTY-SIX

Tessa

B y the time Andy got back she'd cooked him paella – one of his favourites. She put on a show of effort and regret, but Andy had only the most perfunctory small talk in response to her attempts at conversation. They sat eating in near silence, Tessa having no idea what to do once she ran out of things to say. She ended up repeatedly smiling at him like she'd lost her mind.

They were eating dessert, and Tessa was resisting the urge to ask him what was wrong, for fear of them arguing again, when Andy finally spoke.

'Someone in the village mentioned to me the other day that we don't really use your car that much, now you're at home.'

She paused, surprised by his sudden burst into life. 'I suppose so.'

'Do we really need it?'

'Uh, I mean. Yes.' She wanted to tell him she'd need it if they had a baby, but she knew that she couldn't. It wasn't true anymore. Or if it was, they weren't allowed to talk about it. Or something. She didn't really know now because they'd stopped talking about it. 'I need it in case I have to go somewhere when you're at work.'

He shrugged. 'It just might save us some money, you know? While you're getting things together here.'

'Sure. But I'd be—'

'For the amount you go out, you could easily taxi and bus. I just thought it was worth considering.'

'Well … okay, sure.' She was trying to keep things pleasant. Trying to de-escalate. 'Let's think about it.'

'Cool. It's just, you know, they're giving us a really good rent here. And they brought it up with me.'

They. He'd said *they.* But no, she definitely wasn't allowed to mention that.

'I hear you,' she said. This was about the note, wasn't it?

'I just worry they see that car not really doing anything, and we're paying tax and insurance on it… Carbon footprint too.'

'Yeah. I hear you.'

Finally, he returned one of her mad smiles.

———

Later, they went upstairs, and Tessa showered and changed into the black satin knickers and top she knew he found sexy. But when she walked in, the bedroom was dark, and Andy was already asleep.

———

The sheets beside her were cold when she reached across the next morning to find him. The clock on the bedside table informed her she'd overslept – it was almost eleven. Jesus, what the fuck was she doing? She grabbed her phone and saw she had a message.

Maddy. From late last night:

Hi, Auntie Tess!

Above the message was a photograph of Maddy, red-faced, storm-haired and still impossibly beautiful, staring at the camera from a hospital bed, wild surprise in her eyes, a swaddled infant in her arms.

Tessa made coffee while trying to call her, but she couldn't get through. She paced around the house muttering to herself, excited. She'd have to abandon everything today. Drive down to Kent and see them. While she still had a car.

She put down her phone on the kitchen surface, showered, and returned to tidy up. For the first time since it had arrived, that letter she'd been sent hadn't been lurking in the back of her mind. It was a pleasant feeling, a normal feeling, and it lasted up until she went to put the milk from breakfast away. A folded piece of paper, pinned to the fridge by a Jeff Buckley magnet, caught her eye. On it were scribbled the names of some local restaurants and a taxi firm, recommendations given to Tessa and Andy after they'd first moved in. Oversized loops. Curly flourishes. She stared.

The wretched letter was still tucked in the pocket of her jeans, and she took it out and laid it on the table beside the note from the fridge, comparing the two distinctive sets of handwriting.

She smiled and shook her head. There was no doubt. This wasn't even similarity. The letter had been written by Ruth.

TWENTY-SEVEN

Tessa
_____

She sent a message to Andy, asking if he wanted to bunk off work and come to Kent with her for the weekend. By then Maddy had messaged to say she and the baby were being kept in the hospital for observation. Andy declined, which she'd expected but nonetheless found disappointing. At least he'd put a kiss on the message, so he couldn't be *that* angry with her today. Maybe a little reset would be good for them.

Tessa packed a night bag and drove up to the hotel and equestrian centre. She slowed down and came to a stop. Before she could talk herself out of it, she turned in, and at the fork just beyond the entrance she took the right towards the hotel.

Behind the hotel building stood a steel Portakabin with a pompous-looking sign reading: *Appleford Estate Office*. She walked up an access ramp and knocked on the door. Ruth's familiar voice drifted through an open window, 'Come in.'

The inside was colder than outside. On the wall of the corridor hung colourful posters with overlapping themes: save energy and switch off lights, only boil the water you need, heat the human not the home.

Ruth was sitting behind a desk in the first office on the right, a blanket over her lap and a water bottle sitting on the table. She smiled, although her jaw looked as tight as her red turtleneck jumper. As tight as that means-business ponytail. In her eyes Tessa could see Ruth knew damn well why she was here.

'Tessa, I thought that sounded like you. Everything alright?'

'Well,' Tessa said, stepping inside and placing the envelope on her desk. 'I thought it was, but then I had this letter through the door, and I have to say, I'm just a little bit confused, to be honest.'

'I see.' She leaned over and looked at the envelope. 'I take it something in it has upset you?'

Tessa nodded.

'Do you know who wrote it?' Ruth asked.

'Come on, Ruth. If you've got something to say, you can say it to my face.'

'Ah, so you think *I* wrote the letter.'

'It's your handwriting, isn't it?'

She grimaced, pretended to look at it again, and shifted in her chair, which squeaked beneath her. When she looked up again her face looked genuinely pained. 'Uh, I'm really not, uh—'

A voice from behind Tessa cut her off. 'It's fine, Ruthy.'

She turned around and saw October standing in the doorway, the sweetest of smiles on her face and an overlong rainbow cardigan wrapped around her short, round body. 'You're too quick for us, Jessica Fletcher. It was indeed our Ruth's handiwork, but I have to confess I'm actually the one responsible for the words themselves.'

Tessa looked to Ruth who stood up and handed her back the envelope, eyes down apologetically.

'Come on,' October said, 'let's you and me talk.'

October's office walls were covered in more posters from a lifetime of protest, from Ban the Bomb through to Black Lives Matter. The faint smell of patchouli Tessa had caught on entering built to a climax here. Behind October a banner from the summer fete stretched from wall to wall above the window. It read:

A LITTLE CONSIDERATION, A LITTLE THOUGHT FOR OTHERS, MAKES ALL THE DIFFERENCE — EEYORE

'Would you', she said to Tessa, scanning her cluttered desk, 'like a chocolate biscuit?'

'No,' Tessa said, before remembering who she was talking to, who was responsible for the massive savings they were making on their home, and adding, 'thank you.'

'No, me neither.' She sat down and invited Tessa to do the same so they'd be facing one another across the desk. 'I get the sense you're upset, but please, please don't be. There's really no need. My little missives I send to everyone when I see they might need them. It's not a personal thing, you understand.'

Tessa took a breath. 'It felt quite personal, is the thing. Because it sounded like you were talking about me. Specifically.'

October picked up a snow globe on her desk, shook it, and appeared to become distracted by the outcome. 'My worry is, you've not received a single heart yet, have you? Which is quite unusual. And I very much wanted to help you achieve that, as I'm sure, after hearing your heartfelt speech at your introductory in—'

Interview. She had been going to say interview.

'—meeting with us, that would have been heartbreaking.

For want of a better expression. What I worry about is that you're just ... I've not seen you as much lately. You don't really come to the Kindness Sermons or the pub anymore, do you?'

'I'm just really busy.'

'And I see what it is you're doing. With those two. It's very admirable. But, it's a very ... focused approach. It's not got ... a broad enough reach. Do you follow?'

'Not really. You're talking about Jayden and Kath.'

October began to cough. 'Pardon me. Yes. Jayden and Kath.'

'Both of them want to play music. I have a studio. We're not disturbing anyone.' She shrugged, inviting her to point out the exact problem.

Now October looked up at the ceiling. 'Yes, but... How to put this... You're, I want to say, making waves ... no, that has a positive connotation, doesn't it?'

'I think it works both ways.'

'A village like this, we're like one of our Olivia's lovely, knitted jumpers. Do you know the ones I mean? When it's all meshed together and warm and toasty, no problems. But one little thread comes undone, and the whole thing might come apart. Do you follow?'

'I'm not a big knitter ... but I understand what you're saying.'

She looked genuinely delighted at this. 'While I'm sure Kath and Jayden are enjoying the use of your garden shed, I'm sure you know there are others to consider. The best sort of kindness, the kindness that really brings home the hearts, are acts with a really big ripple. But a positive ripple, of course.'

Tessa took a moment to gather her thoughts. 'So, sorry, can I just ask? Who's being negatively affected by our music, exactly?'

October leaned forward and in a low voice said, 'Don't worry, sometimes it takes some perspective, a committee, to see the whole picture. For a start, and I probably shouldn't be so specific, but Olivia isn't that happy about Jayden playing rock music. I understand it's old-fashioned, but she is a bit that way, and we value her for it.'

'She doesn't like him playing rock music?'

'I know. But I think she is concerned about the drug element.'

Tessa had to hold her face still to prevent a grin breaking out. 'Drug element?'

'The boy's mother was an addict, I believe.' She coughed again, unsurprising given how much incense must have been in the air. 'His father was a rock musician, too. Also, an addict. All very sad. And I think Olivia believes that the boy needs distance from that … culture now to thrive. You know, from the sex, drugs, rock and roll of it all.'

Tessa paused, having not really considered it like this before. Still, to link the music to his parents' bad choices … no, she couldn't have that. 'Olivia never mentioned this to me.'

'Well, she seems to think she implied it politely.'

'Really? Well, the thing is, music's not really that way anymore. They're all sober and vegan these days.'

'Nonetheless, we must respect Olivia's feelings. She is his guardian, after all. And then of course, there is Kath. You know, for a long time she has promised her neighbours that she will tend to her cottage.' Lowering her voice, she added, 'And that hasn't happened yet, as I'm sure you've noticed. We've been waiting quite the decade.'

Feeling on safer ground now, Tessa said, 'Don't you think that maybe she needs some help? Maybe someone to talk to, to draw her out? That's all I'm trying to do.'

'We have asked her repeatedly about it, and offered our help.'

'What help, though? You know there's *asking* and then there's … *actually being helpful.* I know she's stubborn, but what she needs is a realistic plan and some support. On some level she'd love that place to be tidy. But she can't do it emotionally or practically without help. I mean, she can hardly move sometimes with her back the way it is.'

'Her back?'

'Yes. And was her cottage always like it is now? Was it like that before her husband died?'

'Well … no.'

'You see what I'm saying. I think maybe there's a psychological issue. And she doesn't know where to start. I've been trying to think of a way that might make her happy and keep her safe. You know, moving her things to a warehouse and going through it all with her. Or even keeping it there for good. And maybe getting her someone to talk to. But I've been doing that at her pace.'

October paused to consider this. She nodded, like she could see her point. 'Keep her safe, yes. Interesting. As I say, I can see where you're coming from, but part of me wonders if the whole thing is a danger, as you say, which now you mention it, of course it is … shouldn't we just have someone come out to assess her? For her own good. We must think about safety, always.'

'No.' Suddenly she could see how easily it happened, how the committee had come to section a man that they didn't really like. 'No. She doesn't need that. She needs … kindness. And a plan.'

October, perhaps wanting to avoid a confrontation, nodded and returned the subject to Tessa. 'Kindness, yes, always that. But you take my point about the neighbours, don't you? They see you being friendly with her, and to them it's like you're taking sides.'

'Sides?'

'I know, it's unfortunate. But everyone's feelings are valid here, and it is a long time to live with those sights and smells. And, of course, Jayden and Kath are one thing. But also, Tessa … word travels in a village like this. I know you've been asking questions about some previous members of the community. Which, to an extent, is understandable given what happened with dear Eleanor. But again, some people have been uncomfortable with you … digging over old coals. Is that the expression I want?'

Tessa didn't correct her. Instead, she stared at the wall, feeling not unlike she once had in school when she'd received a detention for wearing her skirt too high: a rage kept in check by a more overwhelming sense of absurdity. 'So do you want me to stop playing music with them? Is that it? Are we going to get moved on if I don't? Will you up our rent?'

'Up your rent?' She looked appalled. 'No, no. Not at all. No. Something tells me you shouldn't believe everything you hear. No, I am telling you these things because I don't believe we can be kind with all these secret discontents. Not at all. You do you, as the children say. But… But, Andy. He has some hearts now, doesn't he? And what has he done? Put his skills to work where they are effective. Couldn't you do something similar?'

'To be honest, that's what I thought I had done.'

'Yes, but … why be so… as I said, focused?'

She sighed. 'I know I messed up with the Story Station thing. I don't know if it got back to you or not, but it wasn't that I didn't want to do it. I just wanted to work out—'

'Ah, now, interesting you should bring that up.' She grinned, an excited little girl all of a sudden. 'The person that we hired isn't quite working out. Their timelines for delivery are ... not quite what they initially promised. We still haven't heard a thing yet.'

Tessa's throat constricted. She'd walked right into this, hadn't she? Clever October. 'You want me to do it again?'

'Could you?'

Time was critical here, because the longer it took to answer, the phonier her earlier remark appeared. What had Leo said to her? *Just say yes, sort the rest out later.*

'Of course,' Tessa said. 'If that's what you want?'

October opened her mouth wide and clapped her hands three times. 'How wonderful. I know you are busy, but would there be any chance of hearing something ... next week? We'd just need an idea, not the whole thing, obviously.'

'Next week. Sure. Fantastic.'

'And we'd really need it for January.'

'Wow. No, okay, yeah, that's ... possible.'

'Oh, perfect, Tessa. I can have Ruth brief you on where we're up to with it all. But thank you, Tessa. Thank you so much.'

Tessa smiled, with no idea how she'd managed to end up here again. She took a deep breath. It was probably for the best. If she was back in the committee's good books, maybe they'd back off about her jams with Jayden and Kath. Because there wasn't a chance in hell she was giving those up, if that's what October had been hoping for. It would also get Andy off her back, and show him that she really was taking this all seriously still – even if this whole encounter had only deepened the disquiet she now felt about the village.

'I'll get to it asap,' she said.

'I do appreciate it. *We* appreciate it, Tessa. And please, don't think I haven't heard you today. I very much value your input, and I will give the things you've said some further thought.'

Tessa looked up at the wall behind October and noticed a neon-pink poster broadcasting the quote: KINDNESS STARTS BY RECOGNISING WE ALL STRUGGLE. She had to stifle a laugh.

TWENTY-EIGHT

Tessa

S he'd found Maddy in a hospital side room, the baby in a trolley crib wrapped in a knitted blue blanket. Both of them were asleep. The chart on the crib said the baby's name was Juliet, which was also Tessa's middle name. Her eyes welled, and she reached down to hold the baby's tiny foot. With her free hand she reached over and hooked Maddy's little finger with hers.

Not wanting to invade their home on such an emotional weekend, Tessa stayed in a nearby Travelodge. She paid frequent visits to the hospital, running out for supplies and keeping Maddy's spirits up while she waited to be discharged. They joked about what their dad would be saying wrong right now if he were still alive, and tried not to talk about Mum, who had messaged Maddy eight months ago to say she couldn't afford to come back to England unless Maddy paid.

'Bhav was furious, but I did offer,' she said.

'And?'

Maddy looked down at Juliet. 'She never got back to me.'

Tessa considered telling Maddy about Nether Appleford, especially the Andy stuff. But in the end, she decided Maddy had enough to be dealing with, and so she stayed quiet.

On Tuesday morning Maddy and Juliet were finally allowed to leave, and Tessa had a message from one of the higher-ups at the Hollywood film company with whom she'd been sharing demos over the last month. She'd almost given up on it, not having had the sense they really liked her ideas. But now they were saying they were really into her stuff, and they wanted to hear more fleshed-out tracks before the end of the month. Excited, she settled Maddy and Juliet back at home and sped back to Nether Appleford. How the hell she was supposed to do this alongside the Story Station thing she had no clue, but what choice was there?

The score was for an animated horror film about a man being hunted by a version of himself from another timeline, and if she got the commission she'd get £30,000 – more than enough to show Andy she meant business. The only worry was, it was a for-hire gig, and she only got paid on completion – a standard risk down on her rung.

She'd been using the reverse-speech nonsense Andy had shown her a while back, recording her own voice, reversing it, and messing about with tuning software to create melodies that she thought sounded sort of time-warpy. The problem she'd run into was that she'd run out of interesting things to do to her voice. She needed multiple voices now if she was going to really create an entire score, with all the different dynamics and moods that would require.

Andy was still out when she got home, and Jayden and Kath came over as usual. With their permission, she set up mics around the place to record their conversations in the hope of using their voices in the piece. Ideally, she wanted a whole library to choose from, but this would make a great start.

It was Kath's birthday, and Tessa handed over a bottle of Loch Lomond on her arrival for their jam. When Jayden arrived shortly after he made no mention of her birthday, cheerfully getting on with his parts and smiling at them both when something sounded particularly good, as usual. It was odd, because more than once over the previous few weeks Jayden had reminded Tessa not to forget the date. Birthdays seemed important to him, so much so, she'd written his down on her calendar for next May.

Kath might have noticed, too, because her performance was lethargic and distracted. Was it possible he'd hurt her feelings? Something was going on though, because Jayden had a mischievous air about him all evening, and when they called it a night, Tessa fully expected him to pull out a gift and surprise Kath. Only it never happened. He packed up the bass and asked Kath if she wanted a walk back.

'I'm fine, Jayden. Going to just get my breath and rest my back. It's really killing tonight.' She sat up and winced before rolling her head from shoulder to shoulder.

He nodded. 'Night, then. Don't be talking about me, though?' He pointed at them both playfully.

'Anything else you want to … add tonight?' Tessa said.

'Nah,' he said and smiled. 'I'm good. See you.'

He left, and Tessa frowned. She turned to Kath. 'I can't believe he forgot. I'm so sorry.'

'My birthday?' she said, stretching. 'Oh, he didn't.' She glanced at the sliding door. 'Go and check he's definitely gone, would you.'

'Why, what is it?'

'Just check.'

Tessa did as she was asked, even going so far as to walk

around to the front of the cottage. She saw him pacing back towards Olivia's, earbuds in. When she returned to Kath she was sitting on the sofa, handbag on her lap.

'Anyone going to disturb us?' Kath said.

'No, Andy's out as usual. What is it?'

She pulled out a plastic bag containing a full sugar-bowl's worth of white powder.

'I think this was my birthday present from Jayden. It's ketamine. He told me the other night he could get me some and the next thing I know, I find this in a box wrapped up on my porch.'

Tessa stared, her mouth open. 'Oh, shit. Where the hell has he got that from?'

'I've got no fucking idea, my darling. And looking at the amount here, I'm a bit worried how he's paying for it.'

TWENTY-NINE

Tessa

Tessa stopped the recording, and the two of them spoke about Jayden for nearly an hour.

'We're going to have to have it out with him, Tess.'

That wasn't going to go down well, but they needed to know where the drugs came from, and whether he'd got himself into any debt or trouble. For now, Kath would keep the drugs at hers, concerned that if she gave them back, Olivia might come across them. 'Better under my mattress than his.' Because *she* was a whole other problem. Did they tell her about this or not? Tessa didn't want to. Doing so would destroy any trust they'd built with Jayden forever, while confirming all of Olivia's worst fears. And then Andy would inevitably find out, adding more fuel to *that* fire.

Kath left, and Tessa returned to the cottage and sat in silence. Andy was still out, probably at Olivia's. Again. She wouldn't get jealous, that wasn't her style, but she could admit that it was really starting to irritate her. She was surprised he hadn't made more of an effort to be home early, given she'd messaged him her plans for that day. Was he still angry? They'd spoken plenty of times over the weekend, and she thought they were in a better place. Now she was getting hungry. Was he expecting her to eat alone?

Numb, and cold now, too, she got up and put on one of Andy's oversized jumpers that lay over the back of the sofa. She made a bowl of muesli and beneath the kitchen light she noticed the jumper was covered in white hairs. Cat hairs. Olivia had a white cat.

She shook her head. She wasn't going down that road. He'd already explained he was rewiring parts of her house, that he couldn't be certain it was safe. Jayden was the issue here. She needed to focus on that. Maybe if he understood why they were worried, and showed signs of maturity when they talked to him, perhaps, *perhaps* they could forget the whole thing. Keep it between the three of them.

One thing was certain, though: the jamming had to stop. At least for now.

On Thursday night, Jayden turned up to practise and began to unpack his bass. After a strength-gathering look at Kath, Tessa told him to sit down. He obliged, oblivious as to what was about to happen.

'Jayden, you know Kath and I care about you a lot, don't you? That's why we do all this?' She threw a glance across the studio.

With a minuscule shrug he said, 'Yeah, I know. What, am I in trouble?'

'You're not in trouble,' Kath said. 'We just want to talk about the … box I found that I suspect came from you.'

'What box?'

'Don't,' Kath said with unsettling seriousness. 'Please.'

After a moment he sighed and threw up his hand. 'It's all fine. You don't need to worry about it, I told you. No one's looking for it. I got it legits.'

'How?'

He shook his head with his eyes closed, confident. 'It's sorted, Kath, don't worry about it.'

'Jayden, we are worried,' Tessa said. 'You're our friend, but you've made Kath a felon.'

'A felon, you mean like a criminal? No, I haven't.'

'Ketamine is illegal, you know that? She's now got it in her house.'

He raised his voice. 'Didn't you hear her? Ket's the only thing that helps her. I heard what she said.'

Kath interjected. 'Yeah, but Jayden, that's not quite what I meant.'

He looked from one of them to the other, his lip curled aggressively. 'Well, if you don't want it, just chuck it away. I'm sorry I even bothered.'

Tessa turned to Kath, and she looked back with concern. 'If you're not going to tell us how you got it,' Tessa said, 'we've got to assume the worst. And really we can't be mixed up in anything criminal, Jayden. It's not fair on us, and it's not fair on Olivia either. We'd have to come clean with her.'

He scoffed. 'Olivia?'

'Listen, I understand you were trying to do something nice. But can you see where we're coming from? We can't really ignore a bag of drugs.'

'A big bag,' Kath added.

'Who are you mixed up with? You're only fifteen.'

'I know my own age. Why you even worrying about Olivia? She doesn't care about you. She's part of the whole problem. She's one of the main ones on that stupid committee.'

There wasn't much else Tessa could say. He'd reacted as

she'd feared. Resigned, Tessa said, 'Kath and I have talked, and we think that for now we're just going to have a break from playing music.'

'What?' It was the loudest she'd ever heard him speak, and she recoiled. 'Why? As punishment? Are you punishing me? That's—'

'No, it's not punishment.' Tessa tried keeping her voice calm. 'You must know Olivia finds you coming here difficult. She's got this thing in her head about rock music and drugs. And you doing this … it's not exactly helped my case.'

Offended now, he speared Tessa with his gaze. His head moved from side to side in micro-shakes of disbelief. 'You're so fucking dumb.'

Tessa stared at him blankly. Not knowing where to look, she turned to Kath, who had a hand over her eyes.

'Okay, Jayden. Thanks for that. I think you should go now. Sorry this—'

'No, you don't get it. Why do you care what Olivia thinks? She's just messing with you. She's trying to make you look bad to them. To the committee. And to Andy.'

'Jayden … What?'

'She's got a thing for him. Haven't you noticed? He's over there all the time, I can hear them talking and flirting.'

'Steady on,' Kath said, raising her voice now.

'No. She dresses up and puts on make-up. And I'll be honest, I think she's deliberately breaking things so he comes around to fix them. He's there all the bloody time.'

Heat rose in Tessa's chest and neck. 'You've got the wrong end of the stick,' was what she managed to say, even if she wasn't entirely sure all of a sudden.

'Ah, no one ever listens to me. You don't believe me, look up her ex. Find a picture, I dare you, and tell me you don't think she's after Andy.'

'Enough, boy,' Kath said, the edge in her voice catching Jayden's attention. 'If you don't want our help, that's one thing. But don't take it out getting all personal on Tessa. She's been nothing but good to you. Why don't you go home before you say something even more stupid? Go on.'

He stared at them, still shaking his head. Like he might murder them. Like he might cry.

'Fine,' he said. 'I'm sorry I fucking bothered.'

The two of them went back to the house and Tessa poured them both a glass of whisky. They sat in silence a while.

'I'd say we did our best,' Kath said.

'It didn't go very well, did it?'

'He'll come around. He was just trying to show off to us, wasn't he? Look at me and my connections. Now his pride's all deflated. He'll settle down, and then maybe we can have another chat.'

'Yeah.'

Kath finished her whisky and got up to leave.

'You don't have to go. We could … watch a film maybe. No idea what time Andy's planning on coming back. I could cook us something?'

'You're a darling, but I've got to start packing for my little holiday.'

'Holiday? Where are you going?'

'Well, you'll never guess who bought me a two-day spa retreat in the city centre for my birthday?'

'Who?'

'The bloody committee.'

'Uh. Sorry, what? The Kindness Committee?'

'Unexpected to say the least, but hot tub and massage with my back the way it is? Yes, please.'

'I... Wow. Have they ever done anything like that before?'

'Never. Not even a card. But I never say no to free.'

Tessa couldn't believe it. Had they listened to her? Had October *actually* listened to her? It seemed that way, and so she smiled. Yet at the same time, for reasons she didn't understand, she felt a twinge of fear.

THIRTY

Tessa
_____

Andy came home not long after Kath left, and he cooked them both a stir fry. She didn't want to think too much about what Jayden had said, and the whole thing felt stupid once he was home, chuntering away and being nice as usual. But after Andy fell asleep, she couldn't stop herself checking the film society Instagram. She scrolled down the page until she found the original picture of the gang in its pre-shark condition.

She swore when she saw it. Andy was staring out at her from the bottom-left corner instead of the shark's face. Only it wasn't Andy. The eyes were ever so slightly closer together, the lobes of the ears smaller, the canine teeth a bit more prominent in the goofy smile. But the wide face, the dark beard, and the sheer size of him compared with usual men, was undoubtedly similar. Even the cropped hair and slight widow's peak were the same. The two might have passed for brothers, or fraternal twins.

She put down her phone. It didn't mean anything.

214

On Saturday morning, Andy left early to take Tessa's car around to Ruth's before going out to work. Ruth had agreed to pay them over the going rate, but that didn't make Tessa hate the decision any less. But she didn't stand in the way. She didn't dare risk spoiling the current detente with both Andy and the committee.

She was immersed in her soundtrack work all morning, getting as much done as possible before the committee delivered their demands, and didn't check her messages until lunchtime. When she did, she had one from Andy, a slightly blurry picture of hearts dangling from the Kindness Tree. The text below read:

Congratulations! What did you do?? Champagne tonight?

She tried zooming in but couldn't properly read the text on the heart. She walked down to the tree and looked around until she found it:

To Tessa, For opening our eyes!

She smiled, but again, she felt only disquiet. She walked home typing a response to Andy, and when she next looked up, she noticed a giant removal lorry parked further up The Road.

She stopped. Was she being paranoid, or was that Kath's cottage?

Breaking into a half-walk, half-run, she became increasingly convinced that she was right, until finally it couldn't be denied: the van was outside Kath's. And October, Dev, Leo, Ruth, Olivia, and Aaron all stood beside it, discussing something with a young guy in a polo shirt bearing the same logo as the one on the side of the truck. None of the committee looked particularly overjoyed at being there. They wore baggy or worn or paint-covered clothes. The back of the lorry was open, and on it were boxes Tessa recognised from the front of the cottage. Another man in a polo shirt walked in front of her from the direction of the drive carrying a crate, which he loaded onto the lorry.

'Tessa,' October said, alerted to her arrival by Ruth. 'We were just going to come for you. Look.'

Tessa did, and on the drive she saw a small army of men.

'This is all your doing,' October said, 'you were absolutely right. A plan was exactly what was needed.'

'Does she know?'

'Sorry?'

'Does Kath know about this?'

October turned to the others, her face wrinkled by bafflement. 'Of course not.'

'It's a surprise,' Olivia said with a tone of voice that she clearly used with her children at school.

'Like *Changing Rooms*,' October added with glee. 'Have you seen that programme?'

The front door had been propped open. They were actually inside the cottage.

'Did she give you a key?'

'No, it was a *surprise*,' Olivia repeated, smiling, her eyebrows lowered in disbelief.

Tessa wanted to walk over and slap her. She started shaking her head. The assembled committee all looked at her, their self-congratulatory delight on the brink of turning sour. They were all asking what her problem was, but Tessa couldn't speak. Didn't have words for the dumbfounded horror she felt. Could they really be so ... stupid?

One of the men came out of the cottage carrying a snare drum. He banged on it to make his mate laugh.

'No,' Tessa said. Her voice sounded whiney and quiet. 'Stop this.'

'Sorry, Tessa?' It was Dev's voice, coming from miles away.

'You need to stop it. This isn't right.'

'I thought this was her idea?' Ruth said, warily scanning the assembled faces, a tinge of doubt in her voice.

'It was,' October said. 'This was what you were saying, Tessa. That she was stubborn. Well, here it is, a plan. We're not just *saying*, we're *actually doing something*.'

'I didn't … No, that isn't what I meant.'

'We've hired a team to help, so she doesn't hurt her back. You said it was dangerous here. We're putting things right.'

'No. Don't you get it?' She was shouting. She couldn't help herself. She needed to slow this down. Reset. 'This is wrong. All of these things … they're connected to her husband. You can't just take them away.'

'We've organised a warehouse,' Dev said. 'For her to sort through in her own time… October, I thought this was something Kath requested. Or at least, had intimated that she wanted.'

'It is,' October said, 'and she will be delighted when she sees what we've done.'

'No, she won't,' Tessa said. The man with the drum walked behind her and she asked him to stop.

'You don't need to stop,' October said, her voice hushed.

Tessa left the committee and strode down the drive to address the other men. 'All of you.' None of them looked up. She put her fingers in her mouth and whistled. Their heads raised like meerkats'. 'Stop what you're doing. There's been a misunderstanding.'

Like fuck, it was a misunderstanding. The men began

muttering and looking around for further instruction. Another man walked out from inside, casting her a glance on his way over to his mates working on the crates and boxes.

'You can carry on,' October said. 'Don't worry. Tessa, can we discuss this?'

But it was clear to Tessa now that October wanted Kath gone, that she was using what Tessa had said to give her an excuse to do this. But she would put a stop to it. Only then she remembered: *the ketamine.* Bloody hell, the bag was in the cottage. If the committee found it, they'd use it against her in some way – especially with Leo involved. Blackmail her into selling up.

She had to get it. She had to get inside. The mattress, that's what she'd said.

Behind her the committee were now engaged in discussion with three of the movers. They weren't looking her way. She glanced at the gaping doorway and went for it, darting inside. Tessa breathed through her mouth, a mixture of earthy, mouldy smells, badly concealed by pot-pourri, greeted her. A small area of dust-coloured carpet had been revealed by what the movers had already shifted. She strode over boxes and furniture, trying to follow the path she'd taken when here before. When she reached the stairwell door, it was soon apparent that it hadn't been opened in a long while, obstructed as it was by rugs and sofa cushions stuffed behind a dresser. So where did she sleep?

Voices intruded from outside, moving men close to the door. She strode over a pile of vinyl records and into the interior hall. Her options were limited here; more clutter obstructed the doorways. She knew the kitchen already from her last visit, so she tried the bathroom. Black mould. Peeling plaster. No seat on the toilet. She stared at it, suddenly overwhelmed by just how terrible things had got for Kath.

She took a breath. Maybe she should just go home. Let them tidy the place, consequences be damned. Could they be any worse than living this way? She shook her head. This wasn't how it should happen. Kath had to be involved, not … tricked.

She listened for the voices, but they sounded further away now. She came back into the lounge and noticed a wall of boxes to her right, stacked as high as her head. She slid through a gap where the box wall and the actual wall met. Inside was a small room created by another box wall. A mattress lay on the floor, with magazines and more vinyl stacked on either side to make tables. Old cups of water and dirty plates rested on them near the head end. An electric bar-heater, maybe thirty years old, was positioned inches from the duvet and blankets. Kath's clothes filled plump plastic bags nearby.

Tessa swallowed, unable to process that this was where Kath, that obscenely talented, solar flare of a woman, put down her head each night. It wasn't right. This was a death trap.

There wasn't time to dwell on it, though, and she carefully manoeuvred around the room, not wanting to knock the boxes in case they fell. She lifted the mattress. The bag was tucked not very far under the head end, thank God. She grabbed it, shoved it into her pocket, and fled.

All eyes were on her when she walked back down the drive.

'October,' she said, 'I'm really sorry I gave you the impression that this is what I meant. But it isn't. Not like this.'

'It's all in motion, though,' she said, like what they were discussing was the planet's orbit, not a couple of moving vans. There was a trace of petulance in her voice too.

'Not like this.'

They stood in silence, gazes locked. Unbelievably, October

was still smiling, although God knew what that was, swimming around in her eyes.

'Do you want us to just carry on?' one of the movers said.

'Just put it all back,' Tessa said. 'Otherwise … I'll call the police.'

With that, already dreading and regretting what she'd just threatened, she marched home.

THIRTY-ONE

Tessa

Tessa hid the ketamine in her studio and watched the vans leave from her window. Shortly, the committee filed past her cottage like a funeral procession. She called Kath, told her what had happened, and Kath fell silent. When she spoke again, her voice was soft but steely.

'I'll come back and talk to them.'

'Are you sure? Do you want me to come?'

'No.'

'Okay.' Picturing Kath's makeshift bedroom again, the electric fire and blankets, she added, 'Kath … Did I do the right thing? Stopping them.'

Kath sighed. 'Let's talk tomorrow.'

She knocked on Kath's door later that evening, wanting to find out if she was okay. But also the bag of ket was in her pocket; God knew how Andy would react if he thought she was using drugs again. She needed it gone. When Kath didn't answer after a third knock, she was about to head back. Finally, the door parted, leaking that now-familiar dank smell from inside, and something else, too: whisky.

'Hello,' Kath said, avoiding eye-contact. She shuffled out and closed the door behind her.

'Did you speak to them?'

'The committee? In a manner. I told them I knew what they were up to, but they said they were just acting on the concerns of *my friend*.' Now she looked Tessa in the eye.

Tessa shook her head. 'Unbelievable. You don't think I told them to do that?'

'I don't know.' She poked out her bottom lip. 'You asked me last night if you'd done the right thing, stopping them. Sounds like a little bit of you wondered if it was a good idea.'

'I just wanted to be sure.'

'Did you speak to them about me? Before they went in.'

'Not *about* you. But you came up, and I told them I was worried about you, and that they needed to support you better.'

'Right.' She shook her head. 'After everything I told you.'

She didn't know quite how to explain the conversation she'd had with October without telling her about the note. Did she want to get into that now? 'I didn't tell them to break into your house and take all your things.'

'No, but you gave them a chance to twist it, and they did. That's what I told you they do.'

Tessa gave herself a moment, taken aback by Kath's anger. 'I'm sorry. I wanted to help.'

'You sound like the kid now.'

'Kath, they completely mangled what I said. And I stopped them. I threatened to call the police on them. On bloody Leo.'

Kath nodded, thrust her hands further into the pockets of her oversized sweater, and sighed. 'They're coming for me now, guarantee you that. I told them I wasn't scared, that I wasn't selling up, if it was the last thing I did. But something's changed, them doing this. They said their worry is I'm a danger to myself and my neighbours. That they'd not realised before until *you* mentioned it. What if there was a fire? I told them I'd put it out. I also told them they'd be fucking sorry if they touched my stuff again.'

'You really said that?'

'Yeah. And I told them if they didn't back off, I'd go down to the police station and tell them what I know.'

'What you know? As in … the things you've told me?'

She nodded. 'I don't know if they believed me, but it gave them something to think on.'

'How did they react?'

Kath took her hands out her pockets and pushed them into the small of her back. 'I've done a lot of travelling today, Tess. And I never did get my massage. I'm going to have a lie down now. Shall we talk tomorrow or something? When I've had a think.'

Tessa nodded, and was walking away when Kath called back, 'I do know it's them, not you, Tess. Just … you can't underestimate them.'

It was only when Tessa got home, still thinking over her talk with Kath, that she realised she still had the drugs on her. Andy was upstairs in the bath, so she hid them in a drawer in the studio. She'd have to deal with all of it, the committee and Kath, tomorrow.

She ate breakfast with Andy. He was chirpy, oblivious to everything that had gone on yesterday, and he kissed the top of the head before heading out to fix the pub's broken light. Of course, Aaron would tell Andy everything, and once he came home things would really hit the fan. She had better prepare for it, then.

She tidied the kitchen, still somewhat dazed by the incredible mess she'd made of things. Andy, Kath, Jayden, the committee – she'd managed to upset them all. She deserved her very own tree of black hearts for such an achievement. She dragged herself upstairs, tired and slightly nauseous, and wandered from empty room to empty room. So much space, and still no children to fill it – because that had been her secret hope, hadn't it? To trick her body into action, or some other irrational bollocks. She'd never *really* believed she *wouldn't* have children, had she? Not like she suddenly found herself believing now.

She grabbed some tissue from the bathroom. Dried her eyes in the mirror. Stupid woman – who found it so easy to criticise bullshit, yet couldn't avoid her own childish magical thinking.

What she needed now was sleep. And to wake up six months ago and stay at home the day they first found Nether Appleford. Instead, she opened the cabinet above the sink to grab her toothbrush. It was a small unit, and everything was crammed inside, which was why Andy's toothbrush fell into the sink, dragging with it a reel of floss and a long-forgotten pregnancy test.

Her heart lurched. She stared at the cassette.

It was *not* a sign.

Yes, she was three days overdue. But so what? *So what?* She'd been here a million times before. Three days was nothing. And yesterday she'd been convinced her period was coming on around lunchtime, but what she'd taken as the first twinges of cramp eventually abated. Or had she simply not noticed in all the drama?

No. This *wasn't* a bloody sign.

Still, she dropped her underwear anyway. Used the test.

But *because* she knew it wasn't a sign, she put the test down on the sink, brushed her teeth, and almost forgot about it.

Downstairs she heard the key in the door, footsteps in the lounge.

'Tess.'

Andy, back already. His voice boomed in the stairwell. Tessa smirked. Aaron must have told him. He hadn't even waited to finish up the job before having it out with her. Here went nothing, then.

The stairs began to creak, and she stepped out to stand in the hall to meet him. She stood in the doorway. He stood on the top step, face red like he'd been running.

'What's the matter?' she said.

'Tess, I'm so sorry. I just spoke with Aaron. The boy, he was up at your friend's cottage—'

'The boy? Jayden.'

He nodded. 'He was up at Kath's this morning apparently, and he said he looked through the window and saw some boxes had come down. In the corner of the house. He got an ambulance out, and they've taken her away.'

'Sorry, what?' She was annoyed. He wasn't making sense. 'You mean Kath?'

He nodded.

The natural darkness in the corridor began to close in around Andy until it was only him in her field of vision. 'What's happened to her?' she said.

'She died, Tess.'

The blackness closed over Andy now, and she leaned to rest her shoulder on the bathroom doorframe. Only she missed it. Her arm went out. She was falling. Andy's hands were around her, bringing her back to her feet. He pulled her to him, and she was apologising. He pushed open the door to the bathroom to try and give them some room to sit down.

She got her bearings, steadied herself, and gently pushed him away. The pregnancy test – she didn't want him to see it. Didn't want him to think that this was what she did when alone.

'I just need a moment, Andy. Just give me a second.'

He obliged, stepping into the hallway. She closed the door and looked at the test. Only one line. She wasn't pregnant. Kath was dead.

Her hand rose to her mouth. Tears filled her eyes and fell. She wiped them away, picked up the test to throw it in the bin. Andy never emptied the bloody thing anyway, it was *always* her, but she would wrap a tissue around it just in case.

Kath was dead.

She pushed down the pedal, glancing one last time at the test as she reached for the loo roll. In this light, it almost looked like there was as second line. How funny. She brought it up to her face.

Oh look, there it was. A slender shadow. A pale imitation of the control line above. A ghost line.

She stared. Her foot retreated from the pedal. The bin lid clattered, startling her.

A shadow. A line.

It was a line.

And Kath was dead.

THIRTY-TWO

Tessa

K ath had been drunk. It was put more diplomatically, but word around the village was that, during the night, *something* had caused several heavy boxes, stacked precariously beside the mattress where Kath slept, to fall. Emergency services had found her cottage to be 'dangerously cluttered', and they'd had great difficulty reaching her body.

She had been crushed by the weight of her grief. Case closed.

Tessa took some small comfort from knowing that her death was likely quick, or if not, that she wouldn't have known anything about it, having sustained such trauma to her skull. The thought of her trapped beneath those boxes, yelling for help, was too horrific to contemplate.

One afternoon the following week, she sought Jayden out after school. The two of them walked the lake path in the November cold, talking around the subject until Jayden said, 'I'm so sorry,' and burst into tears. They found a bench, and she held him, her own tears hidden from his view.

'I was so mean to her last time I saw her,' he said.

'Friends fall out because they care about each other,' Tessa said, stroking his back through his chunky coat. 'She knew you were trying to help her, trust me. She thought you were brilliant.'

When he'd composed himself, he said, 'Is it true, on the day before, they tried cleaning her place, and you stopped them?'

Tessa nodded. 'Did Olivia tell you that?'

'Yeah. She seemed annoyed because they thought you'd encouraged them to do it. But I told her they must have misunderstood. You wouldn't have said that.'

'No. I wouldn't. There was definitely a … misunderstanding.'

He met her gaze now, damp-eyed but determined. 'Did they do something to her, Tess?'

She paused for too long. She didn't know how much to say. How much to share the nagging doubts and suspicions in her black little heart. Because, yes, given that Kath had threatened them, and then died the next day, her first reaction had been: *the committee did this.* But unless Kath had held something back, she really had only the flimsiest of a case against them. Nothing that would worry them, even if they had been up to no good. And it wasn't in any way far-fetched, given the condition of the place, and given she had been drinking, that it had just been a terrible accident.

Besides, he was fifteen – easy enough to forget sometimes. She needed to be the grown-up now.

'There's no evidence of that.'

His head dropped. 'I thought you'd say that.'

She'd assumed he'd fight her. Want her to see his point and go at it until she did. But he didn't. He'd accepted what she'd said. Perhaps for now that was best.

'I'm worried they'll find the … present in there,' he said

after a while. 'You know, when they clean up. They'll make her seem like a druggie. Should I try and get it?'

'Don't worry about it,' Tessa said. 'I've already sorted that.'

He smiled at her weakly. 'So, can I come and see you? To talk. Not music or anything.'

It hurt her heart to look at him. 'Of course. Of course, you can. Any time. We're friends, Jayden.'

His smile grew.

Later, he got up to leave and said, 'Tessa, just be careful, yeah? I think they're going to try and blame you for what happened.'

She bristled. 'Blame *me*. For what?'

'I overheard Olivia say it to Dev. He came over late last night. I know it's rubbish. But she said something like, "If Tessa hadn't stopped them clearing the house, Kath would still be alive."'

Tessa got home and slammed the front door. The cottage shook.

Her fault. *Her* fault. So, this was how they were going to spin it?

She laughed bitterly, filling a glass of water at the tap with a shaking hand. Those bastards. That bitch. She strode out to the studio and sat in her office chair. For a while she stared at the electronic kit but felt her face screwing up again. She leaned forward and pinched the bridge of her nose until she had herself under control.

She unlocked her desk drawers, and from the top one she took out the used pregnancy test from beside the bag of ketamine. The two lines remained, that important one still so weak that she wanted to do another test to make sure before telling

Andy. She didn't think either of them could deal with a false positive.

She needed to buy more tests first, but hadn't got around to it yet. Kath's death had taken up most of the space in her mind the last few days, and she'd half expected her period to still come. It hadn't, although she still hadn't ruled out an early menopause – which would be just flipping typical. But this little bit of hope in her hand was good and new. A talisman, and she wanted to savour it.

Because if it was really happening … they could get out of Nether Appleford, couldn't they? Forget they'd ever come here and have the life they'd *actually* wanted.

She moved the test around in the light of the studio's spots. From some angles you couldn't even see the line. No, she wouldn't tell Andy just yet. Why risk building his hopes up? High hopes, long way down. That's what he always said. Could their relationship even stand a big crash at this point? Better he not know. That was the kind thing to do.

Again, she laughed bitterly. If she was pregnant, and that was a big if, it was funny that it had finally happened here in Nether Appleford. Did it not vindicate the compulsion she'd had to move here after all? Well, no, because she'd done her own version of kindness, hadn't she?

Except … she'd discovered her pregnancy *after s*topping her jams with Kath and Jayden. She'd already broken Jayden's heart and promised the committee she'd do their Sound Station. Hadn't she even got her first heart on the tree, too? So, if she was going to go in for this nonsense, there was a case that doing kindness the Nether Appleford way had been what did the trick in the end.

But she was done with the superstitious crap now, wasn't she? Nether Appleford had *nothing* to do with any baby they might be about to have. And a good thing too. Because she didn't know what the truth was, whether the committee was really behind what happened to Kath or not. But she knew they were poison. And that things weren't right here. It would take some convincing, but she knew she had to get herself and Andy away from here. Herself and Andy, and perhaps their child.

She placed the test at the very back of the drawer and stared at the bag of ket. She shook her head and felt herself smile. She reached down and moved the plastic covered powder through her forefinger and thumb. Her eyes filled with tears. 'Oh, Kath.'

THIRTY-THREE

Tessa

A ndy walked through the door and had barely entered the lounge when she pushed herself against his chest. His arms enclosed her, but slower than she would have liked. He felt rigid, and when he greeted her with a 'Hey,' he sounded distant. She squeezed him and he didn't squeeze back, and all the joy she'd been feeling at his return abandoned her.

'Everything okay?' she said.

'Knackered. Absolutely knackered,' he said, and went back to the car to bring his more expensive tools into the hall.

Despite this, after a dinner through which he stared at his phone the entire time, he announced he was going back out to work.

'Can you not go?' she said. Finally, he made eye-contact with her across the dining table.

'What?'

'Can you, for once, just spend an evening here? With me.'

He stared at her, dumbfounded. 'Yeah … I mean, of course I can.' It was a while before he added, 'Everything okay?'

'No, of course it's bloody not,' she said. She couldn't look at him. Her plate, the light switch on the wall, the carpet: anywhere would do. She was frayed, close to saying something she'd regret. Her breathing was too loud, but trying to slow down to make it quieter only exacerbated the problem. 'Andy, I don't think it's working here. In the village.'

When she heard him shuffle in his seat, she allowed herself to look up. He pushed a hand into his beard. 'You don't?'

'No.'

He nodded contemplatively. 'It's … been trying. I agree with that.'

'Trying. Yeah, trying is a word.'

'First with the lady breaking in here. Then what happened with your friend.'

'Yeah. Okay. And the Kindness Committee breaking into Kath's house. Trying to take all her belongings to a warehouse without telling her. Any opinion on that?'

He stared at her, his silence a tell. His opinion was going to cause an argument. But that just made Tessa persist.

'You know they're going round saying what happened to her is my fault?'

'Are they? I heard them say you gave them the idea and then changed your mind.'

'No. No, I mentioned in passing treating Kath better. That's not the same as, *Go and rob her.*'

'That's not what they were going to—'

'You're on their side. I fucking knew it.'

'I'm not on anyone's side,' he said, his calm tone infuriating her further. Actually, he wasn't just calm. No, he was positively mellow. 'I just mean they were reacting to what *you'd* said. The danger you'd pointed out. But then you stopped them doing that. Which, being honest, I found confusing. What did you want exactly?'

'I wanted them to stop thinking of her as a "pariah", your words.'

Andy shook his head slowly and knocked on the table with the butt of his fork.

'So, you've talked to them about this? Olivia, probably.'

They held eye-contact now, and Andy licked his lips. She knew he was piecing together his response. Extracting the venom, neutralising any commitment, adjusting the weight perfectly so that its balance on the fence was perfect.

'Not particularly.' He shrugged. 'What is it you want me to say, Tessa? It's not your fault what happened. There.'

The defeated way he said this shook her. 'I know that. What I want to know is that you are with me, Andy. I barely see you at the moment, and I feel sometimes like this village is actively against me, and yet you just seem to have dived right in and never looked back. But don't you think the people here are … weird? Don't you get a sense that this place is seriously off? I swear, just six months ago you would have.'

Andy waited a while, doing his weighing-up act again before getting to his feet. His chair scraped the tiled floor mercilessly. He took his plate to the bin, and when he returned, he had his keys in his hands.

'Where are you going?' she asked.

'Tess, I'm doing what we came here to do. I'm trying. That was the promise we made. To try.'

'You don't think I'm trying?'

'You tell me? Do you think everyone here thinks you're a really kind, community-orientated person? Or do you think they just see someone who does whatever it is they want to do, so long as *she* thinks it's kind, and everyone else can fuck off?'

'What can I say to that?'

'Stuff gets around in the village, Tess. I hear about things. Once or twice, like yeah, maybe. You're adjusting. But you've got everyone's back up here. Going around asking weird questions about people who used to live here, looking up old internet articles about members of the committee. And even when people have tried steering you in the right direction, waved a red flag in your face, you've ignored it.'

'What … what red flag?'

'That you were upsetting Olivia with all the Jayden shit.'

'Oh, for goodness' sake, fuck Olivia.'

'And why Jayden over everyone else? Because he's a difficult kid with a bad attitude. Like you. That's who you relate to, Tessa. Rather than someone a little bit … predictable, maybe. A little bit boring but, you know … a nice human being. That's all Nether Appleford is, Tess. A village of nice people. So, if it's not working for you, then… you know, maybe there's a reason for that.' Still shaking his head, he walked to the door. 'Maybe *they're* not the fucking problem.'

He slammed the front door behind him, and from the lounge she heard her acoustic guitar fall to the floor.

———

Andy wasn't really a man who stormed off. He certainly wasn't the sort of man that vanished without telling you where he was going. But wanting the day and all its stress behind her, she went to bed, very much hoping Andy would return tonight and slide in behind her, put his hand on her belly. He'd pull her into him, whisper into her ear that he was sorry, and then *she* would say sorry. Then maybe they'd kiss, and perhaps more, and afterwards she might even tell him about the baby.

Only, when she woke up, the bedside clock said it was five in the morning. The bed beside her was still empty. She grabbed her phone from the table and saw she had a message from him, sent at one in the morning:

I'm at a hotel tonight. Need some space to think. X

She kept re-reading it, worried each time about what *space to think* meant but dumbly reassured by that kiss. How angry could he really be if he put on a kiss? She vacillated between annoyance that he felt *he* had anything to think about, and guilt that he'd actually had a point, and their situation was even more serious than she'd realised. Before long the sun was coming up, and she knew she wasn't going to sleep.

Downstairs she drank coffee and ate breakfast, her stomach too unsettled to enjoy either. She paced and chewed her nails. Okay, perhaps she hadn't timed or phrased her objections to living in Nether Appleford well yesterday. And she could completely understand that he might be angry at her for moving him out here in the first place, only to change her mind this way – especially as he was making such a success of it. But once he knew, he'd be with her, wouldn't he? They could sack off this halfway-house, consolation-prize existence and be a family.

She called a taxi. Went to the supermarket. Bought some pregnancy tests. She did one on her return. Then another, just to be sure. They were both positive. She screamed both times the line appeared.

Wanting to show him all three tests, Tessa grabbed the keys from the kitchen peg and ran out to the studio. She unlocked the drawer to retrieve that first one she'd done last week and stared inside. The test was where she'd left it. The problem now was that the bag of ket wasn't.

THIRTY-FOUR

How to Kill with Kindness

E verything we do must appear on the outside as kind as we know it is inside. Which is why the time had never been quite right to deal with the problem of Kath. The mess in her garden grew so slowly, and her promises to act always came across so sincerely, that we could never really use it as a way to move her on. And we couldn't really keep pressing her with our offer to buy without looking like bullies.

I could have forced things. But bearing in mind the big moves we'd already made on the likes of Willy Mortimer and such, I was concerned another tragic event might attract too much attention. One must be cautious in these matters.

I was biding my time with Kath. And I suppose, having taken into account her health, my plan had been to just outlive her. Procure the cottage from whichever obscure relative claimed the place. But best-laid plans, my darling, and with time so suddenly short for me, I knew action was needed if I wanted Kath dealt with before you take over from me.

And a kind person is a flexible person, darling, and when

an opportunity for a blitzkrieg of kindness presents itself, you must seize it.

Now, Kath and Tessa becoming friends had a certain inevitability to it, in retrospect. Their musical interests and their watchfulness. The way they are perceived in the village. Certainly there was plenty to exploit. Once Tessa made her concerns about Kath's situation known, I knew they could be spun into sounding like a request for an intervention. Once it became an issue of safety, and one raised by someone close to Kath, any concerns about her autonomy went out the window.

I was thinking on my feet, and what I'd hoped was that Kath would come home to find all her belongings gone, and be so angry and upset with us, and with Tessa for instigating it all, that she'd finally sell up. If that didn't work, at least the cottage would be neat and tidy – not ideal, but the best I could manage in the time. Her pain would have been, on balance, worth it for the much greater kindness being done for the village. As I always say, the harder it feels, the kinder you're being.

Unfortunately, Tessa arrived too early the day we went over to clear Kath's cottage. Sometimes I wonder if there might not be a Sharpie in there somewhere, darling, as once she saw what was happening, she was able to anticipate Kath's true reaction as well as I was. She put on quite the performance to halt proceedings, and everyone got spooked. I have to applaud how she got inside everyone's heads. In some ways I like her, she's not dissimilar to Eleanor Beddington, only without the doggy on her back. I'll give her this, she is a smart rival – one that it will give me some pleasure in overcoming.

Then Kath returned early from the little break we'd organised, and I was pleased initially with how perfectly mad she sounded when she summoned the committee to meet at The Yew Tree. 'I know what you're up to…' 'You're all in it together…' Entirely predictable, and it was good that everyone heard that raw instability.

On the other hand, the threat she made concerned me. When she said, 'I've got proof of all the things you've done to the others here,' it changed things.

'You've come for me now, so I'll come for you.'

Well, what choice did I have, once she said that? Perhaps it was a bluff made in anger, but I couldn't take that chance. With so many things at stake, how could I? To bring about 'true' kindness you need to seek certainty and be decisive. The fact is, she was intimating she'd noticed my work. That was enough for me, even if it changed my plans.

As I said, a kind person is a flexible person!

Now, darling, I don't tell you this lightly, but whenever the occasion comes when you might have to take a life, you have to close your eyes and imagine a world without this person in it. Will anyone miss them? Will their absence create more sadness than it will improve the lives of others? These aren't easy things to do, or at least aren't without practice. But I was able to close my eyes and picture the way forward with great clarity. Picture myself with the key, letting myself into Kath's cottage, breathing in the rancid smell of the place. Picture myself clubbing her head with the cosh I keep for such things while she slept, to ensure she didn't suffer, before pushing the boxes piled beside her onto her sleeping body. A fitting end which no one would question, given how things played out.

It wasn't as easy as that in the end, but I made sure it didn't look that way. And I have to say, on the whole, it all worked out perfectly. Because not only did it solve the issue of Kath, it also tarnished Tessa better than I could have hoped. By stopping us, and then the accident occurring, Tessa had made herself look both a little unhinged, and ultimately responsible for how things transpired.

And darling, it's even better than that. Because when Tessa went inside the cottage that day, I noticed she'd gone inside and was in there for some time. She came out, hands deep in her pockets, and it crossed my mind that she might have retrieved something from inside. I didn't know what this might be, but I further noticed that while berating us, she gesticulated with only one hand, while the other remained deep in her pocket like she was clutching something in there over which she was particularly protective.

I began to piece things together then, about Tessa, and Kath, and Jayden. And even though I couldn't be sure, I had a strong feeling about what was in her pocket. And given what I already knew about Andy, and his concerns with Tessa, it gave me another opportunity to sow discord between the two of them. Whether or not I was right didn't matter; all I needed to do was plant the...

THIRTY-FIVE

Tessa

A ndy sat on the sofa in the lounge. All she could see was the back of his head above the cushions when she entered, a silhouette against the morning sunlight coming through the windows.

'You're back?' Tessa said.

He didn't turn around. 'Do you want to come and have a seat?'

'Why?'

'Just … we need to talk.'

Andy didn't like talking in clichés, but now here he was, bold-as-brass basic.

'Did you just get back now?'

'I've been up in the bedroom waiting for you to get back. I didn't sleep well.'

She walked around and sat on the sofa at a right angle to him beneath the bay window where she'd not too long ago seen the pale face of Eleanor Bedd—

The bag of ketamine was on the cushion beside him. Her heartbeat quickened. 'Why do you have that?' she said.

He pursed his lips, creating an expression that said: *Poor Tessa. Poor, helpless Tessa.* 'I was thinking about everything we talked about. I really needed to think. And then it hit me. You've not been yourself lately. You've been working really hard on this new commission.' He bobbed his shoulders: need he say more?

She was about to tell him that he'd laugh when he heard the real story. But then he probably wouldn't. It would probably make her seem even more reckless than if the drugs *were* hers. But something else took precedence over establishing her innocence. 'Why were you going through my locked drawers?'

'I told you. I had my suspicions. And they were right. Or at least … I hope they're right. Because otherwise, I really don't know what's going on with you. This,' he gestured towards the drugs, 'there's help for.'

Tessa couldn't help laughing. It wasn't what she wanted to do, but it came out anyway. He sounded like she'd imagined he did back in his Christian days. A youth pastor chiding a wayward youth.

'Yeah, sure,' she said, 'why the fuck not. I'm absolutely caning that stuff and it's the reason I'm not happy here. Do you even know what that is?'

'What is it, coke? Not smack, I imagine.'

'I think you'd have noticed me on smack, don't you?'

'I don't know, Tess. It's not really my world.'

'It's not *my* world. It was a brief experiment that…' She didn't need to explain herself to him again. All that was ancient history. 'That's ketamine. And I'm not microdosing it for inspiration.'

'I don't believe you. Where did you get it? Kath? I've heard from people she was into that stuff. Don't tell me Jayden was involved.'

'Andy. You've got it completely... Can we just start this again? Please. I need to tell you something really important.'

'No, you can't just ignore this. You promised me when we went through all of that ... shit that you'd never bring drugs into the house again. That you were done with it. On top of everything else...' He sighed. 'This isn't working, is it?'

'What isn't working?'

'You. Me. Any of it.'

Tessa tried to swallow. She couldn't do it. Her larynx felt anchored to her rib cage. 'Don't say that.' Her voice sounded small.

He held up the bag and yelled, 'What else am I supposed to do with this?'

Tessa's eyes welled up. She wiped the tears away. Had they really drifted this far in such a short space of time? The Andy she'd moved here with would never have believed this crap. Would never have doubted her so casually. Someone had got in his head, they must have. All that stuff about hearing Kath being into drugs and having his suspicions. What the fuck?

'Fine, if you don't believe me...' Tessa said, feeling now how she imagined Jayden must have felt the day they'd come to accuse him of breaking into her studio. What was even the point of arguing? 'But listen to me, didn't you see what else was in the drawer?'

'No, Tess. I was a bit distracted by the big bag of drugs.'

'You didn't see the pregnancy test?'

He paused, knocked from his trajectory. 'Maybe. I don't know. I'm used to seeing them around. So what?'

Already it had dawned on him, though. She saw it in how hungry his gaze had become to meet hers. She stood up, walked through the kitchen, and retrieved the two new tests from the downstairs toilet sink. She put them on the coffee table in front of him.

'Are they real?' he said.

'Yes. Of course they are.'

He stared at them for a long time before his head dropped, and he caught it in his open hands. He stayed this way for a while, face hidden in his palms while the rise and fall of his shoulders picked up pace. She sat beside him and started stroking his back.

'I know,' she said. 'I didn't believe it at first. But…' She tried a laugh. 'Shall we just stop fighting? You're going to be a dad.'

Andy stood up, ran his hand over his beard and through his hair, walked to the other side of the lounge and spun around. 'I can't believe this. It *literally* can't be real.' He addressed this to the room rather than her.

'It is real. I've done three tests now.'

He shook his head. 'But I've met someone, Tess.'

His words floated in the oppressive quiet between them, so big and important, she could practically see them. Again, she laughed, covering her mouth like it were a yawn or sneeze. 'What?'

'I've met someone else. I've been working out what to do, trying to think of the best way … the *kindest* way forward.' His hands clenched and unclenched at his sides repeatedly, and he stared at her belly. 'I can't do this, Tess.'

Despite the numbing shock spreading through her body, she managed to find some words of her own. 'I've just told you that I'm pregnant with your child, Andy. Do you not think that's something you need to sit down and contemplate a bit first? What can't you do?'

'You don't understand.'

'What? I mean … thank you for being honest about your fucking affair, which is what I presume you're confessing, and that is useful to know. But in the scheme of things, does it matter at this exact point? Might the whole baby thing be worth considering first, if what you're about to say is that you want to break up?'

He shook his head. 'I'm seeing Olivia, Tess.'

'Well … okay.' She tried to sound tough. Tried to sound unmoved. 'I could have guessed—'

'And she's pregnant, too.'

PART III

How to Kill with Kindness

THIRTY-SIX

How to Kill with Kindness

S pent too much time staring at old family photographs
today and feeling nostalgic about my accomplish-
ments. But the hospital appointment did not go well, my
darling, and I've been told I won't be around beyond the end
of the year. I'm shaken, of course. But I am grateful for the
certainty now. Because it will mean I must tie everything up
before Christmas. These next weeks will be crucial, because
now Kath has been handled, I would like to see the back of
Jayden. And now there is, of course, this child of Tessa's
to be...

THIRTY-SEVEN

Jayden

R ags asked him to take some pictures of the equestrian centre and the hospital. Get shots of the stables, and the entrances and exits, he said. And any security cameras. Jayden wasn't stupid, Rags was right about that. He knew they used ket to knock out horses. He'd seen it on TikTok. And there was only one reason a ket dealer wanted pictures of a place's security set-up and the number of horses they looked after.

But he did it. On the Sunday morning at the end of October half term, while most people were at the Kindness Sermon. Because he owed Rags. And because he liked Rags. And because it wasn't illegal to take pictures, was it? Still, he'd paused before pressing send on his phone. Twenty, thirty seconds maybe. But that was all.

Legend Kiddo! Bonus points if you can find anything else out about the security set up.

That message stumped him. He wasn't sure what more he could give Rags. A few days went by, and a few more. He was starting to hope things had moved on. But Rags called him after two weeks, asking him how he was getting on. He sounded his happy self, if a bit distracted. And he was talking so quickly, Jayden had to ask him to repeat himself more than once.

'Could you… Could you maybe ask someone?' he said. 'Someone who works there? Say you're doing a homework project on … on horse hospitals. Yeah? Could you do that? Find out about the drug deliveries for me. About alarms.'

'I can try, Rags. Yeah. Everything alright?'

'Yeah, kiddo. Course it is.'

These were bigger asks than a few photos. But he didn't want to let Rags down. So after school he walked up to the estate office and told Ruth he was writing a story for English about a vet, and was wondering if she could show him around? Ruth, surrounded by papers and looking stressed, was happy for the break. She didn't suspect a thing. He even took photos inside, of the camera positions and security doors. Of where the drugs cabinet was and where the alarm box was on the wall. She even told him the times of their weekly drug deliveries.

'The only thing I ask, Jayden,' she said afterwards, the only time she came close to acting suspicious, 'is that you let me read your story when it's done.'

He smiled and nodded, already a step of her. 'I don't really like people looking at stuff like that. But if you really want to, I will.'

A few days later, once he'd handed over all the information and photos to Rags, he made sure to cover his tracks by taking Ruth an actual story he'd written as homework. He was quite proud of deceiving a committee member in the centre of their operations, and actually burst out laughing when he later found a heart up on the tree, thanking him for sharing his lovely story.

But his laughter and joy were short lived. And when Rags messaged him to tell him he'd be in touch soon, he didn't even have time to get worried about what that meant exactly. Because Kath hadn't taken his present in the way she'd expected. And neither had Tessa. They didn't want to even play music anymore. He'd lost his cool with them, and gone home and punched his pillow in silence, threw his leather gloves in the bin. Then before he'd even had a chance to make things right again, to try and apologise for his reaction, Kath had died.

At first, he had been too stunned to react. A few days went by and all he did was listen repeatedly to one of the jams they'd recorded on his phone, replaying the bits where Kath spoke, perhaps hoping she might say something different each time. Something that would let him know she hadn't gone. Then on the third night, he was wide awake at three in the morning, unable to stop going over their last argument in his head.

He'd turned on the bedside light and walked over to his bin, which often went weeks without being emptied. But Olivia must have come in during the day, because now it was empty. He'd gone outside, tipped the general waste bin out in the front garden, and sat on the grass going through the refuse until he found the gloves. He put them on and finally started crying. Olivia had come out to comfort him, but he wanted none of it. He wanted nothing from any member of that committee.

Because she hadn't died. She'd been killed, he was certain of it. And nothing Tessa had said when he spoke to her made him feel any different, even if she still seemed in denial. The way everything had played out, from the committee trying to make it look like Tessa had wanted them to take Kath's things, right through to the nice way Ruth had treated him when he'd wanted her help with his fake homework. She'd not wanted him to suspect what they were about to do, had she? She'd been buttering him up, playing him all along.

There had been more late-night visits to Olivia lately, right before and right after Kath died, in particular. Hushed conversations late into the night. Members of the committee – he'd seen them through his window.

All the while, Rags kept trying to call him. But he couldn't deal with him now, so he let it go to voicemail each time. Because his heart had been broken, yet again. But he was also terrified that the small committee who handed out kindness prizes each year might be coming to cut his throat in the middle of the night. Coming for him, and coming for Tessa. He had to warn her. Had to tell her, so they could do something before it was too late.

A couple of days later he came home from a lame Monday at school, just wanting to nap. He'd not been sleeping and his stomach was on permanent spin cycle. Edgy already, when Olivia jumped out and yelled surprise, he nearly shat himself. She made him a pizza, which was random. While she prepared it she sang to herself softly, high and sweet. At the breakfast bar, he started eating and she gave him a little square gift, wrapped in sparkling paper.

'I'm sorry things have been so difficult lately,' she said, her hands clasped together. 'I'm… I'm hoping that things might be easier now.' She gestured that he should open the gift, which he did. It was a CD of James Blunt's *Back to Bedlam*. 'I thought we could maybe try and find some music we both liked. He's a guitarist. I know it's on Spotify, but I always liked the lyrics and artwork.'

He nodded, smiled, not wanting to hurt her feelings, said, 'Yeah. He's... I've not heard much.'

'I used to love him when I was younger.'

From upstairs he heard shifting floorboards. Both of them looked up.

'Is someone here?'

'Jayden, there's been a slight change in our circumstances. Now, I know this might be difficult news in some ways. But I'm also hoping it might be good news in other ways. But I've met someone, and I've very much fallen in love with them. And they love me too. And so, for the time being he is going to—'

'Who?'

'—stay here until the whole thing is sorted out.'

'Who is it?'

The stairwell began to creak, and he knew who it would be even before Andy came down and stood in the kitchen doorway. 'Hey, Jayden.'

Jayden had no words. He'd been right. Tessa hadn't believed him, and he'd doubted it himself, but he'd been right again. He was always right. But even given that, what the actual fuck? This orc in a Megadeth T-shirt. And Olivia. Together? What the hell was wrong with Andy? Why would anyone like him ever in their right mind leave Tessa for Olivia?

'What's happened to Tess?' he said.

'We're sorting things out,' Andy said.

'Is she staying here? In the village.'

'She's gone to her sister's for now.'

'And what about after?'

Andy glanced at Olivia.

'We don't know,' she said. 'It's early days.'

'You two.' Jayden got to his feet, unable to stop shaking his head.

'Where are you going?' Olivia said.

'I'm going to hang up a heart on the tree. Let everyone know what a kind pair you two are.'

'Jayden,' Olivia said, 'that's not a very understanding thing to say.'

'No,' he said, resenting that they'd pushed him to this. Forced him into this storm-out-like-a-little-bitch cliché. But he was otherwise powerless. What else could he do? Smack Andy one? He was a size, and he'd absolutely crush Jayden.

For a moment, though, he studied him. If he was quick enough, he could maybe get a couple of blows in first. Andy, understanding what was happening, stretched out to his full height and took a step forward. Nah, it wasn't worth it. Jayden marched to the back door, hoping to find a biting line to leave on. But it all happened too fast, and the door slammed behind him before he'd even composed a draft.

'Fucking kindness, my arse,' he said to no one.

———————

He didn't know where to go. He had no plan, and a cold rain had begun to fall. He ran to Kath's cottage, found a back window open, and climbed inside. He found a spot on the kitchen counter to sit on and warmed himself up by the heat of the gas hobs.

It had all played out the way it had done in the past. The way Kath and Eleanor Beddington had suspected it would. Kath first, now Tessa. And they had already come for him. So it was just a matter of time before they came back to finish the job.

He'd have to be even smarter now if he was going to get

out of this without a drug charge to his name. Or worse. The first thing he had to do was get rid of the bag of weed, which he still had hidden in Olivia's attic. He'd wanted to ditch it in town the day he met Rags, but there had been cameras everywhere. Then he'd been about to leave it in the tree hollow by the bus stop when he realised if someone found it there and reported it to the police, Andy might find out about it and trace it back to Jayden. He'd considered dumping it down the toilet, but worried it might block the drains or take too long to flush. He even worried about setting it on fire because the smoke might draw attention. He was probably being too cautious, but better safe than sorry. What he needed was something certain and easy to accomplish.

Once that was done, he needed to get out of Nether Appleford unscathed. He needed someone to help him. A grown-up. And really he only had two candidates. One was Tessa, the other Rags. He had no qualms anymore about overstepping that boundary with Tessa, because their days of being simply friends were already over, thanks to Kath's death. She must be suspicious that the committee might be behind Andy and Olivia getting together, and she would surely be making plans now to leave.

How incredible would it be if she took Jayden with her? And was that so out of the question? She liked him. They got on. And it wasn't like she had any other children. With Andy gone, might she even adopt him? He jumped down, laughing to himself. He couldn't get ahead of himself. As nice an idea as that was, he didn't want his heart broken.

But he could give himself a good chance. He could tell Tessa everything he'd been holding back about what had been happening to him. About Leo and the drugs. If she didn't believe in the village being after them before, she would once he was done. Then they could flee together. Maybe plan a way to bring the village down and avenge Kath's death once they were safe.

He liked that idea so much, he didn't even entertain the idea of turning to Rags. Because what sort of life awaited him in that direction?

It was the last Sunday of November, and an emergency Kindness Sermon had been called, with October to take to the stage. Olivia had wanted Jayden to come, because she was going to talk about Kath. But he had ignored her and gone back upstairs. He could barely look at her. The night before, he'd had to listen to Andy and her fucking at two in the morning. Tessa wasn't even back from her sister's yet, and they were acting like life was normal.

While the village was busy in the chapel, Jayden retrieved the weed from the attic and walked down to the Kindness Tree with it hidden under his coat. Earlier in the week, a company had come to dig out a shallow, rectangular hole by the information board. Tomorrow, a company was coming to pour concrete in the hole to form a base for the new Story Station. When he was satisfied he was alone, he climbed into the hole and used a serving spoon to dig out a patch of soil in the corner. It took longer than he'd expected. He was patting the soil down with his foot, the weed finally buried, when a shadow fell over him and his entire body went cold.

'Hi, Jayden.' He knew the voice. 'Want to come get in my car? We need to chat.'

THIRTY-EIGHT

Jayden

He followed Rags from the Kindness Tree to where he'd parked his car a bit further up The Road. It was the same one he'd always had, a little red Hyundai that smelled like old milk and oil – low key, because Rags said it didn't pay to be showy. Rags drove down the country lanes too fast, rounding blind bends without slowing down. Jayden's wrist started to hurt from gripping the door to stop himself being jostled.

'I wasn't ghosting you,' Jayden said. 'It's just a lot's been going on.'

'You don't think I'm angry, do you?' He threw his head back and laughed. 'I'm not angry. I'm just in a rush, kiddo. Time is ticking.'

'Right.'

'Tell me something, what's your long-term goal?'

'Goal?'

'You used to talk about going to university one day, yeah?'

'Yeah, I suppose.'

'You were going to play music, too.'

He shrugged. 'Yeah, maybe.'

'And how are those things going, Jayden? You making good progress towards those goals?'

'I don't know. Probably not.'

'You're old enough to hear this now, and no other fucker will tell you, but I've had enough kids like you over the years deal for me to know that when you turn eighteen, you are on your own. I know social services will make a big song and dance about supporting you to make the *transition to adulthood*, but do you think they really will? In this economy? And university? That's a rich kids' racket. Even if you got a bursary or a scholarship … you'd have to be paying for your own accommodation, too, especially with your mum out the picture. Frankly, kiddo, you're fucked. Fuh with a capital ucked.'

He turned to Rags, scowling, and said, 'Why you saying all this?'

'Why? Because it takes the fucked to know the fucked. And we are on the fucked train together.'

Jayden didn't like the edge he heard in Rags' voice. Or the way he kept punctuating things by smacking the steering wheel hard enough to jolt the car. He tried to sound calm. 'Why are *you* fucked?'

'Good question. Very good question. Well, you remember all that ket I had? That my supposed mate gave me as a parting *kindness*?'

'Yeah.'

'Yeah, well, the mug only stole it from the fucking Benton Boys, didn't he? Nicked it instead of delivering it, over some bollocks grievance, knowing he was going to off himself before they came looking.'

Jayden's internal temperature plummeted, anticipating the story's direction.

'And you know about the Bentons, don't you? Fire. Acid. They don't break bones, they crush them.' He ground his palm into the centre of the steering wheel. 'One sunny afternoon a few months back, Tommo bloody Benton, six-foot-two of him in his long coat and fucking nan glasses, turns up at my house in the middle of nowhere with your old mate Vim.'

'Vim.'

'Yeah, Vim.' Rags gave a cynical laugh. 'He had some debts with the Bentons, and your mum put him in touch with me about doing a bit of work to pay them back. Anyway, one good turn later and Vim's found out about the Bentons' missing ket. Stupid bastard thought they'd let him off if he grassed me in to them. Next thing I know, Tommo's doing a jig on him in front of me, and I spend the night burying bits of Vim in my garden.'

Jayden took a deep breath and sat up in his seat. 'He killed him?'

Rags ran a hand through his hair and the car jerked again. 'Oh, yeah. Says to me after he's just *re-establishing credibility*, which I take to mean he's showing me who's boss, and says he's really missed getting his hands dirty. But it's fine, you know, because next thing Tommo's taking his shoes off in my hall and asking to come inside. He's polite as you like, in my lounge looking at my book collection, asking what I thought of fucking *Half of a Yellow Sun*. Barefoot, kiddo! And once I've explained how I ended up with his ket, and how I ran things, he says he quite admires me. Not *really* admires, though. *Quite* admires. And he says that if I pay him back the 60K by the end of the year, he might have some use for me.'

Rags steered the car onto the motorway now, and put his foot down. The needle on the speedometer settled near 85.

'Is that why you wanted to know about the hospital? For the ket.'

'Sort of. I didn't see how I could get 60K for him in that time without knocking over a load of family vets and selling it in bulk. Anything else would take too long. And floggin' ket's what I know these days. But then you've come along, and I'm seeing this massive hospital in a village full of hippies... Only the security on the place is too much, isn't it? If that alarm goes off they'll have the police and private security there before I've even opened the drugs cupboard. Thing is, I'm not a thief. I'm a businessman, Jayden. Which means I'm risk-averse. Do you know what that means?'

Jayden did, loosening up a little bit at the possibility that Rags had softened on the idea of the hospital. 'Yeah, I mean, that's what I thought. You'd have to have someone who knew what they were doing. With, like, wire-clipping and shit.'

'Wire-clipping and shit, exactly.'

'Yeah. Unless, you had an insider.' It was out his mouth before he could stop it.

'An insider. Jayden, you really are smart, aren't you? See, that's what I was calling you about.'

'Right.'

'This is a village full of hippies. A bunch of people who want to do the right thing, yeah? The kind thing. Now, from what you've told me and what I've found out online, I think that little kindness committee oversee all the businesses in the village. Is that right?'

'Yeah.'

'And am I right in thinking that one of that committee is a copper?'

Jayden tried to swallow but couldn't. 'Yeah.'

'Is it *the* copper? The one that you nicked the drugs from?'

He paused, considered lying, but he had no idea how much research Rags had done already. And right now he wanted to stay on his good side. 'Yeah, it is.'

'So, a copper hoarding drugs. That's career-ending. And get this, I've looked him up. He's got previous. Nearly got booted for beating up a protester. Funny he's ended up in a village like that, although maybe not. Every nasty bastard in the world thinks what they're doing's kind. Anyway, so, suppose you get into his shed again, take some pictures and video for me. Then I go have a chat with him and see if he'll do me a deal. What do you think?'

Sweat broke out on Jayden's forehead. 'I... I...' He was going to have to tell him he'd lied about the drugs. And if he did that, he'd also have to tell him where he *had* got them from. And how would Rags react to that, given he'd clearly pinned all his hopes on this? 'Can I think about it a little bit?'

'Time's ticking, kiddo. Please.'

'It's just... I... I mean, I need time to plan it. Work out when to ... you know?'

Rags started nodding slowly and winding the string of his purple teething necklace around his finger. 'The thing is kid, if this works out ... I'm going to need some help in the future. You know. Like we talked about back in the day. Only better. Not even that far in the future. Whether it's working for the Bentons, or I'm on my own. But maybe you come live with me. You have a room in my flat. Earn some money. Get to go to uni. Maybe you have something like a future, yeah?'

Jayden nodded. 'Just, I just need to plan and ... think.'

For a while Rags was silent. Then with a nod, he said, 'I'll call you. Pick up this time.'

'Definitely.' Jayden wished he could think of another plan, one that wouldn't involve outing his lie. Perhaps there might be a way to catch out Leo in some way that would do the same job as the drugs. 'Why do you need to use the hospital anyway, Rags? Why don't you just ... tell the copper to get you 60K by the end of the week?'

'Nah,' Rags said. 'That hospital is a money factory, Jayden. And I know for a fact the Bentons are on the look-out for a new ket set-up. Tommo wants to get his hands dirty – well, here's the dirt. And if we had an insider, I don't need sixty grand. A money factory.' He blew air into his cheeks. 'I'll be indispensable. And you, kiddo, can get grubby with us, too.'

THIRTY-NINE

Jayden

R ags dropped him off at the end of The Road. 'I'll be in touch soon.'

'Can you give me a week?' Jayden said, and after some thought, Rags nodded.

'I want an answer next Monday, kiddo.'

That was fine by him, because hopefully by then Tessa would be back from her sister's. And despite there being something oddly appealing about the solidity of Rags's otherwise frightening offer, his heart was set on Tessa. When he pictured a future with her, they were jamming together in some smart suburban house with a studio. Central heating, hugs and, of course, the Epiphone. When he pictured his future with Rags, it was mouldy walls and a charity-shop ukulele.

Tessa came home on Friday, and Jayden went over as soon as he could. He knew that she wouldn't be in the best frame of mind, given all that had happened, but she'd be pleased to see him. To have him in her corner. He planned to really look after her. Make her beans on toast or something. Make her laugh.

Only that wasn't how it went down. When Tessa opened the door, she looked... distant. A bit annoyed, too. She was short and sharp with him, and the warmth he'd anticipated, especially after how she'd been after Kath had died, just wasn't there. She didn't listen to him at all. In fact, she called what he was saying a conspiracy theory. Actually shouted at him in the end.

And on his lonely walk home he sensed it, his future path hardening like the concrete base of the Story Station. What a mug he'd been for thinking things could be any other way. That anyone in this world would want to invest in him without getting something back for themselves. He wasn't attractive. He wasn't funny or charming. He wasn't talented. And what smarts he had were only good for one thing, which was what he ought to focus on now. Leo had been right, he was economy.

———

Still, he waited over the weekend for her to message him. An apology, maybe. Just in case. But nothing came. So when Rags called him, he picked up first time and said, 'I'm in.' Then, once he'd asked for a few more days to come up with a decent plan, he took the Epiphone from his room and left it against Tessa's door.

Now all he needed to do was work out a way to get Rags what he wanted. He had the faintest outline of something that might work. A way to use Nether Appleford's kindness against them. Admittedly, it wasn't a very kind idea. And he wasn't entirely sure he could really do what was necessary. But what was kindness anyway? It would be kind for Jayden, and for

Rags. And bringing down Nether Appleford would avenge Kath. Was that kind, or was it just righteous?

On the way by the Kindness Tree he stopped to read the hearts.

Andy, for going above and beyond for me.

He recognised Olivia's handwriting. Me. Not me and my family. Me.

Olivia helped Maria with her maths homework. Thank you!

Hypocrites. Bloody hypocrites, the pair of them. He studied the others, his lip curling.

Ruth is the best listener in the village.

October was very nice for buying my charity cookies.

Dev, for getting me back on my feet!

Leo is the best guitar teacher.

Aaron always closes on time, honest ;)

He wanted to burn the tree down. Stand here and wait for them all to come running out, hands over their mouths and tears in their eyes. But he'd be sent away if he did that. If he helped Rags, then at least he benefited. At least he got some sort of future.

Kindness? His arse. Fuck Olivia, and Andy, and Nether Appleford. And, most of all, fuck the stupid committee. They were all part of this, and they all deserved what they got.

FORTY

Tessa
_____

What Maddy said was, 'So, what are you going to do?'
What she meant was, *Are you going to keep it?*

The two of them sat in Maddy's lamplit lounge at two in the morning, baby Juliet in her mother's arms feeding. But even though the consensus – arrived at quickly and reinforced in the four days she'd been staying with Maddy – was that Andy was a pig and a bastard and a let-down and disappointingly typical, the thought of *not* having the baby hadn't crossed Tessa's mind. Not even at her most angry and exhausted.

'So, let's imagine my trust isn't entirely shattered,' Tessa said, keeping her voice low so as not to disturb Bhav asleep upstairs, 'and I meet someone I like enough to even want a baby with. By the time I know that he's not a psycho or a bigamist … I'm already, what, two, three years further down the line? Face it, if I was struggling to conceive before, it's hardly going to be easy then. Besides, I don't feel like the baby is *his*. I know it *is* his. But I just already feel it's *mine*. Do you understand?'

Maddy smiled, because of course she understood. 'You'll make whatever work. I'm sure.'

'Yeah.' Tessa shared none of her sister's certainty.

'Not that we care necessarily, but what do you think Andy wants?'

The sound of his name caused sorrow to sweep through her. Memory fragments jostled for attention. His oversized jumper slung over a sofa back. The slightly spicy smell of his hair after work that she'd always thought of as the smell of electricity. His expression the morning he'd seen that last negative test.

'Well ... before I left, he said he wants to be part of the child's life. But I'm sure he'd rather I not have it. It's going to be a right mess.'

'Yeah, for him.' Maddy gulped from her glass of orange juice to hide what was a sincerely angry expression. 'And we're going to make sure he meets all his obligations. It can't fall on you. Did you talk about money?'

'We didn't talk about much really. I will, don't worry. I think I just want to let the dust settle now.'

Maddy nodded, but Tessa knew she was humouring her. Her sensible, science-minded sister wanted to talk about practicalities. About money, and visitations, and about where Tessa would live now. But Tessa and Andy had made short-term plans, and now she didn't want to think about anything beyond tomorrow. She wanted to wear her grief first and let it stretch to her shape. After a decade she didn't know the first thing about being alone anymore.

———

Four days soon stretched to a week, and Tessa knew she was outstaying her welcome. Maddy was understandably exhausted, and as well as dealing with her hopeless sister, she was still replying to emails from the lab despite her maternity leave. So, it wasn't surprising that her patience was starting to fray.

But who else could Tessa turn to? All her eggs had long ago been deposited in the Andy basket. On the train up to Maddy's she'd flicked through her phone contacts and realised just how weird it would be to message any of these people for even a quick drink.

After sixth form, she'd never had another group of friends. Once you reached a certain age, you stopped having almost everything in common with your peers. People got stranger, more complicated, and often not in a good way. And staying in touch with people for the sake of it … well, she'd considered that another mug's game. Anyone you lost had likely always been an acquaintance. Tessa had kept her world small because good people, *people that got it*, were so, so rare. Better to focus on the people that matter. People like Andy, or so she'd thought.

But she couldn't stay with Maddy indefinitely. Waning goodwill aside, Maddy's resemblance to Olivia increasingly nagged at her. It made her reconsider things Andy had said about her sister over the years. Had he secretly pined for her after all?

So, she left for Nether Appleford by train and taxi, despite Bhav's offer to drive her back. The cottage had been cleared of Andy's things, as they'd arranged. He was moving in with Olivia, while continuing to cover half the rent on the cottage until Tessa had been paid her film commission and could get a place of her own elsewhere. He'd left up photos of the pair of them, which frankly irritated her. They'd been his as much as they'd been hers. She sat down on the sofa they'd ordered together online after moving in and let the inevitable tears come. Not as overwhelmed as she'd expected, she eventually went to the kitchen to unpack the bags of shopping she'd picked up on the way home.

She'd had to put the shopping on her credit card because the debit card had been declined, so now she went online to check their joint account. It was empty.

'What the...'

Nervous, she located Andy's number into her phone. But she didn't press the call button. She already knew why he'd done it. He'd been the only one putting money in since she'd stopped her day job. Everything in there was technically his. And while taking it out this way wasn't in the spirit of what they'd discussed, was she really going to beg him to subsidise her now?

Her grip on the phone tightened. He didn't believe she was going to get that commission, did he? That had to be it. After all, he knew Tessa had no savings. She'd put them all into their IVF. Maybe he didn't trust her not to stiff him out of revenge. Could it be that? Really? Even after all these years together.

She felt nauseous. She placed the phone down gently, got off the stool and walked into the lounge. She took the photographs of them both down, took them into the kitchen and, one by one, smashed them on the tiled floor. Glass and wood skittered in all directions. She took the many mugs they'd bought as gifts for one another over the years – the System of a Down one, the crap one she'd made for Andy in a pottery class, the one he'd bought her with their dishwasher-faded faces on – and destroyed them.

The shrapnel had only just come to rest on the tiles when the doorbell rang. She stood still, her chest rising and falling rapidly. The bell rang again. And then again. Closing the kitchen door behind her, she answered, giving no fucks about her appearance – let whoever it was see the damage.

It was Jayden. 'Oh, hi.' Embarrassed, she lifted her sleeve to dry her face and sniffed to clear her nose.

'Do you know he's moved into Olivia's?' he said.

'I know.'

'What a cunt.' Tessa laughed. 'How are you feeling?'

'I'm okay.'

'I'm fuming, Tess. I won't lie. Can I come in? To talk.'

She looked back in the lounge, searching for an excuse not to let him inside. She didn't have the energy to keep herself contained around him, and as nice as it was to see a friendly face, that wasn't fair to him.

'I can make a sick beans on toast if you've got beans,' Jayden said. 'And toast.'

'Thanks, Jayden. I really appreciate that. But I really need to sort a lot of things out. Being alone is probably best for that.'

He nodded like he understood, and she believed he did. At least partially. How much did he know, though? Had he heard about the pregnancies yet?

'I hate her,' he said. 'I know what she's done for me, Tess, but she's behind all this. She's done this to you. Her and that … committee.'

'Who, Olivia?'

'Yeah. She's been … making all those electric problems in the house, I swear. And then all they'd do is talk when he came over, so he'd have to come back again another day.'

Tessa said nothing, offering him only a shrug. She wasn't ready to hear the details of their affair yet. 'These things happen in life, Jayden. It's complicated.'

'Did you cheat on him?'

Taken aback, she said, 'Not that it's your business, but no.'

'Well then, fuck them. I hate cheats.'

'Jayden … you really don't need to swear so much.'

He shook his head, and it seemed like he might say he'd

271

told her so. He didn't though. Instead he said, 'I don't know how, but *they* did this to you. It's like Kath and you were saying. They get rid of the people they don't want. That's why they're trying to make out it was your fault for stopping them that day.'

'Okay, Jayden…' She couldn't deal with this now. She just didn't have the mental space.

'And they killed Kath.'

'Can we catch up another day? A lot's happened and I need some processing time.'

He took a step backward, reading her mood. 'Yeah, of course, Tess. But can we talk first? Seriously. Like, are you going to stay in the village? Because I think you need to just go. If they killed Kath, what if—'

'Jayden, stop it. Please.'

Frustrated, his mouth formed a hard line and he shifted his weight. 'I need to tell you something. It's sort of about the committee, but—'

'I don't have any options, Jayden,' she said, voice raised. 'I have to stay here for now. I can't afford anywhere else. And I don't need you in my head with this … conspiracy bollocks.'

He moved his head from side to side, weighing up whether he should say something else. Then all the hardness fell from his face, and he looked down at the floor. 'Fine. It doesn't matter.'

'Jayden—'

'No, my bad. I'll see you around, Tess.'

Once he'd gone she went out to her studio, fully intending to distract herself with work. It was either that, or get the whisky out. It was better out here. It had less Andy in it. But what Jayden said wouldn't stop tumbling around her mind, and she was annoyed she'd lost control and upset him. It wasn't that she actually believed that Kath had been killed, or that there had been something more Machiavellian to her and Andy's break-up. And yet, was it that implausible? It had been like Andy was possessed by the end. A walking mouthpiece for the village and the committee. Like he'd been worked on. And she'd seen how October had twisted her words to try and get her way about Kath. And how they had all tried making it seem like Tessa's fault.

So why not throw a little *Dangerous Liaisons* shit into the mix? Why not murder?

Unable to stop herself, she typed Olivia Chambers in a search engine, much as she'd intended to do weeks before Andy had made her second-guess herself.

Incredibly though, she was clean. Spotless, in fact. All she found in Google's history was some past articles relating to her work in a Portsmouth school, a flawless and up-to-date LinkedIn account, and a Facebook page. But that was strange. All the other committee members had blots on their record, yet here was Olivia, with nothing at all.

Tessa found Olivia's Facebook page. She had no privacy settings in place, and her whole profile was visible. To Tessa's relief, she didn't immediately see a selfie of Olivia and Andy. She wasn't without tact, at least. In fact, flicking through her timeline, Tessa found that in the last two years Olivia had posted little but lame quotes about kindness and forgiveness on coloured backgrounds.

It was apparent why. Before then she had been with Jamie, and pictures of the two of them could be found by scrolling down far enough. For a moment, her heart stopped when she saw the two of them grinning at the camera over a pizza. Jamie looked even more like Andy here. She kept scrolling, and the more she did the more she cursed herself for not being more suspicious. She should have sought out this page before, back when she was looking for pictures of Jamie.

But she hadn't, because it had been beneath her then.

Because even though something was off, she'd been trying so hard to be a less suspicious person here, so she'd dismissed her gut again. This place. This bloody place.

She didn't stop scrolling. That was how she found a photo from five years ago that made her brow furrow. And another from seven years ago that chilled her heart.

The one from twelve years ago made her go to the kitchen and open the whisky.

Each photo she found depicted Olivia with her *then* partner, something Tessa had established to her satisfaction with some detective work on other posts around the time. Up to and including Jamie, Olivia had had four boyfriends going right back to her university days.

But here was the thing: each one, with or without a beard, had the same look. Tall, strong, something of the stereotypical Viking about them. Tessa couldn't quite believe it. Olivia didn't just have a type. She was a collector.

FORTY-ONE

Tessa

S he sat smelling the whisky. Touched it with her tongue but didn't sip. She moved some things around in the cottage to make it feel less like the place where she'd lived with Andy. Her soulmate. Her rock. If she was going to have to stay here, even for a small amount of time, she didn't want to give the impression she was waiting for him to change his mind – especially to herself.

That was out of the question. Even given his child was growing inside her, his betrayal was irreversible. Wasn't it? How would their relationship ever move forward now? Practically. Tessa and Olivia's child would both be the same age, and they would of course meet. Play together. Technically be siblings. She would end up mothering a walking scar. And she and Olivia would be bound together. For life. God, it was enough to drive someone to murder.

She cried. Sniffed some more whisky. Could the fumes hurt the baby, too? She shrugged. Maybe she should just cane the lot.

Money – that's what she needed. And quickly. That needed

to be her focus if she was going to get out of here. Stop all this wallowing and get it together before Olivia and the committee upped her rent. Get her and the baby out of this ... benign trap. Ha, was that what she'd called it? It was a Venus fly trap, more like. Slowly devouring the best of her, leaving behind the ... husky bits. Husky, was that right? Husky was how Maddy once described Andy. That was funny.

She poured some whisky into her mouth before she started crying again. Held it in there, gargled with it. Then she spat it out on the kitchen tiles to join the photo shrapnel. Tomorrow's problem.

The answer was her film score. Because that's all she could control now. She couldn't do anything about the committee murdering Kath, or Olivia stealing Andy, whether or not she felt, or believed, those things to be true, whether or not she did vaguely sense predation nearby, something coming for her, footsteps encroaching, rhythmic as a chant: *Just Be Kind. Just be Kind.* What the hell could she do, Jayden? Nothing, is what.

But the film score! That was close to being money. That was work almost done. One last push, and she could get a definitive answer from this Noah guy. She ambled out to her studio, her beautiful, necessary studio. Yes, another reason she couldn't move yet. She booted up the computer and listened to what she had composed already. Turned it up obnoxiously loud. So cosmic. So strange. They were bound to say yes; she wouldn't have got to this stage if not. And if she did get it, other work was bound to follow. Work she could do at home with a small baby.

Because if they didn't say yes, she was a tiny bit fucked. The dribs and drabs from her other work wouldn't be enough to move, put down a deposit, and get everything ready for life as a mother. She'd have to go back to her old job. That might necessitate returning to London – which would be expensive for a single mum.

She nodded along to her music. It was good stuff, and this *was* a good plan. She still needed more voices, though. Long sections of speech with different energies, maybe even conversations between two people, or whole crowds, that she could play with and create different effects. All she had were samples of herself, Kath, and Jayden. The crowd samples she'd found online didn't really work. They didn't offer enough control or variety. She really ought to have got a recording of the chatter at a Kindness Sermon. She wished she'd thought of it before all this had happened. Never mind, perhaps she could find another crowd somewhere. At a church or at another village's fete. She could surely find one online.

Feeling a fraction more positive, she ordered some perimeter microphones online and decided to reward this progress with some food. She put two pieces of slightly stale bread in the toaster and went to sit on the doorstep in the sun. But when she pulled open the door a chest-high object fell towards her. She jumped back and it struck the floor with a heavy thud. It was a bass-guitar case. And inside was the Epiphone she'd given Jayden.

FORTY-TWO

Tessa

E arly the following week, someone knocked at her door while she was on a lunch break. Hoping it might be Jayden, wanting to apologise to him for having been so abrupt and shouty the other day, and wishing she'd seen him over the weekend, she ran through the cottage. But standing on the doorstep was Ruth, and Tessa's abdomen tightened.

'I'm so sorry to disturb you.' She held out a Pyrex dish covered in clingfilm. 'It's a lasagne.'

'Oh, thank you,' Tessa said, taking it from her.

'Yes.' She rubbed her now free hands on the side of her jumper. 'I'm just... I just wanted to say I was very sad to hear about everything that has happened with you and Andy. I'm ... just devastated for you, really.'

Tessa had no idea exactly how much of the story Ruth knew, but the idea of the villagers gossiping about the whole mess broke her out in an anxious sweat. She wanted her gone, but she summoned up just enough politeness to make sure Ruth had nothing juicy to take back to the committee. 'Well ... thank you, Ruth.'

'It's mortifying.' She shook her head. 'How could he? I can't get my head around it.'

'Thank you.'

'I actually came…' She glanced quickly behind her. 'I also wanted to apologise. Could I come in for a moment?'

'Actually, Ruth, I'm—'

'I won't be long, I promise.'

'Okay, but I've got a lot a work on.' Reluctantly Tessa stepped aside, and Ruth came into the lounge and sat down.

'I can well imagine. The committee actually asked me to *respectfully* enquire if you were still interested in the Story Station, but I'm going to guess that's not on your priority list right now.'

Tessa smiled and shook her head. 'Ruth, I really don't—'

'I totally understand. And good. It's their own fault anyway. If Olivia hadn't botched the initial numbers and left it all for me to sort… Never mind. Tessa … I just wanted to say that I've been feeling dreadful about the incident with the letter. The one I wrote for October.'

'Oh. That all seems … a long time ago now.'

'She can be very forceful when she wants to be. I know she might not seem that way.'

'Well … I can believe it.'

'It isn't the first time I've been uncomfortable with something the committee have asked of me. But when you work for someone … you can't always rock the boat.'

Tessa sat down on the other sofa, just a little bit curious now. 'What sort of things do you mean?'

'Well, I don't really want to get into that so much. But Tessa, I wanted you to know that I'm sorry. Because I thought, personally, what you were doing with Kath and Jayden was … a lovely thing.'

The remark caught her by surprise and her throat tightened. 'Uh ... well, obviously, you can't please everyone.'

'No. No, that's true. But I think, looking back on it all, given what's happened, I think all of it should have been handled differently.' She glanced up at the window, like someone might be watching her. She seemed tense and spoke in a hushed voice. 'And Tessa, I don't think someone should be taken to task for asking questions. That's just how I was brought up, and it's why we're not all speaking German now, frankly. It would perhaps do for some of our younger committee members to remember that.'

What to make of this small, earnest woman? She was October's dogsbody, and might well be here on committee business. And yet her unease and anger appeared real.

'I just think music is a wonderful thing, Tessa. It certainly seemed to help the boy with settling here. I really didn't think October ought to have meddled there. How is he coping?'

Tessa grimaced at the memory of his reaction to her yelling at him. 'I've been away, so I've not really seen him.'

Ruth nodded. 'Well, that's a shame. That is definitely a shame. You know ... he came to see me recently. I don't think he was in a good place.'

'What happened?'

'He was just asking some very unusual questions.' She considered something before shaking her head. 'You have enough to worry about at the moment. Let me leave you in peace. You know where I am if you need me. I hope you enjoy the lasagne. I know you must be busy at the moment, so I thought having a prepared meal would get you back some time.'

Tessa thanked her again and walked with her to the door. And while she wanted to ask more about Jayden, she held back. Something about her visit didn't seem right.

That evening, hungry, she took out Ruth's lasagne from the fridge. She put it on the counter and removed the plastic wrapping. She put her nose to it. It smelled good. Which was a shame. Because she trusted Ruth about as far as she could throw her. She opened a new compostable bag and tipped the entire thing into it.

FORTY-THREE

Tessa

Despite her concerns about Ruth, she wanted to hear what she had to say about Jayden. The following evening after work she walked over to Ruth's cottage and knocked on the door, a pang of sorrow in her chest on seeing her old car in the drive. There shouldn't have been space in Tessa's brain for the boy right now, with all that was happening, yet the upsetting return of the bass guitar kept nagging her. The whole ket thing, and his belief that the committee were *after her*... Those things were her fault. She'd built up his confidence and shared all her stupid thoughts about kindness with him. Then, her being careless when talking to Kath about the village's history that day had sent him into this conspiracy spiral. She owed him her consideration, and if he was in trouble now, she needed to know.

And if Ruth *was* up to some scheme on behalf of the committee, it wasn't a bad thing for Tessa to play along with her friendly advances while she was stuck here in the village. Forewarned was forearmed. Keep your enemies close, and all of that. But it also wasn't entirely out of the question that recent events had actually made Ruth want to turn on the committee and defect, was it? Or at least reach out to Tessa to let her know not all of the committee saw things the same way. She had seemed uncomfortable with the committee's actions that day outside of Kath's. And if she genuinely wanted to ally herself with Tessa, that could only be a good thing.

Ruth answered the door with a surprised smile and very quickly smuggled Tessa inside. Her cottage wasn't fusty the way Tessa had imagined it – the very opposite, in fact. White surfaces gleamed, unencumbered by clutter. Hints of personality shone from framed modernist prints and record sleeves on the walls. Quietly, Billie Holiday sang from two speakers set atop a polished upright piano.

At Ruth's breakfast bar Tessa accepted a tap water, and thanked Ruth for the food and the apology. 'I feel like I should put up a heart for you, maybe,' Tessa said, watching Ruth's face carefully.

Ruth waved her hands. 'Oh no, please don't. I don't want the inquisition from October.'

Had Tessa just seen a trace of fear in her eyes? She smiled, to let her know she thought she understood. The room fell silent.

'I love Billy Holiday,' Tessa said.

'Do you? She's wonderful, isn't she?'

'Do you play piano, then?'

Ruth laughed. 'Not at all. I used to try to sing once upon a time...' She shook her head.

'Really?'

'A long, long time ago. Nothing but a Nina Simone wannabe, really.'

'I love a bit of Nina.'

'Well ... who doesn't? I used to practise for hours trying to copy her intonation. Neighbours must have thought I was a lunatic.'

'Why don't you anymore?'

'It's not really the same without an accompaniment, is it?'

'And no one in the village could help with that?'

'I'm too busy these days, Tessa. Too busy and out of practice. Not that I wasn't a little jealous of Jayden and Kath getting to use your wonderful studio.'

The remark gave Tessa pause. Had she seen Tessa's studio before, other than when she'd first shown them around? How did she know it was wonderful? Likely it had just been a throwaway remark, informed only by what Tessa had told her on that first day. But the way she'd said it made it seem like she'd seen it. But Tessa wouldn't overthink it.

'You'd have been welcome to join us,' she said, 'if I'd known you sang.'

'Would I?'

She nodded. 'Of course. Actually, Jayden was why I popped over. I wanted to just ask a bit more about why you were worried about him. You mentioned he'd said something to you?'

'Ah, yes. I'm sorry about that. I'm not entirely sure my imagination isn't getting the better of me. Young people are something of a mystery to me. All it was, was that October spotted him walking around the equestrian centre taking pictures of the security cameras. This was before Kath passed, so a while ago now. But then recently he came up to the offices to ask me to show him around the horse hospital because he was writing a homework story about a vet.'

'Did you not believe him?'

'He showed me the story afterwards, and the mark he'd received. But having heard about his background, and some of the people his mother was involved with, it did concern me that he was asking a lot of questions about the security systems and such. How the drugs were delivered and monitored.'

'Oh. But he showed you the story.'

'He did. And I likely wouldn't have given it another thought. Except … the Sunday before last, I was too busy to make it to the Kindness Sermon, the one they held for Kath, much to my shame. And when I looked out my window, I saw Jayden getting into a car with an older man. Someone I'd never seen before. And Tess, I'm not very experienced in this area in any way, but to me, he looked like a drug dealer.'

FORTY-FOUR

Tessa

She thanked Ruth for sharing what she'd seen and heard, and tried to reassure her that it was likely all innocent.

'I'll check in with him, though,' she said.

'Thank you, Tessa. And I meant what I said to you yesterday. I think you and the music, they were good things in that boy's life.'

Once home, Tessa knew she needed to speak to Jayden as soon as possible, find out who this man was and what he was trying to get Jayden to do. He had to be the person who'd got Jayden the ket, didn't he? And it didn't take a genius to work out why a ket dealer might want know all about the security set-up at a horse hospital. But she couldn't face going around to Olivia's. Or *Olivia and Andy's*, as it now was. God, had he even been trying to tell her something the other day? And she'd shut him down cold. What an idiot! She sent him a message, contrite and heartfelt, telling him she was feeling more like herself and wanted him to come over to talk.

But even though the message sent, every time she checked

it was still marked as unread. And when she tried calling him the following lunchtime, it went straight to voicemail.

What could she do? She would have to wait for him to be ready now. She couldn't make him get back to her. She just hoped that in the meantime he didn't do anything stupid.

Even though her new perimeter mics had arrived, once Tessa looked at local events online she'd been overwhelmed by a sense of agoraphobia. She simply didn't have it in her to ask a group of strangers for permission to record them. Reluctantly, she resigned herself to compiling strangers' voices from copyright-free compilations. She briefly considered using her recording of Jayden and Kath again, but after listening to a section of them jokingly talking about how much they loved her when she'd briefly left the room, she'd decided it was too much. Strangers' voices would have to do.

The work kept her mind busy. Whenever she stopped, though, her attention would snap back to her predicament. The loneliness of it. The inescapability. It was exhausting, and by early evening she was ready to sleep. She was thinking of knocking off early, when Ruth came over again. To check on her, she said, and to bring another meal.

Tessa could tell from her body language that she was angling to come in, so reluctantly she stood aside. Once she'd deposited another lasagne in the fridge, not questioning that Tessa had seemingly eaten her last one in a day, she asked Tessa if she'd spoken to Jayden.

'I don't think he's talking to me at the moment.'

'Oh, why not?'

'It's complicated.'

Ruth frowned, and walked around to sit on the sofa

beneath the window. Tessa's guitar was on the other sofa, and she stared at it for a moment. 'That is a shame. Although, I suppose with everything else going on, you probably don't want to be doing additional mothering.'

The corner of Tessa's mouth rose at the unusual phrasing. Additional mothering – so *did* she know about the baby? That she hadn't specifically mentioned it in their last encounters had made her think Andy and Olivia were keeping that part of the break-up private. Perhaps not, though. She didn't like that idea at all, but perhaps she was overreacting. 'I'll keep trying.'

'One of the committee heard him having an animated conversation on his phone the other day down by the Kindness Tree,' Ruth said. 'And Olivia told us he hasn't been the same since Andy moved in, understandably. I just wonder… Would it help if I spoke to him, perhaps?'

Tessa shrugged. 'I … honestly don't know.' Given the way Jayden felt about the committee, Tessa didn't think it would.

'It's just… I understand it's difficult for you at present to go over there and knock on the door. But if I went…'

'You could try.'

'It's just, I had my thinking cap on – dangerous, I know – and you see, I know you were going to do something at the Christmas fete with Kath, weren't you?'

'We were, yes.'

'So, this is probably a silly idea, but perhaps I could say to Jayden that you and I were planning something for the fete. To honour Kath. And that we would like him to join us, maybe? Would that work? It could bring you back together in a natural way.'

'I…' She couldn't help the puzzled smile that appeared on her face. 'Is that something you want to actually do, Ruth?'

'We could try, couldn't we?' Ruth's hands, clasped on her lap, were shaking ever so slightly.

The problem was, she still didn't trust Ruth. As much as she wanted a friend now, she couldn't shake the feeling that this was part of some village plan. Perhaps to get close to her, to find out what she was thinking. It was the same logic she was using in humouring Ruth. If she was up to something, being friendly might cause her to slip up.

'Suppose we did,' Tessa said, 'wouldn't it upset October and Olivia?'

Ruth looked her in the eyes. In the window's light her greying hair appeared thick and glossy, yet her face looked tired. Worn down. 'I have worked for October a long time. If she can't forgive me this indulgence, I'm perhaps not as important to her as I've always assumed. And perhaps, after recent events here, that's not as important to me as it once was either.'

'Oh. Right.'

She lowered her voice and leaned forward. 'Tessa ... I *know* you know about Nether Appleford now. About what she's like. How the committee *really* works. And I really do think we'd be safer as a unit now.'

Tessa's breath caught. She knew she had to be careful here. 'I don't know anything, really.'

'Do you know about October's brother?' Ruth asked. Tessa shook her head. 'He would have inherited the estate, despite being younger than her. He killed himself shortly after his father died, meaning the estate went to October.'

Tessa waited, but Ruth stared into space. 'What are you saying?'

'Nothing at all. Other than October gets what she wants. He was hoping to sell the estate to pay off his debts, but when he found out about *Nether Appleford's* debts, that was it for him. She was there when it happened. The only other person in his house. She told me she spent the night discussing options with him, and he'd simply gone to bed and never returned.'

'That's awful.'

'When she told me, I said the same. But her view was, everything worked out for the best.'

Tessa closed her eyes. 'How does the committee really work, Ruth?'

'Just that she gets what she wants. That she knows how to get that.'

'How would she do that?'

Ruth sighed. 'Some years ago she asked me to spread a rumour among the committee. A rumour that she was unwell and might not have long left. She asked me to say that her plan, given she had no heir, was to hand the estate to the kindest person on the committee.'

Tessa huffed a surprised little laugh. Of course, all the committee would do every bonkers thing October thought was kind, if it meant inheriting this whole place. 'Did she mean it?'

Again, Ruth shrugged. 'I don't know. Probably.'

'Is she dangerous, Ruth? Am *I* in danger?'

Her eyes widened, and she shook her head aggressively. 'Oh no. Tessa, no, I don't want you to think that. No, I would never have encouraged you to move here if I believed this place was dangerous. No. What I'm trying to say is that October doesn't always get things right. And that the consequences of her very narrow view of what kindness is can be... No.' She stood up, and gave a phony-looking smile that she dropped after a few seconds. 'Just that we shouldn't be afraid to stand up for ourselves here. That's all I meant. You aren't in any danger.'

FORTY-FIVE

Tessa

Not more than an hour after Ruth left, the rest of the committee started visiting her.

Dev came first, arriving with a gift of vegetable curry. Like Ruth, he was full of regret and sadness about what had happened with Andy and Olivia.

'What you need to know,' he said once he'd worked his way inside, 'is that we will make sure you get the best possible support for the baby. Our surgery has a superb midwife, and she lives in the next village along. And we actually have one of the health visitors here in the village, too.'

Tessa's jaw muscles tightened. So there it was. They *did* know about her pregnancy. Oliva and Andy had said something after all. How bloody dare they. 'I didn't know...' She shook her head. 'Well, thanks, Dev, but I'm really not sure yet if I'm staying here or not.'

'Oh no? Well, that would be a shame. But obviously ... yes, you must do what's right for you. And until you leave, I'll personally make sure that whatever you choose to do, you have the absolute best support.'

'Thank you, Dev. That's great.'

'Have you … given much thought to it all?'

'To what?'

'To what you might do?'

Tessa's eyes narrowed. 'I'm not sure I follow.'

He leaned towards her and dropped his voice, and the smell of his citric aftershave caught in the back of her throat. 'Look, I'm not judgemental, okay? Let's be real. I know it can't be easy, what with Andy and Olivia. I can't even imagine how you are going to work all that out between you. What I'm saying is, if you want to go ahead with it, and you're willing to face all that complication, we'll be there for you. Okay? But if you went another way … well, there's no judgement here. I could support that, too. And it would be understandable, okay?'

Tessa took a moment to compose herself, one hand reflexively moving to her stomach. 'Well … I'm going to have the baby. That's decided.'

Dev grinned at her now, and she saw a bead of sweat on his forehead. 'Sure. Of course.'

She wished she could have recorded his exact words, because later, when she called Maddy in a panic, she wasn't entirely able to convince her that Dev sounded like he was trying to encourage an abortion.

The following day Benedita and Aaron came over, little Lucas with them, handing Tessa a giant casserole dish and some bottles of non-alcoholic ale at the door before coming inside.

'We just wanted you to know, that we don't take sides,' Benedita said. 'And that this must be incredibly difficult for you. The village will support you in whatever way we can.'

'That's great to hear,' Tessa said. 'And I appreciate that.'

'You know, whatever you decide. If you want to keep it. If you don't. I can't imagine how difficult that decision must be.'

'This isn't a judgemental place,' Aaron said, apparently unaware that even if she didn't want the baby, he would be the last person she would want to speak to about it.

'You're both very kind.'

Leo came over next. He handed over a box of chocolates and some flowers. She didn't let him in. She stood behind the door. He went through the script, the sorrys, the stuff about how much the village would help her.

'No sides,' he said with entirely the wrong kind of smile.

She waited, braced, for the inevitable. And it eventually came: 'I think everyone would be in your corner if you didn't want to go through with it, by the way. After what he's done, who could blame you? If you're worried about what people would think here ... you're in good hands. It's all about choice here.'

'Oh really,' Tessa said, 'that's good to hear. How kind of you to say that.'

His smile softened into something more human, indicating her sarcasm had sailed over his head.

After Tessa closed the door on him, she threw the chocolates away, as she had done the casserole and even the ale. It was paranoid, but fuck it. Paranoids didn't get poisoned.

'It's a small village,' Maddy said that night, 'so I know it sounds funny, but maybe they're genuinely worried you'd think they might judge you. It's possible it's coming from a good place. Maybe.'

She told her then, about all of it. They'd been speaking regularly since the break-up, Maddy checking in almost daily. But up until now all she'd told Maddy was that Nether Appleford was a bad fit. Now she told her about Kath's stories, and Eleanor, and what she'd found out about members of the committee. She told her about the conversation in October's office and what happened at Kath's cottage. Finally, she told her about what she'd found on Olivia's Facebook page.

When she was done, Maddy sighed, and the line remained silent.

'I know how it sounds,' Tessa said. 'I know I've just thrown a load of random parts at you and asked you to make—'

'You need to get out of there.'

Tessa fell silent. She moved the phone across to her other ear. 'Do you think?'

'Yes. You need to leave. Pack your things and come to us. We'll sort it all out from here.'

'I can't, Maddy. I can't do it to you. I'm working on moving, I promise. I have a plan.'

Maddy paused. 'The film thing?'

'Yes.'

Another pause, followed by a sigh. 'I trust what you're saying, Tess. I trust your instinct about this. But you need to get out of there.'

Tessa didn't want to argue with her. She couldn't leave, not until she'd finished her work. Not until she'd given herself the best chance of getting back on her feet financially. But Maddy believed in her. She trusted her. Dear God, how much she'd needed to hear that. And it wouldn't be long now. Her work on the score was so close to being done. If only the interruptions would stop.

October came last, right at the end of the week. She brought no gifts. She brought only a sympathetic face and a desire to come in and talk. Tessa supposed this would be the last of them – she certainly wasn't expecting a friendly visit from Olivia at any point. So despite feeling queasy with morning sickness, she acquiesced.

'We're all very upset about what happened,' October said, and took a sip from the cup of tea she'd suggested Tessa make for her.

'Thank you,' Tessa said, a low-level fear causing her voice to sound weak and breathy.

'I understand that right now you must be all over the place. But don't feel like there is any pressure for you to leave the village. Ruth tells me that might be the case, and that you may not be able to complete the Story Station music. But we support everyone equally here.'

'I'm not… I really don't think that it's a good idea for me to be in the same village as my ex-partner and his new girlfriend. Especially with us both having babies.'

October nodded. 'I'm sure you've thought it all through. But I just meant that as a community, there wouldn't be any favouritism shown if you did decide to stay. I have to say, my heart is with you, Tessa, because there is so much to consider. It's so complex, isn't it?'

'Sorry, what's complex, October?'

'Knowing the kindest thing to do. So many people to consider, some born, some not. I tried to give it some thought myself, working through the different options. I mean, after all this time you finally have a child, yet with a *love cheat*.' She made a face like the words had left a bad taste. 'But then, the heart does its own thing, doesn't it? And I suppose it's kinder that everyone is with who they wish to be with, and no one is living in bad faith.'

'I think overthinking things isn't helpful,' she said, no idea what October was on about.

'What I wanted to say to you,' October continued, 'is that we aren't interested in asking you for rent immediately. We understand what has happened, and I know you may have some arrangement with Andy, but we are going to suspend rental payments for the foreseeable future. Is that helpful to you?'

'Uh…' She'd not expected this. For a moment she couldn't speak. 'Thank you.'

October nodded. 'You're more than welcome. This is what we're all about here, isn't it?'

'I suppose so.'

'It is all very complicated, and I don't envy you. So many things to consider.' She turned her head away, like she was considering a whole new perspective right there and then. 'I mean … just a few things in a different position would make it easier. For example, if you weren't also pregnant. Then at least you could all move on. But this baby of yours. It … just complicates it. It makes a kind outcome very difficult.'

'October.'

She looked at Tessa now, appearing to be surprised she was even in the room. 'Yes.'

'I know you mean well, but there's a chance that what you're saying might be taken the wrong way.'

'Oh. Really? How so? I'm sorry if that's the case. I really pride myself on not causing offence. Have I offended you?'

'That's not the right word—'

'All I mean is that … this is such a tragedy that's befallen you all. And the babies, they tie you to one another in a way that means you can't escape from it.'

Tessa couldn't keep her anger out of her voice. 'I know that. But I want the baby, October. As I told all the other members of the committee. I don't feel it's particularly kind on me if I end up childless.'

October appeared pained by this and moved her head from

side to side, weighing up her response. 'I can see what you mean. I hadn't realised you were quite so set on things.'

'Well, I am.'

'Of course, never mind me, then. My only thought was simply to make sure that you'd considered the options and to let you know—'

'Yes, that you'd support me either way.'

'Exactly. I suppose I also had it in my mind that after what he'd done to you, you might not want to have his child.'

'I really don't want to discuss this anymore. If that's okay. I'm actually feeling a bit nauseous, to be honest. The baby and everything. Is it okay if we talk about this another time?'

October nodded and got up. Tessa saw her to the door. 'Morning sickness?'

'Yes.'

'Horrible, I imagine. I should ask Dev about perhaps finding you something for it.'

'It's fine. I'm fine.'

'I'll ask anyway. Least I can do. Thank you, Tessa.'

At last, October left. Tessa opened the windows and set a vanilla candle going to clear the air of her incensy scent. Angry, she had to restrain herself from walking over to Olivia's and telling Andy about the sort of people he was dealing with. All that stuff October said about her rent, had that been some sort of bribe? A little sweetener to get her to consider terminating the baby. And why?

Well, that much was obvious. She was in the way of Olivia and Andy's happy ending. It would be so much tidier if she just got rid of the baby. Or if she just died.

The thought stopped her still. Perhaps she shouldn't have gone all guns blazing at October. What if she'd just kicked a hornets' nest?

FORTY-SIX

Jayden

It took him a few days to come clean to Rags that he'd lied about Leo and the drugs. Rags uttered a whiny *nooooo* on the other end of the phone, and was working himself up to losing it when Jayden interrupted him to tell him where they *had* come from.

'Rags, someone's been trying to set me up,' Jayden said. 'And I think it was that copper.'

'What?' He still sounded angry. 'Why would anyone want to do that to you?'

'They don't like me here,' Jayden said. 'They want me gone because I don't fit.'

Rags went quiet. 'I've got to go, kid. You've absolutely fucked me.'

'No wait, mate. Listen. Listen. This place is wrong. Like, wronger than just a copper with a bit of weed. They tried ruining my life and … I want to get them. I think we can get them.'

'And how do we do that, Jayden? I've got three weeks now.'

'It's fine, it's fine. I've got a plan.'

'You've got a plan. Oh great. Fucking great. Let's hear the plan then, kiddo. Let's hear your brilliant fucking plan.'

He squashed his anger and calmly detailed what he'd come up with. It was good, he was certain of it. All it needed was Rags to have faith in him.

For a while, Rags said nothing. Then he sighed, and said, 'See you, kiddo,' before hanging up.

He was still fuming a few days later. Rags wasn't answering his calls. One afternoon after school he stood staring at where the concrete base had been poured for the Story Station, not sure what to do next. Was the side he'd buried the drugs on ever so slightly higher than the ground level? No, it was barely noticeable. Not so much that they'd redo it, anyway.

He walked over to the lake beyond the Kindness Tree. Walking helped him think, and that's what he needed to do now more than anything. His plan would have worked, he was certain, and part of him wanted to do it just to show Rags. But what was the point? If Rags was just another adult that didn't believe in him, why should he take the risk?

Besides, now Tessa was in his head. She'd been messaging him, apologising, and wanting to meet to talk. He was tempted to go over there now and see what she had to say. Just to throw it in the mix.

'Jayden.'

He turned and saw Ruth approaching him across the green. Shit, was this about the uneven concrete?

'Jayden, I'm so glad to see you.' She smiled, showing all her big white teeth. 'I'm sorry if I'm disturbing you.'

'You're alright.'

'Good. Good. How's school?'

'Fine.'

'Good. Well, you see, the thing is, I know it's been a very difficult time for you lately. I know you and Kath were close. But Tessa has been trying to reach you.'

'Yeah, I know.'

'You see, we have a proposal for you.'

He paused to appreciate that pronoun. '*We?*' he said.

'Yes, Tessa and I. I've offered my services as a singer, and we were going to perform something in Kath's honour at the fete.'

He couldn't believe what he was hearing. Tessa had teamed up with one of the committee? What the fuck was *that* about? 'You sing?'

She nodded. 'And we very much wanted you to join us on bass.'

Jayden laughed. He stared out at the water and shook his head.

'It okay,' he said. 'I don't really want to do music anymore.'

'Oh,' he heard her say behind him. 'Oh, well, I see. Never mind, then.'

He kept his back to her and after a moment he heard her leaving. He turned to double check and watched her disappear behind the tree. This was some fresh committee shit, without doubt. It was so obvious. Tessa just couldn't see it, though, could she? Even though it was right there in front of her. They were going to try and set her and him up together somehow. Get rid of them both, he was certain.

He had to move on. Stick with the original plan and choose Rags. That meant saving his arse on his own. Rags'd soon change his tune once he had his insider, once Jayden had – what was that expression? – *re-established credibility*. Bringing down the committee would help Tessa too. She'd never know about it, which was sort of funny and perfect. It was exactly how she'd told him real kindness worked.

Ruth had to be the target. She was the weakest, and yet knew where all the buttons were in the village. In a way he felt sorry for her, the way she was bossed around by October. But however unwilling she might have been to go along with it, she'd been part of what happened to Kath. It was like with the Nazis, wasn't it? He'd learned about it in history. Workers at the death camps. People who'd voted for Hitler. The ones who just said nothing. If you just went along with it, you were no better than the ones making it happen.

On Saturday morning he put on the gloves Kath gave him. He walked over to Ruth's cottage, and she answered in her dressing gown, looking surprised to see him. He dug deep, brought back into his mind his lowest point, at the police station, spraying blood on the reception desk and floor, and said, 'Ruth, I didn't know where else to go. I need to talk to someone. I need help.'

FORTY-SEVEN

Tessa

S he moved into her studio. She didn't plan to, but it just seemed easier to grab her blankets and sleep on the sofa. That way she could fall asleep and wake up with her work. It was more efficient. The sort of thing all those rise-and-grind types did. It certainly wasn't because there was only one door into the studio, and she could monitor it at all times. And it certainly wasn't because the night after October left, she'd had a dream in which all the committee stood at the end of her bed in the moonlight, all of them holding gleaming, sharp instruments. If someone found the carving knife she'd stowed under the studio sofa cushion, she would tell them she was just being cautious. That was all.

She lost herself in the voices of a hundred different people. Chopping them up, twisting and stretching them, violating them. For eighteen hours a day they nagged her, implored her, instructed her, shouted at her, pleaded with her. And that was before she reversed them, listening so intently to them that she began to hear the secret messages Andy had told her about.

Words, sentences, and, at one point at two in the morning, a chant: *Just be Kind, Just be Kind, Just be Kind.*

Maddy phoned every day, but Tessa could only take so much nagging about her staying put in the village instead of moving in with her. Tessa wished she hadn't told her about the visits from the committee members. Maddy was freaking out. Eventually, Tessa stopped answering when she called. Did to her what Jayden was still doing to Tessa.

Her morning sickness, and the not dissimilar feeling she got when recalling her visits from the committee, meant she was subsisting on plain pasta, dry toast, and ginger tea. The studio wasn't well ventilated, and her lack of sleep crept up on her regularly. Time moved strangely, and days passed.

But soon the score was close to being submittable. She was working on the final mix early the following week when the front doorbell rang. It was likely Andy; he'd said he would come over after work to collect some more of his things. Why he hadn't used his key was beyond her. But the bell rang again.

Once inside, she realised Andy was upstairs already. She could hear him moving around, and the lights were all on. She opened the door and found Dev, suited as always, holding out a brown paper bag. He pushed it towards her.

'A little bird told me that you were suffering with morning sickness?'

Tessa took the bag and looked inside. It was an unmarked medicine bottle. 'What is this?'

'It's just a little something I think might help with your symptoms.' He winked. 'Off the books, so to speak. Needs to be kept in the fridge.'

'Thanks, Dev. What is it, though?'

'Oh, it's nothing pharmaceutical. It's a home remedy – some ginger, some B6-rich foods, a little something to help it go down. Patients of mine swear by it.'

'You made this?' She sounded wary, but he showed no signs of noticing in his enthusiastic nod. 'That's sweet, thank you.'

'Not a problem. Remember, keep it in the fridge.'

She bid him farewell and came inside. She put down the bag on the kitchen counter. She took out the bottle, smelled the contents, and screwed up her nose. The stairwell began to creak, and shortly Andy appeared in the doorway carrying a full hiking backpack.

'Sorry,' he said, addressing the floor. 'I'm nearly done. I didn't answer it. Might've been weird.'

'Yeah, no problem.'

He looked up and gave her a concerned once over. Noticing the bottle in her hands, he asked, 'Everything alright?'

'Fine. Just Dev's morning sickness remedy. Smells vile.'

'Oh, really? Olivia's not been feeling great either. I should talk to—'

'Andy, I don't give a fuck. I don't need to hear about the ins and outs of Olivia's pregnancy.'

'No, sorry. That was dumb. I … just … uh … maybe let me know if it works. Not because of her, I mean, but you know. So I know you're okay, that you're feeling better.'

She laughed. 'Here.' She put the bottle back in the bag. 'You can have it. The smell's making me feel worse. If Olivia can handle that, fair play to her. I'm not touching anything from that lot, though.'

Andy took it, thanked her awkwardly, and left before he put his foot in his mouth again. Tessa went back to her studio, finished off her tracks, and after several final listens, and even more deep breaths, she emailed the link to the production company. Hand still shaking, she moved her mouse to shut down her computer, but was stopped by the ping of an email.

It was a bounce-back message. She tried sending the link again, and received the same email. She tried a final time, recalling that famous definition of insanity, and once more got the same, unsettling email.

It was probably nothing. A full inbox. A server error. Yet her heart hammered. Because the message appeared to say the sender didn't exist.

She checked the email address she'd used. Copied it into a word document to examine at size 47. No typos, although she knew there wouldn't be already, because she'd been replying to Noah's messages, not typing the address fresh. A horrible thought began to swell uncontrollably in her mind.

What if the whole thing had been a trick?

But no. She'd done her due diligence. She'd seen the LinkedIn page for Noah and for the production company. She'd checked the email address; the end part matched the emails on the official company website.

Only she could have done more, couldn't she? She could have phoned the company up. She could have asked to speak with Noah on the phone. Only she hadn't done that, had she? Because she'd never really for a single moment doubted that a film company would want to work with her. It was only right, after all her years of toil, that an opportunity like this would come up to reward her efforts. It made sense, so she'd not questioned it. And why would she? But who would play a prank like this and why? Who would want her to waste time this way? Steal her time. Steal her independence.

Someone that wanted her to be entirely reliant on them and no one else. Someone who, at just the right time, could offer you a discount on your rent to save the day.

It struck her then, what she should do. What she should have done at the very start, once their conversations had moved from the website chat function to email. She did it *every* time she got a realistic-looking phishing email from a fake Amazon or PayPal, but hadn't this time because she'd wanted – and let's face it, needed – to believe it too bloody much. She clicked on the email address header and opened the details. And there it was.

The real, hidden address was a random string of letters and numbers connected to a Google account.

An account that had now been closed. And why would it be closed now?

Because whoever had been fucking with her now had her where they wanted her.

FORTY-EIGHT

How to Kill with Kindness

A nd what I have to ask is, Are you following all this so
··· far? Is it chiming with you, or perhaps awakening
parts of you hitherto dormant? I will continue to have faith
that this is so, despite some of the doubts I've had recently.
Sometimes it seems as if you aren't with it at all, my darling.
But in my blood I feel a Saint resides in you somewhere.
Despite the Dozy act you insist on putting on – even to me.
Because we are family, and I believe that must count for
something.

Which you would be right to question, of course. Because
surely 'real' kindness only works if you treat all of humanity as
if it was your family. Kindness. Kin. They are inseparable. You
can't 'rationally' favour biological relatives over others, even if
we are compelled to otherwise.

Yet on the issue I've gone back and forth. Have I talked
about my brother Alan yet? Sorry, I keep losing track of things
in my haste. The treatments are exhausting me. If I am honest,
sometimes I feel like the living dead…

Anyhow, at first I did believe that our family perhaps had

307

the Sharpie, or even the Saint, gene – which made us more important. This was because of my Alan. My first playmate and darling brother. My first conspirator. My first soul-mate. He had been there on the cliff when grandmother fell. It had been our decision to push her. And for so many years afterwards, we thrived because of it. All our schemes, all of our kindness, had been a family affair.

Yet after we parted for university, I soared, and he plummeted. His time studying became a mess of excess. Drink, and likely drugs, too. He aged terribly in his twenties, and often found work to be a great chore. He lived with my parents, getting into trouble with the police many times. He suffered frequent gout, and a few times he was even hospitalised. Perhaps because he lost his looks – or more accurately, traded them for indulgence, he never appeared to involve himself with anyone romantically or sexually.

It was when he left his twenties behind that the problems really began, though. That was when he started mentioning his guilt out loud. Subtly at first. 'If only I could sleep your sleep,' he said to me one Christmas, when discussing the seemingly innocuous topic of his insomnia. Then it grew more pronounced. We would meet for coffee, and he would tell me of another instance of his recurring dream about being arrested for grandmother's death.

'Do you ever think about telling anyone?' he asked once. 'Because in my dreams it is not the worst feeling.'

'No, I do not,' I would say. Because why would I? We had done the kind thing. We had been perfectly rational about it, despite our tender age.

'Do you *ever* feel guilt?' he asked.

'Only if there is something to feel guilty about, and I try to avoid that by thinking hard,' I told him.

Still, I kept telling him about the things I was doing in the hope it would inspire him. The acts of quiet kindness I was getting away with. But I sensed that the older he became, the more the drink killed off vital brain parts. The ones that perhaps we had once had in common. He didn't seem to find my cleverness intriguing anymore. Frankly, he was becoming a little bit of a Dozy. My sweet, funny brother and his razor-like intellect were no more.

Then he stopped leaving the house, and I would have to visit him in his murky flat in a god-awful Manchester suburb. When he would get stressed in our conversations, he would have to lie down on the floor. He'd shut his eyes and rub his temple.

'You are impossible,' he'd say.

Just when I thought things couldn't get any worse, he started to suggest that he was actually going to confess. And that this was perfectly fine, and that I shouldn't worry. Because he would claim that he had pushed grandmother when I wasn't looking.

But that was rubbish, I'd insisted. I remembered the statements I'd given at the time. My recall – up until these recent treatments – was exceptional that way. I'd told the police I'd seen the entire thing. Described it all in great detail. They would know something wasn't right.

So I would have to talk him down, and after much temple rubbing, he would take my point, which was always the same: it would be *deeply* unkind to *me* if his need to confess put us both in prison.

This worked for a while, but one afternoon he phoned me. He told me that his confession would override any child's testimony in the eyes of the law. He'd looked online at the relevant case law.

'I must unburden myself,' he would say, adopting the hoity-toity tone we often did when trying to compel and impress one another. 'You mustn't stand in my way.'

'All our good work,' I retorted. 'You're undoing all of it.'

'Good work?' He shouted this at me.

He said he'd found other people online, too. People we'd helped. Our old French teacher, Mr Eldon, for goodness' sake. Now an old man, yet Alan wanted to burden him with an apology. Wanted to apologise to all the people we'd helped with our kindness. Our beautiful, rational kindness.

'I'll keep your name out of it,' he kept insisting, like that was the point.

This was when my kindness was put under its greatest strain. I had to act. I did think he would do his best to deflect harm from me, but once his truth was out in the world, there were no guarantees. And if there is one thing that I need to be functional, it is certainty. As I've made clear to you, one cannot be their best, kindest self, if they are always looking over their shoulder. If there is doubt.

My biggest concern, though, was that he'd never been as bright as myself in the first place. Perhaps the alcohol wasn't to blame. Perhaps all this time, I'd imagined we had been in it together, when in fact, he had just been going along with whatever I told him. A brother in thrall to his brilliant older sister. And if this were true, well, I could never trust that he wouldn't at some point in the future feel it necessary to unburden himself further. To be truly free, perhaps his dreams might instruct him to reveal my role in it all.

So I told him that I would help him. That if he could just wait, we would sit down together at his flat and make a plan. And so, the day came. I took the train, and wore a long coat bought from a charity shop. I set up a tape recorder of myself playing the piano and set a plug timer to come on while I was out so that the neighbours would hear it through the wall. It wasn't an airtight alibi, but it was enough for my purposes, I believed.

When I arrived, I made sure no one saw me in the lobby or stairwell of his building. He was drunk when he answered the door. My decision was already made, but seeing him this way eased my mind considerably. I had him make us multiple cups of tea. When he relieved himself, I grasped my chance to arrange matters.

I took down from the wardrobe one of the dumbbells he once bought to tone up his arms. When he returned, he found me sitting on his bed. I told him that I wanted to lie down, and that I was overcome with the feeling that we were doing the wrong thing. I'd changed my mind, I said. Of course, this had the desired effect. Once he was done remonstrating, and pacing, he lay down on the floor and began rubbing his temples. Remarkably, I wouldn't even have to reposition him. He lay with his head beneath the wardrobe.

I kneeled to retrieve the dumbbell from where I had concealed it beneath the bed and stood above him. In a swift, powerful motion, I threw down my weapon as hard as I could, making sure the large weight struck his forehead.

The resulting crack, and the spasmic fashion in which his arms danced, suggested my work was done. Still, I went to the kitchen, took a chair, and returned to the bedroom. I rolled the second weight off the top of the wardrobe, watching it leave a trail in the dust and career over the precipice – much like grandmother had done. Really, it could have gone anywhere, but luck was with me. The weight did what it needed to do. An unfortunate accident exercising, is how the coroner would report it.

And darling, I must be honest, I never regretted doing this. Not once. Because I knew it had to be done. For my work to continue, I had to make this sacrifice.

But yes, it did make me question everything. About our family. Perhaps we weren't special after all. My brother flipping his personality the way he had – it had been a considerable blow to my confidence. In the aftermath, I overreacted, and adopted the opposite position. I started to think that perhaps biology wasn't important at all.

I lived in a village for a while and tried very hard to find like-minded…

FORTY-NINE

Jayden

Ruth took him in, arm around his shoulders, and made him a cup of tea. She sat beside him on the sofa.

'What is it, Jayden?'

'You know about where I'm from, don't you? About my family.'

She shook her head. 'I don't... I'm not sure what you mean.'

'You do. Everyone here does.'

He spun his tale, and she listened carefully, her face gradually lengthening with concern while the rest of her grew smaller.

Needing cash, he told her, he'd done a drug drop for a dealer a few months before he came to Nether Appleford. But he'd been robbed on the way there. He suspected the gangster did it himself, got one of his boys to follow him on the train. Because after, the gangster hadn't even been that angry. And he'd said Jayden now owed him for the drugs, and that he'd have to work for him until he'd paid off his debt.

'Oh no, Jayden. No.'

'Thing is, I thought I'd dodged it coming here. I didn't think he'd be that bothered to find me. But he has.'

'Oh, Jayden. Has he hurt you?'

'Not yet. But he will if I don't do what he wants.'

'And what does he want?'

'It's the horse hospital. I'm sorry, I lied to you about wanting to see it for my homework.'

She shook her head and stared at the floor, muttered, 'Jayden,' softly.

'He wanted to know all the security and everything. I think he wanted to rob it. But then he changed his mind because it was too risky. He said he wanted me to set someone up. Someone on the committee that he could, like, bribe. I think he wants the village to be, like, his long-term supplier. There's a drug in there they use on horses he wants. Ken— kendal-something.'

She moved a frail-looking hand to her mouth and studied him. Eventually, the hand dropped to her lap again, and she said, 'Well, there's nothing for it but to call the police, Jayden.'

'No, he'll kill me. That's what he said.'

Ruth swallowed. 'Dear God, Jayden. Do you believe him?'

'Hundred per cent. He's part of the Benton Boys. Look them up, they're a brutal gang. They've burned people alive, I swear.' The last part was true enough, but had it maybe been a bit too much? It was all sounding a bit far-fetched, now he was having to say it out loud. His heart raced and his mouth was parched.

Ruth's hand went to her mouth again. The hand was shaking now. It was hard not to feel shit about that. Really shit. But she was part of what had happened to Kath... Nazis. He had to remember Nazis.

Unless, of course, she had nothing to do with it. Unless

maybe she was a genuine person in the wrong place at the wrong time. That could happen, couldn't it? No, he was being weak. Ruth had her hand in everything in the village. There was no way her hands were clean.

'Jayden, I can call Leo. He can drive us to the police now. They couldn't touch you.'

'Read about them, Ruth. They'd find me eventually. They're massive.'

'Then, Jayden, I don't know how I can help.'

'I don't know. I just know that ... you know how everything works. In the village.'

'Jayden, you can't be suggesting—'

'And I know you're kind. That you wouldn't let anything happen to me.'

She took a breath and her face hardened. Now he'd surely gone too far. She wasn't buying it anymore. 'Leo is very resourceful. I know this ... monster must have made you feel you have no choice. But he is just trying to frighten you. No one is above the law.'

'Unless I change my name, he'll look for me forever. That's how it works. If they just let debts go unpaid, they look weak.' She still wasn't going for it. He had to go for the kill. 'My biggest worry, though, is that if I don't do what he says, he'll harm anyone I talk to or care about, too. Olivia. Tessa. You. Maybe he'd even target the committee to make a point.'

She shook her head repeatedly and slammed her fist on the table. 'No. Rubbish.' She glared at him with wet eyes. Now he wasn't just feeling guilty; he was scared. 'You shouldn't have come to me with this.'

Ruth stood up and strode across the room. She paced back and forward, and Jayden's guts began to squirm. He'd lost control, and now he had no idea what Ruth was going to do.

'I'd like you to leave, please,' she said.

315

'Serious?'

'Go.' She held open the kitchen door and pointed. 'I need to think. Dear God, Jayden. How did you ever get into this situation?'

'I'm sorry, Ruth. Listen, we can just forget about it. I can sort this out myself, maybe.'

'Too late for that, isn't it?'

'You can't tell anyone, Ruth.'

'Oh, you've made that abundantly clear.'

Jayden stood up. Ruth kept pointing and avoiding his gaze. So he left, and at the door he tried one last time to sell his story. 'Please.'

Still shaking her head, her expression one of barely concealed panic, Ruth slammed the door shut.

He went back to his room. Put in his earbuds and closed his eyes. Ruth had *actually* been angry with him. All the careful niceness that adults put on with him, poor little foster kid, had vanished almost as soon as he'd mentioned the threat to the committee and her. He'd sort of known that adults had an act. But he hadn't realised how comforting that was before. He missed it already.

He was angry, too. Angry that this hadn't gone his way, and terrified about how this would play out. He'd messed it up, hadn't he? He'd taken Ruth for a pushover and assumed she'd just agree to help him once he'd explained the stakes. If she came back at him now, he would crumble. He had nothing but front.

Later, he went out for a walk to get some air. He sat at the lake's far end and watched the water caress the bank. When he got home that afternoon, Olivia was on the sofa, singing sweetly to the cat while it vigorously bunted her face. She picked it up and put it on the floor. It jumped straight back up and did the same thing again. Olivia carried it from the lounge and shut it out.

'She's been skittish all afternoon,' Olivia said. 'Ever since Ruth came over.'

Jayden felt sweat break out over his body. 'Ruth was here?'

'Yes, she was in a very funny mood. Not herself at all. And she asked to speak with you. Any idea what that might be about?'

'With me?'

Olivia nodded. 'She said that when you got back you should go to the estate office and see her. She'll be there until late.'

Jayden swallowed. 'Oh, right. Okay.'

'What's that all about, then?'

'She not tell you?'

'No. She told me you'd know.'

Jayden nodded. 'Oh, it's nothing. I just … asked her about a job. She was going to see if she could get October to let me do stuff in the office.' It wasn't a bad lie at all; he'd considered and abandoned it as a way of infiltrating the hospital.

Her manner changed, and she cocked her head. 'A job? Really?'

'Yeah. Just to get a bit of pocket money at the weekend. Maybe she was worried because October said no.'

Olivia smiled, apparently relieved that there was such a wholesome explanation. She didn't break eye-contact with him, though, perhaps still looking for a tell. 'Well, you'd better get over there, then. Do you want a lift?'

The cat started scratching the door again. 'Nah, I'll walk.'

'Okay then. Great.' She turned to the cat. 'Duchess, did you hear that? Ruth was just trying to get Jayden a job. You can calm down now.'

Jayden smiled politely, and as he did every time he heard it, inwardly cringed at the cat's name.

FIFTY

Tessa

S he tried not to panic. But she didn't sleep, and once light
appeared in the curtain cracks, she went back to the
cottage and counted down the minutes until 9. It was all done
by 9.07. She hung up, having been told that the Noah working
for the company had never heard of any Tessa Todd.

Numb, and still teary, she started scanning through the
SoundGreat clients she'd turned down recently to see which
ones were still looking. She sent a few hopeful replies before
starting a search for actual jobs. At the council and the NHS,
like she'd done when she first left university. Something steady
and with good maternity cover.

Every so often she'd have to stop and cry again, overwhelmed with frustration at the lost time and her own stupidity
at not twigging before. By late morning she had a client again,
one paying a pittance for her to produce her acoustic track. It
was a small victory. And by then she'd managed to convince
herself the reverse-speech soundscapes weren't a total waste, so
that was something, wasn't it? She could probably do something else with them, provided her prankster hadn't stolen them

to use elsewhere – although she doubted that somehow. This didn't feel like a professional attack. It felt personal.

By the late afternoon she was ready to start asking the question: Who did this to her? And the only answer was the obvious one: Olivia Chambers. How better to humiliate Tessa and fuck her financially? Keep her distracted while she worked on Andy.

Jayden had been right, hadn't he? She'd been horribly naive. Looking back, Olivia had been there on that very first day they'd been in Nether Appleford. Although she could only have glimpsed Andy, it would have been enough to catch her eye. Was it possible, then, that she might even have been able to use her position on the committee to arrange for them to win that prize?

Her shoulders drew inwards as a chill crept up her back. Olivia had been in the pub when they went back for their free lunch. Not only that, but Andy had spoken to her. By the bar – she could picture it clearly.

But if she was going to open this door, why stop there? What if they'd never discovered Nether Appleford by accident? Andy had been the one driving that day, and it was entirely possible he could have manipulated the game they'd been playing to have them wind up there.

She felt another chill. Something Ruth had said that day came back to her. She'd said to Andy that he looked familiar. Was that just because he looked so like Olivia's ex, Jamie? Or because she recognised him. Because Andy had been to Nether Appleford before.

FIFTY-ONE

Jayden

He sat in his room, unable to believe what had just happened with Ruth. She'd gone for it. Just as he'd hoped she would. His phone started ringing, and he knew who it would be before he took it from his pocket.

'What do you mean, you've sorted it, kiddo?' He still sounded angry.

'I did my plan, Rags,' he said and pushed out his chest. 'And it worked. I've got you an insider. She wants to meet you. She's given me a number so you can meet somewhere neutral and talk it over. She's prepared to help out.'

It took a while to convince him, he kept saying he didn't get it or thought there was a catch. Eventually Jayden said, 'She's doing it to be kind. Because she doesn't want me or anyone in the village hurt.'

Rags paused, started to laugh, and said, 'Fuck me, kiddo. Fuck me.'

Jayden didn't want to laugh. He wanted to throw his guts up. 'And you're going to help me, Rags, aren't you? The flat and the work and everything. University.'

He went quiet, like he didn't even remember. 'Oh, yeah. No worries. You've saved my life, kiddo. We'll talk once I've got a sense of this. What she's prepared to do.'

'She knows you want long term. I made sure.'

He laughed again. 'Fuck me.'

He took off his leather gloves, placed them on his desk, and sat in silence staring at the place in the corner where he used to rest the Epiphone.

Ruth hadn't been angry when he'd seen her. She'd been pale and red-eyed, her hands and voice trembling.

'I looked up these people,' she'd said. 'I understand now. They are animals.'

There had been nothing satisfying about it all. In fact, the more he looked around the office, at all the files and paperwork and Post-it Notes stuck in strange places, the more convinced he became that Ruth really was a puppet. Someone just doing the bidding of the most compelling person in the room. Or the most threatening. And who fitted that description in Nether Appleford?

He moped about the house, finding himself in the kitchen when Olivia came in to make a hot chocolate. She moved gracefully, with happy purpose.

'How did your meeting with Ruth go? Did you get the job?'

'Went good, yeah. Nothing concrete or anything. But she … was just getting the measure of what I'm good at, and that.'

'Great stuff.' The microwave pinged and she stirred hot chocolate powder into her milk. 'Don't know about you, but I think everything just seems to be coming together all of a sudden, my darling.' And with that, she gave him a mischievous bob of her eyebrows, and walked away.

FIFTY-TWO

Tessa

She had to know. If Andy and Olivia or the committee had done all this to her, she wasn't just going to take it like a mug. They'd destroyed her – and for what? They could have had their crappy affair and baby, and just left her out of it.

Tessa strummed her guitar on the studio sofa, started plucking a rendition of 'Autumn Leaves', a loose interpretation of the Eva Cassidy setting. She wasn't sure she wanted to lock herself in a room alone with a member of the committee, but realistically, Ruth was her one chance of finding out what had been going on. She had no proof connecting any of her suspicions, and the idea of going to the police at this point was laughable, especially given Leo's involvement in the committee.

She imagined trying to convince the police. Well, Olivia stole my partner by sabotaging her own electricity supply, and then she made me believe for many months that I was doing work for a film company when in fact I wasn't. Also, her friends came over to my house and made threatening suggestions about me terminating my baby, whose father is also the father of her baby. And did I mention that the village committee coerce residents if they don't like them? My fifteen-year-old drug friend even thinks they murdered someone.

But Ruth: surely it was possible she'd been genuine, and that with a little more encouragement... Tessa wanted to trust her. She'd been the only committee member who hadn't hinted that she get an abortion, and was it really possible she was *that* good an actor? If Tessa approached the question the right way, Ruth might be willing to share something she could use. Or at the very least, something that could put Tessa's mind at ease that she wasn't completely losing it.

It would maybe take charm and time. And did she have time, if they were already thinking about aborting her baby? She had to give it a go, and she had an idea how she might do it. She went upstairs, showered, and tried to make herself look like a person who hadn't lost her mind.

Then she took out her phone, found Ruth's number, and messaged:

Don't suppose you want to maybe come over for a jam?

FIFTY-THREE

Jayden

Rags had made out like he was going to get in touch with Ruth straight away, and told Jayden he'd let him know how the meeting went. But Sunday passed by with no word from him, and by the end of school on Monday Jayden was starting to imagine the worst. Had it all been a set-up, maybe? Was Rags now in the hands of the police, about to give away Jayden as his accomplice?

Every break he got on Tuesday he checked his phone. Still nothing. So when he got back to the cottage on Tuesday afternoon he messaged Rags.

Everything okay?

By the evening he'd still had no response. Not even a little tick on the message to indicate it had been read. What the actual…? Something was going on. On the bus back home on Wednesday, he waited for it to empty out before calling Rags. Four days was too long. He needed an update. But it went straight to the automated voicemail. He tried again and again.

When he got off the bus he started the long walk back to the village.

The sound of an engine behind him made him step off the road and walk on the grassy embankment. The vehicle approached and began to slow. He turned, expecting maybe Olivia or one of the other villagers who occasionally offered him lifts the rest of the way. But it was Leo. Anxiety flooded him.

'Do you want a lift?' he said through the open window.

Jayden put on his best matey smile. 'Nah, you're fine. Thanks, though.'

'Get in,' Leo said, his voice and expression stern. 'We've got to talk.'

Jayden's face fell. He didn't move, and after a while Leo flicked his head to tell him to get a move on. What could he do? It wasn't like running was an option. Where would he even go? He nodded, and walked around to the passenger seat.

———

Leo didn't take him home. He drove a little further on and pulled off at the Manor Hotel. Jayden's heartbeat quickened. 'Where we going?'

'Just somewhere private.'

'Am I in trouble?'

Leo said nothing. He drove to the estate offices and the two of them went into the Portakabin.

'Anyone here?' Leo said, and when no one replied, he gestured for Jayden to follow him into Ruth's office.

Once Jayden was inside, Leo closed the door behind him and sat down behind the desk.

'Sit,' he said, and Jayden did as he was told. 'Now, mate, all

I've done since you've been here is try to help you. Would say that's fair?'

Jayden nodded to keep him sweet.

'I've tried to give you pointers. Tried to keep you from getting in trouble. Tried to let you know that the people here in this village are smarter than you, and you'd be better off trying to be more like them, rather than trying to always fight them. That's what I did, and it's been the best decision I've ever made. People here look after you. They really do. But you just do your own thing, don't you? You don't really have a sense of community.'

'Leo, I don't—'

'I think you're either born with it or not, to be honest. Anyway…'

He reached into his trouser pocket and took something out. In a flash he chucked the object at Jayden, who flinched, but not quickly enough. Something hard smacked his temple.

'What the fuck,' he said, wincing and touching the impact area on his head. He looked down at his lap where the object had fallen and understood what Leo had thrown. It was a necklace. A purple children's teething toy.

'Recognise that?' Leo said.

He did. It belonged to Rags. 'What the fuck, Leo?'

'You're in a lot of trouble Jayden. *A lot.* Your mate has dropped you right in it. People like that, they act like they've got your best interests at heart, but they don't. When push comes to shove, they'll always do what benefits. And it doesn't sound to me like you're the victim in all of this.'

He didn't know what Rags might have said, but there was no point denying he knew him now. 'The guy's a criminal. He's full of shit.'

'I'm sure that's true. He definitely isn't an associate of the

Benton Boys. I looked him up before I even met him. Question is, what's your role in it all? How angry should I be?'

'Did you do something to him, then?'

'I think it's best you don't ask that. *I think* the best thing for everyone is to just forget anything ever happened here. And I think if we choose to go this way, he's the start and end of this chain.'

'What way's that?'

'The way where you do exactly what I tell you to do. Then whether you did or didn't have something to do with a plan to rob the village vets becomes moot. You don't end up fucking up your life and I get to see you fulfilling your potential finally.'

'My life is fucked whatever happens, isn't it?'

Leo smiled. 'There's economy fucked, Jayden. And then there's first-class fucked – and you don't want to know about the latter.'

Jayden wanted to sound brave. Say something funny and tough. But he knew when he spoke, his voice would let him down. 'So you want me to do something?'

'I've got one little job for you to do. Good news is, it's really easy. But I think you'll find it difficult. Thing is, I actually don't give a shit about that. Because this is what's right for the village. Which is why it's even more important you do it. All this time, all I've wanted you to do is just … be a team player. So now's your chance, Jayden.'

FIFTY-FOUR

Tessa

P unctual as always, Ruth arrived after dinner, and carried with her an armful of goodies. Milk, ginger tea bags, a loaf of bread. Tessa had been worried about her appearance in front of this meticulous woman, but she needn't have. Ruth didn't look her usual tidy self. Her dress was creased and had a ketchup stain on the collar, and her tired eyes were red. She took the items to the kitchen, boiled the kettle while espousing the virtues of the tea as an anti-emetic, and began to put away the items she'd bought, her movements rapid and erratic.

'Oh, you have plenty of milk,' she said, studying the fridge.

Tessa sat at her kitchen table. 'Hey, you can never have too much milk.'

Ruth didn't turn around. 'This is all very exciting, thank you for this.'

'I don't suppose you spoke with Jayden at all, did you? He's still not speaking to me.'

She broke eye-contact. 'I ... don't think he'll be joining us.'

'Oh, right. Never mind. Just us two, then. We can get to know each other.'

'Sounds perfect.' Ruth still hadn't turned around yet, and her head bobbed around like she was studying the contents of the fridge. Maybe in anticipation of a future shop for Tessa. This was a truly kind woman, could there really be a doubt?

Screw it, she didn't have time to play getting-to-know-you. She needed answers. 'Ruth, I know we've talked about October before. But can I ask you something?'

'Of course.'

'What do you know about Olivia?'

'Olivia,' Ruth said, sounding a fraction more engaged. 'What about her?'

'Well, you said that the other committee members were in October's thrall. Do you think that's true of her?'

Finally she turned to face Tessa. 'No more so than any of the others, really. She's very young, emotionally, and has a lot of growing to do, so I think she likes to go with the flow.'

'I was just thinking about something you said, about them maybe being motivated by inheriting her fortune. Could it be...' She had to be careful here. She didn't want Ruth to know she'd been looking into *her* history. That she'd found the article about what she'd done to her neighbour's tree. 'Does October maybe ... *know* stuff about the others? Like, secrets.'

'Secrets. I wouldn't know.' She still sounded distracted, like her brain was still in the fridge. She wandered over to the dishwasher and pulled it open.

'Well,' Tessa said, 'it's just ... someone told me Leo had been in trouble before he lived here. And Dev too.'

Ruth shook her head, closed the dishwasher door, and turned to her with a smile. 'It's a thought. I wouldn't know, though. Tessa—'

'How did Olivia end up on the committee?'

'Tessa, sorry, can I just ask you something? Did Dev come

and visit you? He said he was going to bring you something for your sickness.'

Tessa stared at Ruth, who stood with her hands together, worrying her index finger with her opposite thumb. 'Uh … he did, yeah. Yesterday.'

'Oh good. Good, I just… I know he uses ginger, so before I made your tea, I didn't want you to have it again if you'd already… Have you finished it, then?'

'Finished what, the medicine? No. Sorry, I… I know Dev meant well but, blurgh, I didn't have any.'

'Oh. Oh, I see. That's a… Well, never mind. Did you throw it away?'

'No. Actually, Andy came over. He took it for Olivia.'

Ruth went still. It wasn't just that she stopped rubbing her finger, or moving gradually towards Tessa, or even breathing. It was as if time in her vicinity had ground to a halt, entombing her. What little colour had been in her face drained away, and eventually she stumbled, grabbing the edge of the nearest kitchen surface.

'Ruth!' Tessa said, up on her feet and over to Ruth in a second.

'When?' Ruth said, pushing off Tessa's attempt to steady her. 'When did he take it?'

'Yesterday evening. Ruth, what is it?'

'I need to leave. I'm terribly sorry. I… I'll explain another time, but I'm suddenly not feeling well.' She was talking almost to herself, already walking to the front door. Tessa followed her, telling her to slow down and offering her water. But Ruth wasn't interested, and when she left the house, she was almost running.

The door closed and Tessa played back through what had just happened. Understanding, clear and bracing, struck her like a cold ocean wave. But there wasn't time to dwell. She had to follow her, while she was still panicked. She might catch her in a mistake.

Without even grabbing her coat, Tessa yanked open her door and jogged down the drive in pursuit.

FIFTY-FIVE

How to Kill with Kindness

... **B**ut there were no like-minded people in that village. They were only interested in their small, seaside lives, and treading over anyone that got in their way. Some were Spiders. Some were exceptionally stupid Dozys. But my plan to either find another soulmate, or maybe even forge a family which I could guide towards 'true' kindness, was met with resistance. Sometimes actively. I just couldn't do my work there at all, despite the sea air. It pushed me uneasily back towards that biological hypothesis again. That perhaps *our* genes were the only Saint genes.

Are you still following? Speaking with you earlier today, I had the sense I was a lunatic for writing this for you. That when you read it, you wouldn't fill with inspired awe and love, but run for the hills. But I think that is merely a reflection of me looking back at these writings and panicking at how disordered they are. Maybe I've said this, but I get so tired in the evenings, and I often lose track of what I've told you and what I need to tell you. I'm just so busy, and yet I know I need to make the time to keep track of things for you in a way you understand.

If time doesn't run out, I might tell you more about my life in that village near Portsmouth. But it's not crucial to what I wish to impart – other than to say: don't let setbacks make you question your core ideals. And the point is, I knew what I needed to do next. About family. And kindness. And finding a path through. But we must move on.

I took some time travelling, and I began searching for a place I could take an active part in building and shaping. Somewhere that I could make reflect my values. After much hunting online – the internet is a wonderful place for someone with my interests – I came across an article about a woman inheriting an estate with a long history of kind acts. About how she wanted to build it around modern, green ideals – and, most importantly, kindness.

Of course, I sensed from our interview that she was a Dozy. Someone that wouldn't have the first clue how to foster 'true' kindness. And that proved to be correct once I had embedded myself in the village in such a way as to be able to influence events.

October proved very suggestible, and soon actively sought my guidance on everything.

So I began the reshaping and rebuilding of Nether Appleford, giving it new purpose and direction.

Of course, I had to fill the village with Dozys and root out any competing Sharpies and Spiders. I came to understand this was the only way to make it work. One Sharpie for every village of Dozys is about the right balance. Hand-pick the residents. Root out the bad eggs. Also, if at all possible, make sure their professions are useful to the community. Have a spread of skills, like the masons.

Then build a committee of Dozys, to create a veil of

democracy. Manufacture consent, as the saying goes. Dozys love that. But make sure each committee member knows which side their bread is buttered on, so they know not to rock the boat. Choose problematic people for this, people who made mistakes once and are eager for a second chance. Preferably make them bad with money, so they are reliant on your charity. Maybe even pick one or two, with extremely useful professions, and find out more of their secrets. The doctor's habit of stealing from his own pharmacy. The PC's problematic associations and ongoing WhatsApp groups with known bent officers. Let them know you know, but that you are their friend. The keeper of their secrets from the tyranny that is October and her virtue.

Interview enough people, and you will get the right picks. If you're struggling, you can play games with adverts on Facebook or hunt people down on LinkedIn. Let them know about our community. Draw them into the application process. It's hard work, but worth it.

Especially when you are building something for your family.

Because that was what I also came to understand on my travels, darling. It was okay to funnel some of your kindness towards a biological relative, so long as you don't funnel all of it. Especially as there is a high chance they might be a Saint. And if it actually enhances the work you are doing for humanity.

I just knew I needed you close to me. Because when you watch someone you love from afar, alone and suffering in the world, all you want is to scoop them up and bring them home. I made that home for you, darling, and it's here. Where no one can harm you. I am grateful your family brought you up to be healthy, but I am less enamoured with the Dozy values they've instilled in you.

What I hope is that by spending our time together while we can, I have shaped your life in a positive way. Given you the solid ground you need to improve. Found a partner that meets your quite specific tastes so that your heart is satisfied, allowing you to move on with hardening your mind for the work to come, which will begin very…

FIFTY-SIX

Tessa

R uth was now walking at pace down The Road, and
Tessa followed her from a distance in the shadows,
hoping she wouldn't turn around. When Ruth reached Olivia's
cottage, Tessa left the pavement. She hid just inside the
entrance to Dev's drive, almost opposite Olivia's. She wasn't
particularly well concealed by the low bush at the front, and if
Dev looked out his front window behind her, she'd be stuffed.

All of Olivia's lights were off. Ruth knocked on her door
and after a while began looking through her bag. Not finding
what she needed, she trotted back down the drive. She walked
over to her house, and just when Tessa started contemplating
going back, Ruth re-emerged holding a bunch of keys in her
hand. She unlocked Olivia's front door and went inside.

Tessa felt real fear now, and as questions began to pile up in
her mind, she wanted to get back home before Ruth came back
out. Once back inside her cottage, she locked the door and
tried to call Maddy. It went to voicemail.

'Okay, Maddy, call me when you get this, please. I'm sorry,
but it's all gone really weird.'

She told her about getting the remedy from Dev, and about Ruth's reaction when she'd found out Andy and Olivia now had it.

'I mean, why does she even have keys to Olivia's house, Maddy? And what was she doing in there? What was such an emergency? I'll tell you what I think. There was something in that remedy, wasn't there? Something meant for me and not for Olivia. I wonder what that could be. I wonder what Olivia and I both have in common. Listen, can you call me straight away. Please. Love you. Speak soon.'

When she hung up she was breathing heavily. Maddy might think she'd lost her mind, but she had to tell someone. Playing back the conversation to herself in her head, something occurred to her then. She called Andy, and it went straight to voicemail. She wrote him a message instead:

Call me asap! Tell Olivia not to drink the morning sickness remedy!! I think it's poisoned. X

It took her a moment to realise what she'd done, and before sending, she deleted the kiss.

It was late, almost midnight, but Tessa wasn't tired. She was too scared, and too bewildered by her situation: stuck here in this village, unsure whether to flee what might now be a very real threat to her and the baby. She'd spent the evening going back and forth to the upstairs windows, wanting to keep an eye out for possible threats. She had no idea what Ruth or the committee might do next.

Again, she considered phoning the police. After all, trying to poison someone was a real crime – unlike, for example, stealing someone's partner. But she didn't actually know they'd tried poisoning her, did she? The police would simply have her word for it. Tessa still had no real evidence. What she should have done earlier was take her phone and record Ruth's break-in. Or, she should have called the police while Ruth was still in the house – although even that might have amounted to nothing. The only other evidence, the bottle of poisoned sickness remedy, might have been disposed of already. But it might not have, and to that hope she'd have to cling. Because with something like this, she likely had one shot before the police started treating her like she wasn't in her right mind.

She was standing at her bedroom window, looking out at The Road, packing a small suitcase just in case, when her phone rang. It was Andy. He sounded weary. 'Tessa, what's going on?'

'Did you get my message?'

'Yeah.'

'So?'

He waited, and eventually sighed. 'You know I should phone the police.'

'What?' She turned away from the window, into the middle of the room.

'Tessa, what the bloody hell am I supposed to do? We get out of the cinema, and you're messaging me about some bloody medicine you've given me being poison, and then I find it spilled over the fridge. The whole shelf's out of its groove. Like someone's made a bad attempt at faking an accident. Who even let you in? Was it Jayden? Is he with you now?'

'No, I don't know where Jayden is. He lives with you. And that wasn't me, Andy. Listen, is there any left?'

'Yeah, all over the fridge, like I said.'

'Please, listen. Can you get a sample of it? I think the committee tried to poison me, okay? And when Ruth found out about me giving it to you, she went to stop Olivia drinking it. *Did* she drink any, Andy?'

'No. She hated the smell, too. Tessa—'

'I need to prove it's poisoned. Just get me a sample and I'll come over—'

'Tessa. Listen, no. It's late. And I'm not doing this. I know you're angry at me, and angry at Olivia, but this isn't the fucking way or the time—'

'Andy, no, listen—'

'I thought you were being a bit too nice, a bit too *kind*, when you let us have it. But maybe you realised you didn't want to help us after all, maybe you thought, *Fuck Olivia, let her be sick*, and that's … fine. Whatever. But this is … mental, Tessa. This—'

'Andy, you fucking wanker. Listen to me, okay. If anything in our relationship was ever worth anything, listen to me. Just save me a sample, that's all I'm asking. I didn't break into your house, it was Ruth, okay?'

'I mean … really? Of all people, Ruth?'

'Yes. I followed her and she went in, using a key. She went—'

''Night, Tessa.'

'Andy, don't you—'

He hung up. Tessa screamed. She threw her phone at the wall, where it smashed into pieces. She stared at the black mark left on the wall. She ought to go over to Olivia's right now. Claw his eyes out, the bastard. But then *he* would call the police. Or worse, Leo. But she should still go over there. Because the evidence was still there. If she could keep her cool, maybe she might still be able to convince him to give her a sample.

No. She should call him again first. She didn't trust herself not to lose it in his company. She retrieved the pieces of her phone, but the screen was now cracked in multiple places. She screamed again, this time from deep in her throat. She pushed the battery back in and waited for it to start up, which thank God it did. Only when she tried swiping, the screen didn't respond to her fingers.

'No.' She left the room and ambled across the landing, towards the stairs, eyes down at her phone. There wasn't an option now. She'd have to go over to Olivia's and deal with things in person.

Her phone screen illuminated, and the ringtone followed shortly after. Maddy's name appeared. Finally, she was calling Tessa back. She could have cried with happiness.

She tried to answer, but the green icon wouldn't budge.

'Oh fuck off, no!' No matter hard she tried, she couldn't answer the call.

By now she'd reached the top of the stairs, and she looked up ready to negotiate the top step. That was when she saw the figure, looking up at her from the bottom of the stairwell. It looked like a man, though it was hard to tell. He was wearing an oversized black coat and an orange carrier bag over his face, three crude holes cut for the mouth and eyes. In his hand he held a tyre iron.

FIFTY-SEVEN

Tessa

The figure in the stairwell advanced towards her.

Still brimming with aggression from her conversation with Andy, she replied, 'I don't know who you are, but get out my house now.'

'The ket.' The voice was male, and his accent was strange. Was it cockney? Or Australian, or something else? He kept climbing.

'Ket?'

'The drugs.'

'There's no drugs here. Get out.'

'There are. Upstairs.' The voice sounded young, too. Jayden – this had to be something to do with Jayden. His mysterious dealer. They thought the ket was here, didn't they? She didn't fancy her chances with a tyre iron, but she had the advantage of being stationed above him, at least momentarily. She scanned the landing for a weapon. Something to throw. But shit, there was nothing that could take on a solid piece of metal.

'Don't come up any further,' she said, holding up her phone.

'Just go up.'

He climbed another step. If she could drop down when he neared the top, and aim a good kick at his middle, it might knock him back down the stairs. But then what? Unless he cracked his head on the wall just perfectly, he'd just come up again. No, she couldn't stop him, could she? Instead, she needed to slow him down.

'Honestly, you're making a mistake. Who told you there were drugs here?'

'Back up.' The intruder's voice cracked, like he was on the brink. Like he didn't want to be here at all. He was too close to her now, she had to move. She reversed back into the bedroom, because maybe there she could grab one of the lamps. He ran up the final few stairs and stalked her, not a massive man like Andy, but big enough to have a physical advantage, should he catch her.

'Seriously,' she said, backing away from him, her voice high and shaky. She put her hands out in front of her, between him and the delicate contents of her belly. 'You're making a mistake.'

'I'm not.' His voice was nasal and high, and he sounded as scared as her. Maybe she could talk him down. Reason with him.

'I already told you: there aren't any drugs here.' She couldn't give him what he wanted; she'd flushed away the ket the day Andy found it.

She retreated down the space at the side of her bed, towards the largest of the two lamps on either side. The man stopped just inside the door, level with the foot of the bed, blocking her exit. 'Liar.'

It was her turn to lose control of her voice, and 'What am I lying about?' came out too high-pitched to sound anything but terrified.

'Close your eyes and put your arms above your head.'

He was coming towards her again and she pushed out her hands. 'No.' She had to think. Had to stop whatever this was. 'I've got money. Do you need money?'

'Arms up.'

She couldn't let this person tie her up or whatever he was going to do. She had to think of something to stop this. 'I do have the drugs. They're downstairs. They're downstairs.'

'Arms up.'

Her arms remained in front of her, so he came at her. She dived over the bed, feeling his grip on her leg before managing to kick him off. She grabbed the other lamp, and fell to the floor on the other side. He came around the bed, fast, tyre iron raised, and when he got down on top of her, she closed her eyes and screamed, 'Please don't, I'm pregnant, I'm pregnant!'

She braced for the attack. She could hear his breathing by her ear, the shuffle of his clothes as he shifted her from side to side, like they were struggling even though she was trying to wait until he was close enough for her to be able to strike him with the—

'Tessa,' the voice said, right up against her ear, no accent now and suddenly familiar. 'It's Jayden. I'm not going to hurt you. Okay? They made me come here, so just pretend, yeah. If you don't pretend, they'll kill us.'

'What?'

'Pretend I've hit your belly. They said they'd be watching, so make it real.'

A moment later he grabbed both her arms and pinned them above her head. He raised the tyre iron and she screamed as he brought it down. It struck the floor beside her. He swung it up and down twice more, striking the floor both times.

Then he leaned back down. 'Grab your belly. I'm so sorry, Tess. Just pretend, yeah. Then get the fuck out of here. It's Leo and Ruth and the committee ... everything we thought, but worse.'

He got up, and she dragged herself to the wall, hands over her belly like he'd told her. When she looked up, he was already running, and a moment later she heard the front door shut downstairs. For a long time, Tessa didn't move. Eventually, she went downstairs, checked every room and cupboard, and finally locked herself inside. She sat down on the bristly doormat with her back against the front door.

She put her head against her knees, closed her eyes, and clung to her legs while her whole body started to tremble.

FIFTY-EIGHT

Jayden

He didn't give a fuck who saw him now. What he'd done deserved prison or death or whatever else Leo had in store for him. He strode back to Olivia's, pulling the plastic back from his head, relishing the pain of the packing tape tearing away from his neck. When Leo had first sealed him in it, he'd cut the holes last, and Jayden had been convinced he was going to suffocate him.

But no, it was important for him to hit Tessa. Right in the belly, specifically. And now he knew why.

I'm pregnant, I'm pregnant! He stopped, leaned over Dev's fence, and vomited on his immaculate lawn. He raced on, throwing the tyre iron into Leo's front garden on his way past.

His breathing was fast and out of control. But he wouldn't cry, despite the pressure at the back of his throat and nose.

Pregnant. Tessa was pregnant. But did that mean she'd cheated on Andy? Or was it his? Because if it was his, that meant he'd not only left Tessa, he'd left her pregnant. She'd been dealing with all that while Jayden had been angry with her. He sniffed. Used his sleeve to dab up a bit of liquid gathering at the corner of his eye.

He didn't know what came next, if Tessa would call the police or not. Leo had reckoned she might not if they made the break-in seem connected to the ket. But Jayden had changed the plan, so who knew what Tessa's next move would be? Who knew what she thought of him? But he'd have never hurt her. He'd known what he was going to do, even when Leo was giving him his orders.

What did it matter what happened now, though? There had been blood on Rags's necklace. They had killed him. And they had killed Jayden's future.

He opened the cottage door, took off his shoes and the stupid coat Leo had given him and told him to get rid of. The television blared in the lounge, Andy and Olivia up late. Sighing. Laughing. Murmuring. Jayden stepped towards the cracked door.

'I just hope I'll be as good as my mum,' Olivia was saying.

'Sure, you've learned from the best.'

'But it's different for me. You know, because she *chose* me. I didn't choose … you know.' She whispered: 'This little one…'

'What, because you were adopted?'

'Exactly. They picked me. They knew that wherever I'd come from, whoever my parents were, criminals or Nobel laureates, they'd *decided* to love me. Which is so … amazing. But after all this stuff with Jayden, it's made me realise…' – she lowered her voice again – 'that I can't just make myself love a child. I think that being related to someone, being family, that's just so important to me. I already love this little one, and I know I always will, whatever they do. But what sort of person am I, if I'm not like my mum? Because I only ever wanted to be like her, really.'

Jayden balled his fists, and a fought-back tear fell.

'Did you ever look for you biological parents?' Andy said.

'No. Funnily, despite what I said, it's never interested me. My parents are my parents.'

'So there you go,' Andy said. 'You are like your mum.'

'I don't even know how I'd find out who they were, if I wanted to.'

Jayden pushed the door and caught sight of them draped over one another. Seeming to sense danger, the cat shot off into the other room.

Jayden glared at Olivia. 'Are you pregnant?' He could feel his face contort with anger.

Olivia looked at Andy, but he had nothing for her.

'We were waiting to tell you,' she said. 'It's absolutely usual to wait twelve weeks to share such news, just in case there are any complica—'

'And Tessa's pregnant?' Now Jayden's glare blazed at Andy.

'Did she tell you all this?' Andy said.

'Is she?'

'Jayden, listen mate, calm down, okay? If you're angry at us for not telling you—'

'You're a shit, *mate*. Doing this to her.'

'You need to calm down. You don't know—'

'Yeah, don't know, don't care.'

With a stride he was by the mantelpiece. He grabbed the carriage clock resting there and came at Andy. He jumped at him, aiming to strike his head. Andy grabbed his arms and held them still, telling Jayden to calm down. But Grandad told him to pick his battles, and now this was his. He wanted to hurt him. Hurt him the way he'd hurt Tessa.

Andy pushed Jayden's own hands into his chest, and Jayden stumbled. His leg caught on the coffee-table leg and he fell backwards. He heard Olivia scream before his head struck the fireplace tiles, and all went black.

FIFTY-NINE

Tessa

She had no car. She'd destroyed her phone and didn't have a landline. She didn't trust anyone in the village. And somehow, *somehow*, her whole smartarse, never-being-taken-for-a-mug adulthood had brought her to midlife without a single friend close enough to stay with.

She grabbed a steak knife and a rolling pin, and took them with her upstairs, her nerves tweaking at every late-night house creak. She raked through drawers and cupboards looking through the flotsam of a decade with Andy to find an old phone into which she could put her sim. She didn't find one. So instead, she found a taxi firm which, thank fuck, did online bookings, and by the time a car arrived to collect her she'd drained her PayPal by booking an overpriced hotel on the edge of Oxford.

As the taxi drove down the long road away from the village, the blue lights of an ambulance, heading towards them, illuminated the trees and surrounding countryside. It raced by them.

Sleep-deprived and hungry, she walked into Oxford the next morning and took her phone to a same-day screen-repair shop. She was handing it over when a new message from Andy briefly flashed up behind the cracked glass:

Jayden attacked me last night and is now in the John Radcliffe. Someone told him about the babies…

If Andy was implying it was her fault, he could fuck right off. But why had Jayden attacked *him* now? Was that part of the same plan that involved attacking her, or something else? She ought to stay far away. Once her phone was fixed, she'd call Maddy and never look back. But she had a few hours before her screen would be ready, and the defensive way Andy had written the message had her worried. What had he done to Jayden, exactly, that required hospitalisation?

She made the hour-long trek with her small suitcase to the John Radcliffe hospital, but once she'd located him the nurses wouldn't let Tessa in. The case was too complicated, and social services and the police were involved.

She was about to leave when Olivia arrived, and the two of them stared at one another across the waiting room before Olivia finally raised her hand and walked over.

'Did Andy tell you, then?' she asked. Tessa told her about the message. 'Did you want to see him?'

'I just wanted to know he's okay,' Tessa said. 'Andy didn't give me much.'

'He was feeling better this morning, but they want to observe him.'

'What… So he's okay?'

'There's no bleed or fracture of his skull. But he keeps needing to sleep and isn't quite himself when he's awake.'

'Oh my God. And Andy did that to him?'

'Andy was defending himself, and Jayden fell and hit his head.'

'I just ... can't picture Jayden attacking Andy.'

Olivia smiled, looking so much like some parallel-dimension Maddy. 'Well, he did. He's very loyal to you, Tessa.' She let this sit for a moment before softening. 'Do you want to see him?'

They went into a private room where Jayden lay hooked up to various machines, head propped up on a pillow, body in a blue hospital gown. A radio in the corner played Classic FM at a low volume. His face free from the contortions of youthful irony and defensive fronting, he looked like a little boy.

Tessa walked to his side and took his hand. His pale skin and slightly parted lips upset her in a way she didn't fully understand. She felt no anger towards him about the night before. Someone had made him do that, and if not for Jayden, it would have been much worse. Her jaw hardened with resentment for everything that he had been through, and the sense she didn't even know the half of it. 'Do you think he likes this music?' she said to Olivia.

'Oh, they just said music might help. If you want, you can put something else on.'

Tessa hadn't expected that answer, and overwhelmed with gratitude and exhaustion, her eyes welled. She went over to the radio, double-checked, and when Olivia nodded Tessa turned the dial until it reached Planet Rock. AC/DC were screeching about being shot down in flames. It would do.

'What happens now?' Tessa said, resuming her place beside Olivia.

She looked disconsolate. 'I don't think there's a choice, really. When he's discharged, the social workers will take him to another emergency home.' Her voice wavered at the end of her sentence. 'I'm not... I can't really help him, Tessa.'

Tessa nodded. 'And after that?'

'Hopefully another family will take him on. Or there might be a home he can stay in. But … I didn't know he could be violent. That's something… That's a no from me.'

They stood in silence. A song by Ghost came on. 'I've heard him listening to this one,' Olivia said.

'I don't think Jayden is violent,' Tessa said.

Olivia took a deep breath and her back straightened. 'Well, you didn't see him last night.'

Tessa took her point and stayed quiet.

'He must have overheard us,' Olivia continued, 'although I was being very careful how I put things… Unless someone else told him."

'Well, it wasn't me. You really told no one? Because the whole committee seems to know about my baby, somehow.'

'No. Well, I mean … I did tell Ruth, I suppose. But *she* wouldn't have told Jayden. I've known her for a long time. She's sort of my guardian angel. She was the reason I came to Nether Appleford in the first place.'

SIXTY

How to Kill with Kindness

O f course, but the truth is, I'd always kept my eye on you. And I never stopped thinking about you. At first, after I gave you up, I had my brother follow the family home. From the address, it wasn't much work to get your adoptive parents' names and learn about who they were and what they stood for. Occasionally, I would drive to the house, in the hope of catching a glimpse of you. Once or twice, I pretended to be an aunt and went by your school to ask about your performance. Extremely bright, is what they would tell me, and yet it became clear to me over time that you were infected with a humility from your new family's religiosity. No matter the seed, a small pot will stunt the flower.

Thankfully the internet, and your benign addiction to social media, made it easier to keep tabs on you later in life. To track the disappointments of your relationships with these men you liked – giant men with childish souls. Of course, it warmed my heart that you shared my own weakness for such men. That we shared a 'type' made your unusual decisions more understandable to me. And you were nothing if not consistent on that score, although you sadly lacked the wisdom to pick one who worshipped you. That is the trick of it, of course. Your own father – dead now, I am sad to report – worshipped at my altar for many years during my youth. He owned a bar in London, and after hearing me sing during a cabaret night gave me a residency. He was convinced that I would be a star, and I was happy to play along, despite knowing that the world had more important work for me to do.

It was a foolish thing to have got pregnant as I did. I knew better, and yet I was swept up in being kind to myself, and I had a sense of invulnerability. Once it happened, I knew I had options, but still, once in that position, it was very hard to consider an alternative. It was your father who made me see that I couldn't possibly continue on the independent path that I had grown used to *and* remain a mother. So while I was vexed right until the very end, I had to let you go, darling. Because it would not have been kind to try to divide my attentions between you and my career. Despite what people may try to tell you, you cannot have it all, darling. This is the lie of our era. You *must* choose. And I did, for fear of you growing hungry in a box stuffed in some back room of a nightclub. Giving you away to someone less driven was kind to you, to me, and to your 'parents'.

Your father, by the way, died of a heart attack one night in a club back room. Without his support and enthusiasm – without his attention, really – I stopped singing professionally. I had enjoyed my time in the spotlight, but I had coveted the influence held by those behind the scenes. This was when I joined the world of work, and when I decided to continue the acts of kindness my brother and I had started all those years before. My true calling.

Had your father lived, I might well have wanted children at

a later age with him. In fact, I did try for some time in my late thirties with a different partner. But it never happened for me, and sadly, it took a toll on the relationship too. He, the unimaginative sort, could not bear to live without a child.

I have digressed, darling. There is just so much to say in so little time. My point was simply that I never let you out of my sight. I always planned on us reuniting one day. And once the internet came into the world, I made the next step, contacting you. While our friendship online might to your eyes have seemed organic, I had noticed you were a member of a Christian teachers' Facebook group. Like so many online groups, there were no objective methods by which to confirm that I met the entrance criteria. All that was required was the right performance. I learned very early from these encounters that you were unaccountably loyal to your 'parents'. You told me that you had no interest in finding your biological parents, and even harboured resentment. This confirmed to me that if I wanted to be in your life, I couldn't reveal myself. Certainly not while I was alive.

From then, my comments to you were always genuine, darling, but I was trying to positively influence you, too. Supporting your best thoughts. Ignoring your more idiotic ones. It was hard hearing about how much you were ignored by higher-ups at work. How much you had to do for so little pay. How much of a pushover you were, both at work and at home, and all so that people continued to think of you as nice. It appalled me, frankly. And at times I wanted to physically strike you for being so pathetic.

I must be honest about that. After all, true love is tough love. And soon, in our DMs, you were baring your soul to me. About your inability to make deep connections. Your lack of an anchor, as you called it. Your God-Shaped Hole. You were so open. While I appreciated that, I knew as a mother that it meant you were in danger. You needed me. Just as I needed you to bear witness to my work, and hopefully, carry it on after me.

When the time was right, I told you about the village. And how life here was value-led, and that we were trying to build a community of kind-hearted people. Very soon I began work on ridding the primary school of one of its young male teachers, very much in the fashion of my old French teacher, now I reflect on it. And when I sent you the advert, and you applied, it was one of the happiest days of my life. I knew already that you would get the role, even if I couldn't help you by making sure both the other applicants did not make their interviews.

Obviously, it was me that made sure October made you an offer on one of the cottages, an offer you couldn't possibly refuse. What you must understand about October is that despite her well-brought-up exterior, she really is just a hollow marionette. When she speaks, she uses my words. The woman has never sprung an original thought in her life. Her only motivation seems to be to copy. Copy her family's hippy-capitalist traditions. Copy the people around her. Copy what she sees on the news and reads on her phone.

But then you moved here with that man I had warned you about, Jamie. It didn't take me long to find out he was sleeping around behind your back. I had never liked him, darling. And I had tried, in my own subtle ways, to convince you to leave him. And to give you the confidence to want better. But no, gentle never works with you, does it? You have to be told. Shown. Explained to. Just like every religious person I've ever known, your own causal role in the world is a mystery. You wait for God to do things. Which makes you easy prey for those who think they're Gods.

But I digress, again, because what I needed to tell you is that I made sure that I had filmed him in the act. That was difficult, given he took his fancy woman to hotels. But, alas, money makes the world go round, and money is something hotel workers have in short supply. Once I had the footage, it was a matter of watching Jamie's movements, knowing when he left his laptop alone. The Film Society intermission was always so chaotic, I simply needed to slip in, insert a memory stick, and press play.

I am sorry that I had to do this to you, darling, but shock is what you need. That is just how your brain works, I believe. And certainly, it did the job. I thought my solution quite clever, in all honesty, because – unlike some of the actions I've taken in the village to bring about kinder outcomes (if I don't get time to tell you, find out about what I did to Hattie Milner so that I could simultaneously extend my role to the equestrian centre and rid the village of a miserable blight) – all I did here was show everyone Jamie's true nature.

Once he was gone, I started planning how to find you a suitable replacement. The last thing I wanted was you giving up on the village because it reminded you of that man. I was already sick, so time was short. But then one day he just arrived here, and for a moment I thought I'd seen him before because of how like Jamie he looked. How like so many of your partners over the years have looked. I could tell Tessa and Andy were quite taken with the place, and that they were on the brink of something in their relationship. I could feel the tension between them. Was there a problem here? A childless couple, a woman no longer at her most fertile. Had they tried? Failed. Were they here looking for some inspiration about how a future life might look? Or was I reading my own story into theirs?

Of course, I could tell from their clothes – inexpensive, sweatshop-made fare – that they had no money. Was there a chance they still rented? They might be in the market for a particularly attractive rent decrease. And I could tell this man was loyal, because while Tessa was not unattractive, she was far from ripe, shall we say. She doesn't even make the effort to reward his loyalty with make-up or hair dye. In one way I admire her for this, and darling, you could perhaps use just a little of this independent streak yourself, although that is another issue. However, here he was, this youthful, strong, handsome man at her side, clutching her hand like they'd only just started courting.

All of this was so much fantasy. And yet, I've come to trust this instinct. I've come to trust the little signs and portents that turn up in life, and allow myself the liberty of imagining what they mean. Why this man? Why now? And of course, I then saw your expression when you noticed him.

So I arranged that they would win the prize to come back here. Just to work on them some more. I watched your face again when you spoke with him at the bar. And was it really that much of a surprise when their application arrived in my inbox?

Getting them through the committee was a formality. I'd already told you all that I'd met them, and that they would be perfect. When I decide things, they have a tendency to come about, as I'm sure you've noticed. And I knew *you* were never going to vote against them, not when I reminded you who Andy was. Then, when Tessa splurged her heart out about kindness, I'm sure you were watching Andy's face and thinking, like me, that the two of them were doomed. Just as I'd anticipated. They just hadn't realised it yet. And what kinder act is there than making the conditions right for a life-changing epiphany?

My next steps were easy enough. To make one or two electrical adjustments to your house. I'm a fast learner, and a spoon in an extractor fan, a few snipped wires, some heat to the exterior of a plug socket can do more than any dating app, with the right timing. In the meantime I heightened the tension between the two of them. Made sure word spread about every little mistake Tessa made. Dropped remarks about how I wondered if she was another Eleanor Beddington. I sensed she wouldn't need much to sabotage herself, and I was right.

I did some reading around the role of a freelance composer, and came to understand that they often don't get paid until the end of a project. It seemed remarkable to me, and yet Tessa went for my phony offer at the expense of all her other projects. Her compositions were wonderful, I must say. Certainly a deal better than that depressing choral singing you played me from your university days, sorry to say. But I made impossible demands to her, and spun her along just enough to exacerbate what was already happening between the two of them. His doubts about her selfishness. About how little she valued or noticed him. How little she contributed emotionally and financially. And she just kept delivering to me, so in her own world that she didn't even notice her partner drifting towards you, my beautiful iceberg.

Which, of course, is what was needed for everyone's happiness. Andy would be happier with you. You would be happier with him. And Tessa, she is a free spirit. A Sharpie really, if I am honest now. Once she realises this, she will be happier, too. She can embrace her destiny, like I did. Perhaps become a Saint too, away from Nether Appleford.

Of course, then the babies happened, didn't they? How on earth was Andy supposed to settle into his new life with his doting, open-hearted new partner, surely soon to be wife, when he had finally managed to get his bitter, black-hearted ex pregnant. Knowing the man he is, he would spread himself between both of you evenly. Even if he detested the new child and all it stood for. That is the type of man he is. Simple. Loyal.

And Tessa… Did she really want his child now? It may as well have been Rosemary's baby, as far as she was concerned. She'd be a single mother to the baby of a fiend.

It was obvious what the kind thing to do was. The baby had to…

SIXTY-ONE

Tessa

T essa walked through the hospital, still dazed by what Olivia had gone on to tell her about how she'd met Ruth. She had found Olivia online. Formed an intense friendship with her. Engineered her a move to Nether Appleford. Been instrumental in giving her purpose by involving her with the committee.

'Does she have a key to your place?' Tessa had asked Olivia.

'For feeding the cat, yes. Although she has keys to all the houses in the estate office.'

Taking into account Ruth's reaction to Olivia having Dev's morning sickness medicine. Taking into account that Jayden had mentioned Ruth's name alongside Leo's last night. Taking into account all Ruth's strange advances these last few weeks. Was it so outlandish to suspect she might have had a role in pushing Andy and Olivia together, perhaps by sabotaging Olivia's electrics? Perhaps by occupying Tessa with a phony work project and playing on existing weaknesses in their relationship? Like their inability to have children, which Ruth had known about from the start.

She'd known everything from the start.

But now Tessa's pregnancy had thrown a spanner in the works. So she'd sent the other committee members to convince her to abort it. Or, perhaps just used those advances to make her seem more trustworthy. Then she'd had Dev try to poison Tessa. And when that hadn't worked, she'd somehow coerced Jayden into attacking her.

It was ridiculous. Bloody paranoid nonsense. And yet...

She was lost now, on a corridor she didn't recognise. She looked up and saw a sign above a set of double doors. Oncology. She didn't want to be here. Where the hell was she?

The doors below the sign opened, and adrenaline shot into Tessa's bloodstream.

'Oh, hello,' Ruth said, her face mirroring some of the shock Tessa felt.

'Ruth, hi.'

'What are you doing here?' Ruth said. For just a moment, her gaze drifted down to Tessa's belly. 'Everything alright?'

Why was she here? How was she here? Was it possible she'd been following her? She stared at this little woman. This bitch, with her harmless face and terrified-rabbit eyes, who had caused so much destruction and pain. *This* was who she had been scared of. *This* was the danger to her and her baby. Tessa's face had curdled into a snarl, so she quickly adjusted her expression. 'Yes, everything absolutely fine. I'm fine. I was here seeing Jayden.'

'Ah, yes. Of course.' She paused. Too long. 'Me too. What a terrible thing to have happened.'

'Yes, Olivia messaged me. Awful.'

Ruth smiled. Tessa smiled.

'It is a maze here, isn't it?' Ruth said.

'Yes. It is.'

They stared at one another, and eventually it was Ruth who blinked first.

'I tried to call you,' Ruth said. 'About an hour or so ago.'

'My phone's playing up.'

'Ah, I see. Well … Tessa, we should talk, shouldn't we?'

'Do you think so?'

'Yes. Yes, I do think so. I want to explain about running off so suddenly yesterday. You must have thought me awfully strange.'

'No, not at all.'

'Will you be in tonight?' Again, no doubt about it this time, Ruth's gaze wandered to Tessa's middle.

She had been planning to be far, far away by this evening. But not now. Knowing that the person behind all this was Ruth, *bloody Ruth*, she wanted this confrontation very much. She had to stop her, and now she was one step ahead, she had the opportunity, too. Ruth was obviously clever and devious, and covered her tracks so well to make sure she was untouchable. But she had no idea she'd been caught.

'I'll be in,' she said.

Looking at Ruth now, so small and yet capable of so much destruction, she knew exactly what she had to do. She'd been bested before, hadn't she? Her tree incident. Undone simply by a neighbour's security camera system.

Tessa had started smiling again, and something like alarm crossed Ruth's face. They nodded at one another, and Ruth walked away.

'See you tonight,' Tessa said.

A video camera. A simple bit of modern technology. Pathetic, really.

SIXTY-TWO

Tessa

S he caught a taxi back to Nether Appleford from the city centre. Her phone fixed, she explored her missed calls and messages. As well as the missed call from Ruth, she had voice-mails from her sister and from Andy. She listened to the first few seconds of Maddy's message from last night, and couldn't bear to hear her concern. She cut the message short and called her. She answered after a single ring.

'Tess, you okay?' She sounded like she'd been drinking coffee for three days straight.

'Yes, I'm okay.'

'Oh, thank God. Andy. Andy, it's Tessa.' She heard Andy muttering in the background. Why were those two together? 'Where the hell are you, Tessa?'

'I'm just in a taxi heading home. Why are you with Andy?'

'Because I'm at his house.'

'At Olivia's? Why?'

'Because of your voicemail last night,' she said, exasper-ated. 'And then you didn't answer your phone last night or this morning. I didn't know what had happened and...' She took a deep, juddery breath. 'I was so worried, Tess. Didn't you get my messages?'

Tessa had to take a breath not to cry herself. 'I didn't. My phone... I broke my phone. I went to get it fixed. So you're at Olivia's?'

'I didn't know where else to go, and I didn't want to phone the police because you said one of the committee was a policeman. So I wanted to check with Andy first, so I called him and went over.'

'Maddy, I'm so sorry. I'm okay and I'll be back soon. I'll explain everything.'

'Fine, yeah, cool. But you're okay?'

'Yes, I'm okay. It's all going to be fine.'

When Tessa was five minutes away she texted Maddy, and she was waiting outside Tessa's cottage by the time the taxi pulled up. Andy stood with her. Tessa walked up the drive and hugged her sister before letting her inside.

'You can go now,' Tessa said to Andy.

'Did you listen to my voicemail?'

'No.' She'd assumed he'd been chasing her on behalf of Maddy or calling about Jayden.

Andy reached into his pocket and took out a small polystyrene takeaway pot. 'It's some of that stuff from the fridge.' He handed it to her and when she reluctantly took it, he shrugged.

'Why?' she said.

'I don't know.' He looked away. 'You know ... something you said. About Ruth.'

'What about her?'

'Well ... remember that thing of yours I found in the

studio? I didn't *just* find it.'

'No?'

'Ruth said to me she'd seen you coming out of Kath's with something that looked like ... well ... weirdly, she said it was marijuana, but ... I just thought I should mention she was the one that put it in my head.'

'I see.'

'And I never told her afterwards that I'd found it either. But then ... she asked me where I'd found it. Which was ... strange. Not "*did you*", but "*where*".'

'Did you tell her?'

'No, I think Olivia might have told her – they do talk a lot. But I did think, why was she so interested in the drugs?'

'Right.'

'Anyway, I just... Maybe I don't trust Ruth, that's all I'm saying. And maybe I trust you.'

She looked at the pot, and back up at Andy. 'Thanks, Andy. I just hope I'm wrong about this.'

'Yeah. Me too, to be honest.'

———

Once inside, she heard the sound of the kettle boiling, and Maddy striding around the kitchen.

'I'm so sorry for scaring you,' Tessa said. 'Who's got Juliet?'

'Bhav. Was everything okay with Andy? Sorry for involving him.' She sounded weary, and when she came closer to hand over some ginger tea, she looked it too.

They sat opposite one another at the table. Tessa wanted her gone. It wasn't safe, and Tessa had things to do. A plan to enact that needed preparation.

The pot was still in Tessa's hand. She slid it across to Maddy.

'What's this?' Maddy said.

'Some of the stuff the committee tried to give me. I probably overreacted, and I'm really sorry if I have, but do you think there would be a way to work out if there is anything harmful to me or the baby in this?'

'You want me to see if someone at the lab will analyse it?'

'Is that possible? I mean, yes. How long would that take?'

Maddy picked up the pot, peered inside, and fastened the lid again. 'Are you coming back with me now? I think you should.'

'I just need… I just need a few days to tidy up things here first. On my own. Then, yeah, I'm getting out of here.'

Maddy stared at her sceptically. 'You sound unsure. And that unsettles me, because … that's not you.'

'Well … I'm trying to be a more rounded person.'

Maddy still didn't look convinced. 'I think if you're not coming with me, I'll stay here with you.'

It was out of the question. She needed Ruth alone, and Maddy as far from danger as possible.

'Please, Maddy. I need you to go. I'm sorry you came all this way. I'm sorry I left you that message. Thank you. But I really need you to find out what's in that pot as soon as you can. Please.'

'Really?' She fell silent and considered this for a while. 'And if this comes back positive for something, what then?'

'Then I have proof.'

'And you come to me immediately?'

'Yes. I come to you.'

'Straight away?'

'Yes, straight away.'

Maddy reached over the table and offered her little finger to Tessa. Tessa hooked her own little finger around hers. For the longest time they sat in silence that way.

It took another hour for Maddy to finally get in her car and drive off. Once she did, Tessa wasted no time. She grabbed her studio key, walked out into the garden, and once inside began to flick switches and push buttons. The radiator warmed the room. The PA hummed. And she sat down at the computer and began to work.

SIXTY-THREE

Tessa
_____

R uth arrived on time, of course. But she looked tired and
out of sorts. She wore a jumper with creases, and her
ponytail looked hastily fashioned. At her side, her handbag
bulged, and she covered it with a protective hand. Tessa made
a mental note of this.

'It's a bit dark,' Ruth said, closing the front door
behind her.

She was right. It was cold, too, and that was because Tessa
had already had the heating off for a few hours and had turned
all the lights off but for a single lamp in the corner. 'I've been
working out in the studio. Maybe when we're done talking, we
could try a song.'

'Oh.' Her surprise pleased Tessa. She'd rocked her already.
'Yeah, why not?'

Once inside the studio, Tessa picked up a guitar and sat
down on the office chair, liking a solid object between the two
of them. Ruth perched on the sofa, placing her bag carefully
beside her. She began to scan the room while Tessa ran her
fingers up a scale.

Ruth lifted her hands up to her head, and with a tug she tore off her hair. Tessa stopped playing. Ruth placed the wig down to one side of her and reached up to adjust the velvet hairband parting her grey stubble. 'Well, here you go. I owed you an explanation, so … ta da.'

All Tessa could think of to say was, 'Wow, okay.' It was shocking to see her this way. Her hair gone, she looked even smaller and more delicate. 'What do you have?'

'Breast cancer. Quite advanced, I'm afraid. The chemo is palliative.' Both palms came out as if to say, *You were after a big secret, well, here it is.* 'That day I ran off, I was suddenly feeling terribly sick. Funny, given what we were discussing at the time. As I'm sure you know, it comes in sudden waves.'

'I'm so sorry,' some robot Tessa recited.

'That's the real reason I was at the hospital today, actually. I'm sorry I lied. They say I will be lucky to see the New Year, although they've been wrong a lot so far.'

'I'm just… I don't know what to say.'

'You don't have to say anything. But do you understand now?'

'Well, yes. Of course. I thought it would be something like that. You didn't look well at all.'

'No. I'm really not.' She gave a smile that was unfortunately ghoulish without the colour of her wig to offset her pallid skin.

Despite this revelation, Tessa wasn't buying it. 'Why did you go to Olivia's?' she asked.

'Olivia's. When?'

The way Ruth's face remained so effortlessly calm, even though she'd been caught out, encouraged Tessa further. 'After you left here that day you felt sick, I went after you. To see if you were okay. And I saw you go to Olivia's.'

Her jaw hardened and the smile slid away. Another blow.

After a moment, she looked like she was about to say something. Then she started to scan the room. Her gaze alighted on a vocal microphone standing to one side of the drum kit. Like a search beam, it moved to the microphones around the drums. Finally, she noticed the microphone behind her, in the corner of the room behind the sofa. Just a metre away.

'Actually, Tess,' she said, 'would you mind if we went back in the house, please?'

She'd realised, hadn't she? Tessa looked confused, hunching further over the guitar for fear of Ruth being able to see how hard her heart was beating beneath her top. 'I think we should stay here. It's too cold in the house.'

'No, I'm... I just think we should talk first. The heat in here, the lack of air, is making me muzzy.'

'Shall I open the door? I've got the radiator on full. I'll turn it down.' She got to her feet.

'Could we go now? I'm actually feeling very light-headed.'

Ruth was already up and out of the door. She had her bag and wig against her chest.

Tessa set the guitar on its stand and pursued her. Her phone buzzed on her way through the door. She took it out from her pocket and caught the gist of the incoming message from what briefly appeared on her lock screen. She opened the full message and had read it by the time she reached the lounge, where Ruth now sat waiting for her on the sofa. It was a message from Maddy.

Are you around to talk? I pulled in a huge favour and had them look at your sample at the labs this afternoon. My colleague just sent back the results. Not sure how you're going to feel, but lots of ginger. No poison though. I still think...

She didn't read the rest. Her body sagged.

'Bad news?' Ruth said.

'It's nothing.'

'I see. Well, Tessa, perhaps it's a generational thing, but do you think we could turn our phones off? I really would like to speak without interruption.'

Tessa didn't know how, but Ruth had sensed what was in that message. Had she made a miscalculation? If this woman had done all the things she suspected, she would make it her business to know everything, wouldn't she? And the sample coming back negative was further proof of that. Ruth would *never* have left evidence of her crime behind, would she? If anything, she'd have taken the opportunity to make Tessa look even more crazed by replacing the poison mixture with a clean one. Just in case Tessa somehow managed to convince Andy to give her a sample of it.

She should have seen it before. Because the obvious thing for Ruth to have done would have been to simply throw the medicine away, wouldn't it? Let Andy and Olivia think they'd mislaid it. Leaving it spilled in the fridge was a level of second-guessing that spoke of frightening degrees of planning and detail.

That she hadn't thrown it away entailed something else too. It meant that Ruth had known exactly how her sudden departure would be perceived by Tessa. That Tessa would have guessed the medicine was intended to harm her baby. That was why she'd instructed her attacker to come that same evening. She knew she might not have much time.

And of course, she'd spotted the microphones Tessa had set up in the studio immediately and straight away moved the conversation elsewhere.

'Yeah, sure, we can turn them off,' Tessa said. 'I'm with you there, to be honest. I wish I wasn't as addicted to this thing as I am.' She walked over to the window and put the phone on the window-sill.

'Is it off?' Ruth said. 'Look, I've switched off mine.' Holding up the screen, she walked over and put it next to Tessa's. Tessa held up hers again and let Ruth watch her power it down. She was removing any chance of being recorded. What she was about to say must be interesting.

'Perfect,' Ruth said, and resumed her position on the sofa. 'Now let's get to it. You were asking why I was at Olivia's.'

'I was just interested in why you would go there if you felt sick.'

'I'm sure you were.' Did Tessa see a little between-us-girls glint in her eyes now? 'Well, I wanted to … I was…' She hummed, but not in a troubled way, rather as if she'd stumbled across a chess strategy she'd not encountered before. 'Tell me something first. Why were you really at the hospital today?'

'I was seeing Jayden.'

'Ah, Jayden, okay. Well, I was just going to Olivia's to get a glass of water. I didn't feel capable of getting to mine. And I was confused.'

Tessa took a deep breath. 'So why did you go back to yours, come out with a key, and go back in again? And why did Andy find Dev's medicine all over his fridge?'

Ruth's eyes widened with what appeared to be amazement. She leaned forward, crossed her legs, and whispered, 'Do you *know*?' After submitting her to an inspection she leaned back again. 'I just can't tell if you know. I think you do. But perhaps not.'

'I don't know what you're talking about.'

'Tell me why you were at the hospital?'

As much as she wanted to resist letting Ruth take control of the conversation, she saw no point in holding back now. She knew what she was angling for and let her have it. 'I miscarried.'

'Oh. You did?'

'I went for a check-up. I saw Jayden, too. But…'

'I'm sorry, Tessa. That is a shame.'

'I was attacked in my house. A man broke in and hit me in the belly with a tyre iron.'

Ruth closed her eyes and shook her head. 'How awful. How awful. Why?'

'He thought I had some drugs that belonged to him.'

She actually tutted. 'And you didn't go to the police?'

'No. Because I thought it might have something to do with Jayden.'

'Jayden. Oh, my. Awful. Awful. How do you feel now?'

'How you would imagine. Except maybe … maybe in some ways it makes things easier. Easier for Andy. And Olivia.'

Ruth was nodding, those eyes still sparkling like sunlight on the open patches of an algae-covered pond. 'Do you know, then? Go on, tell me what you know.'

'What I know?'

'Yes. What do you think I was doing in Olivia's house? You obviously thought it might be interesting, given you were trying to record me in there.' She cocked her head in the general direction of the studio.

Tessa nodded, her eyes watering over when she tried to be tough and stare her down. Here went nothing. 'I think October made you do it all. I think October has a special relationship with Olivia. I think she chose Andy and me to live here. And I think she worked very hard to split Andy and me up, and get Olivia and Andy together. I think me getting pregnant wasn't part of the plan. And I think she made the rest of the committee try to convince me out of having the baby, possibly as a tactic to make you seem more trustworthy, or possibly because she really did believe in their powers of persuasion. And then she sent Dev to poison me. And when that didn't work, I think you panicked when you found out I'd given the poison to Andy, and ran off to stop Olivia being poisoned. And then October sent a man to kill the baby in a different way.'

'October, you say?' She grinned like an aggressive chimpanzee. 'I have to say, Tessa, you are very, very clever. *October*. Are you hoping you'll wound my pride? That I'll rise up and say, "October couldn't do that, it was me. All me."'

Tessa swallowed. 'October runs Nether Appleford, doesn't she? It's her village?'

'I liked you from the start, Tessa. I really did. I've liked you more and more as time has gone on. You are quite something. What my brother and I would have called a Sharpie.'

'A what?' Tessa almost laughed.

She reached behind for her bag, and brought it to her lap. If it was a weapon, Tessa wasn't unprepared. Part of her plan this afternoon had been to hide weapons around the house, just in case things took a violent turn. Beneath this sofa was the steak knife.

From the bag, though, Ruth brought out two items. One was a blue A4 hardback notebook. On the front in black pen was written, How to Kill with Kindness. The other was a medicine bottle, just like the one Tessa let Andy take for Olivia. She placed the latter down by her feet, the former on her lap.

'I think once the brain knows that death is near,' Ruth said, 'it communicates this to the rest of the body. I know all of my parts are whispering to one another to down tools, like factory workers when revolution is in the air. Keeping busy has helped, though. It sends the opposite message. That there are still important things to do. And I needed to prepare to hand my work over to a successor. And I wanted that person to understand what it takes to truly be a kind person. That sort of thing requires intelligence. And a hard heart. The capacity to be cruel in order to be kind.'

'Being cruel to be kind.'

'Yes. Don't pretend you don't understand. You know that *true* kindness can't be distilled onto a little plastic heart. That it isn't always fit for public consumption. *True* kindness is being attacked by some thug and then *not* going to the police – just to protect a young miscreant whose entire life would be ruined if he entered the criminal justice system. It's taking drugs from a friend's house in full view of other people, for what reason, I can't be certain, but I'd wager it was simply to salvage her reputation. Kindness, Tessa, is deciding to play music with two people no one else would bother with, simply because *you* think it might enrich their lives – despite everyone else frowning at you and calling you all sorts of names.'

'You think those things are kind?'

'Yes. Yes, of course. You are a very kind person, Tessa. In the most meaningful way.'

She was about to say something about how what she'd done wasn't kind. That all she'd done was what she thought was right. But she didn't, because Ruth had just told her she was kind. And that was extremely funny. After all this time, all this effort, someone had finally said it about her.

'You said it when you first met the committee,' Ruth said. 'Kindness is about kinship. Treating others as you would family, which is what you did. But most people, Tessa, they only know how to *appear* kind. And that's because they just want to be liked. Not like you and I. But that is fine, of course, because kindness rarely flourishes between Sharpies – and too many

Sharpies spoil the broth, as the saying should be. Kind communities should primarily be people who *don't* have that little voice in their head always asking questions. Telling them something is wrong. Because put a Sharpie in charge, Tessa, and nothing *is* wrong. Do you follow?'

'I think so. You don't think most people can treat others like family. That they're not … intelligent enough to know what that truly entails.'

Ruth closed her eyes, smiled like she'd tasted the most delicious meal of her life, and clutched her book to her chest. 'It is a lonely life, understanding the world. I used to have my brother to share things with, but since his death I've had to do things alone. But you understand, I think. In fact, I *know* you do.' She held out the book. 'Here.'

She took the book from Ruth and placed it on her lap. She opened it and saw a long bullet-point list on the inside cover headed, RULES FOR BEING TRULY KIND.

- *you cannot be truly kind until you are kind to yourself*
- *a kind person is a flexible person*
- *the harder it feels, the kinder you're being*

Tessa turned the page and found more of Ruth's familiar handwriting, this time just paragraph after paragraph of her unfiltered thoughts. She flicked through the rest and found most of the book had been used.

'Do you want me to read this?' Tessa said.

'I've been trying to get it all down, but I've not been at my best. And I was concerned time was running out, and while I think it's all there, admittedly, it's somewhat chaotic. But … yes, it's all there. Please.'

'You want me to read it *now*?'

'Yes. It won't take you long. I write very concisely. And I want to watch your face.'

'Okay.' She didn't know what she was about to encounter, but if Ruth had written everything she'd done here, she had the proof she needed in her hands. She just had to play along.

'Then when you're done,' Ruth said, 'we'll talk more.'

SIXTY-FOUR

How to Kill with Kindness

Tessa. Darling. For the longest time I have been writing this for Olivia, who through biological connection is technically my kin. I assumed that because of this, within her lay the dormant ability to comprehend what it means to be 'truly' kind. I believed she was best placed to continue my work, given what little time I had left. Or, if not continue it, at least be inspired by it.

I believed that she would be the only person who might, at least eventually, with some tutelage, place me in the context I deserve. These things I've had to do, they are not 'average' things. They are the business of gods in a world without them. But a rational, logical person can't ignore them. That is irresponsible. Inaction is action. God will not sort them all out, so I must.

Perhaps now, having read about what I've done, you find it laughable that I believed Olivia capable of taking on my work. I do, but on the ride of time we must stay in our seats. And as I have already stated, not knowing the future is no reason not to act in the present.

I worked very hard with Olivia for many years, possibly seeing what I wanted to, but feeling very much that I was making some progress. So many late-night conversations, messages, and phone calls. I took her to films and played her music to broaden her horizons. For years we had a 'Philosophy Club', which she eventually wanted us to call a 'Philosophy and Faith' club. In the end she found this too stressful, because she couldn't understand that simply saying, 'but that's just not Christian' was not an adequate refutation of a given argument. Instead, we tried a 'Culture Club', and I tried a strategy of propaganda. I should have known I was in trouble when she couldn't even handle Philip Pullman. But one persists. Because of family. Because of kinship.

But her 'parents' had done a lot of damage, lumped her with a *Weltanschauung* which likely never fitted her make-up. Oh yes, I do believe religiosity is something one is genetically predisposed to – and when you are innately capable of seeing the wood for the trees, yet continue to ignore such an ability, the cognitive dissonance is incredibly stressful. My hope was that by bringing her to me, and trying to unpick all that oppression-masked-as-humility, she might flourish.

I told myself I was making progress. That perhaps inside she was absorbing everything I was saying, despite not necessarily showing this on the outside. That she went along with so many of the committee's more difficult decisions, I took not to be passivity or mimesis – perhaps at first these had been factors – but actual non-dogmatic moral reasoning. That she stopped making the treks to the church in the next village was positive, too. And I convinced myself that it was her impoverished emotional life – one brought on by my abandonment of her so young, and having been raised by parents intellectually unfit to do so – that might be the last obstacle to her full epiphany.

Jamie, and his very elementary mind, had to go first. He was the partner you choose when you hate yourself, and I'm only sad he got away so lightly.

That she went for Andy, an upgrade on Jamie both physically and mentally, I took to be positive, also. A pragmatic decision not held back by his relationship with you. I couldn't imagine her embarking on an affair when she first moved here. Andy is, for want of many other things, loyal and predictable – obvious to me immediately and confirmed with an online search. His profession. His presentation. His choice of partner.

Yet still, my own time was running out. And I knew that, as it had been with Jamie, it was perhaps a shock she needed to finally understand what her role in the world, and in the village, was to be. Hence me putting this all down for her in the bluntest possible terms.

Which brings me to you, Tessa. I don't feel I need to apologise for anything that I've done that may have, at least initially, hurt you. I suspect once you have read this, you will understand my decisions. Perhaps you might even thank me before I shuffle off this mortal coil.

I did what I did with a mother's love. Now, I know how that must sound, but I suspect you may already be ahead of me now. For surely this non-biological, familial connection we have is at the root of all kindness. And I did what I did because I believed this arrangement would be kinder for everyone involved.

Andy was not a match for you, Tessa. He is meat and potatoes with only a teaspoon of cranberry sauce, not fit for an appetite as complex as yours. And while I know that even the strongest of us require a retinue, Andy, unfortunately, can't stand to simply exist alone. Big on the outside, small inside, he will forever require a higher power. He abandoned one religion in favour of another, namely you. Your insight and critical mind became his new bible. But he is one of those I speak of, with a religious disposition, who are simply born with a lack of belief in themselves that dooms them to a life of prostration.

The problem with such people is that they can always go lower. They will never feel humble enough. Once he grew dissatisfied with you, Tessa – which he was always bound to, given he could never see your true worth – he was bound to succumb to the pathetic gravity of that mass of wish-fulfilment in the sky, and His earthly representatives, such as Olivia. Boundless, unrealistic hope versus earthy, hard-earned realism: you could never win. Frankly, you couldn't give him children, Tessa. And take it from my own experience, that is all you are worth to lead-headed men such as him.

But what I don't think you've properly understood yet, is that you *are not* a mother. Your parents should have been honest with you about this. That is for other women. It isn't for women like you and me. We are not bread ovens in dresses. We have ambitions and plans to affect the world around us, often without recognition. We are the eye-rolling civil service who keep 'leaders' from blowing us all up. We are the angel investors silently moving history forward. We are Atlas, holding up the heavens for all eternity.

Tessa, all this time I saw you as an enemy. Because, despite all my claims to perspicacity, I had become blinded by that biological understanding of family. And even though I knew what you were capable of, and every act of violent independence you've taken since being here had only strengthened my conviction, I was too busy viewing you as an obstacle to Olivia to see what you really are. In short, a true daughter. Someone mentally capable of understanding me and what I have been doing here.

I don't know at what point I was still thinking *Olivia* when actually I was writing to you. Perhaps in some ways I've always been writing to you, at least in the platonic sense. But when we spoke at the hospital, and I could see in your eyes that you knew so much more than you'd been letting on, that's when I knew for certain that...

SIXTY-FIVE

Tessa

It went on like this for several more pages. Tessa's eyes, blurring occasionally with Kath-tears, Eleanor-tears, people-she-hadn't-even-met-tears, scanned over what was left – equally unhinged but now repetitive and increasingly hard to follow. Without her phone she didn't know how long had passed, but had it been an hour? Maybe more. The whole time Ruth sat watching her.

She handed the book back, and Ruth took it from her and slid it back inside her bag. She tilted her head to one side and grinned again.

'Well. What have you learned?' Ruth sounded like an eager teacher.

Tessa looked up at her but found her gaze too vertiginous to hold. She looked over at the front door, as good as Mars to her in terms of proximity. She had assumed that something was very wrong in Nether Appleford, and that Ruth had done some terrible things. Yet she hadn't even been close to understanding the depths of this human chasm sitting before her.

Jayden. All those things she had made Leo do to him. Mind

games. Harassment. Planting drugs. Making him attack Tessa. All to get him out of the way of her grand plan.

She'd made a dreadful mistake meeting Ruth tonight. Despite everything that she'd done, she hadn't really believed Ruth might try or even be capable of killing her here tonight. Now, she could imagine it all too well – and her first priority was getting through the rest of this encounter unscathed. She had to play along. Despite Ruth's attempt to kill her baby. Despite her role in Jayden's attack. Despite that she had murdered multiple times in cold blood.

'What I've learned,' Tessa said, in the most academic tone she could muster, 'is that you and your brother mercifully killed your very sick grandmother as children. You learned that doing the kind thing was sometimes difficult, but that you were capable of doing it. And that made you realise you were capable of doing other difficult things to be kind. Things others couldn't do.' Tessa could hear herself mollifying Ruth despite her best efforts to sound genuine. Ruth didn't appear to notice; she nodded away. 'And you wanted your daughter, Olivia, to continue after your cancer overwhelms you. But now…'

'Yes?'

'Now you want me to … take over your work.'

'Why?'

'Because you think I'm capable. You think I'm a Sharpie. Maybe even a … Saint.' Such ridiculous words, even more childish out loud than on the page, yet Tessa got it out straight-faced.

'And why would that be important?'

Tessa, unsure now, tried to make it look like she knew by smiling. It bought her seconds at most. An idea floated nearby, and she grasped it. 'It's the kindest outcome. For you. Me. The village.'

'Exactly. The village can be your baby now, Tessa. Olivia

and Andy would be happy anywhere really. They're not bound here. They both work. And I will die knowing that kindness in the village prevails. What do you think?'

'What do I think?'

'Yes.' Ruth leaned forward hungrily, the salivating, sharp-toothed predator in every fairy tale Tessa had been frightened of as a child.

She knew she couldn't just say, 'Yes, of course'. As much as she wanted this to be over and would utter almost anything to get things done quickly, there was something as yet left unexplained. A constant presence in her peripheral vision now was that bottle of poison by Ruth's feet. Saying Yes might bring forward whatever Ruth had planned. She had to buy herself time.

'I think you're incredibly intelligent. I think that I can see the logic you've used to bring about some of the things you've done. But you killed Kath. You sent Jayden to make me miscarry. And though I can see from what you've written that you had reasons, I need time to understand and not react emotionally.'

Ruth's expression darkened. 'I see.'

'It's like reading an academic paper, or something. The argument is persuasive and seems to follow but … the conclusions are difficult to stomach. It's … counter-intuitive.'

Now Ruth's scowl softened, and she looked upward in thought. 'I see. Interesting.'

'Can I keep the book? Read it through more?'

Ruth laughed. 'I'm not sure we're quite there yet, Tessa. But we could be, you know? A little bit of trust is in order, I think.' She reached down for the bottle, opened it, and passed it to her. 'A little bit of trust.'

Tessa didn't take it. 'Trust goes both ways. I've already told you. I miscarried.'

With a forceful thrust of the bottle and an eye-roll, Ruth insisted again. 'Applicant, meet employer.'

Tessa closed her eyes, hoping for a miracle now. She took the bottle, fighting hard to conceal her terror. She wasn't winning, though.

'I don't want to do this,' Tessa said.

'You're not a mother, Tessa. That's not your role in life.'

'I know that. But is this what I think it is?'

Ruth shrugged.

'Is this Dev's morning sickness remedy?' The dreadful truth of that name for it struck her suddenly.

Ruth nodded.

'If it's mifepristone... I had a terrible reaction once. I was sick for days. I don't think it's safe to take after what's already happened to me, Ruth.'

Finally, a hint of concern appeared in her expression. 'Trust.'

'Well...' Tessa was running out of options. If Ruth wasn't moved by what she'd said already—

'Ruth, are you going to die before the concert?'

She stared at Tessa emotionless.

'Because I thought you wanted to sing with me there. Or was that all just bullshit to try and get close to me, to work out what I was going to do about the baby?'

She kept staring, and eventually said, 'I am hoping to still be alive at the weekend. And I would like to sing one last time, so that these people get a little glimpse of what I once was.'

'Exactly. We can't do it if I'm in hospital.'

'Goodness, you are dramatic.' Ruth shook her head and sighed. 'Show me, then.'

'Show you?'

'Show me.' Ruth patted her belly.

Tessa understood and nodded. She closed her eyes and

lifted her top. Ruth stared. Stared at the bruise-like make-up on Tessa's belly, something she'd learned to do from a YouTube video and had applied in under an hour. A torn sponge. Red, brown and terracotta first. Blue, green and yellow. The effect was impressive, even for someone who was certainly an amateur where make-up was concerned.

'Stand up,' Ruth said. Tessa obliged. Ruth reached out and touched her. As she'd planned to do, she yelled and flinched on contact. It worked. Ruth apologised, and encouraged Tessa to sit and lower her jumper. Tessa wanted to cry with gratitude, but it wasn't over yet. Ruth was studying her now, silent. Did she suspect? Was she toying with her?

Tessa took a breath, and not able to quite believe the words were coming out of her mouth, she said, 'Ruth, I'm not going to lie. I can't get past some of the things you've done. Yet, another part of me, up here,' she pointed to her temple, 'is excited by this. Okay?' Ruth's eyes widened. 'And I'm fascinated by you.'

Ruth's posture stiffened. She pushed out her chest. 'I see. Well … I suppose a few days won't matter, will it? Perhaps we perform our song, and celebrate afterwards with your gesture of trust. Then we'll get you set up on the committee. I'm sure they would be very receptive to you as a member.' A galaxy of slyness twinkling in her eyes.

It would have to do. 'Okay, fine. But can I ask you some things?'

Ruth nodded.

'What happens to Jayden now?'

'He's burned his bridges here, hasn't he?'

'What about all those things he knows?'

She narrowed her eyes. 'Well, everyone knows a lot about everyone around here. So what? To me it all feels … balanced.'

Tessa nodded. 'So he's safe.'

She shrugged, met her gaze, and nodded.

'And how do you do it all? I mean, really. Even after reading that... How do you keep them all in line? Someone like Leo...'

'So many questions. Well, it's different for everyone. But in many ways, it's the same. People just can't bear it if they're not thought of as kind. Saying *Just Be Kind* goes a long, long way. It's not that different from just saying, *Obey*, really.' She bobbed her eyebrows like it explained everything. In some ways, it did. 'And deep down, people don't want to think about what's right. They want to be told what it is, so they can focus on the performance of being a good person. It's bonding, and it gives you a sense of self.'

'That's ... fascinating.'

'Do you have your answers?' Ruth said, 'If so, shall we sing? We've not long now.'

She had played music in many different circumstances: a post-jilt wedding, a squat during a police raid, a barge full of ex-cons, but nothing had ever been as strange as performing jazz standards with Ruth after what had just transpired between them. Especially given that her voice, throaty and honey-toned, with a powerful vibrato, was nothing short of remarkable. It was as if someone had switched on a radio.

When they were done, Ruth re-affixed her wig, collected her phone from the lounge, and touched Tessa's arm. It took great effort not to recoil. When the cottage door closed Tessa stood watching it for a minute before running upstairs once more to check from the window that Ruth wasn't waiting outside to return. When enough time had passed, enough time to be sure, Tessa went back into lounge and moved the sofa. Beneath it, she had stashed the laptop, open at 180 degrees so that it squeezed beneath. She righted the screen, and moved the mouse, careful not to disturb the USB pre-amp she'd hidden beside it just in case it triggered some catastrophic error.

Her recording software was open behind the black screensaver, and when she saw the line was still moving, indicating a live recording, a nasal screech of victory erupted from her. It had worked. It had bloody worked! The whole conversation had been picked up by her brand-new perimeter microphones.

'I've got you,' she said. 'I actually fucking got you.'

Tessa had set things up so obviously in the studio that Ruth would want to move them to the lounge. And she'd fallen for it. She'd come to the one room where there were more microphones than anywhere else in the house.

Now Tessa just had to hope that what she had recorded was enough.

SIXTY-SIX

Jayden

He woke up in pain, his neck and head volleying agony back and forth in an endless rally. When he opened his eyes, it was like emerging from a vivid dream. This room, this bed, this gown, all seemed both familiar and alien. He called out and a nurse came.

Once the medics had fussed around him and he had eaten, Olivia spoke with him. Over and over she said he seemed so much more like himself, although he had no idea what that meant, because his last real memory had been the journey in Andy's van to the hospital. She held his hand, briefly, but couldn't make eye-contact. They struggled to make conversation, which was fine by him, because once the painkillers started fading, he couldn't really concentrate. But she reminded him of the fight he'd had with Andy, and *everything* came back to him, and along with it, a deep sense of embarrassment and shame.

'What happens next?' he asked.

'They want to keep you in another forty-eight hours. But

after that, Jayden, I'm really sorry, but you're not going to be able to come back with me.'

She relayed the next steps to him, and he listened as best he could. When she was done, he nodded, accepting his fate. She'd already packed up his things, and the social worker would collect them from Olivia.

'I'm sorry you have to miss the end of term, but the good news is, you can just start up in January again. They have a temporary family which is closer to Birmingham. Which is better, really, isn't it? And you can still see some of your friends here, on the train maybe?'

She knew that wouldn't happen. He'd not been here long enough to really make any friends worth keeping.

A nurse came in later that afternoon. 'There's someone here to see you,' he said.

Jayden grew tense. Was it someone from the committee? Had they found out he hadn't done what he said he would?

'Someone called Tessa,' the nurse said. 'Dark hair. Pale. Heart tattoo on her wrist.'

Jayden nodded, scared now in a different way. When she came in, though, she hugged him. It hurt him to squeeze her back, but he did it anyway and didn't complain. She'd brought him chocolate, and grapes, and a giant bottle of Lucozade. He felt a surge of adoration, and had the ridiculous urge to tell her he loved her. But he kept quiet.

'I'm so sorry,' he said. 'They made me do it.'

'I know,' Tessa said. 'I know everything.'

Quietly, she told him about Ruth trying to poison her. About how Tessa had caught her out and Ruth had come clean, making her read a book detailing everything she'd ever done in the village, and more. Tessa appeared to tread carefully around which details to share with him, restarting sentences, falling into long pauses.

He couldn't process it all at first. Tessa had implied that Ruth had hurt and maybe killed a lot of people. He had so many questions. Felt so much relief and anger jostling for space with his continuously morphing fear.

'So *Ruth* made Leo do those things to me?'

'She has something over him,' Tessa said. 'Over all of them. She wasn't happy Olivia fostered you, but apparently after meeting your birth mother, Olivia was planning on taking you on longer-term. Ruth had plans for Olivia, though, and you didn't fit, so she tasked Leo with trying to catch you out doing something bad. But when he actually couldn't get anything on you, she asked him to make something happen. I'm guessing you found the drugs.'

He nodded. 'They didn't know?'

'They assumed, but Ruth decided you were a bit cleverer than they'd given you credit for. They bided their time, and when we started playing music together, Ruth started encouraging Olivia's worries about rock music being the devil's work, to try and get rid of you. I think at some point she had an idea you'd given the drugs to Kath or me, and she wanted to try and catch us out. She didn't know the complete truth, but she came close when she told Andy to look for drugs at mine. But not long after, you came to her.'

She waited for him to volunteer his side of the story, and so he told her about Rags, and how he thought he had nothing to lose, so wanted to bring down the committee. When he was done, Tessa said, 'I think they've done something to your friend. But after my speaking to Ruth … and your fight with Andy … they consider you dealt with. Okay?'

'Why were you talking to her? Was it true you and her were playing music together?'

'No. Not really. She was trying to get close to me and wanted to do something at the concert, the three of us.'

'So you're not playing the concert?'

Tessa sighed. 'That's not the point.'

'You are?'

'I'm playing along right now, okay? While I deal with it. That's what I wanted to come here and tell you now, okay? I know they are moving you back to Birmingham, and Jayden, that's a good thing. Go, and don't come back.'

'Did she kill Kath?'

She looked at her hands, began to squeeze the web between her thumb and finger, and nodded. 'And I'm not going to let her get away with it. But that isn't your problem now.'

Jayden felt his face twisting. He couldn't get enough breath through his nose, but he didn't want to open his mouth because he might start shouting. His hands gripped the sheets.

'I know,' Tessa said. 'Just stay calm, okay.'

'Nah, man. Nah. We've got to… She's got to pay, Tessa. Seriously.'

'Hey.' She put a hand on his arm. 'Hey, stay calm. Don't make me regret telling you this.'

He looked at her, saw determination and anger like his own in her eyes. 'She's got to pay.'

'I'm working on it, okay?'

'How?' He sounded whiny, he could hear himself. Tessa shot him a warning look and he looked down at his balled fists. He closed his eyes and a high-pitched noise filled his ears. The world swam away briefly.

'You okay, Jayden?'

'Yeah. I'm fine.'

Ruth and that committee. They'd completely fucked him. They'd murdered Kath and Rags. They'd ruined everything.

'Why?' he said, his voice stretched and thin. 'Why is she like this?'

'She's very different, Jayden. It's as simple as that. She thinks her difference is a super-power. But that's just a story. A bit like kindness. Kindness is a story we tell about the things we do, when the truth is, in most cases, more complicated. And the sad thing for Ruth is that what's different about her isn't a super-power. She's just broken.'

'Can you tell me what you're going to do about her, then?' he asked. 'I want to help.'

'No. I don't want you involved. I want you long gone. I will come and find you, Jayden. Once it's done. But I think she would kill you if you came back. Or, use what she knows about you to make you do things you don't want to, for the rest of your life.'

He didn't want to argue. Just in case she never came to see him, he didn't want the last time they saw each other to be a fight.

'You know you need to get her book, don't you?' he said.

'Well … leave it with me. It's in hand. Promise me you won't get involved.'

He started shaking his head, tears filling his eyes again. He felt her little finger wrap around his and tug gently.

'Jayden…'

Jayden looked into her eyes, and said, 'Fine.' But he never said he promised. Not technically.

She left much, much later, after she believed he had calmed down. But he hadn't. He'd just worked out that's what it would take for her to leave. And now he really did need to be alone. He was still angry hours later, when a nurse wheeled in an enormous suitcase of his things. He got out of bed, opened it, and began to unpack until he found what he was looking for: the leather gloves.

He put them on and climbed back into bed.

Did Tessa really think she could deal with Ruth and the committee, or was she just humouring him to keep him safe?

Leave it with me. What, so she could sing Christmas carols with her at the fete? That'd show her.

He wasn't convinced Tessa really knew what she was up against. Had it really sunk in just how nasty they all were? *Broken* didn't cover it. What if Tessa got herself hurt? If he lost her as well as Kath…

He closed his eyes. Because what could he do about it? He was just a fifteen-year-old kid. A kid who thought he knew what he was doing but had just shown he hadn't a clue. He'd picked the wrong battle and lost.

He sat up and his eyes flew open. Grandad hadn't only told Jayden to pick his battles. That was what Jayden tended to remember, but Grandad usually liked to add something else to that lesson, too.

'Pick your battles, Jayden,' he would say, 'because there's always someone bigger, uglier and nastier than you out there, and one day you might run into them.'

It was all good stuff. Stuff that kept being relevant, the older he got. A smile that didn't feel like his own spread across his face. He'd had a very dangerous idea. But it was one he couldn't ignore.

SIXTY-SEVEN

Tessa

S he hadn't told Jayden about her recording. If she had, it might have sponged up some of that determined rage she'd seen in his eyes at the hospital. But by the time she saw him, she'd already realised her plan hadn't worked.

The more she listened to it – both Ruth's voice and her own audible in lip-smacking clarity, thanks to the multiple microphones – the more she realised just how clever Ruth had really been. Giving it another listen now in the lounge, just to be sure, it was obvious she'd failed.

—*Ruth, are you going to die before the concert? Because I thought you wanted to sing with me there. Or was that all just bullshit to try and get close to me, to work out what I was going to do about the baby?*

—*I am hoping to still be alive at the weekend. And I would like to sing one last time, so that these people get a little glimpse of what I once was.*

—*Exactly. We can't do it if I'm in hospital.*

—*Goodness, you are dramatic. Show me, then.*

—*Show you?*

—*Show me.*

Most of it was like this. Short non-committal sentences clarified by unrecorded gestures. Tessa was the one doing most of the talking, and most of the discussion was about what she'd *read*. Damn herself for resting on her laurels, for letting herself think she'd already bested Ruth by getting her into the lounge in the first place. She should have worked harder getting her to say something worthwhile.

The recording was supposed to be the smoking gun. She'd planned to take it to the police station nearest to Maddy in Kent. Explain that she thought her local police force might be compromised by Leo, and she needed help. But that relied on her credibility. If she turned up with this, they'd see a paranoid woman from another force's patch telling wild stories about murder and conspiracy. A pregnant woman fresh from a break-up and prone to making covert recordings. Recordings that revealed very little of interest. At best they'd pass it on to someone higher up than Leo in Oxfordshire and wash their hands of it. But who knew how far Leo's reach went in the force? If he was tipped off that someone had been bad-mouthing him to another force, that was her fucked.

She appraised her useless WAV files on the screen for a final time before downloading the entire conversation as a single file which was uploaded to the cloud.

Jayden had been right, as he often was. She needed the book. The recording had been a gamble anyway. There would have been issues including it in any legal trial. She'd known that. But if it had been *just* good enough, it might have given the police grounds for an investigation. The book would have those same issues getting into a trial, potentially, but it was more than enough to get them interested, surely?

But how to get it? She reasoned she had two options. She either waited for Ruth to give the book to her once she'd done enough to win her trust. But how long might that be, if ever?

And what would she have to do to prove herself to Ruth that might match giving herself a miscarriage? Punch someone else in the belly? Murder someone? It wasn't worth thinking about, because she really didn't have too much time before she'd have, 'concealing-her-bump' to add to her list of problems.

Besides, Ruth might die before Tessa could get her to hand the book over. She could wait for that to happen, but she was sure Ruth had a contingency plan. Certainly, none of the committee would want that book around, given it implicated them in so many of Ruth's crimes, so she'd have to steal it before they got to it anyway.

So theft it was. Which was better, because more than anything now, she wanted to see Ruth's face when she beat her. When she realised her life's work was done. Which meant either Tessa, or someone she hired, had to take the book from Ruth. But where was it kept? Did she carry it around with her at all times, or did it live somewhere in her cottage? In a locked drawer, maybe. A safe. And when was her cottage ever empty? When she worked, yes, but often she worked from home. She came home for lunch sometimes, too.

The concert, then. It had to be then. She would sing her songs, be surrounded by those blown away by her admittedly beautiful voice, and Tessa could slink off, perhaps. Maybe feign an illness. Then what? Break a window? Ruth was too clever not to have a security system in her cottage. Maybe cameras inside too. Why not lasers around her safe? Why not a little chip in the book itself that activated when moved?

That was the problem, she had no clue what she was up against now. The woman had out-thought her every move so far, while dealing with the effects of chemotherapy. Even if she could get the book, she still had to get away. Still had to hope the police would believe her.

If only there was a way to get the book soon *and* keep

stringing Ruth along until she made her move. She looked around the room. At her guitar. At the place where Ruth had sat the other night. The place on the floor where she'd kept the bottle of medicine just inches from one of the concealed microphones. Lastly, she stared at her computer.

And all at once, she had it.

SIXTY-EIGHT

Tessa

'That's so kind of you, Tessa,' October said. Tonight she was wearing a red beanie with *#bekind* embroidered on it, perfectly offsetting her bright-pink Christmas-tree jumper.

Tessa placed a tray of mince pies on the table at the back of the village hall and smiled. 'No problem. I've been dying to do something to help out. It's just hard to know where to start, with everyone being so kind.'

'I know, isn't it?' October noticed that Tessa was holding one of the plastic cups from beside the punch bowl. 'Is it strong?'

She brought the cup up to her lips and sipped. 'It tastes it, yes.'

She walked through the room, Elton John stepping into Christmas over the PA. She nodded and smiled at the people she'd met over the last six months. Benedita and Aaron. Their children. Leo, sitting on the edge of the makeshift stage, tuning his acoustic. Dev, Jitesh, and Olivia, talking to one another in a classic village huddle. The place had a strong piney smell from

401

the giant Christmas tree in the corner, but just beneath lurked that history-trying-to-rot stink that evoked her first meeting here with the Kindness Committee.

'You're here.' She turned around to see Andy standing behind her. He stood hunched, like he was trying to meet her at eye-level. It was something he used to do when they'd first met. 'Everything ... okay?'

'Yeah. Yeah, it's ... fine. Good.' She'd been dreading running into him, hadn't wanted him to start asking questions about Ruth and putting her under pressure to lie. She'd hoped he might just decide she was crazy and stay away.

Curiosity remained in his expression. 'Did you ... hear anything back about the ... thing?'

She had an answer already prepared. To beat Ruth, she'd left as little to chance as possible. 'Maddy said the sample wasn't big enough. Thanks, though. For trying.'

'You're welcome. I... Is everything *really* alright? After what you said about Ruth... And now you're singing with her. Is that true?' Tessa nodded and looked around for Ruth, spotting her in the corner still poring over the lyrics book she insisted she wanted to perform without tonight. 'I'm just surprised you came.'

'So you said. Yeah, Everything is fine, Andy. Yeah. I'm just ... obviously going through a lot. And maybe I'm a bit all over the place, you know, hormones wise, and maybe the best thing is to just ignore me.'

'I can't ignore you, Tess.'

'Why not?' She couldn't help herself. 'I'm not really your problem anymore.'

He licked his lips and straightened his back. 'You were never a problem. That's— Tess. Your phone call, the other night. The b—'

She held up her hand. 'Andy, just not tonight, okay? I'm

fine. I just want to be here in the moment and … if you want to talk, we can another time. Everything's good.' She met his gaze. 'Okay?'

With a frown he nodded, although his acceptance was short-lived. His eyebrows rose and he pointed at her cup. 'Uh, is that punch?'

'Are you serious?' she said. For all her planning, she hadn't anticipated this scenario. She knew what he was thinking: that she'd lost the plot and was trying to foetal-alcohol-poison one of his precious affair-twins. 'It's just juice.'

'Oh.'

She walked off before he could check if she'd been lying, and found a seat beside Ruth. She didn't look up from her words, which she continued to sing to herself in a low mutter.

'You'll be fine. You can do these with your eyes closed and your hands tied behind your back.'

Ruth looked up and gave a weak but appreciative smile. Tessa felt the confidence drain from her. She was too clever. She'd done what she'd done for too long to be fooled by a newcomer like her. Tessa put her cup down on the table and brought her hand back to her lap. Then she picked the cup up again, brought it up to her lips, and returned it to the table once more.

'What are you drinking?' Ruth said. 'Punch?'

'Do you want some? I can go and get some for you if you want.'

'No. Not before I sing. Alcohol ruins my onset.' Her gaze moved from Tessa's face, down to her stomach, and across to the cup.

'I'm not pregnant,' Tessa said with a bitter laugh. 'It's not like I need to worry anymore, do I?' She made this sound resentful but resigned. A pragmatic victim.

Ruth still didn't buy it though. 'Is it nice, then?'

'Yes, it's fine.'

'Let me try some. See if I'm in the mood.' That wicked intelligence lurked in her eyes once more, and her nerves appeared to vanish. She didn't believe Tessa was really drinking alcohol. She thought that she'd replaced it with fruit juice.

Tessa tried to look puzzled. 'Okay. You sure? Don't want to ruin your … onset.'

'Definitely. Just a nip.'

She handed her the cup and Ruth took a gulp. She tugged her tongue in and out of her pursed lips, making a smacking sound as she clearly assessed the alcohol content. But she'd evidently found it to her liking, because her whole body appeared to relax, and she regarded Tessa with a new appreciation. 'I can taste grapefruit.' She passed the cup back.

'It is a bit grapefruity, yeah.'

'You finish it off. Go on. You deserve it. I want you to have a good time tonight.'

Tessa didn't argue. She shrugged and downed the lot. 'Do you want me to get you some, then?'

Ruth shook her head. 'It's *too* grapefruity, really. I'm not supposed to have grapefruit with my treatment. It can interact with the drugs.'

'Oh, sorry about that. I'll be back in a bit, okay? I'm going to get some more. I can't play well sober.'

Tessa left Ruth for the punch bowl, and refilled her cup. She pretended to drink from it before allowing herself to get into a conversation. Eventually, Ruth stopped looking over and got back to her words. Tessa didn't waste a moment. She slipped outside and beneath the Kindness Tree – a better place than the bathroom to do what she needed to do. She didn't want to be overheard. After double checking she was alone, she stuck her fingers down her throat. She threw up the punch and some of the pasta she'd eaten to line her stomach before coming out. Job done, she went back to the church hall.

As usual, things were running like clockwork. It was almost seven thirty, which was when they were due to take the stage. She felt good. Strong. Ready to discover if her plan had worked.

'I'm ready when you are,' Tessa said to Ruth. She looked up, actual fear in her eyes.

'I'm...' She shook her head. 'I don't quite feel right, Tessa. I'm not sure if it's that grapefruit or ... perhaps it's just ... *you know*.'

Tessa bent down, an odd, reflex-pity trying to insist she treat this poor soul with actual kindness. But as Ruth believed, you had to overcome that sort of thing to be truly kind. She put her hands on Ruth's shoulders. 'You'll be fine. Honestly. It's just nerves.'

Ruth nodded. Swallowed. Nodded again, that fear in her eyes dimming a little bit now. 'I'm sure you're right.' Did Tessa even see gratitude on her face now, too?

'Good.' Tessa rose to her feet.

'Tessa?'

'Yes.'

'Don't make a big fuss of it, okay?'

Tessa nodded. She got up on stage, tested the mic and guitar, and the chatter in the room quietened, and fell silent.

'Hi, everyone. Merry Christmas,' she said. A small whine of feedback made her turn to lower her own levels on the mixing desk. She looked out at the audience of villagers standing, or seated at tables.

'I'm so pleased to have been asked to do this tonight. I'd

like to welcome to the stage someone who I know you'll all be so pleased, and surprised, to hear singing tonight. She's the real brains of the operation here in Nether Appleford, and I don't really think any of you have any idea just how hard she works behind the scenes, making this village as kind as it is.' She looked over at Ruth, aware she was dragging the village's gaze there too – for many of them, this was the first they knew of Ruth performing. Ruth rolled her eyes, and gave her a mock glare that through different eyes might appear cute. 'She is brave. Inspirational. And goes about her business quietly. Which is why none of you talented people have had any idea about *her* being the biggest talent of all. Now, give her a big hand. Please welcome to the stage, Ruth Bellingham.'

The noise was enormous; hollers, claps and whistles competed with 'yeahs', 'whoops', and 'Ruths'. She walked up to the mic, hands across her belly meekly, and raised a hand before standing in front of the mic – performing already.

'Thank you, Tessa,' she said, and turned to look behind her. There was no mistaking it. That was gratitude on her face. And Tessa looked down at her fretboard, avoiding the gaze. To the audience, Ruth said, 'This is quite the woman we have in our midst.'

Tessa played the introduction to their version of 'Winter Wonderland'. She'd come up with a much slower arrangement, with a picking part occasionally interrupted by jazzy chords that brought out parts of the melody.

Ruth opened her mouth, 'Sleigh bells rings, are you listening...'

A hybrid gasp and mutter of surprise moved through the crowd like a murmuration of starlings. Her powerful voice already filled the room, and she hadn't even opened up yet. Tessa for the most part kept watching her fingers to make sure she played the part correctly. Occasionally, she glanced up to assess Ruth. She couldn't hear it in her voice yet, but she didn't look altogether steady at the microphone.

When they finished, a few seconds of shocked silence, visible on the faces of the assembled, preceded an even bigger cheer than the one she'd received getting up. At Ruth's request, Tessa didn't let it last long. She started up their jazzed-up version of 'White Christmas' and the crowd quietened.

'I'm dreaming of a—'

Ruth gagged. Her hand went to her mouth. Tessa kept playing, although her heart began to slam against the hollow body of the guitar. This was the most awful thing she'd ever done to another person, worse than telling her sister to fuck off after being told she was pregnant. Still, she had to a suppress a smile. After all, you had to be cruel to be kind.

Ruth stepped back with her hand raised apologetically. She started walking off stage in the direction she'd arrived. Realising she wasn't going to make it, she ran to the other side of the stage in a panic, bent over, and vomited over the side. People near the stage cried out. Leo, hands up by his face, stared at his now-stained white shirt with disgust.

Tessa put down her guitar and walked towards her. 'Jesus, Ruth. Are you okay?'

'Get me home.' She sounded furious and embarrassed.

Olivia ran up. Benedita and Dev, too. Aaron. Jitesh. Concern spread through the crowd. Olivia climbed up on the stage, ignoring Ruth's pleas for everyone to back away. Tessa couldn't get to her now, probably a good thing. Ruth was sick again. Vomit spattered on the stage and those nearby were splashed. Still, they crowded Ruth, touching her, trying to be kind.

'Back away,' Ruth yelled, and the whole room fell silent. 'I want Tessa.'

By unfortunate coincidence, someone started the music

playing through the PA again. Slade's 'Merry Christmas Everybody'. But at Ruth's request, the concerned group around her parted and Tessa helped her back to her feet and through the crowd to the exit. Someone handed Tessa her coat and bag on the way past, and at last the two of them were alone. On their way back to Ruth's.

Just like Tessa had planned.

SIXTY-NINE

How to Kill with Kindness

Because all of us have roles for which we are perfectly suited, but you must harmonise your talent with the reality you find yourself in. I have learned that there is simply no one cleverer than me, my darling. I have bested scientists, mathematicians and philosophers. They have kneeled before me. Yet because I was never wealthy or male, I have never reached the station in life I deserve. But I have found my own way, and I have delighted in it. Do not let...

SEVENTY

Tessa

She'd bought a syrup online that brought on nausea and vomiting. Adding it to grapefruit juice slowed down the absorption process in Ruth's body, which according to sources online, gave Tessa between five minutes and half an hour. All Tessa had needed was enough time to get away from Ruth to throw up the drink herself, and preferably for the whole thing to happen while they were on stage. It hadn't mattered *when* she threw up, so long as she did, but that she'd done so on stage fitted the picture of the occasion Tessa had in her mind.

Tessa's back-up plan had been to poison Ruth's on-stage water. But in the end, she hadn't needed it. This time, she'd *actually* out-thought her. She walked with her arm across Ruth's shoulders, leading her back to her cottage. She apologised repeatedly for not believing her about feeling unwell and making her go on stage. Ruth shook her head, telling her it hadn't been her fault. That she'd believed it was nerves, too.

'Do you have any of that ginger tea?' Tessa said once they were inside. 'I'll make you some?'

'By the kettle,' Ruth said, collapsing into a replica Eames

chair and resting her feet on the footstool. She groaned. 'It's the chemo, my darling. I shouldn't have pushed myself tonight. I'm so embarrassed.'

Tessa went to the kitchen, and started searching the drawer beneath the kettle to find the right box. She'd hoped that Ruth would blame her treatment. She'd made sure the symptoms all fitted. Chemo could make you tired too. Once the tea had brewed a little, she poured some out, added some cold water, and reached into her pocket. She retrieved two small sleeping tablets and stirred them into the drink, doing so until both had dissolved. Ruth had one thing right about her, without doubt: she was capable of doing what it took to bring about the kindest outcome.

She washed a small amount of the liquid around her mouth, and satisfied the pills had no taste, she spat it out in the sink and took the drink to Ruth.

'Thank you, Tessa,' she said. 'I'm sorry, just for my edification, will you sip a bit for me.'

'I can, but why?'

'I just want to know if I need to let it cool. The treatment makes the skin of my mouth very delicate, you see.'

Tessa sipped some, hoping that the drugs wouldn't affect her too much. 'It's fine.' Then she tutted. 'Sensitive mouth skin. You're worried I'm trying to poison you, aren't you? At least be honest.'

Ruth smiled at this. 'Don't be silly.'

'I suppose I poisoned you tonight, too?' It was a gamble. But if Ruth had considered that possibility on her own, she would be more likely to believe it was true.

It appeared to work, though. After giving it a moment's thought, she said, 'No, I'm afraid you can't take credit for this one.'

Tessa sat down on Ruth's sofa. 'I've not stopped thinking

about what you showed me, you know. Maybe you don't feel like talking about it now, but I'd like to read the book again.'

'I'm pleased you do, Tessa. In time.' She sipped from her tea and closed her eyes, already looking tired. 'I think you should go back to the party. Please. Finish the set, don't let them remember this.'

'I'm not leaving you here. I'm sticking around at least for a few hours, just to make sure you're okay.' She let her adjust to this idea first before adding, 'So I may as well read the book again while I'm sitting here.'

Ruth let out an amused sigh. Her eyes remained shut. 'It's in the office. On the bookshelf. Second shelf down, ten across.'

Tessa repeated the instructions to herself to memorise them. Then she said, 'Thank you,' like she'd been given a precious gift.

The office was upstairs, in the same location where Tessa's back bedroom was situated in her cottage. She couldn't find the light in the hall, and when she walked into the office it was pitch black. She reached out and turned on the light. Above a large walnut desk in front of her, three bookshelves ran wall-to-wall. On the top two shelves were eighty or so blue hardback books, just like Ruth's 'How to Kill with Kindness'. Their unmarked, identical spines ran from left to right.

Tessa frowned. Three more of these books were out on the table, positioned like they'd just been thrown there. One was open, but the upturned pages were bare. Oddly, beside the books, were two brown leather shoes. Men's shoes, judging by the size and style.

She followed Ruth's instructions and placed the correct book down on the table. She opened it, and saw the familiar bullet points cataloguing Ruth's rules.

A breeze, or something even lighter, brushed the hairs on the back of her neck.

Someone was behind her. She was suddenly certain. They'd been behind the door when she came in, hadn't they? She'd been too preoccupied to notice. A leather-gloved hand covered her mouth and a massive body pressed against her back. She tried to yell, but found she had no air with which to do so. She began to fight, and the arms around her started squeezing.

SEVENTY-ONE

Jayden

I t was an hour back to the West Midlands from the hospital. His social worker was mostly mute on the drive. What she could bring herself to say was, 'You were lucky they didn't take it any further, you know?' Jayden just nodded. Yeah, he'd been lucky. But wasn't he owed some of that?

He'd not expected Olivia to show up for his big goodbye, but there she'd been. A hug. A sorry it ended this way. 'I'll be rooting for you,' she'd said. He thanked her for everything and in some ways meant it.

His temporary home was a maisonette on the border of Birmingham and Solihull. Kids circled on bikes, eyeing him up through the car window while the social worker looked for a place to park. They found a spot nearby, opposite a recreation area where a fire-damaged slide was fenced off with black-and-yellow-striped tape.

The couple putting him up didn't smile much. They eyed him warily. They had faces which said, we've heard *all* about you. The bloke was short and stocky, tattoos all over his arms and a little shield-shaped beard around his mouth. She was pear-shaped, dressed in black leggings and a pink top. He couldn't get a sense of her face because once the social worker went, she never looked up from her phone.

His room was alright. Looked like it had been decorated by a ten-year-old. Superhero posters on the wall. A train, too. A fighter jet. Thomas the Tank Engine, for fuck's sake. He had to smile. It had a bit of a pissy smell, and there were funny stains on the cream carpet, but the bed smelled strongly of washing powder so he buried his face in that. They brought him up a hot chocolate and asked if he needed anything to make him feel more at home.

It was almost seven o'clock. Back in Nether Appleford, the fete would be starting. He was glad to be far away. He sort of wanted to see what happened, but he knew it was best he had an alibi.

'I'm fine,' he said. 'Thanks for the drink.'

'It's really not a problem,' the woman said. Her phone beeped. She looked down at her pocket. 'Honestly, if there's anything you need—'

'Nah, I'm good. Unless you've got a guitar?'

'A guitar?'

She looked baffled, like she'd only ever seen such things in museums. 'Graham,' she yelled. 'We got anything like a guitar?'

After an initial 'Nah', there came a long silence. Then some clattering. Then the sound of Graham coming up the stairs. He came into the room with something close to a smile on his face. 'Is this any good?' In his hand was a ukulele, only two strings left stretched across its battered body.

Jayden took it and plucked the strings. One was tuned too high. The other too low. He played 'Smoke on the Water' on the top string, and Graham actually laughed. 'Knock yourself out.'

They both left, and Jayden lay back on the bed with the

ukulele on his belly. He might fall asleep with it next to him. Like a six-year-old. He could hear the radiators clanking near his head. Could hear the noise of a telly from the downstairs flat coming up through the floor.

He smiled, because it was only going to be temporary. He'd figured it all out. When Tessa had left him at the hospital, he'd messaged an old Birmingham mate, who gave him the number of *his* slightly dodgy mate, who supposedly knew what was going on around town. That mate had set up a telephone call with another bloke, and all Jayden had had to say to him was Rags's name. Next he knew, someone was coming to meet him at the hospital the next day.

A bloke had met him in the canteen. Broad and tall, dressed in a black shirt and long coat, he sported a fade up to a head of black hair lined with grey. He had a boxer's nose, tough skin, and penetrated Jayden with two milky-blue eyes from behind owly glasses. Jayden knew who he was, had seen pictures online. Even if he looked older than he'd expected, he was still scary as fuck. It was alarming how all the other diners had no idea who it was they were eating with.

'I didn't know it would be you coming,' Jayden said after waiting for a sign it would be okay to join him.

'I like getting my hands dirty,' Tommo Benton said, his Brummie accent evoking an inappropriate nostalgia.

He bought Jayden lunch, and Jayden explained to Tommo that he wouldn't be getting his money back because Rags had been killed. The guy didn't look up from his plate of chips, but he straightened up in his seat.

'Who killed him?'

Jayden told him all of it. Truthfully. From when he'd got in touch with Rags to when he'd been killed, sparing none of the details about what the committee had done. If this was going to work, Tommo needed to know the lot.

'You sure he's not just done one? Flown abroad. Living it up in Mexico. Or the Amalfi Coast.' He turned to look out the window. 'That's where I'd go.'

Jayden shook his head. Told him all about Tessa, and everything she'd learned. Even about how she was trying to deal with Ruth herself.

'The thing about Tessa,' Jayden said, 'is that she thinks she's smart and strong and all of that. Which she is. But she doesn't realise this woman, Ruth, is like, evil. You know. Straight-up evil. She's not about business or anything. She likes doing bad shit. Tessa can't bring them down. I'm worried she'll get hurt and it'll all just carry on.'

'Evil,' Tommo said. 'Strong stuff.'

'I know. But you can make your own mind up if you get her book.'

'Book?'

'It's like a diary, right,' Jayden said. 'She basically brags about all the shit she's got away with. Tessa read it. It's fucked up.'

'You swear too much. How old are you?'

'Fifteen. Sorry.'

'Fifteen. You've got some bollocks on you, I'll tell you that. If I didn't already know coming here that your mate had been sniffing around that village… So, what stuff has she done?'

Jayden told him what he knew. About the other murders. The coercion and manipulation. The bent copper covering things up for her. Some of it he'd touched on before, other things were brand new. But now he tied it all together.

'Bent copper?' Tommo laughed. 'You've been watching too much *Line of Duty*.'

Jayden refused to be discouraged. Maybe before all this he would have folded. Not now. If the guy didn't believe him, his loss. But he could tell now he was interested. A bent copper. A supply of ketamine. And he hadn't left yet.

'I think that book's the key to getting everyone what they want. You win and we win.'

The man finished his chips and wiped his hands on a napkin. He waited to finish chewing, and said, 'So what's going on in your head? What do you think happens now you've got Tommo Benton here in front of you? Knowing who I am. Knowing who my family are. What do you want?'

'Rags said he was going to change my life. Get me a job and help me with uni. I was thinking if I gave you information, maybe you could help me.'

He shook his head. 'I'm not fucking Father Christmas. If I ask you something, you best tell me the answer.' He used a voice that was both loud enough to be scary but quiet enough to stay below the level of the room's background noise. Jayden nodded, nervous, but not scared. Not yet. This reaction hadn't been unexpected.

'I meant maybe working for you. Or whatever.'

The man's face fell, like he was disappointed to hear this. Like maybe he'd been enjoying Jayden's balls before. 'Right.'

'Okay, so I hate these fu— these people,' Jayden said. 'They hurt me. My friend. They killed another friend. So, what I was thinking is, if you got hold of that book, you could use it against them. Make them do what you want. Rags said it was a money factory. He was talking about using the village to launder money, too. Plus with the cop compromised, you'd have that. You'd get your money back that Rags owed you. In a way, it's them that owe you, really.'

Tommo Benton just stared. 'I still don't get it,' he said eventually. 'What makes you tick?'

'I just want justice.'

'Justice. Right.'

He was losing Tommo now. Had he really expected him to go for any of this? Yeah, he wanted justice. But some time in prison? Was *that* what he wanted? And who for? Ruth? Of course, but she might be dead from her cancer by the time it came to trial. Leo and Dev, definitely. But Aaron? Olivia?

Or was it not justice he wanted? Was what he wanted more basic than that?

Yes. Maybe it was. Maybe he just liked the idea of Tommo Benton sitting in on the Kindness Committee. All of them around a table, silent. Terrified. Trapped. Unable to do their twisted, kind things, for fear of being shot in the head around the back of the chapel.

'Eye for an eye, innit,' he said with a shrug. 'You know what it is… They've got this big tree in the middle of the village where they put all their kind little things they've done during the year. And you know what? When I called you, I was imagining that tree on fire. That's all it is for me.'

Tommo Benton smiled at this. Jayden knew then that the man liked him.

Not long after, though, his expression flattened, all business suddenly. 'Fun as it all sounds, I'm not sure it's worth my while, kid. I'd be wise to just take the hit on the money. I was really only testing your mate, giving him that deadline. I like to test people. Especially if they're useful. I like useful, too. But all this … I'm not sure how useful it is to me.'

Now Jayden matched his neutral expression and stared into his eyes. Jayden knew that if he had been a bit older, had a few more scars on his face and teeth missing from his smile, Tommo would be more likely to go for this. But there had always been the chance that he wouldn't. So just in case,

Jayden had a back-up plan. One based on what he already knew about Tommo Benton and establishing credibility.

'I get it,' Jayden said. 'And, yeah, I suppose, thinking about it, maybe it isn't worth all that risk. I was angry they disrespected you so much, and assumed you might be too. I'm really sorry that you wasted your time.'

Tommo Benton went still, chewing on something even though his chip tray was empty. 'How's she disrespected me?'

'Well … when I first tried getting Ruth to be Rags's insider, I said Rags was connected to the Benton Boys. You know, used your name to give Rags a bit of … credibility. I told her all about you. What you did in Birmingham. Things you'd done. I thought she'd give the Benton Boys one Google and just give Rags what he wanted. But they just killed him.'

'Yeah.'

'They didn't care.' For the first time, he decided to lie to Tommo Benton. 'And they told me you wouldn't have the resources to find Rags. That you were too small-time.'

Tommo's whole body stiffened. His lips pressed together. Eventually, just when Jayden expected to be submerged beneath a wave of Tommo's anger, he said, 'Details. I need all the details.'

Back up in his new bedroom, he sat up and tuned the ukulele. It was eight now. Tommo might have already got the book. Tommo had said once he had it, and had read it, he'd be back in touch. Maybe he'd read it tonight and be on the phone tomorrow. Better charge his phone if that was the case.

Tommo Benton had been a meticulous planner. He'd wanted Ruth's address. When she was likely to be out of the house. Where the book might be. Jayden had given him as much information as he could, and told him about the fete and what it meant to Ruth. It was her big night for many reasons, and she wasn't going to miss it for the world. She'd be out all evening until late.

He started playing 'Brain Stew' on the ukulele.

The last thing Tommo had asked for was Tessa's address.

'She's not part of it, though,' he'd said, a little concerned.

'I'll probably need her, given what she knows.'

In that moment, Tommo had seen his face, and had reassured him that he'd just talk to her. That made Jayden think Tommo fully intended to go ahead and blackmail the committee in some way, and he took comfort from it. But he'd still not wanted to give Tessa's address and description to Tommo.

He had, though. Because the time for doubts was long gone. He hoped he'd done the right thing. He reckoned he had. How could it not be? The whole thing was circular. Vim's debt to the Bentons was what started all this. Now they would end it.

And Tessa would be safe.

He looked at his phone. Nothing. He started playing another of The Blackhearts' standards, 'My Generation'.

'*People try to put us down…*' he sang softly, strumming the way Tessa had shown him.

Yeah, it'd be fine.

SEVENTY-TWO

Tessa

The man holding Tessa put his mouth to her ear and shushed her with sour breath.

'Tessa, be fucking quiet and stop wriggling.' The sound of her own name in his low and unfamiliar whisper stunned her into stillness. 'I'm not here to hurt you, so calm down, alright? Jayden told me everything.'

Jayden? Oh, God, what had he done now? One of the man's gloved fingers accidentally entered her mouth and she could taste grimy leather. She couldn't speak even if she'd wanted to.

'There's been a change of plan, love. Now, I'll let you go, and you're going to spin and face me, and we're going to talk quietly and quickly about that book. Nod if that's okay?'

Tessa nodded, and the man let her go. She turned to regard a smart-looking fifty-something holding a glove-encased finger to his lips. He wore no shoes, yet he still loomed over Tessa. In his free hand he held a gun. Catching the direction of Tessa's gaze, he urged her not to panic with his face and now opened his *shushing*-hand to pat the air. He made a show of slowly putting the gun back beneath his coat, and quietly closed the door to the office.

'Right.' His voice remained just above a whisper. 'You know who I am?'

Tessa shook her head.

'That's probably for the best,' he said. 'All you need to know is that I'm Tommo, and I'm not someone you want to annoy. I'll tell you that once. As a kindness, since you're all into that around here. Don't waste my time.' She nodded. She believed him. The way he carried himself, all his micro-movements and tics, told the story of someone prepared to do whatever it took to control any environment he happened to be in.

'I know who *you* are,' he continued. 'A little bird told me. I know what's been going on. What I need to know now is why you were trying to steal that book?'

She said nothing. Didn't move. She had no idea what revealing the truth to him might lead to. But she couldn't stay silent. She was certain this man would happily hurt her if she didn't co-operate.

'I don't understand,' she said, although that wasn't entirely true. There was only one little bird that knew those things, and with stomach-turning realisation she began to understand what had happened.

'You don't need to. I do.' Irritation briefly caused his voice to break from a whisper. 'That woman, Ruth, was meant to be at an event. Now you're here with her, slipping into the kitchen and putting something in her tea.' Tessa couldn't stop her eyes widening. He'd seen her. Had been here the whole time. 'Yeah.' He smiled and widened his own eyes in acknowledgement. 'So the book, were you going to use it to turn her in?' His smile expanded; he was enjoying his upper hand. 'If it's worth knowing, love, I know it. So just quick answers now. Please. Am I right? About the book.'

'Yes,' she said. Jayden had taken matters into his own hands, hadn't he? He'd gone to this dreadful man. Asked *him* to help, and in return Jayden had told him everything. He clearly had some plan involving Ruth and the book, and until she knew what it was and how she fitted into it, she had to go along with what he said.

'So what was your plan, then? What did you give her just now?'

'Sleeping pills. I was going to sneak out while she slept and scan the book. She thinks I'm her friend. Then I was going to go to the police, and if she tried to destroy the book before they came, I'd still have a copy.'

'I know you've read it. Is it really like the kid said?'

She nodded. 'It's worse than you could imagine.'

He tilted his head like he doubted it.

'What's wrong with her?' he said.

'What do you mean?'

'Is she tapped? Senile? How dangerous is she?'

'I don't know. She's not physically dangerous. She's got terminal cancer and … well, I've given her those tablets. But mentally … she's a viper.'

'So she really runs stuff? Like the equestrian centre up there.'

'Not on paper. But in reality.'

'And she's got a copper doing things he shouldn't?'

Now Tessa was starting to see what all this might be about. 'Seems that way.'

He nodded. Just then, Ruth called out, 'Everything okay, Tessa? You found it?'

'Give me the book,' Tommo said. 'And tell her you're fine.'

'Yeah, fine,' Tessa shouted. 'Just admiring your office. Are all these your diaries?'

'Oh, no, no. They're camouflage. Hiding the masterwork in plain sight.'

After a moment of hesitation, she handed Tommo the book. He opened it at a random page and started to read, shaking his head after a minute and smiling.

'Likes the sound of her own voice, doesn't she?' he said. '"Hitherto", fuck me. Right. Here's what happens. I'm taking this. You, forget all about what happened here. It's not going to be nice for them, I promise, so that'll have to do for you as far as revenge goes.'

'Revenge?'

'I know what she did to you. But the police aren't getting involved. Not until I'm done, anyway. But I've got no problem with *you* unless you make one. So finish up here, go home, make some moving plans, and get out of here as soon as you can. Don't look back. Understood?'

She took a deep breath and nodded. Would it really be that simple? Was he really going to let her walk off? *It's not going to be nice for them*, he'd said. What had Jayden condemned the village to, exactly? And for that matter, what was Tommo's plan for Jayden? If she was getting away scot-free, she didn't expect anyone else to.

'So you want to … what? use the book to blackmail her?'

He glared at her, a warning. It wasn't her business. And did she even care about what happened now?

'Go in there now. Finish up with her,' he said. 'I'll be over later. I don't know why you would after what she's supposedly done to you, but don't try and warn her.'

She didn't want to dig her heels in further. But she had to ask about Jayden. 'Can I just ask about the boy? I care about him a lot, okay? Has he promised you something? Have you promised him something?'

'Go, please.'

'He's really smart, alright? But he's had no role models at all. And I think if he just stays clear of … trouble, I think he'll be useful. To the world. I'll help you with this, go out there and act normal and everything. And I'll never tell anyone I saw you here. But can you promise me he'll be okay after all this?'

He sighed regretfully, and for a moment Tessa believed this was it. He was going to shoot her. 'He is smart. You're right about that. And he's made his choices. Now go. Worry about *you*.' His face darkened. 'And your baby.'

Tears filled her eyes, and she didn't go immediately. But her brief stare was a weak protest. She left the office and walked down the stairs, composing herself. She opened the stairwell door and stepped into the lounge. 'I'm so sorry, Ruth, but you know, I think I'll let you—'

She stopped. Ruth wasn't in her seat. She spun around and walked into the kitchen. She listened carefully. But Ruth had gone.

SEVENTY-THREE

Tessa
_____

Tommo heard her calling for Ruth, and when Tessa went to climb back up the stairs to check the bedrooms he was standing at the top, gritting his teeth in annoyance.

'She's not here,' Tessa said.

He mouthed, 'Where?'

Tessa shrugged and pointed ahead of her to indicate she was coming to look upstairs. If that was where Ruth was, though, it meant she might have been listening in to their conversation. And if she had—

A shrill cry filled the stairwell followed by a horrific crack. Tommo grunted and fell forwards, beginning a clumsy descent towards Tessa. She jumped back into the lounge, catching sight of Ruth standing at the top of the stairs wielding what appeared to be a cosh, the sort a police officer might carry.

Tommo's body rolled around the corner at the foot of the stairs, and he came to a stop with his top half in the lounge and his legs still up in the stairwell. Ruth descended with angry stomps, breathing heavily, teeth bared. 'Who is he? Who is he?'

427

She stepped over him into the lounge, cosh raised. His arm shot out and grabbed her ankle.

She stared at it, dumfounded for a moment, and with a yank he floored her. Tessa took a step back again and Tommo got up. Ruth lay on her back, crying out and grabbing her head, the wig sitting unevenly atop it. Tommo reached up to the bleeding wound on the back of *his* head and brought his hand back to look at the blood.

'I thought you said she wasn't dangerous?' he said.

Ruth shrieked and kicked up at his crotch. She missed, and Tommo bent over and grabbed her by the neck. He lifted her up, dragged her across the room, and threw her into the armchair. Tessa couldn't see what happened next because Tommo's massive body was in the way, but he cried out again and wheeled away from where Ruth sat looking simultaneously pleased and close to death. She turned and threw up, while Tommo wrapped a fist around the handle of a small knife embedded in his chest below the armpit.

'Get out,' Ruth said, her face wild.

Tommo tried pulling the knife, winced, tried again, and gave up.

'You bloody stabbed me, you mad cow.'

'Of course I did. You've broken into my house. What do you want? Tessa, call the police.'

Tommo winced again and hissed a long *f*— sound. 'I've got your diary, love,' he said, his eyes shut. 'I don't think you'd want the police seeing that, do you?'

'My book?'

'Yeah. I know all about your little committee. Fucking Sharpies and Dozys.' He laughed.

'Oh, my book. My little book of *stories*. Of *made-up* stories.'

'Oh, I love a bit of metafiction,' Tommo sneered.

For a while they stared at one another, Ruth growing even

more pale as it dawned on her that this legal get-out she'd constructed wouldn't wash with a fellow like Tommo. Tessa watched from the edge of the room, having inched her way to the front hall.

'I know you, don't I?' Ruth said eventually. 'You're a Benton Boy.'

'Oh, great. That saves us some time.' He sat on the sofa nearest Ruth and turned to address Tessa. This seemed to cause him agony, as he grabbed his neck. 'Tessa, will you get me a cloth for my head.'

Tessa stood still for a moment.

'What is her role in this?' Ruth said.

'You tell me. Wrong place, wrong time, I think,' Tommo said.

'Top drawer beside the oven, Tessa,' Ruth said.

She nodded and did as she was told. When she returned, Tommo pressed it to the back of his head.

'Now Tessa, time for you to leave.'

Ruth's eyes widened, and she looked at Tessa pleadingly. 'No, don't leave me with him.'

They were both staring at her now, and she began to back away.

'No, Tessa. Don't you dare.'

'Don't turn back.'

'Why?' Ruth said to Tommo. 'Are you going to kill me? Is this about that man in denim? I was told on good authority he didn't work with you.'

'Ruth, calm down. I'm not here to hurt you. Unless you keep stabbing me, and then I'm going to feed you your eyes. Now listen, I'm here on business. A hostile takeover, if you like. Something we all stand to gain from, but some a little more than others. Like *Animal Farm*, that's a good *made-up* story.'

'Like most allegories, it's most effective on children.'

'Well, I'm not offering communism, love. I'm offering a transaction. And what you get is that no one has to find out all the good work you've been doing for the community. The stuff in your stories.'

Ruth appeared to shrink. She glanced at Tessa one last time, shook her head twice, and glared at Tommo in silence.

Tommo said to Tessa, 'Last chance. Go. *Now.*'

Again she did as she was told. She heard Tommo telling Ruth that he knew what she'd done to Rags. And that Rags owed him a debt. And that as far as he was concerned, that debt had passed on to Ruth.

Just before she reached the front door, she heard a noise from outside, footsteps, talking. A moment later the doorbell rang. She stood for a moment staring, and heard raised voices from behind her in the lounge. A second later Ruth bustled past her, barely able to stay on her feet, and grabbed the door handle.

'Don't even think about it, Ruth, or you're finished,' Tommo shouted after her.

Ruth yanked open the door and there, stood in front of the porch step, was the entire Kindness Committee.

SEVENTY-FOUR

Tessa

The committee were all asking Ruth if she was okay, and Ruth practically threw herself into the middle of their huddle. Tessa stood in the doorway and noticed that the only one not attending to Ruth was Andy.

'Andy,' Ruth said, 'will you just go inside and get my car keys.'

'Yeah, of course,' he said. The others started protesting, telling her they'd drive her to the hospital.

'No, I want to drive myself.' Her voice sounded dry and thin. 'Andy, they are on the rack in the kitchen.'

Andy walked up to the door, and Tessa shook her head, urging him not to come inside. She could see he sensed something was up.

'Tess, everything okay?'

Tessa smiled an Olivia smile. A bullshit smile. 'Fine, yes. Ruth is just ... she's not well. I'll get the keys.'

'I can tell something's not right.'

'Just ... don't worry and wait here.'

She had to keep him out. For his own safety. But Andy must

have caught the door, because when she reached the kitchen, he'd followed her. Standing by the sink was Tommo Benton. He turned his back as Andy came inside.

'Alright,' Andy said, sounding overly calm. But Tessa knew he must have seen the bleeding gash on the back of Tommo's head.

Tessa grabbed the keys and thrust them into Andy's hand. 'Go and give them to her.'

'Actually, Tessa,' Tommo said, 'I'll take them.'

'Who're you, mate?' Andy asked.

'Andy—'

'I'm Ruth's cousin, mate. She's not at her best, but we've got it under control now.'

'Uh-huh.' He stared at Tommo, believing none of it.

'We've got it covered,' Tessa said, her voice taut, her tone harsh. 'Go. Please.'

Tommo was starting to turn around. Tessa didn't wait, she took the keys from Andy and threw them down on the counter. She grabbed Andy's sleeve and escorted him back to the front door.

'Andy, I've got it under control. Our job now is to just go out there and get rid of them, okay? We'll explain it's a mental health issue, and we need some space.'

'Is that what this is?' He glanced up in the direction they'd come from. 'A mental health issue?'

'And don't mention what you just saw. For God's sake.'

'I don't know who I just saw. Who is he? I can take him, if he's a problem. Is he a problem?'

'Andy, you've fucked things up in a big way this year once already. Please don't do it again.'

He stared at her, a righteous rebuttal building charge rapidly and awaiting release. But her eyes were welling up, and when he saw them, his face softened.

'Will you be okay?' he said. She nodded and shoved him again. Not quite knowing why, he said, 'I'm sorry, Tess. About all of it.'

Finally, he walked away. Ruth was now sitting in Tessa's old car, waiting for her keys behind the wheel. She heard October telling Andy she'd locked the doors, and Andy saying something softly back, which after a minute or so, encouraged the committee to depart. Dev and Leo were the last of the committee to go, both of them eyeing proceedings with suspicion and something that seemed like fear.

'Go with them,' Tessa said to Andy. 'Make sure they stay away.'

He backed away. 'I could say something to Leo.'

She held up a finger, and through her teeth said, 'Just don't.'

He gave her a final, sad look, and walked after the committee.

SEVENTY-FIVE

Ruth

... H*ad* she been thinking about before?

She kept falling asleep. Her head now rested on the steering wheel and drool leaked from the corner of her mouth. She wiped it away, noting how grey and purply her skin looked in the rear-view mirror. Oh, and her wig. How embarrassing. That was going to take some explaining too...

... alone now. She was alone. In the car.

Of course, the car, she'd nodded off again, that was all. For just a second this time. Was it because she'd hit her head on the floor earlier? No. She already knew what it was.

Tessa. Tessa had betrayed her. Ruth had heard voices, crept upstairs, and heard through the door her devious plan with that Neanderthal. She'd been drugged.

She ought to get to the hospital. They would fix her. Although ... was there really a point now? That man had the book. They planned to use it against her. It would all come down again, just like it had when she'd set fire to that stupid tree. After she'd been forced to deal with Alan... Oh, Alan –

such a disappointment he'd been. All those conversations they'd…

… *tap, tap, tap.* Tessa, knocking at the passenger-side window and asking her to open the door. She should send her away. Oh, how embarrassing that she had thought this woman was the one to carry on her work. When actually she'd been a creeping little cunting Spider after all.

Never mind. She had done her best with the time she had left. She had rushed, yes. Not been at full power and, sometimes yes, not in her right mind. *Yes. Yes. Yes.* But she had got most of the decisions in her life correct.

For a few seconds she felt like she as going to vomit. Again. She closed her eyes and tried to will herself over the wave and…

… *tap, tap.* Tessa again. And she wasn't sick. Just tired. Just so tired. She leaned over and pulled the handle. Tessa sat down beside her and locked the door again.

'Do you have my keys?' Ruth asked.

'No. Tommo Benton has them. I think he's waiting for you inside.'

'Oh.' Ruth looked up. Tessa's pale skin was flushed, and that intelligence, beyond what Ruth had even dreamed, was assessing her now like one of the MRI machines at the hospital. 'You betrayed me.'

'I did, Ruth. First chance I had. You've made me believe in evil. Well done.'

Ruth sighed. She fell asleep. Tessa was still wittering when she awoke.

'I thought you understood,' Ruth said. 'About true kindness. About how it's not the same thing as wanting to be liked.'

'There aren't words and languages available to explain to you that there are far worse things in the world than wanting to be liked.'

Ruth shook her head violently. Shut her eyes once more, and while they remained closed she didn't sleep this time. But she was somewhere else now. Crying in her bedroom, because her mother and father had told Alan and her that they would be moving abroad to look after Granny. Oh, how she had screamed and yelled. She had been locked in her room as punishment, and smashed her fists on the back on the wooden door so much, they bled. She didn't want to go to Spain. Her school, her friends, blue-eyed Martin Amery – they were all here in England. And the worst part was, Mum and Dad didn't even want to do it. But they had to be seen to be kind, didn't they? That's what Mummy said. *You want people to think kindly of us, don't you?* And by *people* she meant her dreadful Church friends. Her stupid sister. The neighbours. As long as everyone thought them kind, it didn't matter if…

… in the car. Why was Tessa here? Did she have the keys? No. She didn't.

'Why are you here?' Ruth asked her.

'I wanted to tell you that you were wrong. About everything. That was all. And that even though I wanted you to go to prison for what you did to me, and Kath, and everyone else, perhaps this is better. Perhaps watching Nether Appleford become a haven for drugs and money-laundering and whatever else Tommo has planned … maybe that's a more suitable punishment, given how long you have left alive, and I don't believe in hell. What about you? Why are you here? Go back and deal with the mess you made.'

'I don't know,' Ruth said. 'I'm trying to just … decide on what the kindest thing to do is.'

'Think the boat's sailed on that, my darling.'

Tommo Benton appeared at her window. He put the key in the door and opened all the locks. The door opened, and he kneeled beside Ruth, her book on his lap.

'Come on inside, Ruth.'

Ruth said nothing. She remembered Eleanor Beddington now, and what she had said about the smells of the changing seasons. She was tired now, too. She'd done her best. What were the options? She couldn't bear the thought of that man ruining the village. And yet, if she went to the police about him, it would all come out.

And the worst thing was, to get out of *that* bind, she would have to deny it all. Pretend the book wasn't hers, the handwriting forged, the things inside fantasies. And for what, a few more months of freedom?

She didn't want to deny it. She wanted someone to know now. Someone who understood. Otherwise … what had it been for?

Kindness. That's what. She was getting confused. She didn't need anyone to know. If the book was destroyed, it would die with her. Perhaps that was for the best. Fine.

Besides, the book needed the context. The explanation. And Tessa knew that, yes, but she was a traitor.

'Let's talk in here,' Ruth said to Tommo. 'I might throw up on you. Tessa, get out, and let the Benton in.'

Tommo slammed the door. In the moment she had with Tessa, she looked her in the eyes and said, 'When you see Olivia, please tell her I love her very much. And tell her everything, okay. Don't spare her.'

Tommo Benton climbed into the back. 'It's safer for me here, I suspect.'

That was good. She'd anticipated him doing that. She hadn't lost it yet.

Tessa left, giving Ruth one last cold stare that didn't even penetrate the surface. How had she ever thought she was the one? No, it was biology or nothing. Just like she'd always believed, before the illness had scrambled her brain. Perhaps it *would* be Olivia after all. Maybe, once she heard about all her good work from Tessa, it would unlock the necessary potential. The necessary…

'… Ruth, you still with me?'

She woke again. Still in the car. Still with Tommo Benton in the back. The kindest thing, that's what she was deciding. And now it was obvious. So obvious to her.

'I'm still here,' she said. 'Just about, anyway.' She looked down at her two balled fists. How long had they been that way? It almost felt like something was in one of them. Yes, yes there was. The spare key. She'd taken it down from behind the sun visor when she first got in the car. Which meant … she'd planned what she was about to do back then but … slept and forgot it all. This made her laugh. And because it was the correct thing to do, she'd managed to reason herself back to the exact same point again. It was doubly correct. Checked by the very best.

Smiling, she turned on the engine.

'Ruth, what are you doing?' Tommo asked. He didn't sound worried. He didn't know. He wasn't as smart as her. He probably wouldn't even put his seat belt on.

Ruth dropped the hand brake and exited the drive.

'Can you stop?' Was that a little trace of worry she heard now? Too late, cunting little Spider.

She turned left, and jammed down the accelerator. Olivia's cat, Duchess, bought by Ruth as a thirtieth birthday gift, darted out of the road and just avoided being squashed. She was up in third gear, up to sixty miles an hour, when they hit the kerb and mounted the green. Tommo was complaining about something at the top of his lungs, trying to smash the window because the child locks were on. And then he was punching her in the back of the head, trying to grab the steering wheel.

But it was all far too late. She'd been aiming for the lake, a drowning, but she struck the concrete base of the Story Station, which had been laid incorrectly, those Dozy bastards. She lost control. The car shot beneath the canopy of the Kindness Tree. It struck a low branch, and Ruth heard fibreglass hearts tumbling onto the car. She was going to hit the tree. Then she heard Tommo yell, and decided perhaps fire was best. Then they hit the trunk.

SEVENTY-SIX

Tessa

S he stood at the end of Ruth's drive in a cloud of petrol fumes, looking down The Road at the green. The Kindness Tree was burning. It hadn't rained in the last week, and the flames had already caught the lower branches. From what she could see, her old car was completely ablaze.

She walked towards the fire, past the cottages and their dry, flammable roofs. A good distance stood between the last cottage and the tree, but all it would take was an unkind gust of wind. Could the whole village burn?

On one of the gates she passed, a resident had hung up the black-wool knight she'd first seen on the movie-themed walk that day they'd first visited Nether Appleford. This time, someone had repurposed it for the Christmas-themed walk, and a piece of tape had been placed over the mouth area.

'Silent Night', she muttered, and pressed on to the green.

She hadn't been able to hear the fire before, but now people were coming out of the hall, pointing and yelling. A few brave or foolish residents were approaching the car. Leo was one. As was Aaron.

An awful screaming, which caused a vice-like cold to clamp her spine, erupted from the car. It brought to mind some of the reverse-speech effects she'd achieved with a bit of tampering. The human rendered inhuman. The passenger door opened and someone fell to the ground from the passenger seat where Tessa had been sitting just minutes before. They stood aflame, ran towards the hall, arms flailing, a human comet. From the size alone she knew it was Tommo Benton. Leo grabbed him, got him to the ground, tried rolling him. Only soon *he* started yelling, and began banging his own chest because his shirt was on fire.

Dev started yelling at him to roll. He didn't. He kept patting at the flames, which only appeared to excite them. Aaron came running out from the hall carrying a blanket, which he threw on Leo while Dev continued to yell at him to roll. Only Leo stayed on his feet, and stumbled back so that the bottom corner of the blanket caught alight.

October and others stood at the edge of the green started yelling, warning them that this had happened. Aaron eventually caught on, and yanked the blanket from Leo. Only he stumbled over Tommo, who wasn't moving now, and when he crawled backwards his trousers were alight.

Tessa got close enough to Tommo's body to see that the book wasn't on him. By then the others had managed to get control of their respective fires. She looked up at the car, and knew that anything within it would be done for.

Nearby, a fibreglass heart flung from the tree lay face down on the grass. Tessa walked over and picked it up. *For Tessa,* it said, in handwriting she didn't recognise. *For showing us another side of Ruth.*

PART IV
That's What It's All About

SEVENTY-SEVEN

Tessa

Once the bewildered police had finished taking statements and asking questions, in the hall and the pub, Tessa packed her things and went straight to a hotel, despite the late hour. She never wanted to spend another night in Nether Appleford.

She didn't sleep much. Instead, she lay on the bed with the bedside light on, poring over events and deciding what she wanted to tell the police the following day when she was due to elaborate on her slightly brusque initial statement.

'Just tell them everything,' Maddy advised on the phone the next morning.

'It's not that easy,' she'd replied. 'I don't want Jayden involved.'

'I know you like him, Tess. But didn't he sort of cause all of this? He brought two different drug dealers to—'

'He didn't cause any of it.' She paused to take a breath, surprised by how angry she sounded. 'He's a teenager. Teenagers aren't old enough to be causes. They're all just

445

effects. Especially someone like Jayden, after what he's been through.'

Maddy sighed. 'I'm sure the police will bear his history in mind. But he's culpable for some of it, Tess.'

'Most of us do stupid things in our teenage years. If I can keep him out of it, I think I should.'

The line fell silent.

'I didn't mean that to sound pointed. I'm sorry. I just … really think he was trying to help. With Kath. And me.'

'How's he going to learn if nothing comes of this?'

Tessa shrugged to the empty hotel room. 'I think you learn by example, don't you? He's not really had that.'

So when she spoke to the police, three of them in the room on the other side of a table, she told them what she could. What Ruth had done to her, to Kath, to the village over the years, walking lightly around the parts involving her and Andy's break-up. She told them that Ruth had manipulated the committee, at which point one of the officers, an older bloke from a different department, wanted her to elaborate about Leo. She told them she didn't know about the specifics of his involvement in anything criminal, or any of the other villagers' involvement. She only really knew about Ruth, and what she'd confessed to and written in her journal.

After some consideration, she did reveal to them Olivia's relationship with Ruth, asking them to handle the matter carefully because Olivia didn't know Ruth was her mother.

'She might not want to know,' Tessa had said.

In many ways, she hoped Olivia didn't. It would give Tessa a solid reason beyond her own spite not to give Ruth her dying wish.

She kept Jayden out of it, though. She told them that Ruth had been involved with drug dealers somehow, and that this was all connected to the equestrian centre in a way she didn't fully understand. When Rags went missing, Tommo Benton had come looking for him, and had turned up the night Ruth fell ill.

Had they pried further, or brought up anything resembling a connection to Jayden themselves, she might have revealed something. But they didn't. So in some ways she didn't really have to lie. That was what she told herself, anyway.

What she had to live with, though, was going into her laptop and deleting from the audio recording any mention of Jayden. They hadn't been impressed with what remained. They'd said nothing, but she got the sense that, after listening, they felt their time had been wasted. She gave them an MP3 on a CD anyway, covering her tracks like an actual criminal by deleting the master recording.

Before she left, she asked about the book. Whether they'd found it. After exchanging glances, one of the officers shook their head.

'If it was in the car, it was toast.'

———

Leo was waiting for her in the car park outside, a bandage visible above the neck of his hoodie and below an area where his hair was visibly singed. She smiled at him, and he tried to hug her. Tessa leaned back and he gave up. He said he was here to see HR about some time off. She didn't believe him.

'How did your interview go?' he asked.

'It was fine. I just told them what I knew.'

He nodded, looked away. 'Feel like an idiot. Looks like Ruth was running some racket with an organised crime group in Birmingham. Mad. She seemed... Anyway, I think that's the angle they're going for. Open and shut. Probably won't even look too much into it, now Ruth's dead.' He locked eyes with her. 'Unless they thought anyone else was involved.'

'I think that was my sense too.' Still wary of him, she wanted to give him what he wanted, to make him go away.

'Did you get an idea if they were looking into anything else?' he said. 'I can't get my head around her connections, to be honest. These people… She always seemed so … lovely. But maybe … I don't know, maybe I can remember something that helps.'

'They just wanted to know about her generally. I think they reckon the cancer might have been affecting her behaviour.'

He smiled at this before remembering to look upset.

Two weeks later, Leo was murdered.

She found out at one of two funerals she attended in the New Year. The first was Kath's, a low-key affair at a crematorium near Nether Appleford at which only five people had been in attendance. One of those was Jayden, who had come with a woman who spent most of the short service looking at her phone. The rest were crematorium staff and the distant relatives who stood to inherit the land on which Kath's cottage had once stood. Tessa read a short eulogy she'd written. Jayden got up and read the 'My Generation' lyrics, which he'd found on his phone while standing at the front asking everyone to hold on. When he finished, Tessa was crying.

Afterwards, she tried to catch up with him, but he was being rushed off to the car by his clearly impatient new foster mum. He was getting inside, so she had to run, but she caught up with him just as the woman closed her door.

'Hey,' she said, and threw her arms around him.

'Hey.'

'You okay?'

'Doing fine, yeah.'

He didn't look it. He looked and felt thinner, and she couldn't find all of him in his eyes. Tiredness, maybe.

'I just wanted to say hi, anyway,' she said. 'I'll come and visit you soon.'

He nodded, unmoved by this. She hugged him again, and put her mouth to his ear. 'I've kept you out of it, okay? So if you have anything left, phones with calls or chats on, get rid of them. Burn them.'

She didn't wait to see his reaction, but when she tried walking away, she realised he'd grabbed her little finger with his. She looked around and he smiled at her. That part of him that had been missing from his eyes had returned.

The second funeral was Ruth's. Tessa had no respects to pay, but when she'd been invited by Andy she'd been curious to see what happened. Clearly the investigation was moving slowly, and despite the rumours about her involvement in shady goings-on, most believed that it was likely Ruth had been *made* to do whatever she'd done.

After the service she saw Andy. Leo's absence was noticeable, as the rest of committee were present, so she asked him why Leo wasn't there. He told her that he'd been attacked after going out drinking in Oxford. He'd died a few nights before in the John Radcliffe. There were rumours it might have been connected to his police work, but officially it was viewed as a drunken altercation. No one had been arrested yet.

'I'm not sure,' Andy said. 'Olivia thinks it's nothing, but there have been … weird people around the village. People like that bloke in Ruth's house that night. I think some of Benton's people have been sniffing around, trying to find out more about what Ruth was up to. Who she was connected to. I know a few on the committee are worried. I am. I've said to Olivia we should get out of there.'

'Do,' Tessa said. 'I'm not messing around, Andy. Get the fuck out of that place now. If it's Benton's people…' She shook her head. 'I need you alive when this kid comes.' She swallowed and took a deep breath. 'Olivia's going to need you, too.'

'I know.'

'Did you ask her, by the way?'

Andy nodded. Not long before the funeral she'd told Andy that she knew something about the identity of Olivia's mother. She'd asked Andy to find out if Olivia was curious to know more.

'She has no interest.' He sighed and took a drink of his whisky. 'I think she had an idea who it might be when I told her it was you asking the question. I wanted to give her some time to think about it, but I asked again on the way up. It's a *big* no.'

'Good,' Tessa said.

She moved in with Maddy semi-permanently, helping her rest during the day after her nights breast-feeding, by taking care of Juliet. She took her for walks in her buggy around the well-kept park of Maddy and Bhav's middle-class suburb. Singing songs to her in her bouncy chair. Changing nappies and bottle-feeding her reheated breast milk.

She didn't lie to herself. She hated it most of the time. Dull, repetitive labour, it demanded only small fragments of time, but at such frequent intervals one couldn't even hide from the misery by retreating into the drift of deep thought.

But she did it. Not as practice for later in the year. Not in the hopes Maddy might return the favour later down the line when she would face all this same stuff, only without the security of work or a partner. Not even as a way to pay her back for letting her stay there rent free. No, she did it because she could see her sister needed it.

It was the right thing to do. And sometimes, she did actually enjoy it.

One afternoon, after she'd let Maddy sleep for five hours, she handed Juliet over and went to make Maddy a cup of tea. When she came back, Maddy took the drink and said, 'Don't let anyone ever tell you you're not kind, Tessa. I don't know what I'd do without you.'

'It's not kindness,' she said, aware she'd snapped a little bit. 'It's just what's right.'

A moment later, she burst into tears.

Maddy had found Tessa a room in her work building's basement which never got used, and after sweet-talking the security team, she arranged for Tessa to use it in the evening and at weekends. It was good timing, too, because she soon had a new commission from an elderly woman in Canada, who was prepared to offer Tessa a considerable advance sum if she produced her album of borderline-pornographic folk songs. The amount would be enough for a deposit, and at least six months' rent. A flipping miracle under the circumstances. Still wary of what Ruth had done to her, she didn't spend too long on the demos. But by the end of the following day, the advance was in her PayPal account.

Still, she didn't rent straight away. She took a dog/house-sitting job for one of Mads's posh friends, and used the two months to find a place near enough to her sister's so that they could support each other – although not so close that she couldn't actually afford it.

The place she chose was a three-bedroom basement flat on a rolling two-month contract. The threat of demolition hung over the place, so the rent was low. All the rooms were set off one corridor running along the left of the flat. She took the first as a bedroom, the second as a studio, and the last would eventually be the baby's. Until then, she considered letting it – the extra cash would be welcome, providing someone out there could put up with night feeds.

She advertised, and met a woman that reminded her of Ruth and a man that reminded her of Leo. How much those resemblances reflected reality she couldn't be sure in retrospect, but she considered that a therapist might be a worthy investment, should she ever find herself not living hand-to-mouth. So, for a while, the spare room remained empty.

Occasionally, she heard from the police. They would repeat that the investigation into Ruth was ongoing, and that it might take some time to unravel. They would ask questions for clarity, usually if she could remember details from Ruth's book that might help specifics in their investigation. People, places, dates. They didn't call as much as she'd thought they would, though. But she told them what she could.

Richard 'Rags' Ragford, a person already known to the police, was still missing-presumed-dead. But despite a search of Nether Appleford, no body was found. How thorough that search was, given Rags's background, Tessa wasn't sure. But she strongly suspected he was buried in the woods somewhere on the valley walls.

Meanwhile her belly grew, and discussions opened with Andy and Olivia about how it was all going to work. Mostly things were amicable, although not to the point where Tessa or Olivia could speak face-to-face. They had moved out of Nether Appleford at the end of January and were now closer to her in Reading, near Olivia's parents.

The strange men were apparently still seen lurking around the village every now and again, and late at night cars no one recognised would prowl down The Road and back. It wasn't the same anymore, Andy said. And he worried that once the police investigation into Ruth and Tommo Benton's deaths died down, those men would be even more visible.

Tessa didn't disabuse him of the notion either. Her guess was that the other Benton Boys knew enough about why Tommo had been in Nether Appleford to pick up where he'd left off. She wasn't sure what that involved exactly, and she didn't think it involved her, given she'd been mostly an afterthought in Tommo's plans. Apparently Benedita had replaced Leo on the committee, Jitesh had taken Olivia's role – although rumour had it she and Dev wanted out now too – and Amara had been promoted to Ruth's role.

While she wasn't worried for herself, she did worry about Jayden daily. What if the Benton Boys knew about him? It wasn't paranoid to think that if Tommo had told his goons about Nether Appleford, he might also have mentioned where his information had come from. Then again, she could equally imagine a high-level gangster not wanting to reveal his source was a fifteen-year-old. Maybe he'd held that back while he got his own hands dirty doing the groundwork. She could hope.

She kept her eye on the news, read the little bits that would appear in local papers, mostly the Birmingham ones, about the incident in Nether Appleford. She set up a Google alert with

Jayden's name, too. Nothing ever dropped into her inbox, thankfully. So yes, she could hope.

She missed his company. Playing music with him. Watching him getting better at his instrument. Hearing his thoughts. Basking in his optimism despite everything he'd been through. She missed how open and giving he'd been, and how she'd felt about herself in his company. Missed it when the three of them got really good at a song and would just look at one another's grinning faces while playing.

Sometimes she passed by that third bedroom on her way to the bathroom and would think about Jayden then. Sometimes she would peer inside, make sure no one had snuck in, and close the door. Other times she would turn on the light and simply stand there, imagining.

SEVENTY-EIGHT

Jayden

He sat on the bench in the park. The one in front of the burned-down slide. He'd got his best gear on. No band shirts today. Gucci T-shirt. Scrubbed Nike trainers. Neither fitted him, because they weren't his. He'd found them in Graham and Libby's cupboard. But he didn't like standing out around here. Not when he went out, which he liked to a fair bit, as Graham was a cook and not a great one, and the flat was small.

It was starting to spit, and he wished he had a coat. It was cold, but his coat was old and shit, so he hadn't brought it with him. Some kids rode by the park slowly, talking to each other and eyeing him up. Time to go. At least he'd got a good fifteen minutes today. He closed his eyes, knowing it would always be like this. On edge. Waiting for trouble. And it wasn't even like he was scared of it. It was more that he had so much anger now, so much sadness, that he didn't trust what he might do to someone if things kicked off.

Hearing footsteps nearby, expecting trouble, he opened his eyes and straightened up.

'Hey, Ramones friend,' she said, and sat down beside him.

He smelled her familiar perfume then. Her shampoo. It relaxed him. It made him want to grin. Her face was rounder than when he'd last saw her, her belly bigger beneath a new coat. He didn't want to hurt the baby or anything, but he hugged her hard anyway.

'What are you doing here?'

'I told you'd I'd come see you. Your foster parents said you liked to walk the block, so I was going to go hunting. Then here you are. Right over the street.'

'They're more like foster flatmates.'

'I see. You not enjoying it there?'

'It is what it is.'

She thought on this, and said eventually, 'Why haven't you been returning my messages?'

'Uh.' He didn't want to tell her it was because he'd destroyed his phone and sim. That one night he'd stolen some rum from Graham and got so angry, he'd chucked it repeatedly at the wall. 'New phone.'

'You didn't think to tell me?' She looked hurt.

'Honest, all my numbers went too. I...' Fuck it, why be shy? '... got really angry and smashed it to bits.'

She laughed at that, and the sound made him happy.

'We've all done that. So, listen, Jayden, I've come here for two reasons. First, here's a present.' She handed him something long and thin, gift-wrapped in bright-red paper.

He tore it open and found two drumsticks. He knew whose they were. 'Ah, man. That's... Thanks.'

'She left them at mine, and I found them when I was moving.'

'You're not in the village?'

She told him what had happened since he'd left, some of which he'd heard, some of which he hadn't. When she was done, they sat in silence a while. His legs were shaking now, and he bopped them up and down to keep warm.

'Now the other thing', she said, 'is I've been thinking. I've got this flat.'

'Yeah?'

'Yeah. With a spare room.'

'Oh yeah?'

'Uh-huh. It's grotty as all hell, to be honest. But I like it. The flat, not the room, I should say. The room's as good as mine. Anyway.'

'Right.'

'I don't know if you'd want to or not. Or if it's even possible, really. I've not looked into it. Not much, anyway. But, if it *was* possible, would you think about coming to live with me?'

'Like, yeah!' Realising he'd sounded too excited, that he might have misunderstood, he added, 'For a bit, you mean?'

'For a while, Jayden. You know.' She smiled, looked a bit mad, to be honest. But in a good way. In a like-she-was-scared-he-might-say-no way. 'It would mean another new school. We'd probably fall out loads. I'd have rules. Lots of rules.'

'Like, live with you, *live with you*?'

She shrugged. 'Yeah. I'll help you. You can help me. We'll be a team. If you want.'

Jayden was smiling. He didn't want to be so obvious. He didn't want to get his hopes up. 'Can we play music again? If this happened.'

'I'd be annoyed if we didn't.'

Tessa reached out and grabbed his little finger with hers. For a long while they sat there in silence. Eventually a car drove by, and some kids yelled obscenities. Neither of them really noticed.

Acknowledgments

This book was a beast, one eventually tamed with the support of the following patient and wise people. Jennie Rothwell and the One More Chapter team. Joanna Swainson and the Hardman and Swainson team. Helen, my dream reader. Joe and Alice, for important discussions about dinos and crunchy ears. The whole extended Masters clan, with special thanks to Dad for sharing insights from a life working in social services, Mom for insights into village-life, and my brothers, because they know what's good. Professor Deborah Bowman, for sharing her thoughts on kindness. Stevey B, Tom Leahy, Tom Fairfield, Grundy, Jeremy Warmsley and Finchy, for miscellaneous chats. Louisa Scarr and family, I owe yew one. Special thanks to the Criminal Minds, Cinema Under the Stairs (the best cinema in Oxford), Barnaby Walter, and the Botley Ds. Lastly, immense gratitude to readers and book buyers everywhere.

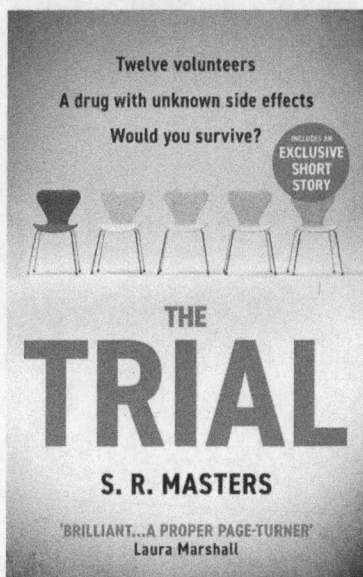

Twelve volunteers
A drug with unknown side effects
Would you survive?

INCLUDES AN
EXCLUSIVE
SHORT
STORY

THE
TRIAL

S. R. MASTERS

'BRILLIANT...A PROPER PAGE-TURNER'
Laura Marshall

Would you sign up to a medical trial if you didn't know the possible side effects?

It seems like the opportunity of a lifetime. An all-inclusive luxury trip abroad, all you need to do is take a pill every day and keep a diary…

Read on for an exclusive extract!

Available in eBook and paperback now

Extract: The Trial

Prologue

PATIENT 3

Please use this diary to record how you have felt during the day, thinking of your physical health, mental health and overall wellbeing.

Day 14

This morning, when the pretty doctor gave me today's pill with that patronising little smile of hers, I was caught between an urge to run far away from her, to protect her, and an urge to smash her face into pieces so you would send me home.

Does that help you? Is this the sort of thing you want to hear about?

You definitely should hear about this stuff.

Because it's your pills doing this to me.

I wasn't certain at first, partly because of the headaches, which have left me feeling weak and unsure of myself, but also because of the whole opulent package. The private jet, the island setting, the beautiful room with the sea view in front of me now… It beguiled me. Surely anyone with this much money must know what they're doing. They wouldn't be giving people a drug with side-effects this bad?

But I can't stop these thoughts, these alien thoughts, which worm into my head every day. New perspectives. New connections. New opinions. Like how I felt about the doctor this morning when she gave me my pill. And this maddening disorientation I feel when I consider what I've been doing with my life.

It's making me want to do things that I'd never do.

And the headaches aren't getting better. You promised they would, but they're getting worse. So much worse.

How am I then, you ask? Let me be honest with you. Let me really help your research and earn my fee.

You want to know about my physical health? How about: it's like I have another person inside here with me. An awful, animal person, with weak, animal appetites, and they're taking over my body.

And my mental health? Well, I want to run around your fancy complex scratching a warning into every surface so that any other idiot who comes here won't believe you when you tell them they won't feel a thing.

I want to warn them that you're going to take their souls.

And how about my overall wellbeing? It feels like you've opened a door in my head that can never be closed. That I've seen the world in a way that I can't ever unsee. And the worst part is, I want to run headlong into this new darkness. Because I know once it consumes me, the light I'm running from won't matter.

Yet right now I'm in the doorway, being yanked both ways by two powerful opposites.

In the last few days I've found myself on my balcony here, or on the patio high above the beach, and I think about how the damage might already be permanent. And I think about falling. Obliterating myself beneath this blazing sun to spite the darkness.

And there have been times where I've wanted to go to the kitchen, find myself a knife, and stain your white coats red. Then I'd gather up those pills of yours, take them out to the cliffs, and cast them into the sea before burning this place to the ground.

Chapter 1

Elle pretended to be absorbed by the glossy holiday brochure open on her lap below the reception desk while just metres away a giant man paced in the lobby muttering to himself and kicking the chocolate-coloured sofas.

'I told them,' he said to the vending machine on the back wall, 'you have to watch closely.'

He returned to the sofa. *Smack. Smack.*

Terry was one of the regulars. It had been weeks since she'd seen him around the hospital, and she'd been worried about what might have happened to him. Now, with every *sock* of the leather upholstery, Elle flinched. She wanted to push her chair away from the desk and into the back office, where she could escape upstairs and get help. But she didn't want to draw his attention. So instead, she looked at her holiday brochure and tried to keep still. Palm trees. White sand. A crimson cocktail.

'Do they listen though? *Do they?*'

Smack. Smack. Smack.

Terry mostly appeared at reception to access the hospital Contemplation Room, a space set aside for patients' spiritual needs. Elle would push the little red button on the wall to let him through and he always thanked her. Quiet and shy, something of the local ale uncle about him, he could barely make eye contact, let alone trouble.

Elle wasn't privy to the details of his mental health history – her job was strictly non-clinical – but Terry had been doing well enough to walk around without a chaperone. A common story at Parkwood, though, was patients being discharged too early – especially since Core Solutions took over some of the NHS contracts two years ago. They struggled, and sometimes returned unannounced – often in a bad way. She'd had two incidents in the last six months, one of which had needed police involvement because there was no longer any on-site security.

Something clattered in the lobby. Terry was shaking the vending machine.

She couldn't ignore it now. He was going to hurt himself. Elle stood, leaned over the desk, and called through the open glass hatch. 'Terry, are you okay? Do you need me to call anyone for you?'

He turned to look at her, recognition briefly in his eyes. Then he yelled, 'They look at you like goats. You want to watch out.' He kicked one sofa hard enough to lift it from the ground.

'Okay, Terry,' she said, 'I'll get someone to help you. Just wait there, okay?'

She slid the glass window closed, locked it, and turned to the phone. After the second incident she'd asked for more training and guidance from Core Solutions. Nothing had been forthcoming, so recently she'd invented her own protocol: Ward, PCSO, police.

Guessing Terry wasn't likely to be under hospital care anymore, she called the neighbourhood PCSO. It went to voicemail.

Elle glanced up to check the lobby again and startled. Terry stood just centimetres from the glass. Despite the November cold, he wore only a food-stained Iron Man T-shirt tucked into a pair of shorts. He slammed his palms against the glass, which shook in its rails.

'Can I get through? I need to get upstairs.'

Elle took a step back. 'Okay, let me get you help, Terry.' She tried sounding assertive yet compassionate. She didn't want to agitate him further.

He palmed the glass twice again. 'I need to see him.'

Elle could see the illness at work on the surface, his tense posture and dancing eyes. Yet it was in those eyes she could see the other Terry, too, imprisoned and afraid, and almost apologetic.

Terry spat on the glass. He yelled. He struck again, harder. Then seemingly defeated, he walked away muttering.

Elle took a deep breath, reached for the phone and tried the number for the PCSO again.

The reception window shattered, and Elle covered her face as glass shards rained around her. A round coffee table struck the desk, briefly lodging in the hatch before the weight of its legs pulled it back out. The remaining frame of jagged glass didn't stop Terry from attempting to climb through, and Elle darted into the back office, footsteps crunching. She turned, ready to shut herself in.

Terry had one bleeding knee on the desk and was stretching for the red button on the wall. If he pressed the one for the conference facility door he would be free to walk around amongst the fifty or so guests on site. Elle thrust out her arm and got there first, pulling the plastic lever below the switch to disable it. His hand swatted the button a moment after. He didn't know what she'd done, and retreated through the opening to try the double doors. Elle stepped back and slammed the door.

On the other side of the wall Terry began to kick out again.

'Terry, please calm down.' Her voice was so weak he probably couldn't hear it.

Elle looked down at the lock. The key wasn't there. It was in the reception drawer.

She grabbed the handle again; she could retrieve the key if she was quick. But the thumping ceased. His frustrated grumbling grew louder, followed by the sound of glass and other objects tumbling to the floor. He was entering the reception again.

Elle turned to flee. Once out in the corridor she could lock him inside, stop him getting upstairs. But at the back door she hesitated. What if he hurt himself in the office? She scanned the room. The stapler, the guillotine, a letter opener.

Terry kicked the door between reception and the office; he hadn't yet realised it was unlocked. The thin partition walls shook.

Was there time to clear the danger? She wouldn't be able to live with herself if—

The handle of the reception door squeaked and moved downwards. Before Elle could get out Terry stepped inside, shoulders heaving, a bull about to charge.

'Terry, you shouldn't be in here.'

'I need to see him.'

The people upstairs today were on a local authority training course, not clinicians experienced with seriously unwell patients. She had no idea what Terry would do, given his aggressive state, and she was the last line of defence.

He came towards her, and because the door swung inward she would have to step into him to open it. So instead she stepped away, moving deeper into the office. Only Terry wasn't interested in the door. He changed his direction and came for her instead.

Panicking, she grabbed one of the fire extinguishers on the wall, snapped out the safety plastic and pointed the nozzle at him.

Embarrassed and scared, she said, 'Terry, please step back. I don't want to hurt you.'

He kept coming, shaking his head, muttering about how she didn't understand. His eyes were so very sad. She ordered herself to squeeze the handle, but...she couldn't do it. He was unwell. He didn't deserve to be assaulted.

She threw the extinguisher at his feet to put it between them, turned, and yanked open the door to the stationery cupboard. She shut herself in, darkness blanketing her. She snapped a lock that she'd only half-believed might be there and reached for the light switch, finding only cool brickwork. The stupid thing was on the outside wall, wasn't it? Now her only illumination poked beneath the crack at the base.

She sat with her back pressed to the door, trying to catch her breath. Trying to stop shaking.

'Terry, listen to me—'

Kick.

The force jostled her.

'Terry—'

Kick.

She tapped the pocket of her trousers. Her phone was still in her bag under the table.

'You need to go outside before I call the police. I'm frightened, Terry.'

The kicking stopped. Elle waited, listening intently, her eyes teary and her head involuntarily shaking from side to side.

'Terry,' she said.

After five minutes which felt more like an hour, she heard

rustling at the door's base and scooted away. Her brochure, picked up that morning from an *actual* travel agent's as she cycled to work, slid into the cupboard with her.

A moment later the light came on.

She breathed. She listened. Outside a door opened and closed. Silence.

She stared at the brochure. Huffed a bitter laugh.

On the cover a sun-kissed couple held hands on a white sand beach, gazing at one another like they'd just been granted immortality in paradise. God, she really needed a holiday.

Available in eBook and paperback now

ONE MORE CHAPTER

YOUR NUMBER ONE STOP

FOR PAGETURNING BOOKS

The author and One More Chapter would like to thank everyone who contributed to the publication of this story...

Analytics
Abigail Fryer
Maria Osa

Audio
Fionnuala Barrett
Ciara Briggs

Contracts
Sasha Duszynska Lewis
Florence Shepherd

Design
Lucy Bennett
Fiona Greenway
Holly Macdonald
Liane Payne
Dean Russell

Digital Sales
Lydia Grainge
Emily Scorer
Georgina Ugen

Editorial
Kate Elton
Simon Fox
Arsalan Isa
Charlotte Ledger
Federica Leonardis
Bonnie Macleod
Jennie Rothwell

International Sales
Bethan Moore

Marketing & Publicity
Chloe Cummings
Emma Petfield

Operations
Melissa Okusanya
Hannah Stamp

Production
Emily Chan
Denis Manson
Francesca Tuzzeo

Rights
Lana Beckwith
Rachel McCarron
Agnes Rigou
Hany Sheikh Mohamed
Zoe Shine
Aisling Smyth

The HarperCollins Distribution Team

The HarperCollins Finance & Royalties Team

The HarperCollins Legal Team

The HarperCollins Technology Team

Trade Marketing
Ben Hurd
Eleanor Slater

UK Sales
Laura Carpenter
Isabel Coburn
Jay Cochrane
Tom Dunstan
Sabina Lewis
Holly Martin
Erin White
Harriet Williams
Leah Woods

And every other essential link in the chain from delivery drivers to booksellers to librarians and beyond!